THE ESSENTIAL CLARENCE MAJOR

THE ESSENTIAL CLARENCE MAJOR

Prose & Poetry

Foreword by Kia Corthron

THE UNIVERSITY OF NORTH CAROLINA PRESS

Chapel Hill

This book was published with the assistance of the
Anniversary Fund of the University of North Carolina Press.

Designed by Jamison Cockerham
Set in Arno, Electra, and Frontage
by Rebecca Evans

Cover photograph © Lynda Koolish

Manufactured in the United States of America

The University of North Carolina Press has been a member
of the Green Press Initiative since 2003.

LIBRARY OF CONGRESS CATALOGING-IN-PUBLICATION DATA
Names: Major, Clarence, author. | Corthron, Kia, writer of foreword.
Title: The essential Clarence Major : prose and poetry / foreword by Kia Corthron.
Description: Chapel Hill : University of North Carolina Press, 2020.
Identifiers: LCCN 2019053525 | ISBN 9781469658780 (cloth) |
ISBN 9781469656007 (paperback) | ISBN 9781469656014 (ebook)
Subjects: LCGFT: Poetry. | Fiction.
Classification: LCC PS3563.A39 A6 2020 | DDC 823/.914—dc23
LC record available at https://lccn.loc.gov/2019053525

Contents

Part Three ESSAYS

Part Four MEMOIR

Part Five POEMS

Foreword

Alive Speech

The eighties: fresh out of undergrad and working a D.C. nine-to-five misery, but there was a fringie. Having grown up in a small town, my every weekend was now a new urban adventure, accessible even with the peanuts of my editing salary: music and theater and galleries and literature—an arts scene I'd somehow missed in college. One day Michele—my new and fast best friend—mentioned an article in a recent *Washington Post* profiling a black experimental novelist, an author she remembered referenced by a former professor. I read the piece, immediately ran out to buy *My Amputations* (what a title!), and devoured it. Thus commenced my lifelong reader-writer relationship with Clarence Major. Of the numerous artists I hungrily embraced in my bright-eyed twenties, few of their books remain with me today, but here in my Harlem apartment I gaze at the spines of assorted Major titles acquired over the decades, lined up on my bookcase shelf the way a different reader might display his James Patterson collection.

Post-discovery, I came quickly to grasp the virtuosity of my newfound scribe—a literary figure recognized in various disciplines of prose and poetry, and an accomplished painter to boot. This artistic fluidity manifests itself in content: protagonists who are painters, composers, poets. A Southern Blues musician struggling in migrant-heavy Chicago just after the Second World War, a sketch artist in France pondering whether there is any worthwhile subject matter left to draw, a Zuni composer wrangling intertribal tensions and the social aftermath of colonialism and genocide. The pieces focusing on music creators tend to be hybrid: fiction, poetry, songs.

Major's perpetual experimentation has resulted in an oeuvre stylistically broad. Written a quarter century apart, *Reflex and Bone Structure* (1975) and "Innocence" (2000) combine terse declarative Hemingwayesque rhythm with a magical realism where dreams and reality merge. A cinematic influence is evident as well in the rapid scene cuts, flash images that are also the foundation of many poems (for example, "Water and Sand," "Faith," "Alchemy"). Major was drawn to visual art before verbal, and this merging of disciplines is palpable. In the essay "Painting and Poetry," he asserts: "In several letters van Gogh says he sees no differences between literature and painting. He was a very writerly painter, and a very painterly writer, writer of letters. He spent as much time writing and reading as painting." In *Reflex and Bone Structure*, the reader pieces together the narrative from the subtle clues Major offers regarding his Manhattan characters. Then, without warning, we are on a road trip:

> Canada and I leave town. It's not easy. In Maryland, we get work operating a crane on a construction site, lifting a hundred and forty tons of mashed potatoes from a vacant lot to another vacant lot. Pay: fifty cents and a fish sandwich. For spending change, we stick up a mail train, swooping with seven million, which lasts us a few days. We live it up in Winnemucca, Nevada; dance with buck-eyed Indians in Pierce, Idaho; do the fox-trot with hippies in Eugene, Oregon; backtracking, we hide out in Swiftbird, South Dakota, where a fella, with alert gentle eyes and red hair, helps us invent new identities. With our new cards, we return east, dressed as limbo dancers, with the false endorsement of Teresa Marquis of the Island of St. Lucia, we get work at the Palace Theatre and Carnegie Hall. We're a smashing success. Our manager, a bird-watcher from Dwaarkill, New York, books us for a tour of Italy, but by now we're exhausted. We separate.

Major's singular and wonderfully quirky voice allows me, as a black American, to recognize myself in his work and simultaneously to see myself anew. After a comb-out (whether or not the comb was hot) or a trim, it has been African American custom, at least through the latter twentieth century, to dispose of the removed hair by burning. When this happened during my own childhood and I would question my mother about it, her only response was that it was "bad luck" not to burn it, likely the same reply she'd gotten from her own mother. As an adult, it finally dawned on me that the ritual must have come down through the generations as a means to prevent the hair from falling into the wrong hands: protection against hexes. Major's poem "Hair" delves deep into black hair superstition, wry but sans judgment:

> My grandmother
> threw a lock of her hair
> into the fireplace.
> It burned brightly.

That is why she lived
to be a hundred and one.

Another example of merging African American familiarity with innovation is the one-sided phone call of "Chicago Heat," wherein the concurrent horror and humor of the African American experience rings painfully true—so many complications that death is not necessarily a prioritized development but rather just one more aggravation thrown on the daily mountain of life's obstacles.

In "My Mother and Mitch," breathtaking in its simplicity and power, fifteen-year-old Tommy lives in his Chicago apartment with his divorced mother, Jayne. (She had divorced Tommy's father twelve years before, when Tommy was barely more than a toddler.) Delicately sown details evoke a mid-twentieth-century America of a feminine "ladylike" ideal and Red Skelton on a black-and-white set. Tommy doesn't appear to have friends; outside of homework, he seems interested in nothing but his mother, but this is apparently enough since there is no indication that he is lonely. Their world is a population of two: parent and child, sometimes reversing roles, often giggling playmates. When a wrong number leads to the hope of romance in Jayne's life, and after concluding the caller is not a psychopath, Tommy doesn't seem threatened by this new development so much as curious as to where it all will lead. The mistaken call is from Mitch, an older white man who apparently assumes the female voice on the other end to be of a white woman, until Tommy overhears his mother clarify: "'I am a colored lady.' Those were her words exactly. She placed the emphasis on 'lady.'" Tommy had never known his mother to show interest in white men before, yet there is poignancy in her expression to her son, "with that fearful look that was hers alone," that she does not think Mitch will call again. Mitch does call, eventually mailing Jayne a photograph of himself and the sister with whom he lives. When a meeting is finally set in a diner in the black neighborhood—Jayne at the counter and Tommy clandestinely (in alliance with his mother) at a nearby table—we are afforded the opportunity through Tommy's eyes to observe Jayne alone in public as she awaits her date: a woman clearly overdressed for this greasy spoon but taking pride in her appearance. Tommy states without judgment, "She had always been something of a snob"—unaffected by the sneers of the regular customers ("Yeah. She must think she's white. What's she doing in here anyway?"). This bit of theater preceding Mitch's entrance is the most compelling drama of the scene; Jayne's quiet conversation with the semi-blind date, out of Tommy's earshot, appears comparably uneventful. In fact, Mitch's entrance into the lives of Tommy and Jayne is significant only in its shedding light on an extraordinarily close mother-son relationship. Now, as Tommy approaches manhood, readers are privy to perhaps the end days of such intimacy: "I knew I loved her, and needed her, and I knew she loved and needed me. I did not yet fear that she needed me too much."

A writer's entire opus could easily be constructed from the multitudinous stories unfolding in the thirty-odd blocks of Chicago's black South Side, the neighborhood of Major's formative years. Indeed, the area has provided the backdrop to many of his imaginative works, but Major has opened himself up to the wide range of American communities. In *Painted Turtle: Woman with Guitar*, Zuni life is examined from the perspective of the narrator, who meets the title character as an adult and, from the stories she has told him, pieces together her existence from childhood on. Major incorporates cultural language ("Her father made a cradleboard while her mother was breastfeeding her. This was right after the sandbed"), traditions (a woman washing the hair of her soon-to-be daughter-in-law), and mental illness linked to the legacy of attempted race extermination. In "One Flesh," John and Susie, a black painter and a Chinese American poet in San Francisco, consider marriage. John's mother is skeptical that Susie's parents would accept the bond, and she turns out to be correct. But, surprisingly, Susie's father asks to have a "man-to-man" talk with John alone. In an exquisite and painful scene, Susie's father opens up to John about the plight of the Chinese in America, from personal experience ("Immigration people keep Chinese people in detention long time. Immigration man say he look for hookworms, but he torture while looking.") as well as in a historical context—but in the latter instance, John is already keenly aware of the web of American racism and its sinister divide-and-conquer reality:

> "Indian and Mexican woman charge white man big money to do laundry, but not Chinese, so Chinese be laundry boy for white people. Cost white man little bit less."
>
> And John remembered his history professor telling the class that in 1870 in Mississippi, black ex-slaves, now sharecroppers, were reluctantly doing the work because of unfair plantation wages. They knew they were being used. They knew the sharecropping system was designed to keep them in debt to the ex-slaveholder. In that same year, the plantation owner brought in hundreds of Chinese men from the West Coast to do the work and thereby set an example. They were scabs.

Major crosses borders again with a recurring setting: the black American ex-pat artist in Europe. In addition to the aforementioned sketch artist in France ("Sketch"), the seminal *My Amputations* chronicles a fictional African American poet in Nice and Oxford for conferences and readings; "'Thanks for the Lunch, Baby'" imagines a posthumous Paris lunch with Major's old friend émigré James Baldwin; and Major—a repeat ex-pat himself—brings his own observations of the complications in the European mecca-utopia with "A Paris Fantasy Transformed": "To be sure," he writes, "there was as much racism in France as in the States, but in Paris, I was not the target of French racism. As soon as the French discovered I was not an African or Arab from one of their former colonies, I was treated well. This was an ironic and ambiguous position to be in." But there was love before disillusion, and in the same essay Major recounts his long fascination with the French capital—not just the Wright-Baldwin heyday of a generation prior to his arrival but Paris's ubiquitous presence in the South Side of his youth, with African American artists of all disciplines constantly hopping between the City of Lights and the Windy City, among them singers Josephine Baker and Lil (ex-wife of Louis) Armstrong. Essay, in this case, makes crossover into memoir.

An essay that could be seen as memoir is "Necessary Distance," in which Major recounts his innate captivation with painting ("My first articulate passion was for the works of Vincent van Gogh"), his scholarship he received as a teenager to attend sketch classes at Chicago's Art Institute, his awareness of the absence of African American work on the walls of mainstream galleries, his fascination with form over content ("What did matter was *how* the painter or storyteller or poet seduced me into the story, into the picture, into the poem"), and his frustration with critical pigeon-holing—for example, the inevitable critique comparing African American writing to jazz ("But what was I to make of the fact that I had also grown up with Tin Pan Alley, bluegrass, *and* European classical music?"). Coming of age as an aspiring writer in America, Major remembers his sense of distress and now sees it as a routine rite of passage: "Every generation is sure it is more disturbed than the previous one and less lucky than the forthcoming one."

The essays profiling renowned writers (Baldwin, Ellison, Wright) are deliberately narrow, addressing aspects of the authors that have been rarely glimpsed. In "Don, Here Is My Peppermint Striped Shirt," the reader is invited into a virtual 1970s Greenwich Village Moveable Feast: a Christmas party hosted by Grace Paley and Kirkpatrick Sale where Major meets the subject of the essay, Donald Barthelme; they run into each other again at a book signing for William Burroughs. There is poignancy in the overview of career highs and lows in "Richard Wright: The Long Hallucination" (an essay resonating with the themes in the rest of this the collection, hearkening back to the *My Amputations* excerpt setting protagonist Mason in a Paris cemetery searching for Wright's ashes) and in "Claude McKay: My 1975 Adventure," a heartbreaking chronicle of one of America's true literary luminaries who spent his last days in sickness and abject poverty, and with the knowledge that all his books were (at the time) out of print.

Major also opens readers up to scribes who are less celebrated, such as fellow writer-painter Kenneth Patchen as well as Wallace Thurman, a jack-of-all-writing trades of the Harlem Renaissance (or more accurately, as Major states, the New Negro Movement). Thurman was a novelist, short story writer, screenwriter, author of articles, Broadway-produced playwright, and the publisher of two short-lived magazines (a single issue of his *Blast* "carried works by Gwendolyn Brooks, Zora Neale Hurston, Langston Hughes, and the artist Aaron Douglas"), and all this before his death, in destitution, at the tragically young age of thirty-two.

In "Rhythm: A Hundred Years of African American Poetry," Major provides a detailed overview of a broad range of black poets, from slavery through the mid-1990s: Wheatley, Dunbar, Toomer, Bontemps, Hayden, Cullen, Sanchez, Baraka, Jordan, Dove, Komunyakaa, Walcott, Lorde, and dozens of others. Major also addresses the question, "Can poetry be both political and didactic and at the same time still be art?" As is made glaringly evident in his own epic poem "The Slave Trade: View from the Middle Passage" and continuing forward in history throughout the work contained in this anthology, that perpetual art-politics question is absurd, especially as it is usually addressed to artists of marginalized communities whose complicated lives rarely provide space for art merely for its own sake. In "Rhythm: Talking That Talk," Major asserts: "I would go so far as to say that *all* alive art is rebellious, and *all* alive speech, slang or otherwise, is rebellious, rebellious in the healthy sense that they challenge the stale and the conventional."

Clarence Major is among that select group of writers whose speech is truly alive, magnificently dynamic. This volume is worth a read and a re-read, and another re-read years from now, the language vigorous and vital, ever incisive, ever changing, ever new.

Kia Corthron
May 2019

PART ONE

NOVEL EXCERPTS

From

Reflex and Bone Structure

I saw some of the work the cops did. One used a flat device to take the fingerprints. Since rigor mortis hadn't yet set in, the spoonlike object wasn't necessary. I helped them. Canada helped too. Everybody in the neighborhood pitched in and gave a hand. They all got their fingerprints taken. Though no one had counted on that. The cops had fingerprint cards they carried in a plastic briefcase along with one of those syringes for injecting silicone beneath the skin. This way prints could be taken effectively. The cops were all over the place looking in crevices. They looked beneath the bed and in the empty closets. They had some desensitizing fluid they didn't use.

These policemen were real. They were very funny. Canada was once a cop, but I don't think he was ever as funny as these. One had a Polaroid MP-3 camera for copy work—the kind that gives an instant negative. He also carried in his pocket a bottle of ultraviolet ink. Another one wore gloves and picked his teeth with a toothpick. Still a third moved around the place with a scalpel scraping up the blood. Dry spots. One was working on the edge of the window with a hacksaw. Why, I don't know. Another held test tubes for the one scraping up blood spots. One was sprinkling powder around the devastated area of the suitcase—rather, what was left of the suitcase. They'd already marked off what was left of the area with a piece of chalk.

But I didn't hang around. . . .

I am in a foreign country in a tiny fishing village. A procession of natives, dressed in black, are following four pallbearers, also in black, carrying a coffin. They are moaning, climbing a hill, and the orange sun is going down behind them. I must have seen this somewhere. Cora is in the coffin. I step closer to make sure it's Cora. It is. She sits up, suddenly. The pallbearers drop their palls and run. The whole procession scatters.

The playbill in hand: It is damp from perspiration. Cora learns her lines well. Good evening, folks. We are in the Concept West Village Theatre on Grove Street near Sheridan Square. In a few moments you will hear Dale's best strongest voice open the performance.

I am backstage. From where I am standing, I see the shabby glow of a red outline. It is Dale's body. Cora isn't in sight, but she knows her part. And she certainly isn't far away. I feel focused as rigidly as one crazed in a trance.

Cora suddenly appears. She is wearing a Fouke-dyed black fur seal coat with side buttons and great deep pockets. Beneath, there is nothing else. Every step she takes exposes her. But she doesn't seem to care.

I simply refuse to go into details. Fragments can be all we have to make the whole. An archaeologist might, of course, look for different clues. Somebody now taps me on the shoulder. The person is a nervous man I have never seen before.

"Don't worry. It will go fine."

"Yeah."

He scratches his keen black nose. He suddenly jerks his arm to see the face of his watch. It gives me a funny feeling. . . .

. . . .

People are served Ritz crackers and Wispride cheese: blue and gold and greenish pink he-gods and she-gods with black wine glasses.

Cora caught the twinkle in some strange man's eye. I traced a line on the ledge and turned fully to the night, looking over the East River toward Brooklyn.

Outside the window I saw a man's childish grin. What was it about him that attracted Cora. The psychedelic lights continued to dance against moving faces.

. . . .

From the turntable the Jimi Hendrix Experience jumps through the room with the force of Goya dancers. . . .

. . . .

Cora is trying to get a part in a play—any play. She stands in line waiting, for a chance to try out for *Peer Gynt*. Nothing happens. She's standing in another line, waiting to try out for *Darkness at Noon*; and she's in another line for *Little Caesar*. It suddenly occurs to her that *Little Caesar* will be a film and she has had no film experience. Her heart beats faster. She leaves and finds another line: this one, for a 1956production of *Middle of the Night,* at the Shubert Theatre, in New Haven.

. . . .

Cora has gone away again. She's driving a rented car around a small bay in a foreign country. The sun is going down. It's raining—just a sprinkle. She drives through the mountains where she picks up a hitchhiker. "Oni's my name." Along the same road, another one. She calls herself "Cathy." And a third: "Eunice." A fourth, "Anita." Huge wind currents, slamming down from the mountains, nearly push the car off the road into the dale. . . .

. . . .

I receive a picture post card. It's from Cora. She's on a beach somewhere in the Pacific Northwest. There's a man with her. They're holding hands and walking along barefoot. The sand is wet and warm. In about twenty minutes they will be in a cottage arranging roses in a vase. After that they will take a Boeing 707 to Victoria, British Columbia, and check into a large room at The Empress where they will stay for five days, sleeping in separate beds. I receive another card. The picture on it shows Cora wearing a delicate taffeta iris-colored dress and smiling. The background is yellow. I draw a blank when I try to remember who the man was. . . .

. . . .

I'm a detective trying to solve a murder; no, not a murder, it's a life. Who hired me? I can't face the question.

I'm tailing Cora and Canada and Dale. The three of them are riding together in a gasoline-powered 1885 Benz, ten miles per hour. Canada is driving, I'm walking. It takes them ninety years to reach the theater. The show has closed. The building is no longer there. The Village has changed. . . .

. . . .

Canada and I leave town. It's not easy. In Maryland, we get work operating a crane on a construction site, lifting a hundred and forty tons of mashed potatoes from a vacant lot to another vacant lot. Pay: fifty cents and a fish sandwich. For spending change, we stick up a mail train, swooping with seven million, which lasts us a few days. We live it up in Winnemucca, Nevada; dance with buck-eyed Indians in Pierce, Idaho; do the fox-trot with hippies in Eugene, Oregon; backtracking, we hide out in Swiftbird, South Dakota, where a fella with alert gentle eyes and red hair, helps us invent new identities. With our new cards, we return east, dressed as limbo dancers, with the false endorsement of Teresa Marquis of the Island of St. Lucia, we get work at the Palace Theatre and Carnegie Hall. We're a smash success. Our manager, a bird-watcher from Dwaarkill, New York, books us for a tour of Italy, but by now we're exhausted. We separate. . . .

. . . .

Canada plays tricks on Cora and she adjusts to his tricks. The action is no big thing. She is soft texture and quivering flesh, and she is a person too. But Canada has trouble. Sometimes it is troublesome for him to see this. He sees the television screen, but he cannot always see the street below their window; or see how Cora opens or the furniture they got from the flea market or see himself reflected in the bathroom mirror. But he means well and often he means to be very good.

He glides his tongue along the edges of Cora's hairline. And I watch from the far side of the dim room. The soft splash of wet vehicles going by outside.

"The living tissue," Cora says.

"Are you pregnant?"

"No, Canada. I'm desperate. I feel tense and desperate." She turns away toward the wall.

I walk closer to see better and the afternoon sunlight touches my face, causing me to retreat.

I hide in the kitchen but do not look at the rubber plants. In here there is no sunlight. But I hear the French horns again and children outside screaming.

In the front Canada and Cora are laughing together. I feel they are probably laughing at me.

I open the silverware drawer again, just to make sure the loaded pistol is still there. Canada might have taken it away, for security—which he shall never have. But it is still in its place in the drawer.

I hate to say each thing has its place but that is the way this house is run. Cora runs this house and she is quite regular. She regulates everything her own way. But I've gotten used to it and it doesn't bother me so much anymore. . . .

. . . .

I'm at the outpost. The nearest seaport is a hundred miles downstream. I'm waiting for Cora's next move.

Canada comes from the woods into the clearing. He's wearing overalls, and he's carrying a shotgun. He squints watching me closely. His mouth opens but he says nothing.

I make up a name. "I'm Dick James." I think fast. "My boat sprung a leak." I think even faster. "It floated off downstream."

. . . .

Cora likes to be alone. She shoots live movies, makes up mysteries and melodramas, and does frame-by-frame animations of her own visions. She's alone in her apartment looking in the mirror. Boris Karloff looks back at her. She smiles at him. Behind her, Peter Lorre murmurs something about being cautious. A tree frog is sitting on her dresser. Cora does a turnabout and sees Charlie Chaplin and W. C. Fields standing in the doorway. . . .

. . . .

I tend to see very little of the surface: Cora's face, for example. Another example: my own face. With Cora one should be more literal. After all she is very physical. She *was* a very physical person. Cora was the opposite of me. She took people and things at face value. She took people at their word. I hardly know how to take people. I spend too much time sunk deep in my own wanderings far down below the surface, dreaming up problems for myself. Where I don't have them, I invent them; and at least I tell myself it is what sustains me. What wakes me up? The challenge of each day . . . Canada is a problem. I mean I have to deal with all kinds of things: people and situations. How will Canada adjust to Cora's death? Who cares about Dale's absence? If no one, why no one? Who was he, where'd he come from? What did Cora see in him, vice versa?

And my being alone so much reinforces the tendency to skin-dive beneath the surface, not that I find solutions. I should ideally strike a balance between the surface and the lower depths. I can do the low stuff very effectively. I need practice on the surface where Cora, Canada, and Dale hang out. . . .

. . . .

The windows rattle because the season is changing. Leaves have dropped from trees and people are wrapping themselves beneath huge coats. We begin with the body and end with the body. Anything else is theory. Soon I doubt if I'll be able to still visualize her face. . . .

. . . .

I want to stop dwelling on her and get myself together. She believed in me, I think. She believed in herself too. Which was probably why she was able to believe in me. But I don't know why she did. I never did anything profound to deserve her trust. I just promised myself to stop thinking about her. But she possessed such an amazing capacity to show affection—even through her dreamy and often even dreary cynicism. Yet I can't knock her too much. It destroys me. . . .

. . . .

I'm driving an early-American mail coach along a long dirt road. Six Iceland ponies are straining to pull me and the load of special deliveries. They're all from Canada. Many of them are addressed to Cora, a few to Dale. I stop in front of the Brooklyn Museum to ask the guard how to get to Manhattan. He takes me on a tour of the museum, showing me various abstract paintings. "These things are about themselves. Look at the paint. By the way, did you put a dime in the parking meter?"

. . . .

The time Canada brought his fist down on the table and shook everything off, I tried to pretend I wasn't sitting there. I didn't want to understand his anger.

Nor could I safely acknowledge it. Cora turned from the kitchen sink to see what was going on. Through his dark glasses he looked at her with disgust. He'd spilled ale on his yellow ochre shirt.

"Bring me the pistol."

Cora opened the silverware drawer and brought the gun to her man. He took it and smiled cynically.

She returned to the dishes in the sink and Canada checked the weapon; then aimed it at me. He held it like that. And I tried not to show fear.

"Light a cigarette for me."

From the pack of Viceroys on the table I took a cigarette, lit it, and handed it to him, cautiously. I squeezed my mind off from thought.

Then from the sink, Cora said, "Canada!"

But he didn't answer.

Again, she said, "Canada." And not waiting for him to reply she continued, "Come unscrew the top of this jar, please!"

From the corners of my eyes I could see her looking at us. I still refused to let my mind work, let alone speak. I felt a word from me at that moment might have been terrible.

"Canada!" Cora shouted.

Finally, he stood up and left the gun lying on the table. While he was at the sink beside Cora fumbling with the jar, I took a close look at the gun. I put on my glasses and leaned halfway across the table. It was not a gun. I was stunned. No, I was only half surprised. The object was clearly a fancy can-opener. Well, I felt better about Canada. We were still friends after all—if we ever were. He was only playing a game? . . .

· ·

I've presently reduced myself to Canada. I'm Canada. Cora and I are picnicking in a dale near Dingmans Falls in the Poconos. We have ham wine cheese nuts. We run out of wine. I fly to California for more. When I return Cora's gone. A note pinned to the picnic basket says: "If you love me come and get me. I'm at Turntable Junction in Jersey with Dale."

· ·

A huge balloon is floating overhead. Cora is up there waving to me. I'm swimming in the swimming pool of a motel in Los Angeles. This morning a picture postcard came from Canada. It shows him defusing a bomb. The New York Police Department will soon give him an award.

Cora is coming down slowly.

I'm now high diving.

Dale is shooting Canada from a cannon up to meet Cora.

. . . .

Organisms live blankly together. But as I say I can't tell you whether or not Dale has meaning. You know he won't focus properly. To know anything specific about his whereabouts is even less likely. Nowadays no one has this particular sort of skill anyway. Take machines: though they break down, they tend to be more precise. Yet the data they offer on Dale (things like social security number, driver's license number, telephone number, or apartment number) are, except in the small way, useless. . . .

. . . .

I've decided to try to make peace with Dale. I rent a car. It's summer and I want to take my three friends on a trip. Cora sits beside me. I'm driving. Dale and Canada are in the back. We move north on 95, through White Plains, on up through Connecticut, Massachusetts and New Hampshire. In New Hampshire we visit a forest full of yellow and pink flowers. We drink tons of spring water and fall asleep in the bottom of a very dry riverbed.

When I wake I am alone. . . .

. . . .

Someone is trying desperately to open the door to the apartment. The wiggling key makes a hell of a noise. Meanwhile I am watching Cora dance. From the mirror, Cora is watching herself, step by ballet step. My stomach aches and my heart swells. Something spectacular is about to happen—though there is evidence. But you know how you know without clues. Are we really clandestine? Why do I feel guilty? I'm innocent. Cora is guilty. Why should I think of hiding in the closet? What sort of tradition is that? What deep fear is this at the root of jealousy?

The person outside continues to turn the key. Cora dances close to the mirror and, without losing rhythm, she kisses her own lips on the mirror.

"Why is it you never give me anything? I like gifts!"

"Rejuvenation."

The noise of the key continues. I feel hungry and thirsty.

"I've got your rejuvenation. I want a gift."

"I give you relaxation."

"You give me menopause."

"I give you tissues."

"You give me your face."

"I give you balance."

"You give me tales."

"I give you muscle."

"You give me sleep."

"I give you sperm."

"The truth is, dear friend, you give me a pain in the age."

"Cora, I give you my vitamins and my growth."

"You give me Canada. He's all."

"Not true. I give you energy."

"I suppose you give me life too."

"I give you life."

"Enzymes."

"Cora, I give you gifts. I gave you a sense of history and art and literature. I gave you man in space."

"You gave me hunger and a male sex organ."

"Taste buds and nerve endings."

"Sure. And they're pointless."

Now at last the door opens. And since no one is there, I understand even less.

We're all saints in the desert buried alive up to our necks. We're praying. Canada, Dale, Cora and I have changed radically. We're asking the Christian God to forgive us for our sinful bodies. To suffer like this is to atone.

I'm alone again on an inland waterway in a rowboat. Rowing is difficult. I'm headed for an inlet called Cora. Wild blackberries and holly trees grace the shores. A kid in a green shirt is on a Dulmen pony, he waves from the roof of a yellow house.

. . . .

I'm restless. I leave New York more and more. Cora travels with me. We're in a hick motel in Elmira. Cora is sitting on the bed playing with her toes. I'm trying to watch television but I can't concentrate on the damned thing. In color, there's a big apple-biting contest going on in Apple Valley Village. Thousands of kids and old folks are on their hands and knees biting apples.

From

My Amputations

Spring was a gentle wrestler holding the body of Nice in an agonizing embrace. Then he made her kiss the canvas. The sky cleared. Mason's first lecture for IHICE would take place the last weekday of April, two weeks away, at the American College in Paris. What was this intense windstorm blowing inside? Alpes-Maritimes Agency d'Immobilieres'd located a furnished three-room apartment for him up on the old Roman Road, Route de Bellet. He could move in the first of May. . . . He'd bought a lemon: a Simca, new and blue and difficult. Parking was a hassle . . . the morning he started driving toward Paris he felt he was in a struggle buggy about to fall apart. Looseness always bothered him. By the time he reached Aix he was cursing himself for not having gotten the Renault. Then just north of the view of Mont Sainte Victoire, as he felt the geometry of Cézanne's landscape, in a BMW speeding south, on the other side, he was sure he saw—would you believe?—Edith Levine: in the passenger seat. The guy driving looked Italian or French. Small world? Mason toyed with the idea of exiting and following her—just to *see* but the next exit was twenty minutes later and by then, well, forget it. He stopped at Arles. The outlying areas, farmland, hadn't changed since that strange, tormented painter cut off his ear here, in, was it 1888. The city itself was now strictly tourist: complete with sidewalk cafés, the type with metal chairs and tables. The drawbridge no longer existed but they'd built a replica. The house he briefly shared with that sailor of the South Sea Islands was bombed during Hitler's efforts to construct his own Roman Empire. Roman ruins in the old center. The postman and his wife were not in sight. The lamplighter café . . . ? The glare of the lighted billiards table. Mason spent the night here—not wanting to push too hard through the late afternoon and early night: and risk not finding a room. He checked into a hotel called Hotel Malchance. He didn't pay any attention. He was tired. Huge succulent plants lined the stairway up to the second floor where he had a room at the end of the hall. After a shower he lay on the bed. Edith . . . in France? Edith:

twenty-one-year-old Jewish Princess from Brooklyn. Calling her a princess was like somebody calling him a nigger. At least Princess was capitalized. Graduated with a bachelor's in sociology from City. She'd irregular, crooked ways even back in sixty-seven: lifting money from his wallet, selling dope to pay back university loans. He always suspected she *sold* a little ass once in a while. Gave away a lot too. Today in that car she was dressed to kill: decked with tons of jewels. A new, upswept hairdo. Back in the old days she was a rags-and-feather hippie. Edith had blown flower petals in cops' faces while dancing around them with other hippies in a mad frenzy of corolla and incantations. She had inbred dignity, but she was a fink. Even stole from her analyst. But that wasn't so bad 'cause he stole from her too: a huge waste of her father's money. A chronic liar, she used to fake orgasm—but was unable to let herself *go:* to go meant a loss of control—the fucking abyss, in its entire irrecoverable large-capacity garbage bag full of anal-tight *nothingness.* Not coming was a defense: a fortress against the brain-shit of the world. She held back except once when she asked him to spank her. She lay across his lap and he whacked her like her dad used to do: she produced, out of her twat, one drop of perfume—smelled like Evening in Paris or Sunrise in Lower Manhattan. He now closed his eyes. Lying prone. Release. He could see her big cayenne-pink hindquarters now, the curl of light pubic hair there at the crack. When his palm struck the flesh there was bounce-back shudders from the hip flash. These were not hard. Not hard enough for her taste. He? He didn't especially dislike it but it was boring: did nothing for his erection. He never did it again and they grew farther apart sexually: she had her own life and he had his. And they had only some vague thing together. Once at a dance party Edith almost got fucked against her will. She only wanted to flirt but the yellow nigger she was belly rubbing with twirled her away off the dance floor, danced her into a dark room from which she shot distressed and yelping five minutes later. Mason was pissed at her stupidity and that night they fought. But she was a smart cookie: she knew the problems of America and could talk them in scientific terms. Her command of higher math awed Mason. She knew changing birth rates by religion; crime rates by ethnic groups; death rates, income rates, you name it. Medians, scales, variables. She used, in her daily life, the jargon: and after a while Mason felt like he had cabin fever. . . . There was the time her father came over. They'd been together a year. Mason was nervous before his arrival: rare is the white man who accepts the black mate of his daughter. Edith's father, kicked out of the family, now ran a fruit vending business up in the Bronx on Pinkney Avenue for his cousin. The old guy got a lot of colored customers from the Boston Road area ("I *know* colored real well—they buy from me . . .") buying his rotten citric "wares"—so said Edith. Maybe Edith was a cold fish and had no integrity, but she did write to Mason once while he was in the joint. That was more than he could say for, well, a lot of so-called compassionate friends. When he got out, he and Edith had dinner together at Ratner's on First—where the waiters (very old Jewish guys) gave them dirty looks. They *knew.* Her pie had a huge green *dead* fly stuck in its whipped cream. Well, you could say old guys had bad eyesight, but . . . such events gave Mason jungle fever. There were times when they were left too long waiting for service in places where the waiters weren't busy. She once said, "New York Jews have some *nerve* hating Black people: a *defenseless* group . . . after the Jewish experience . . ." As a child she'd been to Israel with her parents. Her Brooklyn high school teacher "made" her "lecture" on it: the one thing she wanted to say she never said. She went around for weeks telling her friends she was an altruist—not a Jew. Edith was Edith. There was no fig leaf covering her crotch: even if she couldn't come. Judaism sort of embarrassed her. And she had no intention of becoming a Christian. She liked Mason because, she said, he was gentle and immoral, beyond sin, beyond crime, existential. Plus he *liked* women. When he fell asleep that night in Arles he found himself not in Van Gogh's house but in Cézanne's: upstairs in the place on the hillside in Aix-en-Provence. Cézanne, in a stained suit—complete with vest—was sitting on a stool, before a canvas. He held his pallet with thumb and fingers of the left hand. His sharp eyes darted from the long, bored body of his son, slouched in a chair to the half-finished painting of him, on the easel. Mason left Cézanne to work. He went down the hall and stairway and out into the garden. Skylight was rare here: the trees were thick and close together: it was like having a deliberate roof. He walked peacefully under the shelter.

. . . .

It might be safe over here to quietly assume his "rightful" identity again. Do a few readings for the bread, which he needed already. Signard, head of the International Humanities Institute for Cultural Exchange's Speakers' Bureau had already expressed interest in response to his, Mason's, letter from Nice. Hence this trip . . . not likely to bump into hellcat Brad? Or agents from MFR? But surely that woman was *Edith!*

. . . .

Paris, Paris! IHICE kept a low profile: entrance in a court way (not visible from street) of an old apartment building across the street from the famed cemetery called Père Lachaise. After Signard, a quirky little man, gave Mason an advanced check and his itinerary (he'd read at the University of Paris to a class of grad students studying contemporary American fiction) the booking agent walked out onto Avenue Gambetta with Mason and expressed his delight in the beautiful weather. He also told Mason that the university people would wine and dine him either before or after the event. Mason watched him talk. Signard twitched as he reached for Mason's hand. At that moment another man approached. Signard showed signs of recognition, if not delight. To Mason the guy looked familiar. Very! The fact got his fear churning again. Signard made a nervous leap, yanking the two—Mason and the new-arriver—together; meanwhile, forcing their hands together and introducing them at the same time. Mister Familiar's name was Alm Harr Fawond. Arab? But . . . the American accent? Anyway, the moment lasted less than the time it takes a fly to tune his legs. Then Mason was on his way, with not a second thought.

. . . .

In search of Richard Wright's ashes, he entered the cemetery's profusion of gravestone and leaf and although he didn't find Wright hidden at the foot of a stairway to vaults, he found the lonely graves of Stein and Modigliani and, yes, Balzac and Roussel and one big, blunt tomb marked simply, "Family Radiguet." Bewildered, he came out at a brisk pace. . . . But Mason wasn't ready for Paris. One bookstore on the Left Bank was full of giddy young Americans. Plus he couldn't find his own name (the one, I mean, that he insisted was his) on any spine on the shelves. Pigalle was a flesh hustle that bored him. The lines were too long at the museums. Nightlife was more expensive than it was worth. He thought of going out to Auvers-sur-Oise to lie down on the bedsprings in the tiny room where Van Gogh died, just to feel, or try to feel, the weight of his own body in that moment. No, there was no good reason to spend a lot of time in Paris. He'd give the reading, go to dinner with his hosts, and then split for Nice.

. . . .

Back in Nice he moved into a whitewashed apartment. Sold the Trojan horse—his Simca. Got a Fiat. Felt better. Changed from BNP to Credit Lyonnais. An Italian family, the Rosatis, owned the labyrinthian estate. The villa itself was a credible altar to the sun overlooking the sea. The owner's villa was up at the northern end of the estate. Downstairs beneath Mason's tiny place lived the Barilis. Madame and Monsieur Barili worked for the Rosatis. Mainly they cared for and puzzled over the sturdy carnations. They also exorcised and harvested the pears, grapes, cherries, plums, olives, in season. Rosati—a frail, tiny old man, his wife, daughter, son-in-law and three grandchildren—also worked the land. Being here for Mason was like being in parentheses. Yet—something in Barili's eye. A charm? The look of a spell weaver? Mason felt the eye of a fiend upon him when he passed the fat dark Italian. Surely, he was not some diabolical version of The Impostor? That elusive renegade couldn't possibly be *here!* Here was no place for a prince of rogues: Pegasus somehow had connected the earth and heaven. Every day Mason saw sea horses down there flying up out of the blue. . . . Yet he couldn't get over the feeling of being a lame duck. Next door? In the big apartment lived five women and two men. Mason saw them going and coming. Their motorbikes parked out in the drive. While taking his garbage down to the roadside one morning he met one of the young women—Monique. Since he'd left coffee brewing on the stove, he invited her up for a cup. Skullduggery? She had dark hair and a shy face. While they drank the bitter brew at his kitchen table, they heard the Barilis out in the yard. Some wild smell was in the air. Mason went to the window. Behind him Monique said, "These blood I cannot watch." Mason saw Madame Barili carrying two rabbits by their hind legs. Her husband waited for her by the clothesline where four other—skinned and pink—rabbits were hung by their legs. Monsieur Barili took one of the two rabbits from his wife. Holding it by its hind legs, he quickly, expertly, drove the tip of the blade into the animal's neck—just behind its jaw. Then he stood holding it like that till most of the blood had poured out onto the ground. The other long-eared creatures squirmed and squeaked. Madame Barili, stocky, tough, socked them both in their heads with her fist. They went into shock. Then Monsieur Barili gave his wife the head-end of the still dripping hare. He slit it down the stomach as she held tightly. He then ripped the pelt off as she clung to her end. After that one was hung on the line, she handed him another live one. Mason turned back to Monique. She drained her coffee cup. "I hear the mailman's motorbike." She stood. "Merci. Au revoir." When the postman came up rather than leaving mail in the boxes down by the road, he had a package or an express letter. Mason walked down with her. One of the cats, the black and white one, that hung around the estate came from nowhere and rubbed herself against Mason's jeans. The mailman was coming toward them, looking bewildered. "Pardon. Monsieur, s'il vous plait?" He took the letters and thanked the man. The special delivery was from Schnitzler in London and there was something from Professor Jean Claude Bouffault with the university's return address. Monique was teasing the postman for not bringing her any letters. She told Mason, after the motorbike left the yard, that she had to meet a friend for lunch. This was her day off. What kind of work did she do, where was she from, what were her beliefs, her past? This was not the time, not the place. Eh? Smoke came their way in a sudden gust. He watched her slender body, her shapely bottom as she went toward her Honda parked under the big olive tree at the corner of the yard. . . . Then he went and sat on his doorstep and opened the letter from Schnitzler. He was trying to arrange a lecture/reading tour for Mason in England but probably wouldn't have anything finalized till fall, when the academic year started up again. Bouffault's letter contained an invitation to take part in a detective writers' conference to be held here in Nice at the university. Bouffault explained that he knew Mason wasn't exactly a detective writer, but he thought Mason might find the three-day event fun. There would be detective fans and writers from all over.

He returned to Doctor Wongo's studio. A Nigerian woman greeted him, introduced herself as Adaora Okpewho. "Doctor Wongo is in Nigeria on business. May I help you?" Mason didn't think she could. Yet she was clearly not the sort of person who'd try to cure bad memory or snakebite with calcium tablets. "I came for a body reading." "A body reading's simple. I can give you a body reading. As my ancient mother used to say, 'Him who got text for body way get readers very good.'" And Adaora Okpewho laughed a little musical laugh as erasable as skywriting. Mason immediately trusted her. Emotionally he'd already placed himself in her hands. And he knew she knew it. "Come over where it's warm. You must undress." He followed her past familiar torture-gadgets to the sheet-covered mattress on the floor in a corner. When Mason was lying naked on his back on the mattress Adaora Okpewho bent down placing her knees on a cushion. Here alongside him she looked even larger. He studied her eyes. They possessed the glimmerings of the cudblurbing of a bad dream. Yet his sense of safety didn't lose its tenure. Her alchemy was working. And she hadn't even touched him—yet. Then she did. Her hands were huge and soft with iron and webbed octaves in their rhythm. They turned him to liquid. Then the reading started. Not with her voice but with the music of her flesh. The first thing she touched was his penis. "This," she whispered, "is your khnemu. The fibrous tissue within is a mask for the shredding pages of Baptist Church bibles. Your legs? One at a time. This one, the left: it is a Pond Cypress pretending to be a hawk giving a monkey a ride across a dark sky—to a place of safety. The right one is a parrot who tells the slaveholder the slaves had a dance while he was away in town. You must *watch* this one. Your eyes are not spies; so can't do it with them. But to return to your legs. They're complex limbs: see this bird-like structure at your knee? It's a mule leading a man. The sound you hear behind the plowing is that of a bullfrog pulling off its jacket. You got femur and patella and fibula and tibia down here: they are all counties in High-on-the-Hog and Getting-the-Better-of-Bossman. Then this thing called coccyx. What can I tell you about it? It's close to the center. And the sacrum is too. Legs are important," said the African woman. "They can be trees, every day in the week: milky sap, corky ridges, thorns, twigs, wafer ash, yellow birch. You smell them, taste their sassafras—aromatic, sour sap. Important thing though is this: what the legs connect to." She grinned. And grabbed his cock again. She shook it as she spoke. "This majestic thing is a crab apple one day, a black locust another, a Hercules Club. It has bark. And history. It has fast-moving guys behind it. Nicodemus from Detroit might know more about it than I. Yet, there are times, in the Blues, when the slaveholder gets the better of good old John or Moe or Moses. I'm getting away from—. Never mind. A lot comes from central West. Much from up higher, closer to the sea: Liber Metempsychosis. Ennu. Pu. Teta. So much. I'd take weeks to bend your ear. Ear-tree. And so much that wouldn't fit: everlastingness: kale or collards. Coptic concerns here backed up by all those wonderful tiny Egyptian birds of Thought: facing bowls: or equations: or puzzles." She stopped. "Sorry. I got carried away, chum. Bud. Honey. Pal. I'll start again. Here, your hips are important: and deep inside the sacrum, the femoral artery, cushioned between the hips is the small intestine, the rectum, and your bladder. Hum. Birds with tiny feet dance in your liver, your urine . . . I'm going to move on—up. Your stomach. Ah! This organ pretends to be a fool like a woolly headed black man in the cotton field who wants to evade a confrontation with the overseer who sees nothing. The stomach is also hooked to a plow. It has John Henry sweat on it. The stomach is hooked up with the strength of the bear and the wings of the buzzard. It's the organ that makes it possible for you to run faster than a deer. It's against Friday and Monday. Brer Dog and Brer Rabbit ain't got much to do with this organ." She rubbed it gently. "Yours is flat. Butterflies ain't never been in there, I guess. (You wondering why I, a Nigerian, know so much about you, an Afro-American? No? Good. Your body tells me much.) Here—your chest." She tapped it. "Thorns. Silverbells. Here" (she bent, placing her nose within an inch of his ribs). "We're close to the heartbeat. Yours smell of malt and pine nut. Ginger and goat drifting up from below. Ra must have smelled like that. Isis like pears and perch. I hear a herd of Cayuse ponies galloping in there: Your ribcage is a teepee—gift from your tribal ancestors in North America. Your blood is African: it's a storm: 'de wind and de water fightin' (to quote Doctor Hurston). Pectoralis major? The base of your Talking Bones." She sat erect again without removing her hands. "Now your neck. It's the channel: it gets tight when you have to prove yourself the fastest and the best. (Like your grandfather, you're so fast you could go out in the woods, shoot a wild, gaunt boar, run home, put your rifle away, and get back in time to catch the hog before it fell. But this swiftness gives you trouble. Makes you a dangerous over-achiever.) Your throat is subject to infection: be careful. If you have trouble, the flower of the magnolia will cure it. Just chew it. Stay away from the Crucifixion thorn. Be careful in Utah or Arizona. In the Peach State beware of the one-legged grave robber and anybody who says he can turn a buffalo around. Now, your head. Your brain is sweet gum. It has a history of tricksterism: it's a dog that saves your life, a rabbit that survives the threat of bullies and tyrants. Your ventricles are black locust." She was rubbing his scalp with the firm tips of her fingers. Your brain stem has the aromatic smell of the sassafras. It protected you from being killed by your mother and eaten by your father. Your cerebellum protects you from the return of vengeful ancestors and enemies: from the dead generally. Without it you might be stranded in an endless winter between centuries and races. The fluid surrounding your brain is your incense and it is your own hant and spirit. That's right: keep your eyes closed. Concentrate, my son. Keep the hoodoos out. Mojo workers out, too. There's a two-headed man trying to get inside your epidural space. He has the attractive smell of hemlock. You'll do well to wash your hair with bitter wafer ash ailanthus. Your skull bone is as sturdy as a pyramid and as serious as Zacharias and the Sycamore." Adaora Okpewho stopped. "This is not the end. Your thighs, feet, and your rear are left." She shifted her weight and leaned toward the lower part of his body. "Turn over." He obeyed. "Gluteus maximus. This left cheek keeps the memory of your fear of falling: it remembers what you felt as you sailed through the air when your father threw you out the window. It remembers the thud when your grandfather caught you. This other one is a storehouse too: it holds the passion of sin and crime and the whole morality of your life: guilt for the legacy of hunting possum on Sunday; gambling away the family jewels, it keeps the Lord and the Devil from exchanging places. It reminds you that you need more faith. It keeps you from becoming a grave robber. It's a mulatto hobo who—" At this point, Mason and Adaora Okpewho looked toward the door. Somebody had just entered the room. It was Doctor Wongo.

. . . .

Detection and deception? Possibly. May in Nice was impish: with windswept Terra Amata vibrations beneath its insistent, demanding presence. *Demon* cries! The idea of a conference of detective storywriters? Rare in itself. But, well, why not . . . ? And look: genre people gotta be hipper than, say, all those so-called serious types . . . even if they carry toy pistols in their briefcases! The first session met at nine in the conference room of the library, on a Monday. Mason stole his way in and sat in a corner at the back. A French scholar was lecturing on Himes's domestic novels: the grotesque and twist-of-fate in his ironic picaresques. *Le reine des pommes* was a killer! A blind man with a pistol could shoot out your reflexes! Grave Digger and Coffin Ed hit like metal file cabinets falling from a sixteenth-floor window. The French critic finished and one from Holland lowered the lights and showed them slides as he talked. The jungle was evil? One had to find one's way up a mean, snaky river? Or was this a journey into the mind, deep into the unexplored depths of the criminal vegetation-of-human-existence itself? Should the detective take sides with the villain, help him free himself further from the menacing presence of the—indefinable enemy. Tsetse flies might end your life before you could detect even *why* you're here. Crusaders got in the way of the search, the probing. If you're going to throw your lot in with that of the murderer, then you want to be sure to saddle up properly, pack a gun or take spears. Is your curiosity about that obsessed maniac you're searching for just down right morbid? What about your own contradictions? Your fog, your confusion? And there was the possibility of your crew, and the native dancers—who would not escape the brutality, lust, and good intentions of the Crusaders. This was years after the Roman conquest and long after the beginning of the exploitation of Africans in Africa. What *kind* of detection is this? Through slide after slide, the Dutchman showed his willingness to explore the farthest terrain of his own evolving process: to search every crevice—even into the nose of a Bahr-el-gazel, in the armpit of a Kano trader, between the rear cheeks of a Basuto. Professor Franz Soethoudt's amazing lecture was a concession, a story, a plot, and a line of horses plunging through the desert, carrying riders with muskets. Searching for what? Looking for the cyclical thrust of its own *tale*. . . . The morning session continued in this fashion. Mason went away at noon with a headache.

• •

The next day, more of the same: stolen ponies, shady sandalwood, lost spies, tom-toms, governments in trouble, thoroughbreds in the backs of stolen trucks. But lunch with the detective storywriters was different: noisy, cheerful. He didn't really meet anybody: just the surfaces of people. He couldn't detect any reality behind these surfaces. They possessed good faces, even kind ones, and threw off nice music, sweet, tamed voices. There was a Soviet-approved, neo-Tchaikovsky style in some, in others, German organs or French drums. Ladies sipped bitter red San Pellegrino. One, an American, was working on a whodunit about Brumbies being stolen for a meat grinder in a pet food factory. Her friend, a painter, was with her. They both gave Mason the willies: made him want to go on a crusade to save elephants and the dear rhinoceros. After lunch he went for a walk along the sea. Everybody was out. It was hot.

• •

The conference had a lingering effect: he found himself playing detective. Even bought a black cap pistol, which he carried, strapped to his leg. For days now, Mason went about shooting at shocked people. An old man in a funeral procession at Place de la Beauté swung at him with a walking stick. Mourners filed out of Maria Sine Labe Concerta. They laughed at Mason. He went and bought a *water* pistol. Filled it with *milk*. On rue Foncet, he squirted his first victim: a girl in a yellow dress. She smiled and tried to kiss him, but he ran. He settled down at a sidewalk café at the corner of rue Miralheti and rue Pairoliere. He was carrying this thing too far. What'd come over him?

. . . .

They all go over to a hidden beach at the bottom of a steep hill near Monte Carlo. On the way: Mason remembers a dream he had in the night: a tiny woman in large hooped skirts with many sandwiches packed against her belly and groin—held firm by elastic bloomers—greets him. He reaches for one of her sandwiches and she slaps his hand. She laughs at him. Says: Go suckle the moon! Jean-Pierre is driving insanely fast. Mason's companions are speaking to each other in French. It causes him to want to keep to himself. He wishes he hadn't come. On the beach everybody's like in a Cézanne: nude. Mason and his friends undress. Two fat guys approaching the surf cough and sneeze in each other's face: they seem unaware of the exchange. Mason now is not even conscious of the fact he's a foreigner: everybody who's not pink is brown or tan. Then there's a *very* dark figure coming down the rocky path to the beach. African? Welcome brother! No, not African. Too much *brown* for African. Guy alone. The dark man is coming this way: across the rocks. Carefully. Carrying—what is that? Oh, just a shoulder bag. His white pants are too long. His sandals: loose. Something familiar . . . Oh, no, shit: it's *Clarence McKay!* Mason staggers to his feet and attempts to split: nowhere to hide ("ran to the rock" . . .), nowhere. . . . Ten feet from Mason, The Impostor whipped out a giant Smith and Wesson six-shooter and aimed it at Mason. The Impostor pulled the trigger.

. . . .

There is a tingling breeze coming up from the Alps cutting the fumes from traffic up on the road to Monaco. It's realistic, calm, a friendly day. Mason opens the white wine. Although he's relaxed and enjoying his escape-from-the-bullet-of-guilt, somewhere back there in the glue and glut of his history is a Pony Express rider coming forward, like a bat out of heaven, with an urgent message for him. The word could be anything: that's the problem: it's not clear. From the so-called Impostor? The long-awaited news from Himes of Wright, perhaps Dumas? The messenger has heavy saddlebags. Lots. And the *way—Whew!* Is it news of another divorce, another childbirth? News of being inducted again into the military? Hokum? Word had come from Schnitzler about the England trip. Soon now. He was arrogant enough to be excited. Meanwhile, enjoy. Wasn't accustomed to all of this nakedness: good though: no puritans here ("we're a Catholic country but we're not very religious"). Yet he was chickenman, chickenman—turning on a spit in a cooker (soon to be . . .). Here on the beach, naked and turning blacker, warmer, happier, smoother, he almost dared to feel *complete:* yet—no way. The wine he'd contributed to the beach party he'd picked up at one of his old favorite caves—Caprioglio right across from Paganini's "home" on rue Saint Reparate. He scans the beach. Such grace and lines: curve of pelvis, tilt of tit, and roundedness of buttocks, broadness of chest, slope of thigh. Monique was making a "sand castle" with rocks. Well, dislocation is allowed—even in a straight one, isn't it? Raymonde, intellectual expert on French avant-garde and soon to be shipped to an academy of superior education in Kigali, is spitting out a bitter position pitted against Jean-Pierre's defensive verbal stand on—where'd this conversation come from?—The extent to which France aided the Nazis in exterminating six million Jews. Mason lying prone on his towel with eyes closed beneath sunglasses picks up maybe 80 percent. Scuff. Jean-Pierre says nobody ever *told* him France handed over the Jews till he saw a movie about it. You were in the streets in sixty-eight like everybody else says Raymonde flinging his shoulder-length dark hair back from where it curled over the left eye—a C-shape concealing the figure eight. Chantal butts in to say the deal they got as a result of sixty-eight protests didn't carry with it the guarantee that anti-Semitism would vanish from France. Isabelle sneers: other countries are worse. We do our best: I work every day with the disadvantaged, it's heartbreaking but we at least try. In French. Mason sits up: down the rocky shore Brieuc and Roye are running in all their tiny pinkness with three little female cherubs. A woman with shaved cunt passes going toward the chartreuse tide. He decides to take a dip too. What a cut above Quai Lunel! Monique is already in, a back designed with freckles. How tiny her hands are! In the water he won't have to hear the words he only half understands. That time waiting to cross at rue Desire Neiland the trio of Lycée girls and boys bombarding him with questions in French. How frustrating to have to *be* the dumb foreigner! Selling tickets for charity? You want to hide. And at the entrance to Old Town at Port Fausse on the stairway an old woman asking him *something* as she gestured toward the Cathedrale beyond rue du la Boucherie and Mason's mouth hanging open. . . . She might have been telling him they were dynamiting in the square and he shouldn't go or that city workers in their blue were no longer trimming hedges into square oblong rows but had now gone wild and were castrating on sight. Why always at stairways? And why did the beggars always approach him: did he look so different? They'd come up with their drugged babies telling him a story he couldn't follow: on the mall at the post office—on stairways! One nearly pushed him down the stairway at rue du Pont Vieux and rue du Collet when he refused her. Another spat on his back. Called him a dirty name. Now entering the sea is like throwing one's nakedness into music made with the feudal stones of a chateau. Even Mason feels it.

• •

Celt-spirit here, pre-Roman slush, plunder, spoils, Darkness embraced? Gatwick was snow-cold but under a rainstorm of mice-turds. Professor Frank Poole picked him up, delivered him to the Bickenhall, a modest hotel on Gloucester Place near Baker Street. A little twitchy man, Poole left and Mason was glad. He went for a walk in the neighborhood: had fish and chips in a restaurant just over on York. Even Poole was possibly a spy. In front of the liquor store next door an old toothless hag (also a spy?) surrounded by six police dogs held forth with her begging cup and a cackle. He picked up the *Herald-Tribune* from a vendor at Marylebone Road . . . Betty Boop wasn't going to come. The hotel wasn't there when he got back. The rules here are gonna keep changing? Wrong street. He caught an Al Pacino flick. Slept restlessly: mam'zels teasing him from shadows of lace. He was writing a novel in which he couldn't figure out the difference between what was real and not: Painted Turtle told him it was 'cause he drank too much. His blood sugar. He needed to see a doctor. He was crazy. He accepted her verdict. There were too many women in his novel, he fucked them all too lightly. He needed a conference on morality with the authorities. He was a sinful beast, a pig—a fink. Then he was on this bus that turns a sharp corner on a mountain road and slides off plunging down into the sun-splashed green valley. How could such a thing happen on such a nice day? Naturally he flies up out of the damned thing—Painted Turtle with him. Locked in an embrace they fall in slow motion to the dry riverbed: "We're going to die." When the crew arrives in a yellow metal bird, he and PT are still alive. The letter he'd sent just the day before to an imaginary person has been returned. The helicopter pilot hands it to him. A gunshot goes off in the valley. Sirens start up. Pilot says, "In French it says Return to sender. Are you the person?" In the morning Mason arrived at King's College at nine and after a brief introduction by flubbering, fumbling stuttering Emeritus Professor of American Literature, Basil Llewellyn Ceconhann, he faced his tiny bunch of enigmatic graduate students keen on some word about Afro-American Lit. His talk was a yellow dog. Later, in Mick's, a coterie of these grads bought him beer and chips and revealed themselves as desperately clinging to the end of the rope of academia. He had a double shot of faith-building scotch in a bar off Oxford where a couple of old neighborhood drunks were making a mutt do tricks in exchange for chips. Harry Schnitzler's left word for him to call. In the morning he was expected at Brixton College and tonight at the Young Vic for a poetry reading. What was IHICE up to? Schnitzler sounded (on the phone) like a nervous twit: "We're mindful, too, of the Fulbright people: they might want you. And ICA . . ." Anna Birly called at the last minute: she couldn't pick him up as planned. Could he take the tube? Yes. He was only five six minutes from the Baker Street Station.

Birly, his host and organizer of the Punk Rock Poetry Festival, was waiting in the flurry. They shook. She was visibly hassled. Punk Rock with added Black attraction: like Miles at rock concerts in the sixties? Not quite. Backstage he sat in the dressing room sipping bourbon from a paper cup. Sebastian, the great Punk Rock poet, was combing his long green hair. It stood out in all directions. His eyelashes were orange. From the corner of his mouth hung a weed. Tamara Polese, in Nazi uniform, was helping Etta Schnabel, lesser-known Punk poet, undress. Etta wanted to read in her birthday suit with a rose sticking out of her cunt. Kicks. Her stuff was Protest: biting. Tamara finished Etta and took the bourbon from Mason. "What's this?" she sipped. Burly, uneasily, answered for him: "Hog piss, honey." The trio called Hot Hips (composed of Sylvie—from France, Cornelia and Punk poet Estelle) went on first. Mason with the others went up and stood behind the curtain to watch. They screamed bloody murder at the audience (young punkies mostly): shook their purple short hair at each turn of each line and beat muscled fists out toward screaming voices: "Wash your mother in blood, rinse your father in the comfort of his own suds . . ." It gave Mason the chills. How would such an audience receive him? Tamara went on kicking and screaming for war: "I shoot shots from my M-1 . . . put your fuck-finger in my barrel . . ." Then Etta—as a naked belly-dancer—coughed up and hissed a Goethe poem about deals with the devil and Kafka's doomed soul and the end of the West. Thomas Mann was a jerk who moved to L.A. And so it went: Sebastian. Then Mason: slightly nervous but well received. Politely. And the show ended with straight poet Sven Storm from Sweden, trying to be interestingly dangerous and exciting but not making it: ". . . I come bullets into your military-complex asshole!" In the morning the slicker went out to Brixton in the rain. Spoke sang cried to a group of scorch eyed West Indians Africans Anglos East Indians Palestinians. Shy and untrusting, these kids were not impressed by the author's so-called lack of anger. Their highland was a lowland. How could a black poet write other than *anger*? What emotional osmosis created this freak? At the end one black kid said "You nigger to the white man, like me. What good you think your sweet verse do to liberate us? You waste your time." The audience cheered. Mason's next stop was at Africa Center, that night. Ironically, there were more English than Africans in the audience. Africans were downstairs in the cozy dimly lighted little bar quietly drinking away their London blues. When the show ended Mason and manager Steven Mackie too went down and started working on a cure for the British funk. Mason went back by way of the tube. A shopping bag had just exploded (people were saying) at one station and mobs were being rerouted out of Marylebone Station to other lines. Two dead, six injured. By ten o'clock news some "terrorist" group would phone in word of responsibility. Revolutionaries? Causes and causes. At a Whitechapel community arts center that night he conducted what is known as a creative writing workshop: eight students. The group normally met at this time—eight—every week to read and discuss their works. Mason was added attraction. Simon, group leader, sat next to Mason and as he analyzed a selection of poems by various members, Simon amended him step by step. One girl wanted to know if Mason believed in love. He said he did. But his poems were *so* depressing. He read a love poem. They said but that's not a love poem. He swore to them he had hope. They laughed and gave him cupcakes. He refused to eat with them. They passed around more photocopies of their own poems. One girl there—Colette—who looked not a bit French, in Mason's opinion, wrote excellent poems about peeling vegetables and discovering the nature of the universe through simple acts like shelling peas or following the journey of a bug along a branch, was also looked upon by the rest with some hesitation. They asked Colette why she didn't write about relevant things. She said but I do. By the end of the workshop Colette was depressed. Along with Simon and a couple of others, Colette too, Mason walked back to the tube. They all thanked him and shook his hand. That night the King of Illusion-Deceit-Fraudulence-Cheating-Shenanigan-Confidence pulled his own leg in his sleep: trying to center chubby pretty Colette onto the end of his hard-on, he experienced a disaster: she turned into a faithful photograph of the Milky Way just as he got it in. It was chewed off by the speed of cubistic light. The Great Bear barked at him with his pants down. He shot for cover. Hid behind General Leclerc in the Square. A couple of old vegetable peddlers started beating him over the head with *blette*. (Later Colette sent him a batch of her new poems. He saved them till he felt like going up to Terrasse Frederic Nietzsche. Alone he sat on a stone rail at eight in the morning with Nice beneath him. Blue sea. Full stretch. And Bego to the North snow-capped in crisp contrast with the Cimes du Diable. He read her lines: "... you unbutton my shirt / which is your shirt / and eat / the cabbage tips / of my tits ..." She'd signed all her poems with the pen name: Terry Gottlieb.)

From

Such Was the Season

CHAPTER 1

Last week was a killer-diller! I don't know if Juneboy brought good or bad luck. First news he was coming down here came from Esther. She called me one night from Chicago, where she lives, oh bout a week fore he was to get in. She said, "Annie, my son Adam is coming down there to speak at Spelman bout his research at Howard University Hospital."

I said, "What kinda research, Esther?"

She said, "Annie Eliza, I done told you bout Adam's research so many times, I swear you don't never listen to nothing I say."

Then I said to my baby sister, "You tell that boy he better stay with me when he gets here, I won't stand him staying in some hotel or with nobody else."

It had been many a year since I had seed the boy. He had to be in his mid-forties by now and I hadn't seed him since he was bout eighteen. All the other children come down from everywhere they done scattered to, for funerals and sometimes for weddings and when babies is born in the family, but not Juneboy. He swore when Scoop was shot that he would never set foot again in the South. Everybody in the family knowed how Juneboy felt.

Well, his coming anyway, even for this lecture business, was a kinda homecoming and I was looking forward to seeing him all growed up, but I couldn't imagine he was all that Esther made him up to be. I sure didn't know he was a doctor. Guess I thought he was still in school. Anyways, Esther was just always trying to make it sound like her kids had complished as much in life as mine.

Maybe his homecoming was a way of coming down to earth, finding out bout us, his peoples. I hoped so.

But there was no way to know the whole time he was here was gon be so, so full of all kinds of unexpected things happening. That whole business with Renee. Senator Cooper's mess. And Jeremiah's incident. Seems like every minute of every day—and he finally stayed eight days—something upsetting was going on. And the moon was full part of that time, too.

Then Juneboy hisself called me, the day after I talked with his mother, and told me, "Aunt Annie Eliza, thank you for offering to put me up." He said he sho appreciated it and that he was looking forward to "a reunion with all the folk."

I ast him bout this research he was talking bout. He said, "I'm working on a cure for sickle cell anemia with a group of other pathologists. We hope to find a way to break the hereditary chain." He said, "The interest at Spelman is more social than scientific."

Well, I member thinking while he talked, that he sho talked like a educated man, but then there is these street hoodlums too that can talk real smart, so smart you'd think they knowed something bout everything.

I ast him how was his wife, cause I forgot he was divorced. Then he told me, and I membered Esther telling me. So he would be coming down by hisself.

Though I have a guest room, I always give family guests my own bedroom, and I sleep on the couch out back. Juneboy was family.

Well, child, there was just three or four days to get the house cleaned up and you shoulda seed me rushing round this place of mine, sweeping and vacuuming and dusting and polishing and scrubbing. Everybody say my place is spic and span all the time cause I keep it that way. But they don't know how underneath things there is dust. I was after the hiding dirt, you see. Momma always taught us girls to be clean. Momma kept a clean house. Esther and Kathy like me in this respect. They real partickler. Prudence was like that too all her life.

I called up everybody—Ballard, Donna Mae, Jeremiah and DeSoto, Kathy—everybody I could think of and told them Juneboy was coming down Thursday morning, April tenth. He was flying in direct from Washington, D.C. I told them what he told me: he was gon go straight to Spelman and talk to the social peoples first then take a taxi out here to my place. Spelman just there on Leonard Street Southwest. I told Juneboy I could drive my old Chevy to Spelman and get him. He said no, no it wont necessary. I offered to pick him up at DeKalb or Hartsfield, whichever one he was coming in to. But no, he said the peoples at Spelman was picking him up. So I told everybody so nobody felt like they done let Juneboy down by not picking him up at the airport. He had his own plans already pretty much worked out.

Homecoming. That use to be a big thing, a custom in our family. Nowadays only time folks get together is, like I say, when somebody dies or somebody marries or haves a baby. But we Sommers use to all go down to Monroe to see Momma and Poppa when they was still living. We did it in the spring, in the first week of May. Back in them days country folks round Monroe was still marrying by stepping over the broom. At them homecomings everybody was feeling real good. We all helped Momma cook up a lot of fried chicken and made potato salad and we ate watermelon and drank lots of ice-tea. Sometimes the menfolk would sneak off and drink whiskey but we womens just pretended we didn't know. We singed a lot of happy songs too, songs like "Oh, My Little Soul's Gon Shine," and "Ain't No Grave Can Hold My Body Down," and "Every Time I Feel the Spirit."

We started going back to Monroe a year after Prudence moved up to Chicago. It was our way of getting her back, and we here in Atlanta—Kathy, Ballard, Esther, and me—we too got ourselves back down there. You see, Rutherford never left Momma and Poppa. Then Esther left Scoop and Momma and Poppa took her kids for a while and she went up North to stay with Prudence. Prudence helped her find a job and she been up there ever since.

That first homecoming was real special. I member it better than I member yesterday. Poppa was in good spirits. The fried chicken tasted real good and it was crispy. The watermelon was sweet. The grace said at the table was short so peoples got to eat fore they food got cold. All of our childrens was either not born yet or real little. Poppa, who's real name was Olaudah Equiano Sommer, talked Indian talk and we all laughed. He was proud of his Cherokee relatives. He told us a story bout his father, a important man in the Cherokee Nation, who helped collect money to send colored families to Liberia. You see, back then a lot of Negroes still wanted to go back to Africa. Olay—that's what folks called Poppa—another time he told us how his father made good luck come to the tribe. Grandpoppa built hisself a big bird, a hawk or a eagle. He made this thing out of wood, you see. Then he painted it all the natural colors it was spose to have. He kept it outside the Nation, out in the forest. Nobody knowed bout it cept Grandpoppa hisself. Everyday he took hisself out to this giant bird and he rubbed it with special oils he made from plants and he spoke a secret language to this bird and, after he did this over and over for a very long time, the bird started to talk back to Grandpoppa. He ast Grandpoppa what he wanted, told him he could make a wish, and, if the wish wont selfish, the bird told him he could make it come true. Grandpoppa had to get up on the bird's back and make the wish while sitting up there with his eyes closed. Grandpoppa told the bird not to worry: the wish wont gon be one with self-interest in it. So the bird told Grandpoppa to go on, get up there, and make his wish. He did and he wished the best of everything for the Cherokee Nation, no more war with the white man, no more war with the Creeks. Grandpoppa prayed that the Cherokees would not have any more trouble with the Chickasaws or the Confederates. He prayed for one thing and another for many hours. Then he stopped and the bird told him his wish was a good one and that it would come true, told him to go on back to the tribe and he would see for hisself. He did and at first he looked round but couldn't see how anything was changed. He looked and he looked for days but nothing looked different. Grandpoppa began to think the bird had played a trick on him so he went back to the big bird and told him he couldn't see change. The bird laughed and said change was everywhere, change for the better, there in the Cherokee Nation, and that he only had to learn how to see it. The bird told Grandpoppa to go on back and try again. This time he began to notice how peoples was smiling and speaking kindly to each other and how even the little bitty children wont fighting over toys or nothing. The mommas making corn mush looked happy and the boys going out for the rabbit hunt looked just as happy. This noticing that Grandpoppa was doing went on for days, and before long he started believing the bird's magic had worked.

I member being so struck by that story that I dreamed about it over and over for a long time.

So, homecoming was a time of happiness, storytelling, a time when we all come together and membered we was family and tried to love each other, even if we didn't always do it so well.

Now, Juneboy was having his homecoming, coming back to the South, and, like I said, nobody had any idea what a mess everything would be while he was down here staying with me.

....

I been living here in this same house in East Point for thirty-six years, ever since my husband Bibb bought it with his soldier money, back in 1947. I was the first mongst us children to live in a house I owned. Momma and Poppa course owned the house we growed up in. Me and Bibb planted the trees in the backyard. The big one out front was there when we came. Just as sho as the Chestatee River pours itself into the Chattahoochee, I'll be here in this house till the day I die. It's been a good place and peoples like to visit me. They tell me they feels comfortable here in my house.

I didn't spect Juneboy till round midafternoon. I was straightening up the back room, just a humming, "Somebody Knocking at Your Door," when I heard the doorbell ring one time. I likes visitors who ring only one time. I can't stand peoples who lean on the doorbell like they from the country and ain't never seed a doorbell before.

I went up there to see if it was Juneboy. But it wont. It was that little boy, Edgar Lee, who runs errands for me. He wanted to know if I needed anything from the store.

I didn't need nothing just then.

Then a half hour later, while I was trying to see what was happening on one of my soap operas, the doorbell ringed three times. It made me a little mad but I didn't want to go to the door mad if it was Juneboy.

And it was him. I could see him in that growed up face of his and in that smile. I was seeing him through the screen door but I could see him good enough.

I opened the screen door. "Lord, have mercy! Land sakes," I said. "Boy, look at you! All growed up and fine looking, too."

He hugged me and kissed my cheek. I held onto my wig so he wouldn't upset it.

"You're looking well, too, Aunt Annie Eliza."

"Well, don't stand there in the door letting the flies in, come on in and make yourself at home. You home now, boy."

I led him on in.

"House looks just like I remember it. So neat and pretty."

"Just like your momma keep house, huh?"

"Yes."

We laughed together.

I led him on back to the back and turned to look at him again. "Just let me look at you a minute."

I stood real close so I could see his eyes. He still had them same eyes. I knowed them since he was a baby in a stroller. He was Juneboy all right. Even with that old ugly beard!

Juneboy come just a blushing so I stopped looking at him. Then he held a box out to me. "I brought you a little something."

I took the box and just started ohing and ahing all over the place, acting like I was real surprised but I wont. Not that I spected a present.

I sat down at the table and put the box on it. I looked up at Juneboy. I was like a child at Christmastime. "Can I open it, Juneboy?"

"Sure. It's yours. Open it."

I carefully pulled the ribbon off, lifted the tape off the edge of the paper, and got the box out. At this point I was already trying to guess what it was. I figured it was a blouse or a set of dishtowels, maybe a old lady's dress. The box was lightweight, you see. My mind was trying to talk to me, saying, "Annie Eliza, don't spect much, now. You not a child at Christmastime. It's the thought that counts."

Then, child, I opened the box and wouldn't you know it, it was one of them wall hangings, real pretty one, like Indians maybe made it. That's it right there on the wall. It's made with heavy rope and beads. It don't spose to do nothing:

just hangs there like it's doing. It's got its own way, you see. I knowed it probably didn't cost Juneboy very much, maybe it was real cheap, but it was the thought. I made such a fuss bout it, kept right on raving bout it till I noticed he looked embarrassed. I didn't want him to think I was making fun of his present to me. He sensitive. So I stopped and ast him if he wanted a cup of tea and I ast him if everything went all right at Spelman.

He said, "It was like trying to make an egg stand on its end. The time of year, the season, was wrong. I worked at it; I worked hard at it, Aunt Annie Eliza. I told them what I dream of discovering and they listened as well as any audience can, but I felt sure, in the end, that I had not reached them, they had not understood. Not a single face in the audience gave off that certain light of recognition."

I didn't know what the boy was talking bout but I knowed enough to know he felt like he was a failure with that audience and maybe it was his fault and not theirs. I was ashamed of thinking: maybe Juneboy didn't know as much as he thought he did.

Then I got out some tea. I use Lipton. Renee buy all them fancy teas but, the way I figure it, Lipton just as good as any you can get and you don't have to pay all them high prices.

Juneboy sat there looking real serious, like he had something on his mind. Then he started talking, "You know, I've come here because of the lecture they asked me to give at the university, but I have another reason for returning to the South, especially to Atlanta. I have been suffering spiritually, longing for something I think I lost a long time ago. Aunt Annie Eliza, as old as I am, I should have resolved so many questions that I haven't managed to. Who am I? Where did I come from? My first questions, and they are still unanswered. I've been running from my early self, and now I want to stop. Somehow, I am hoping that I can get back in touch with that little boy I was, looking up into my mother and father's faces and discovering the world. I tried to become a different person and I guess I succeeded. But now I need to find that earlier self and connect it with the new self that I am now. It's funny; I don't think Lauren ever had this conflict. When I see her, she has her problems but they are not the same as mine—and we grew up together, had the same experiences, cried together, laughed together.

"I think back hard and try to remember my father. I loved Scoop so much and felt his pain so deeply. Aunt Annie Eliza, do you understand what I'm trying to say?"

"Sho, Juneboy. You want to get to know your family down here. That's real nice. I'm gon take you to meet everybody, and—"

"Thank you. But it's not just meeting them, it's—"

I couldn't help myself, I cut him off cause I thought he was talking crazy talk. I said, "Juneboy, how was your flight down?"

He gave me a scared look, like he done seed a ghost.

"—There was definitely something wrong with that flight, Aunt Annie Eliza. I thought surely any minute we were going to be hijacked. It was like there was something in the manner of the hostesses and you could see it in the faces of some of the passengers. When the pilot talked to us over the intercom, his voice was shaking. He said he had something important to tell us, but he never got around to saying what it was. Then he called out the name of one of the passengers and this tall hostess found the man because he hadn't responded. She got him up on his feet. He was sitting across the aisle from me. She told him the captain wanted him to come up to the cockpit. Meanwhile, we hit some rough clouds. There were funny buzzing sounds from the middle of the aircraft, probably where the wings join the body.

"I watched that man the captain wanted—his name was Joseph something, some kind of eastern European name. I watched him get up and saw the strain in his face. He was like a man either going to his execution or to the most glorious event in his life. The hostess walked just behind him. He had the grimness of determination. Even when I could no longer see his face, it showed in his shoulders and in his movement. So, curious about what was going on, I got up and followed them, pretending to go to the toilet. It worked out just fine. Somebody was in the toilet so I had an excuse to stand there just outside waiting for it to be free. The cockpit door was open, so I got to watch what was going on in there. Joseph's back was to me but I could see the face of the captain. I couldn't see his copilot. The captain was looking up into Joseph's face. I couldn't hear what he was saying because of the hum of the airplane, but he had this awful pleading expression. I do believe the man was about to cry or was already crying. He was clearly at the mercy of the passenger Joseph."

I brought the tea to the table and got two cups and poured it for us while Juneboy went on telling his story—which, mercy me, was making me feel nervous, not bout what happened but bout Juneboy hisself.

"Then the thing that convinced me, Aunt Annie Eliza, the thing that clinched it for me, was when I saw the captain hand Joseph a little package. Joseph put it in his pocket. He kept shaking his head, saying something to the captain. The captain also went on talking, looking up at Joseph—obviously begging him to do something or not to do something.

"Even when the toilet was free, I continued to stand there watching the exchange. Nobody noticed. I was discreet. I saw that Joseph was about to end his business with the captain. He was pulling away, turning, attempting to come back to the cabin. He was half turned. Without using the toilet, I returned to my seat so I could see his face as he came down the aisle. He was coming down, disappointed but also with a sort of bittersweet victory glowing in his eyes. No hostess escorted him back. He returned alone. Then, just before he sat down, he gave me this look. He looked at me with this twisted smile, the smile of a man who is thinking of suicide. The smile said this but it also said that he thought I had no idea what was going on inside of him. I thought the airplane might explode in midair, to tell you the truth."

I ast Juneboy why.

"Because right after Joseph returned to his seat the captain came over the intercom again and said, 'Fasten your seat belts because we may be entering the worst weather in my experience.' But looking out the window we all could see that it was a sunny and clear day. We were probably at that moment flying over Winston Salem, North Carolina. I looked down and saw a lot of green stretches that looked like they might be tobacco fields."

I couldn't even imagine what Juneboy was talking bout and why he told me this. He sho scared me. Then I recollected that Juneboy always had a vivid imagination ever since he was little. Then, child, I just decided to put my fear of him outta my mind. I was gon enjoy his stay with me if it was the last thing I did.

. . . .

While we drinked our tea Juneboy ast me bout everybody. He wanted to know if his Aunt Kathy and Uncle Donald was okay. He ast bout Donna Mae but I noticed he didn't ast bout her father, Ballard. I told him everybody was excited bout seeing him after all these years. He looked like he was pleased.

I was kinda overcoming my fear of him, you see. Esther told me some years ago that Juneboy wont right in the head. Had something to do with the time he spent in the service. The doctors discovered he had some ghosts or something living in his brains. Nobody knowed what to do for him. I member feeling real sorry for him and I also member thinking the ghosts got there cause of his sadness due to the way his father died.

All of this, I thought, was probably why his marriage didn't work out. Esther had told me that the girl Juneboy married, this Margaret Anthony—funny I member her name, maybe cause it sounds like Mark Anthony—was a real sweet girl. Esther liked her a whole lot. She was the only gal Juneboy ever took up with that Esther liked. This Margaret Anthony was a lady and she had education behind her.

Now, the first day, when Juneboy and I both thought he was gon be here in Atlanta just three or four days, I was trying to figure out how to best get him round so everybody could see him. I still have confidence in my car. I could drive the boy where he wanted to go. I knowed Renee was having some kinda big dinner party Friday night. Well, I figured Juneboy might not be interested in that. He sho wanted to see his cousins—my boys, De Soto and Jeremiah, and Donna Mae. I knowed DeSoto saw Juneboy in New Haven, Connecticut, at least one time when he and Whitney took a trip up North driving around one summer. When he came back, DeSoto told me how Juneboy always regretted not being at his father's burial. So, I sorta thought I might end up having to drive Juneboy to the gravesite where Scoop lay resting his old no good soul.

Not that I minded, mind you. I member the last time I seen Scoop. It was that time when Juneboy was down here, at eighteen years old. I fixed dinner for Scoop and Juneboy then. I used the good tablecloth and the fine china and the best silverware. Scoop, being a street man I never approved of in the first place, probably never preciated the trouble I went to. But I did it for Esther's boy. Esther is my favorite sister. Kathy is too religious—she makes me just want to fall on my knees and pray for the rest of my life. She's a year and a half younger than me. I can't stand too much of Kathy and that husband of hers. Yet I'm stuck with them, being right here in the city. Esther followed Prudence North. Prudence is dead.

We finished our tea and just as I was taking the cups to the sink I was so embarrassed cause it suddenly came into my mind that all the while the television with my soap operas been on. I didn't know it but maybe I had been listening to them with one of my ears and it made me feel sorta guilty.

I went and turned it off but the show had ended.

....

When DeSoto got off duty he came by to see Juneboy. DeSoto was the only one of us who had seed Juneboy growed up. They was real friendly, joking round and stuff.

I started making the supper for us that night while I listened to them talk bout the time in New Haven. Seem like Juneboy musta took DeSoto and Whitney for a night on the town cause the things they keep remembering sounded pretty much out of my sense of the way people ought to live. There was some kinda balloon they was chasing all over town, seem like. Then they was in a tavern drinking beer and the balloon was gone and probably busted somewhere. Then they said something bout this old couple that went out to a cliff in they car and tried to kill theyselves but changed they minds at the last minute and backed the car up. I don't know why they got into the things happening in New Haven. Maybe Juneboy's professor was the man in the car and the woman was the professor's wife.

One thing was clear, DeSoto and Juneboy sho liked each other and that—right off—made me feel less scared of Juneboy.

After a little while DeSoto took Juneboy away with him. Probably out to some bar somewhere. Mens!

I tried picking up on what was happening on "General Hospital" with Luke and Laura and the Quartermaines and Jimmy Lee and the rest of them when my stomach started hurting like I ate something poison. Girl, I thought I was gon die. I kept thinking, "Now, what did I eat that got me to hurting so bad?" And I couldn't think of a thing. For breakfast all I had was Cream of Wheat. For lunch I ate a piece of chicken, the breast, from last night. Couldn't a been the chicken cause I cooked it fresh, like I said, just the night before. I was hurting so bad I could hardly get myself stretched out on the couch. Other than the Cream of Wheat and the piece of chicken all I had was coffee and tea and I ain't never been sick from coffee or tea.

I finally got myself stretched out there but the pain was so sharp I couldn't even concentrate my mind on "General Hospital." My body was talking to me something powerful. I sho wont having no labor pains. Specially since I hadn't been nowhere near no man in that respect in many, many years. I ain't had no use for all the bother that goes with being like that with mens. Oh, I tried it one time after Bibb's death, but it didn't work. Just one time. It wont worth it, child. I might as well had a been shelling peas or shucking corn.

Now, this pain. It was like something growing inside me and not just growing inside me but taking over my whole body, you see. I felt my hands, one with the other, and I couldn't feel nothing but the pain, like it had become me. And there was this feeling of swelling, I mean a giant swelling inside me and not just a swelling inside me but a swelling that was me itself, a swelling that had taken the place of me, my body was it. I member wondering if it was my arthritis gone all the way to the limits but it wont the same kinda pain I know as my arthritis pain. It was this other, much bigger thing. I'm shame to say I even wondered if it had something to do with Juneboy's coming but I couldn't figure out how that could be since all he did was kiss me on the cheek. But you know, in the olden days they used to say that even just a kiss on the cheek by a hootchy-kootchy man could cast a spell on you. The hoodoo mens and ladies used to be afeared something terrible. But that was nonsense in this day and age and besides, Juneboy wont nobody but Juneboy.

When I felt like I swelled as big as I could get, I couldn't move and I wanted to get up and go look in the mirror but I couldn't get off my back cause I had sort of turned into a big round spongy thing, like.

It musta stayed on me, all this pain, being me, for over a hour, maybe two.

Then it slowly just on its own started creeping away, like it was leaving through my fingers and out of my toes and by way of my mouth and eyes and ears. I was like a balloon with the air being let out of it slowly, you know what I mean.

So, by the time DeSoto brought Juneboy back I felt fine. Well, almost like it hadn't happened cept I felt the shakes like I think maybe drunks feel the morning after they been through they cups.

It was a good thing I had already made supper earlier in the afternoon, knowing Juneboy was coming. I ast DeSoto to stay for supper with us, so he called Whitney to let her know he wouldn't be home. I ast Juneboy if he wanted to watch the early news. He did, so I turned the channel to the station with the five-thirty news.

When I walked close by Juneboy I didn't smell no liquor on his breath so I was happy but I couldn't figure where he and DeSoto went off to, so I ast him. He said DeSoto took him up to Martin Luther King's tomb. Then they drove round some. DeSoto knows Atlanta so I guess he was just refreshing Juneboy's memory. But Atlanta done changed so much since Juneboy was down here last time. I think even the house they lived in—even the whole neighborhood Scoop and Esther lived in when Juneboy and Lauren was little—is gone and a park is there with a expressway running through it.

I told DeSoto and Juneboy bout my pain but I didn't make no big fuss over it specially since it had gone. All DeSoto ast me is if I took something for it. I didn't tell him I couldn't even get myself up for two hours. One thing bout pain, that one and other kinds, is it tells you you living—you know you living.

I had cooked a pork roast for Juneboy and some turnip greens and baked potatoes. We musta ate dinner early that Thursday evening. The pork roast was done just before they showed up.

While we ate Juneboy started telling us 'bout being in Poland recently with what he called a delegation of other pathologists. He said something bout visiting some of they universities over there and talking to medical students bout sickle cell. Then he told this story bout being at the airport ready to leave Poland and the Polish police stopped him and took him outta line and made him sit with some Arabs till everybody else was on the plane.

Then, he said, it was while he and the Arabs was sitting together that he got to know these Arabs and they found out who he was and told him they was gon invite him to speak on the same subject in they own country. But you see Juneboy and the Arabs was real mad, sitting there like that with no reason.

And sho nuff the Arabs did invite him to come to Algiers, he said. In Algiers he visited the Casbah and said it was stinking and the peoples were very poor and sick.

He met some Frenchman over there who was staying at this same big fancy hotel where Juneboy hisself was staying. This Frenchman was going round treating the Arabs like they was still his subjects and one time one of them in the travel agency threw his passport on the floor rather than handing it back to him and another one came along and kicked it across the floor just as the poor Frenchman stooped to pick it up. That struck me as real mean.

Juneboy talked so much his food was getting cold.

I could tell now Juneboy was just trying to impress us. I still didn't believe the boy was all he was getting hisself up to be. I wanted DeSoto to stop asting Juneboy so many questions. I started looking at the television again, but I couldn't stop hearing they talk.

I gave in. I ast Juneboy what the older women, women my own age was like. I could play his game too.

"The older women are hidden behind veils and are kept inside. They are in sharp contrast with those young ones in skirts who work in offices. One feels the slush of time in Algiers. It's a tough question. The revolution restored the old order but what do you do with it—especially in its new form?

"And, you know, the cops were gentle. I sensed it. They carry their weapons with a carelessness I admire. They don't seem ready to sling at the first nervous twitch. At the airport, old Arabs sleep stacked against each other in cold, marble corners, waiting for flights that may never come. One feels they live there. Nobody forces them to leave the shelter of the airport.

"There in Algiers one must prove one's words, one's possessions, one's intentions, one's past."

"God, Adam," said DeSoto, "you've been in some strange and crazy places."

After DeSoto was gone, and after dinner, Juneboy and me watched a movie. It was one with Richard Widmark and Lena Horne. He was the town sheriff and she was the town lady. They was in love with each other. I was shocked that they would show a black woman like that on television all wrapped up with a white man. Everybody knowed that it had been going on for hundreds of years but to see it on television—where you don't spect the real world to show itself—was shocking. I was personally shocked.

CHAPTER 2

Like Juneboy, I didn't want to go to Renee's dinner party. All them fancy politician peoples make me nervous. I'm just a plain down-to-earth commonsense person and besides I don't understand none of all that high talk they put on. Course Jeremiah, my oldest, been round them since he was at college. You should hear him talk high and mighty with them bigshots. Sho, I'm proud of him but Lord knows he shouldn't drag his poor old momma into situations where she just end up feeling embarrassed. And poor Juneboy, he just wanted to watch some television.

Sometimes I know I am too hard on Renee. It's just that that gal is so spoilt that it upsets me to see some of the things she do. Seem like all she can think about is mink coats and diamonds and big pretty cars and giant television screens and Lord knows what else. Tried to give me one of her used mink coats a couple of years ago. Child, you should have heard me carry on. Renee, I said, it's so thoughtful of you, honey, and you know I do preciate the offer but my friends would think I'd lost my mind if they saw me in a expensive coat like this. Everybody I know knowed I can't afford mink. Might think I stole it or something. She turned just as red as a big old ripe apple. She one of them red childs anyway, you know, with freckles and them gray cat eyes and all that nappy red hair that she don't never know what to do with.

Anyways, she wont about to spend almost a half a thousand dollars on a catered dinner party for Atlanta's Negro royalty without having some deep dark plan to her own advantage. That child wouldn't know how to do anything for anybody but herself if you paid her. You can see that by the way she treats them children of hers. I feel so sorry for little Curtis, Jane, and Jo, sometimes I just break down and cry. They got everything material they need and ain't ever gone a day hungry like a lot of the children round here but they ain't got the most important thing—a caring and loving mother. Why, when I was bringing mine up I never once let DeSoto and Jeremiah sass me and stay up late the way she lets them children do. I even seed her give Curtis some beer when he was hardly a year old.

They wanted me and Juneboy over there by six, they said. It was Friday night and Jeremiah had got hisself a substitute to preach the sermon at his church, First Christ Church over on Decatur. He never missed preaching his own sermons unless something really important got in the way or he was down sick. When I ast him why not have the dinner party on another night he come just a talking bout Friday being the best time for Renee. Seems everything has to be her way.

I told Juneboy he better get dressed, and then I got out my best wig from the hatbox under my bed. It's blonde but kinda red too. When I was young my hair was like that, so it looks real natural on me. DeSoto says it makes me look young enough to be his sister. Well, I ain't shamed of wearing a wig like some of the ladies I know at church. The good Lord don't say nowhere in the good book that it's a sin to pretty yourself up, if you can. Two summers ago when I went up to Chicago to see Esther, she says to me, "Annie Eliza, take that ugly thing off your head, makes you look like one of these here street hussies."

I told her she never been able to tell me what to do and she wont about to start at sixty-three. I used to change her diapers and when she tries to get smart with me I remind her. It puts her in her place. I wore my wig all over Chicago, strutting my stuff just as pretty as I pleased.

I stood at the mirror adjusting the wig. I could hear Juneboy in the bathroom running water in the face bowl. My alarm clock on the bedside table said five-thirty. We could walk to Jeremiah's in fifteen minutes. His house was the biggest and the prettiest in the whole neighborhood and it was three blocks down in what they call a cul-de-sac. That's a French word. It means dead end. Jeremiah bought the place five years ago from the last white family to move outta the neighborhood. Paid a hundred and fifty thousand dollars for it, but if you ast me that place ain't worth all that much money. God knows ain't no place on this good earth worth a hundred thousand dollars. Sho, it's big and it's got so many rooms you can't count them all and keep a clear head and it's got fluffy carpets and giant television screens in all the bedrooms and antique furniture everywhere. The whole place was designed by some fancy designer who charged them more money than most people round here make in a lifetime, but I wouldn't give you a hundred dollars for it. It wasn't Jeremiah's money no way. All them church ladies bought that house. I never seen so many ladies in love with one plain old man!

. . . .

It was a warm spring night as Juneboy and me walked down to Jeremiah's. I'd been worried some bout Juneboy's pearance. I mean him going to this big dinner party with these high-class peoples. You see, I didn't want him to embarrass our side of the family. Esther's children never had the privileges my boys had. They didn't have a proper father. I mean, they were sorta raised here and there first by Momma and they no-good father and his crazy sisters. Then Esther took them up to Chicago but she had to work all the time. They didn't come up with good strict home training. That's the only way children learn good manners. Now I'm not blaming Esther. God knows she tried the best she could, but she was only sixteen when she got pregnant with Juneboy. By the time the boy was three, Lauren was born. That no-good gambling man of hers. I never knowed if Scoop was his real name or not. Didn't sound like no proper name I ever heard. Anyway, I was pleased to see Juneboy so dressed up in a nice tweed jacket and slacks. I figured we might get through the evening without embarrassment.

On the way over there, we walked past a house with a driveway that showed a view of my backyard in the moonlight. Juneboy come just a telling me bout a time he membered when he and my boys were playing together when they was little out back of the house. Bigger than Jeremiah, he said he had Jeremiah locked up as the bad guy and he made Jeremiah stand gainst that old tree like he was tied to it. DeSoto was spose to be helping him keep Jeremiah gainst the tree. I ast what Jeremiah spose to be guilty of and he just laughed and said it was all just a game but when they played Jeremiah was always the bad guy, you see. I had no memory of them playing like that. I did remember DeSoto picking on Jeremiah though and I use to fuss at DeSoto for giving Jeremiah such a hard time all the time.

Jeremiah's driveway was full of Cadillacs and Mercedes-Benzes and they had them parked all up and down the block. Four of them Cadillacs belonged to Jeremiah. He always say they belong to the church and to God but I never saw the church or God driving them. That boy of mine is a killer, I tell you! We could see all the lights in the house was on. I told Juneboy what a shame it was that that gal was so wasteful. He just smiled. As we walked up the long winding driveway, I told Juneboy bout the time Renee hired the two-day-a-week maid to come in full time to feed the childrens because she was too lazy to get outta bed before twelve. That was back fore the youngest one, Jo, was walking. Thank God, Jeremiah put his foot down, one of the few times! He told that gal if she wanted a full-time baby-feeder she had to get herself a job and pay for the service. But he don't take a firm hand with that gal the way he should. She just one of them nigger gals spoiled something you wouldn't believe, and, child, so full of herself she can't smell her own stink. And all just cause she comes from the Wright family. You know the Wrights is one of the biggest and richest Negro family in politics in Atlanta. My boy gets invited to all they big gatherings and most of them go to his church when they bother to praise the Lord at all. I let Juneboy touch the doorbell just so I could watch the surprise in his face when he heard all them bells in there making all that music as though angels was coming down from heaven. But wouldn't you know it, the poor boy was so unused to such class he just didn't pay no tention to it the way polite people with the right kind of background would have. I could hear them bells in there making all that sweet music and I just gave praise to the Lord that at least one of my boys had made it big in this world.

Little Curtis opened the door.

First thing I heard was Renee's big mouth—and she was way back in the kitchen. It wont the first time Renee done this catering thing. She had her kitchen full of them folk from the catering service. Little Curtis (named after Bibb's brother) told me he didn't want no kiss from me when I ast him to give Grandma a big kiss. That boy is so mannish, just like his father when he was little. Then he ran on off somewhere to play with his tanks and Star Wars. (When I was bringing up DeSoto I had the hardest time keeping them from all them sinful toys like cowboy guns and all that old violent stuff.) Seemed like every television in the house was on and each one on a different channel and the record player in the living room was on too. That's what I disliked bout coming here: always so much confusion.

Then little Jane with her pretty self came running down the hall to meet us. I took her up in my arms and kissed her. She said the mayor was in the den and that the kids was combing his hair and tickling his belly.

Sho nuff, in the den, there was our mayor, Dr. George Watkins-Jones, short and fat and black as ever, stuffed into the usual expensive striped dark blue suit, sitting deep in the couch before the giant screen of the television. Three of his grandchildrens was all over him—pulling at his necktie, unbuttoning his shirt, asting him all kinda silly questions; and all the while him looking like he trying to concentrate on whatever was going on on that television screen. I looked round at the television and there was Mr. Mayor hisself up there on the screen.

I said, "Good evening Mr. Mayor," but he didn't hear me. I don't even think he looked in my direction till he couldn't see hisself on the television anymore. When the Pepsi commercial came on, he looked at me and lifted a hand by way of greeting me. I never did like that kind of casual greeting from nobody. It shows disrespect. I knowed George fore he was mayor and seen him many times since, maybe as many as ten or fifteen times, usually here at Jeremiah's or in church or at one of them dinner parties they give over at Lee Anne's and Congressman Fred Wright's place. I said, "Good evening Mr. Mayor," and he called me Annie Eliza like he always did.

"Mr. Mayor," I said, "This is Dr. Adam North, my nephew—my youngest sister's oldest child."

Juneboy, like a real gentleman, went over and shook the mayor's hand but the mayor didn't stand up.

I put Jane down on the floor cause she started wiggling and she ran off toward the kitchen.

DeSoto, still in his police sergeant uniform, came in from the dining room and kissed me on the cheek just as I was bout to sit my weary bones down in the armchair (the one Renee spilled red wine on last Christmas). I was watching the suspicious look the mayor was giving Juneboy. Then I thought maybe the mayor was afeared Juneboy might assassinate him. It struck me as funny and I laughed. The mayor's bodyguard was nowhere round and that was strange.

While DeSoto stood between me and the screen picking his teeth with a toothpick (a bad habit he's had since high school), I pretended I was watching the television—which I couldn't even see—just so the mayor wouldn't think I was paying mind to what he was saying to Juneboy. He ast Juneboy what he did and Juneboy told him nicely bout the research he was spose to be doing, he said, into sickle cell anemia. The mayor sounded real interested and ast Juneboy all about it and Juneboy talked up a storm like he knowed everything in the world bout this Negro disease. He used big words too, words like hemoglobin. Juneboy told the mayor some organization done give him a grant, which is money, and Juneboy let the mayor know that he was spending a year spending his money from the grant peoples at Howard University Hospital. Then the mayor told Juneboy bout this cousin of his who had sicklemia and I got the impression the mayor didn't think this thing called sicklemia was as bad as sickle cell. And Juneboy agreed. Then the mayor wanted to know where Juneboy lived normally. He said "normally." Juneboy told him he taught internal medicine at Yale University. I kinda laughed to myself.

Then the mayor wanted to know if Juneboy was married and had children and I heard Juneboy say he was divorced and had two boys which is the truth. You shoulda seed the look on the mayor's face. He's a God-fearing family man with many grandchildren, two sons, and three daughters, and everybody can tell you our mayor ain't got no time for people who divorce. It's sort of like they ain't serious bout life. He squinted his little old red ape eyes and frowned with them deep lines between his eyebrows and you could see he was gritting his teeth behind that tight mouth. He kinda pushed one of the kids away from messing with his face. Said to Juneboy, "Sounds like you already made a mess of your life, young man. I admire the work you're doing in sickle cell anemia research but what we black people need are strong, lasting black families." The mayor went on and on, I tell you, reading the boy, so much so I felt sorry for poor Juneboy. Mayor Jones said it was a crime and a sin to leave a wife and two children. Juneboy started sweating as he tried to explain that his wife left him. The mayor paid no tention to the claim; he just went on preaching at the young man bout what was good for Negroes. (He didn't say Negroes. He said blacks but I don't like the word blacks, never did. You can call me old-fashioned if you want, I don't care. Back in the sixties when all the kids started using black I tried for a while to take it up but it just didn't feel right on my tongue cause my generation, you see, always though of black as a bad word. You called somebody black back in the thirties and forties when I was coming up, you insulted them something terrible.)

DeSoto walked out the way he came and that seemed to break the spell for some reason. The mayor stopped talking and just stared at the doorway DeSoto left by. The minute DeSoto left he stuck his head back inside the room and said, "Come here, Momma, I want to talk with you."

We went in the dining room and DeSoto took me by the arm and pulled me into the corner by the cupboard. He started acting this way, like a movie tough guy; round the time he started on the police force. I never did like it. I said, "DeSoto, I'm your mother. Don't pull on my arm like you think I'm some gal you met somewhere on the street."

"Sorry, Momma. Didn't mean no harm." He gave me that old winning grin. "I just want to talk to you about—" he nodded his head toward the den "—that man. I don't care if he is the mayor, he got no right to lash into Juneboy like that. Juneboy is our guest. My first cousin!"

I told DeSoto to calm down.

"It ain't fair, Momma!"

"I know, I know. But you can't deny that the mayor is right about divorce. The mayor is just trying to talk straight Christian talk to Juneboy. Lord knows he probably ain't been nowhere near a church since he was little when Esther used to make him and Lauren go—"

"Momma!"

Then I heard the front doorbell and the kids running up the hallway and the door opening and Reverend Baldridge-Hawkins's big laugh. Then Jeremiah came up from the basement where he has a bar and a pool table and all those video games. Kissed me on the cheek and already he was reeking of booze. Everything seemed to be happening all at once. The front door sounded again and a whole bunch of peoples was up there coming in.

I just wanted to find a corner and hide.

From

Painted Turtle: Woman with Guitar

PROLOGUE

Inkpen sent me to her to make her more commercial, to get her to switch to electric. I never liked the idea all the way, but I wasn't sure it wouldn't be good for her to rake in a little more money and to get off the grimy cantina circuit. I liked her music on the demos he played for me.

If she were telling her own story she'd start it with *Sonahchi*. She was that culturally bound. That seriousness and lack of ambiguity were part of her charm. Did I say charm? I never met a charming southwestern Indian in my life! Even us Navajos (and I'm part Hopi) never went in for good old American charm. They'll tell you my father's people, the Navajos, were like the rest of them, part of nature, but don't believe it.

I kicked around a lot before I decided to try music. That summer when I picked up a guitar, it happened to be electric. It happened one night in a cantina in Sante Fe. This Mexican group let me sit in with them. They said I was a natural. But even then, I knew it wasn't me, that the real me was somewhere else, in a quieter place.

She was on when I went in. A drunk at the bar was talking baseball real loud, arguing scores with the bartender. This was the first time I heard her sing her "Twins of the Sun." That one-string-at-a-time guitar kept leaping between her words like tongue-flames between the toes of a firewalker. I sat quietly in a corner and watched. She went next into another one I had heard on the demo, "Call Me Makki." She didn't bother to tell the audience what makki meant and I liked that. She held her guitar right and the tilt of her chin was just right for the light and her buckskin gave her the right kind of warm contrast to her skin which was only slightly lighter than the buckskin. I watched her eyes. She never once looked in my direction.

When she finished, I took my guitar with me and went over to tell her how good she was—as if she needed to hear that. She smelled of mint and freshly tanned leather. Her necklace and rings and watch were of silver and turquoise and coral and mother-of-pearl and jet agate and they sparkled dimly in the dark light. This was the woman Inkpen said was making hardly enough to get from town to town on, sleeping in bus depots, in flophouses, motels at the end of the line? She gave me only a half-smile—not even that, really. Zunis are like that, especially toward us Navajos. I saw her sizing me up right away. But I didn't let that coldness stop me.

CHAPTER 1: WONDERMENT

Her father made a cradleboard while her mother was breastfeeding her. This was right after the sandbed. It became a family joke that she knocked the ear of corn off the bed. Of course, she didn't. Some of the old folk later said it was the sure sign of bad luck.

She was taken off the cradleboard a month early, in the third. I've seen the old moms keep the babes on till they are a year or older. That's bad news. But that was at Tewa.

That old folks had occasion to gossip again, when the Little Turtle tried to chew the turquoise that had been placed in her cradle to keep the witches and devils away.

. . . .

In my mind I saw her mother as she washed the Little Turtle. When she finished she placed her in the sandbed. The mother's hands were crusty and strong and warm.

. . . .

She was beginning to walk. The first step was very important. The whole family watched. As she took it near the front step, smoke from the bread-baking oven nearby swam into her face and caused her to lose her balance. She sat down in the sand and everybody laughed.

. . . .

The first time she went with her mother up Corn Mountain to gather clay she was still only a toddler. Marelda used the clay to make pottery. The Little Turtle helped—or thought she helped—her mother gather the clay.

Soaked in water
then ground between rocks
The hand-shaped surface
made into a spiral
Mudfrog handles, one
on each side; dung-covered
Fired in hive-shaped oven
Olla carried to the goat-
owner for milk

She played with the older girls in the clan. The chief of the girls and Sakisti called for her to make song. She danced as soon as she learned to walk; she danced, danced, danced, like crazy she danced; danced with the older girls in the Santu at the Sacred Plaza.

. . . .

When she was bad, her mother told her Atoshle would come and get her. She cried out of fear. Her father comforted her with animal stories. But the stories did not always drive away the fear. After all, Atoshle could eat a whole kid without chewing the parts. He kept the bones in his cave. He castrated little boys who played with their shuminne.

. . . .

She learned early to mistrust strangers, to trust the strong odor of yucca soap, to trust its purification powers. She also learned not to wander out of the yard at night. Atoshle or some witch might grab her.

Learning was easy. She played fair in the kick race with the other girls. She avoided, even before first grade, being a bigshot. Before she was two, she developed an appreciation for jewelry. She liked its sparkle; she liked the red and white brightness of her first moccasins, her first headband, and her first shawl. Her father's mantas and breechcloth also attracted her eye. She liked her mother's ceremonial dress so much she put it on one day and wore it all around the house. This earned her a spanking; her first. She tried to wear her father's leggings of buckskin a week later but could only find one thong, so she looked pretty silly to Marelda, so silly in fact that the act of wearing clothes not her own didn't earn her punishment this time. With her courage up, she next ventured into her father's overshoes of undressed sheepskin. She fell. She cried. She recovered. This was learning.

Learning was wonderment. The first time she saw the huge Shalako birds, feeling the excitement and fear together and the other winter dance-figures, and later the summer dancers, she changed—a little bit each time. Her spirit was altered. She lost herself in the change. But she always came back. The sounds of deer hoof-clankers rang in her ears. The smell of cottonwood in bloom and the pussywillow were, at first, stunning and stinging. She heard with surprise the gourd rattles and the sounds of the hoop dancers. In her father's arms at the lady's wood chopping contest, she shuddered from the sight of the big arms and the sound of the ax wrenching the wood apart. Seeing smoke, the first few times drift up from the chimneys of the adobes was the discovery of a silent and strange presence.

Sleeping, as much as the wakeful times, was wonderment. Not only did the dancers come in the night, Atoshle could get you, anything else could happen. The night had no rules. Ghosts came from everywhere, and especially from the graves and from the lake the older people talked about.

Ghost dancer why
do you dance
so slowly
with such menace
while the dwellers
of the pueblo
sleep
Is the night
your sole
companion?

CHAPTER 2: OLD GCHACHU

I can just see Old Gchachu sitting at the head of the table, his only living relative, a childless daughter of fifty, sitting at the other end. I keep watching the Turtle in this setting. Maybe I watch her with the eye in the back of my head or out the corners of my real ones. Old Gchachu waves to Marelda to bring the Little Turtle over to him. The mother takes the child's hand and trots her over to the patriarch. He touches the child's head with fingers that are knotted twigs shaking in a desert storm. He tells her she will grow up to marry a priest who will be a very wise man and she will become legendary among the Zuni for her cooking of shredded lamb stew and blood pudding and hominy and sheep liver and intestines and olla podrido sauces made of chile-colorado and coriander-leaf and that she will be especially good at tchutsikwahnamuwe and legendary also for her love of children and family.

The old man calls Waldo over and Waldo stands beside Marelda and the father-of-the-clan looks at the father of the Little Turtle. Old Gchachu motions toward Marelda's pregnancy and says that the next one will be a boy who will grow up to be a greatly respected member of the Bow Priest Society.

I of course imagine this, making it up from what Painted Turtle told me. She said she was afraid of the old man. She was glad when her mother led her away to help the women and the other girls again.

Being part Navajo and part Hopi myself, I can just imagine the old man Gchachu rapping his staff handle on the tabletop. The chatter ends. He waits till feet beneath the long-scarred table stop moving. When there is only the sound of the grumbling infants and small crawling children, he says, "Everybody here now bow your head with your hands together for prayer."

Another old man whimpers, "But Larry that is the Christian way."

You can just see Old Gchachu lifting his crusted hand to stop the protesting man's words. "Our ancestors are served well. Bow your heads."

The patriarch glances at the rows of children at the children's table. "You children close your eyes and bow your heads, too." He can barely see their faces let alone their eyes but he waits a second or two to give them the chance to obey.

I see the Turtle shiver in confusion. She's sitting between two older children. She closes her eyes and clasps her hands together. I grew up in a family more Catholic than hers and my image of myself at that age cannot match the holy one I have of her. The Little Turtle has her eyes shut and I can see her thoughts. She thinks everybody in the world has closed his eyes and is waiting for something to happen. Only Old Gchachu knows what it will be. She peeks to see if her brother Albion has his eyes closed. He does. She closes hers again. Old Gchachu clears his throat.

The old man begins to speak in a chanting voice, saying words about the Lord God and the Sun and the Moon and the Earth. He asks these things to listen to him. Then he appeals to them, "Receive our thanks to the souls of our ancestors for this food which we are about to eat for the nourishment of our bodies. Dear Ancestors, be with us always in your wonderful spirits and knowledge, be in our hearts, bless us with water and corn, give us the seed we need to make Mother Earth feed us so that we may live long, healthy lives in the spirit of you, our great Ancestors. Amen."

They all repeat his last word. When I was a kid I thought "amen" meant it was time to be happy again.

You can see the Turtle peeking to see if it's time to open her eyes again. I used to do the same thing at Hopi when the priest stopped praying. One was never sure if it was going to be a full stop or a half one.

The Little Turtle turns to look at the daughter who looks old enough to be a grandmother. The grandmother-looking-daughter speaks. She says a long prayer in Zuni. The Little Turtle watches the grandmother-looking-daughter speak these words she has heard her other grandmothers speak. The Turtle notices that the other children and the grown-ups too still have their eyes closed. For opening hers like this, she expects to be punished but nobody says anything. If nobody sees you do wrong maybe wrong doesn't count. She stores away this discovery for future reference. She sneezes in her plate. She looks over at Marelda in fear. Her mother had always told her to cover her mouth when she had to sneeze. This time it had come out before she could catch it.

The women serve the men first then the children then themselves. Painted Turtle waits for the big wooden spoon to plop into her bowl. She looks at her father Waldo who is chewing a locust chrysalide. While she's looking away, the steamy hot stuff is poured from the spoon into her bowl. She smells it before she sees it. When the pouring woman is gone, the Turtle gingerly sticks her finger into the oily surface. She licks her finger. I can see the face she makes. It is a lovely bewilderment at the distance from which I watch. For her, though, it is torment. Her tongue seems to lose sensation. She takes up her spoon and fishes for one of the dumplings, hoping it will taste better. It bobs away like the head of a boy swimming in Spirit Lake. I managed better in my day.

The Turtle climbs down from her chair and goes to her mother who tells her to go back to her place. With her thumb in her mouth, she obeys.

An older girl next to her tells her to eat her mukialiwe. She looks at the slimy stuff in the bowl. Her eyes begin to cloud. She looks around for her Grandma Wilhelmina. She sees her on the other side unwrapping something wrapped in cornhusks.

The Turtle climbs down again and this time goes to her grandmother who asks her if she wants a bite of lepalokia. The Little Turtle says yes. The thing is held for her to bite. She does so. Grandma Wilhelmina now tells her to go eat her soup. She says: But it's green. Her grandmother says: It's good; eat it.

CHAPTER 3: THE SEASONS

If you are a man, it's hard to always know exactly how to write about a woman—even as a girl growing up. Yet you must try your best. You can see she didn't have much time to play with dolls: there were her little brother and sisters; perfect dolls with real diapers.

And the trouble of herself. She had diarrhea and toothache. Even as she played tag and jacks, she had to look forward to emptying the morning slopjar, helping to scrub the floor, fry the mutton, clean the skillets. Slice the onions.

Winter cold drove itself through the logs like nothing you can think of in the Southwest. They say a woman's body is warmer than a man's. Don't believe it. I lay beside her many nights when she was grown. I was warm, and she was cold.

Did she color in coloring books by the stove in the deep of winter? She did.

She wanted to be a boy. Little wonder. Boys at Zuni could look forward to initiation. After that, after the visit with the men to the kivas, they stepped up into daylight like gods born out of the ashes of the dead.

She wanted a sling-shot but her father told her girls didn't need slingshots. She didn't ask for a rifle. She didn't expect a bow and arrows.

Some summers were cold as winter.

It didn't matter that nothing immediately made sense. Her father picked her up in his pickup. She was about the size of a six-year-old but because she was on her period, she figured she must be—at least in this frame—about twelve. He asked her to save some of her blood for the kiva. He told her that while she was at school a Mexican had looked upon a Zuni mask and died. The villagers drove three other Mexicans off into the hills. She rethought this. Her father was not speaking directly to her. He was saying this to her mother. She helped her father later put up a fence around their house. She held the nails. She helped her uncle and her father build a new ladder for her uncle's kiva. The solstice dances came. Anglos came to watch them. She had never before seen so many gathered in one place. She liked the lightness of their hair and eyes.

One winter her aunt—on her father's side—was selected to go up to the top of Corn Mountain to bring the winter flame back from the burning light there and her sisters and grandmothers and other aunts cleaned the winter stoves and fireplaces and ovens and fasted for four days and the sword swallowers that winter were wonderful as they held forth quite seriously in the plaza. Phew!—what a sentence!

In the spring the planting ceremonies started, and this was a lot of fun for the young fast-growing Turtle. She got to dance, dance, dance. Everybody thought she was pretty. She graduated from being cute.

The harvest ceremonies came. The mudheads—children of incest—made the people almost die laughing. For her, laughing was a way of controlling the fear of these monsters.

When spring came, she jumped naked with the other girls into Blackrock Lake and in winter she ice-skated on it. She was old enough to remember some of these things. For instance, one winter, two men fought—using juniper-made swords—on the ice and one, wouldn't you know, lost his kirtle and everybody laughed. She was proudly wearing, as she watched, the new winter black dress and leggings her mother had sewn for her.

Her sisters came along, and they were like her but when her brother came along, last, and different, he was a novelty. He learned to dance in the Muwaiye. She watched him, touched, dressed, undressed him. She got the sense that he was special, being made ready for something she was excluded from. Eventually she learned it was called kiva. There was talk about the things he must learn. One, he must learn to ride a horse. Two, strap a cinch. Three, hold the horn of a saddle. Four, drive a pickup. Five, herd. Six, survive herding with comic books. Seven, survive comic books with soda pop. Eight, survive Life with chewing gum. Nine, he had to learn to chant—his chanting seemed more important than hers. He was half her size, but folks paid more attention to him. He became good at long prayers. She was ashamed of it but happy when she saw him whipped in the Plaza at his initiation. For years, she kept the image of his head stuck between Waldo's legs, on the occasion when he got the breath blown into his mouth: this was the noive's binan. She envied the manta he later got. And the kiva he was taken to after initiation: the act, its privacy, was one of the first acts to seal her off—into herself. Her brother Albion was held between Waldo's legs in the wagon race. She was with her mother and sisters—watching. That was life. Boys, without a doubt, were more interesting. She, therefore, began to think of them as such. They didn't have to squat to pee. And what else?

When her sisters were old enough to do it with her, she danced the virgin dance in the Sword Swallowers Ceremony. She, like her sisters and the others, was dressed in snow-white robes off one shoulder. She loved her peplum ruffles, her white, turned-up moccasins. She cherished her headdress of black fur with the feathers and the star-shaped turquoise tablita. She carried her wands proudly.

She was the first, in her seventh year, to see the Sun priest leave the village and head for the hills. But nobody believed her. The importance of it was lost. Many years later she wondered at the inability of her people to trust the word of a child. Unseen Hands had told her to keep her mouth shut. She had, despite watching for five successive mornings, waiting, expecting. They were going to go to that mysterious, sacred, forbidden, otherworldly lake—way away in another state. There, the travelers gathered yellow or white clay and packed it in jars. It was the stuff that she saw on the faces of Kaklo, Salimopiya, Hainawi, Kokokci, Siwuluhsietsa, and the many, many other kachinas; she saw it on their arms, their legs, their feet.

When she saw the little boy—playing the fire god—strike the match, she was glad she didn't know him and that she didn't have to see him the next day in school. The match set fire to a field of brush which gave the villagers lots of smoke to make the rain clouds come and she listened for the sound of rain to start—she was sure she heard it although she felt nothing like it falling from the sky. With the fire set by the sun god, the restlessness of the villagers began to end.

I'm sure she only imagined it, but she was sure her father—at one point—took a jar of her virginal blood to the kiva where the warriors waited. They painted their faces with it. When the enemy came, they would be ready.

A powerful priest
who has the right mix
of tooshoowe and kyawawulaswe
in his sacred bundle
tells her his secret
the first word
He was on good terms
with Uwanammi
the rain kachina
the Sun Priest
those at the Beginning:
Siiwilu Siwa Suwilu Siyeetsa

CHAPTER 4: SHEEP CAMP

Why is the Turtle in the storeroom? I had a map, but it's limited. I can hear her sobbing. She listens to her father's voice—outside, in the kitchen.

The storeroom door opens, and her father speaks into her darkness. He tells her to get her jacket because at night it gets real cold at the Kechipbowa sheep camp. She doesn't move.

He pulls her out of the storeroom.

She helps her mother pack the food and the goods.

The men sit around the table. Painted Turtle takes the hot bread and the fried mutton and onions and the boiled potatoes to them. They eat, Marelda tells her if she has to be a tom-boy she better stay close to her father. Girls shouldn't go out there.

They leave at sunrise. You can see it the way I see it, coming up along the range. In the Southwest everybody knows the magic and the loneliness and the sorrow of it.

They got to Kechipbowa.

Her father and the other men and boys brought their rolled bedding in from the pickups and dumped it along the walls. A bee was buzzing around up near the ceiling.

The place was mildewed. Painted Turtle had one thing in her mind: the lambs. She wanted to hug each one as they were born. But already she knew most of them would be born in the night and a lot of them would be dead by day.

It was the next morning.

In the pickup beside her father, she rode about a half a mile over to the corrals, which were east of the house. She walked beside her father through the huge place, entering first the main pen. Meanwhile, the hired hands, who were already there, could be heard bringing the sheep down from morning grazing to a lower area where they would remain till sundown. It's the same at Tewa—though we had few sheep. Painted Turtle knew the whole routine because she had listened now for weeks to her father talking with his brother and cousins about what they would do at camp. She followed her father as the other men scattered, going in various directions, back to the shearing pen area, which was empty like the main pen. She climbed up on the rear railing and peeked into the shade at the wide shearing floor with its strands of wool from last year. She kicked her feet and held on with her elbows. Through the west planks she saw a couple of wild horses standing outside in the shade of the fenced horse corral. Their eyes were closed, and each had their left hind leg cocked. She liked the dank, animal smells of this place. They were what she remembered best about it—next to the lambs. Her father called her, and she jumped down and went to him. She followed him out through the doorway into the pens. She could tell he was just checking things. He shook the feed racks to make sure they were sturdy, and he checked for holes. One of her uncles came in and told Waldo part of the west fence needed repairing and the gate to the main-pen needed another latch. She stood up on the fence and walked along the railing. Her father told her to get down.

She got down and went for a walk.

She saw one of her older cousins. He wanted to show her something. She followed him. On the west side of the main corral they came to a place where an ewe and a goat and a lamb were tied with ropes to the fence. The cousin said they belonged to him. The lamb was only two weeks old and it was nursing at its mother's teats. The cousin said his father and uncle gave them to him right after his initiation. Painted Turtle felt envious; although she did not envy the beating she saw him get in the sacred plaza. I was not beaten at Tewa, but I had to go on the rabbit hunt. I may tell you about that one day.

Painted Turtle asked the cousin if she could hug the lamb. He said sure but don't hurt it. She got on her knees and stroked its back. It tried to look around at her without losing its hold on the ewe's teat. Then it stopped trying to see her. She stroked its neck and tickled its ears.

This seemed long, long ago. But I have the clearest view of her in that posture.

. . . .

One of her father's cousins stayed at the house and when they got back at midday, he had dinner cooked. They all sat on the floor and ate fried bread, which they used as spoons to dip into the stew the cook had spooned into their tin plates. After eating, some of the younger boys wanted to go out and practice driving the pickup but her father and his brother told them being at sheep camp was serious business and that they were here to work.

After dinner they drove back out to the corrals. On the way she asked her father if she could help with the lambing and he told her she could watch.

The pregnant ewes had been placed in one corral together. There were about eighty of them.

Those that had not gotten pregnant had been cut off by the hired hands and were earmarked to be watched for slaughter next year. She climbed up on the fence where they were and looked at them. She thought about mutton frying in the cast-iron skillet.

She got down and ran over to the corral of the pregnant. Four newborn lambs were feeding at their mother's teats. She stood there at the fence and watched. They were so eager!

She lifted her cotton shawl from her shoulders and wrapped it around her head. The sun was up in the middle of the sky and it felt extremely hot. It was early May.

. . . .

She watched her father squat in the sheep dung and poke at a ewe's stomach. A cousin squatted with him. Behind her, a man in another corral was yelling at the dogies. Another cousin was hammering at a fence on the west side of the main corral and another inside.

She squatted beside her father who was now pressing the ewe's stomach. After a while she saw the tip of the lamb, but she couldn't tell which end was coming out first. The smell was strong and fetid.

. . . .

Sunrise. Boys herding sheep out of the main pen through the gate and up the path. She watched them leave. She tried to count the sheep but lost count. The ears were marked different ways. She knew her father's mark. She wanted to be a sheep, to bleat sadly. Old Roony barked up on the hillside.

She turned and kicked at the sand.

Her father and his cousins were again at the corral of the pregnant ewes. From the fence she counted eleven new ones. Some were half standing on wobbly hind legs, others on wobbly front legs. One was lying flat on the ground. She went and touched its head. Her father slapped her hand. It was bad luck.

Hot days, cold nights. Her father asked her if she wanted to go back. One of the cousins was about to drive back to the pueblo for more provisions. It was Saturday morning, end of the first week of May. She said she wanted to be a boy. Her father playfully socked her jaw and told her to get in the pickup.

She refused to get in.

She sat on the ground by the motherless lamb and the stubborn ewe. She petted the lamb for a moment, but the ewe kept moving from side to side, dislodging the lamb's grip on her teat. The ewe kicked at the lamb. Painted Turtle spanked the ewe's rump. A cousin forced the ewe against the fence and held her like that till the little one came over and started suckling again.

I've seen this happen many times.

. . . .

They took some of the sheep up a little south of Hampasawa where there was better grazing land. They all came back before dinner time.

. . . .

The shearers gripped the sheep between their thighs and started with the neck, working down the back, then down the sides, clipping close to the skin.

She helped stuff the sacks.

The cousins loaded them on the pickups.

CHAPTER 5: KWELELE

She rolls cornhusks to make her ears. I stick them on her head one at a time. She makes a black face showing herself with white crescent eyes. With my fingers I trace her zigzag nose.

She makes the crouched dance motion of winter. The solstice is near. She's old Kwelele. I trace the outline of her spruce collar. She rattles her beads.

. . . .

I speak to her:

You are in the Coyote Clan. This is your mother's house. Before, it was your great-grandmother Mary Wind Place's, a Bow Priest's daughter.

You crawl with your head stuck up. You get the turtle name. You are counted on.

. . . .

She earns the best grades. Sister Acklam says she draws the best hummingbird.

I speak to her:

You run till you come to the base of Heshota Uhla near the river. Here you beat your tiny fists against the ancient ones at Kechipauan then at Kiakima then at Kwakina.

CHAPTER 6: BLOOD

She felt the blood before she saw it. It was her eleventh birthday. She reached down there and brought up some on her finger. She ran to her mother, scared, thinking she'd hurt herself. Her mother gave her a rag and told her that it was the curse of being a woman. She also said it had something to do with life itself. Her mother told her that long ago, santi inoo as they said, the Bow Priests and the members of the Secret Council of the Apithlanshiwahi kept close watch on this blood.

Painted Turtle went outside and sat in the abandoned car on the other side of the road. She was dizzy with the thought of this blood—her own. She had known deer blood and chicken blood and turkey blood and rat and mouse blood and snake blood and sheep blood and blood from a cut finger and from the inside of her own mouth when her teeth bit into her jaw, but . . .

She sat there a long while. What had her momma meant by curse? Why had the Bow Priests and the members of the Secret Council been so concerned and were no longer concerned these days?

She began to sing a song she made up as she sang. The feelings she pressed into it were forever engraved inside the skin of her face.

I am the crow gut
I am the coyote gut
I am the deer gut
I am the rabbit gut
I am the squirrel gut
I am the mouse gut
I am the fox gut
I am the woodrat gut
I am the raccoon gut
I am the skunk gut
I am the sheep gut
I am the weasel gut
I am the lion gut

I am the shrew gut
I am the badger gut
I am the bighorn gut
I am the lizard gut

Yowejhhheeeeeeeeee
Eeeeee yaaaaaa he

CHAPTER 12: THE RED CLOUD PEACE CRUSADE

They threw her in the mental ward of the Gallup Indian Medical Center the day after she tried to put the boys out of what she called their misery. Doctors from McKinley came over to look at her. Hospital Drive is a long way from Nizhoni Boulevard. They asked her why she wanted to kill her sons. She told them because they would have been better off.

Apparently, they thought she was crazy.

After a few days here, she lost her sense of humor and she began to fear that her sanity might go next.

In the same ward was a big Sioux who claimed to be a descendant of Red Cloud. Her spirit, she told Painted Turtle and the other women, was born at the Fetrerman Massacre and at the Wagon Box Fight. The big Sioux used a lot of vulgar words and chewed tobacco. Painted Turtle thought she was awful. One woman, a Hopi, told the Turtle that behind the big Sioux's back the other woman called her Ground Rat.

The Turtle figured a good way to stay sane was to play crazy like these other women were doing. She began to watch Ground Rat.

One afternoon Ground Rat came to the Turtle in the coffee room and told her that the Red Cloud Peace Crusade was going to strike that night. "If you don't wanna take part just stay in bed." The Turtle wasn't sure what any of this meant but when the lights went off at ten she crawled under her cover as usual. She was a little corn-worm hiding in an ear.

The nurse was down there in his station reading a gun magazine. You could beat a drum in that coyote's ear and he would not lift his eyelids. He was stoned all the time. But he was the nicest guy they had on the staff.

Just minutes into the darkness, the Turtle heard them coming out of their beds and felt goose bumps break out all over her body. She peered through the darkness and saw a herd of fat Navajos and Hopis led by Ground Rat, silhouettes all. They crouched forward as they tipped on toes with arms extended and palms down and fingers ready like claws. The Turtle's heart beat like a gray fox running in her chest.

She heard the first attack.

It was followed by a short, cut-off screech. Obviously, a hand went over somebody's mouth.

This was followed by sounds of muffled cries, struggle and scuffling—flesh pounding flesh. These were the sounds of a blanket party. The Turtle figured Clara the Zuni and Sandy the half-breed were getting it: Ground Rat hated both.

These sounds continued for maybe ten minutes before the lights went on and the nurse came running up the aisle. A moment after the lights came on the alarm went off and this meant that in seconds other nurses from other wards would come running to help. The gun magazine–reading nurse was quickly joined by these others. The Turtle watched them from a sitting position in her bed. They found two women struggling on the floor under blankets. They dragged the two hysterical women up and quickly got them into straitjackets and just as quickly carried them out of the ward.

The next day the word was that in the night Clara the Zuni and the half-breed had flipped out and had to be taken away for emergency shock treatment.

The Turtle felt that her silence was cowardly. Clara the Zuni and the half-breed were subsequently thrown into the Soft Room.

After two months here the Turtle began to fall in love with her doctor and this told her it was time to go. He was East Indian, and his name was Sreenivassan. This love business had to be the first real sign of derangement. His family originated in a place called Kerala. She told him it sounded Zuni. He was planning to go back there to work in the hospital to help poor people. The Turtle dreamed of going with him. Finally, when he only smiled patiently at her innocent expression of love for him, which was not made very directly, she knew that she was just another appreciative patient. She felt rejected.

Doctor Sreenivassan told her she needed to adjust to the outside world again and quickly. He did not tell her she needed to go back to her sons. He did say that whether or not her sons live or die was not her decision to make.

CHAPTER 13: PICKUP

The minute she got in the pickup she knew she had made a mistake. Hadn't she learned from the rape not to do this? The two guys were reeking of booze. She was by the door and the one in the middle put his arm around her and tried to feel her breasts. She knocked his hand away. He tried to unzip her jeans. He and the driver laughed derisively at her anger. She demanded they stop the pickup and let her out; but the driver wouldn't stop. He reached across his buddy and patted her cheek, making a tut-tut sound to show her how deep his scorn was. The one next to her giggled.

The driver began to slow down, getting ready to turn off Thirty-six onto a dirt road a little south of Whitewater. The Turtle made up her mind to try to jump out at the turn even if it killed her. There had to be a better way to get to Gallup to look for work. The driver shifted to first.

Meanwhile, Painted Turtle gave the middle guy a hard elbow in the side and another quick one in the neck, opened the door just as the pickup began to make the turn.

She leaped out into the scrubgrass, rolling over into a gully that separated the road from the cornfield.

She watched the pickup move on a few yards before coming to a complete stop along the road. They would try to come for her, but they would have to run harder than a scared coyote to catch her.

With scratched arms, bruised elbows and knees, she scrambled to her feet and started trotting the short stretch back to Thirty-six. She heard them behind her, cussing and coming.

When she gained the hard surface, she literally was flying south, her oxfords hardly touching the cooling pavement. She didn't even have to look back to know that they were losing ground. Unless they went back to the pickup and drove after her they would have no chance at all. She knew that even if they did that there was still hardly any chance of them catching her. She had become as light as guitar music, as elusive as a song.

After several minutes of intense running she knew they had given up and had turned back. Up ahead she saw the beginning of the footpath she would take. No pickup could be driven onto it safely or sanely.

. . . .

Early that same evening her youngest sister Lupe came running into the house and announced that she was going to be married to a boy named Felix Boone of the Corn Clan whose father was a farmer and sometime sheepherder. It was surprisingly easy for the Turtle to make the shift from anger and outrage to celebratory gaiety.

The courtship period was untraditionally short. Three months later the Turtle's family went with Lupe to the yard of the Boone home. Grandma Wilhelmina handed over a few pieces of jewelry and Marelda surrendered three jugs and a rug. These things were given to Felix's mother. In the yard there was a big jug and a straw chair facing it. Mrs. Boone sat on the chair and Lupe kneeled with her head over the jug. In this manner, Mrs. Boone washed the girl's hair with yucca soap. The woman's hands were thick and strong. She massaged Lupe's scalp vigorously. The Turtle watched with a crisscrossing of feelings; she could not separate one from the other. She and members of both families stood in respectful silence, watching the hair-washing ceremony. One of Mrs. Boone's daughters brought fresh water. Lifting it up in cupsful, Mrs. Boone poured it over the top of Lupe's head. Then she dried the long black hair with a soft cotton towel. Meanwhile, Marelda, who was sitting on a matching chair with Felix on his knees before her holding his head over a similar water jug, washed the bridegroom's hair in the same manner.

So far, so good. After the washing, the two families ate the marriage mush from the marriage basket Marelda had brought with her.

That same day, Felix and Lupe moved into the old bedroom Painted Turtle and her two sisters had shared when they were children and Turtle and her boys moved into the big storage room, off the kitchen. It was cleared out and beds were put in.

CHAPTER 15: DIFFICULT CIRCUMSTANCES

It was winter, and she was wiping the bar. There were two customers at it when her father came in.

She knew right away he was a little drunk when he said he wanted to tell her his life story. She placed a Coors in front of him and continued to nervously wipe the bar around his mug. It was a good thing Mister Fletcher wasn't here. He did not like for the relatives of help to come in while help was working.

Waldo said his story was a gift he wanted to give her for her forgiveness. He added that he didn't know why he needed her forgiveness.

She was as ready as she was going to be under the difficult circumstances.

He talked in a Nawisho voice, as though he had a great black beard hanging heavily from his jaws. She could nearly imagine giant snowflakes spotting his eyebrows and nose. His voice was high and scary and bird-like and low as it varied in tone and she listened to the man who was her father as he transformed himself into words. He reminded her that he had come from a well-to-do family. He had taken kindly to living in Wilhelmina's house. He never questioned customs. He told her he loved her and his other children. He loved his wife and his mother and his mother-in-law. He wanted her to have everything, especially a good education. When she was born he and Marelda had planned a wonderful future for her. But the other children had come so fast one after the other and the drought came. Sheep were lost. He told her she had been a sickly child and when tribal medicine failed the other kind was expensive but they spent what they had on it. Yolanda was also sickly and had to be taken to the hospital at Black Rock many times. Everybody in the clan tried to help the family during these lean years. The women made clothes for the children. Her clothes were passed down to Yolanda and when Yolanda outgrew them, they went to Lupe. She told him she remembered. By the time Lupe was born she had dresses and leggings and moccasins waiting for her. He said he had done the best he could under very trying conditions. Half the time there was no grazing land even when he and his cousins had plenty of sheep. Often, he sold at a loss. In the summer of 1940 when she was just a tot, he said, his sheep came down with a disease that wiped them out. He watched them drop dead in the corrals and in the fields. Had it not been for Wilhelmina's jewelry-making they would not have pulled through that winter. At least she had her license and sold the things she made through shops in Gallup and at the trading posts on the reservation. She had gotten hers before the Agency started charging so much for them. By the fifties you couldn't get started unless you had about seven hundred bucks. Nobody at Zuni ever saw that kind of money back then. He said the family was lucky if it saw five dollars a month. Sure, he had credit at the posts because of the sheep but even that got cut because of the loss. He said he used to pray in the kiva for better luck. He almost lost faith. Even the little garden out front had betrayed them. But he kept coming back to the problem of the sheep loss. He said the original herd belonged to her Grandma Wilhelmina. When he married her mother Marelda he took charge of two hundred head. But after the bad luck he had only about seventy-five and even these were lost in 1940. Most Zunis swore by corn, but you could give him the gentle sheep any day. He liked always to go out where they grazed and just watch them and smell them.

His rambling talk made her nervous. She kept watching the door for Mister Fletcher. He was due any minute. But she could not think of a way to ask her father to leave.

He drank his Coors then talked again. He wanted to know if she remembered going that time to sheep camp when she wanted to pet all the newborn lambs. She assured him she remembered. He told her she was a child pretty as peaches on the trees in spring. He bragged about being a better shearer than his brother and all their cousins put together. He sheared two hundred sheep a day while the others were lucky to get half that amount done. He also bragged about being the best overseer of the lambing. He said that during the season the lambs were coming all hours of the night and day and somebody had to be there all times because of the birth-problems plus the lambs often got mixed up and nobody could tell which was which except when you saw the ewes the lambs went to but if a ewe died and a couple of lambs died it got pretty complicated. He often stayed all night in the corrals for these reasons. He laughed to himself. He then drained the beer from the bottom of his bottle. He laughed again then looked at her. She stopped wiping the bar top. He told her she was a tough girl and always had been. She liked sheep camp better than washing dishes. He said he used to wish she had been born a boy because she was better than all the boys in the clan and much tougher. When he said this, she thought of her brother Albion playing chase-the-stick that summer when he was supposed to be baling fleece.

During this moment of silence, the door opened, and Mister Fletcher came in, shaking the snow off his big boots.

CHAPTER 16: A HUNDRED AND TWENTY-ONE

It was a week after her father stopped in to give her the gift of his story. Mister Fletcher came in bringing a rush of freezing air with him. He stopped just inside the door, stomping his rubber boots on the mat. She watched him bristle and shake his head. He was early: he hardly ever came before five.

One customer had a half-empty mug in his fist. The Turtle went down and asked the guy if he wanted another one. The man said no. He had a face like a mudhead. She went back to the other end of the bar and started wiping it.

Mister Fletcher came over behind the bar and told her he wanted to talk with her. His friendly twinkling eyes had changed. The change in him caused her to turn into a scared little girl, ready to run from the Shalako. They were out of earshot of the lone customer.

He stuttered as he spoke. He had to let her go, he said. He said it was because she had lied about her age. He told her she was seventeen, not twenty-one. She wanted to tell him she was a hundred and twenty-one if a day and ready to spend the rest of her life at the bottom of the earth, suffering and knowing joy, ready too to soar above the earth forever knowing the light and the lightness of moving along on wings, that she was old enough and young enough always and that her age had never started and never stopped and never would start and never would stop, that he did not understand, that she did not either, that none of it made any sense, the rules were one thing here, another there, that people where either trusted for a while or mistrusted then without notice often lost to both trust and mistrust and vanished forever. She wanted to tell him he was wrong not to believe in her but she instead listened to him express his disappointment in her.

She was unable to look into his old sad face because she was learning that age wasn't the same thing as wisdom, as the old ones at Zuni had insisted. He told her he might have lost his license were it not for a friend in the police department who chose to believe he had not willfully violated the law by hiring a minor to serve liquor. Again, he told her how disappointed he was in her lying.

She said she was sorry. She put on her cloth coat and went out into the cold. She would get to the reservation in time to see the Shaliko dancers being led across the river into the pueblo. Snow was falling lightly.

CHAPTER 18: THE BARKING BIRD

Old Gchachu told her to sit on the floor at his knee. When she hesitated, he said that the wisdom of an old rainmaker shouldn't be questioned. He was the one who called for thunder. Uhu ehe yelu. Aha ehe. He told her his spirit was beautiful. She counteracted his claim by telling him she was a singer and a maker of music. At this point she began to suspect she might be dreaming this. He closed his eyes. They were apparently in the sitting room of his house. It did not look like the house of Wilhelmina Loaded-Shotgun Waatsa. She folded her arms and patted her left foot on the floor while resting on her right; then she sighed, as though in resignation, then eased down into a sitting position on crossed legs. She watched him through squinting eyes. He rested his arms on the arms of the chair. He told her, out of the blue, that he was the leader of the party that went to Washington with Zuni grievances which he expressed to the Commissioner of Indian Affairs. He also met that good BIA man John Collier. Kokokei sang a song of Gchachu's success as he danced in the summer dances that year long ago. She was tempted to ask him to get to the point, but he was an old man and the leader of the clan.

Old Gchachu patted the top of her head. He told her she was pretty, and he said he wanted to enter her spirit, to raise her spirit to the level of his own, to help her fulfill her promise.

She told him she had no song for him. Go, old man, and make thunder elsewhere. She got up.

He said he would call upon the punitive kachinas to punish her and she invited him to go right ahead.

He began to chant: Hainawi Hainawi Hainawi Homatci Homatci Homatci Temtemci Temtemci Ahute Ahute Ahute. As he called, they appeared mysteriously at the window, tapping gently on the glass. They were hideous, worse than she remembered!

Old Gchachu whistled like one of the Saiyalia on the way to a winter house.

As though his whistling was a signal, a Saiyalia opened the window and climbed into the room.

Painted Turtle moved toward the door, ready to run.

A few of the Saiyalia's eagle-tail feathers fell from his rear end. The white horsehair of his mask was wet.

The Saiyalia danced around the room, coming menacingly close to her. She grabbed the doorknob but it wouldn't turn. Old Gchachu commanded the Saiyalia to stop. In a language she did not understand the old man talked gently to the dancing-bird.

She shook the doorknob as the Saiyalia again—this time slowly and cautiously—approached her.

When he was close enough for her to feel his feathers, he bent down and whispered, telling her she came into the world for a noble cause but that she had betrayed that cause and must now submit to the love-embrace that would cleanse her of her curse. The bird said he was her spiritual husband and that mating with him would also raise the curse from her sons.

She shouted for Old Gchachu to send Saiyalia away, but he ignored her.

Saiyalia leaped on her, knocking her to the floor.

She screamed.

As the Saiyalia tore at her clothes he clacked his beak again and again, barking the bark of Kanakwe: Huita! Huita! Huita! He shouted in her ear as she continued to scream. She reached down to try to divert his hand and its instrument. She touched a corncob. While this struggle lasted she was dimly aware that the old man had disappeared and that the punitive kachinas were still watching through the dark glass. She shuddered convulsively as she turned her face away from the tobacco smell of the Saiyalia's breath.

From

Dirty Bird Blues

CHAPTER 4

He must have slept dead for six hours, at least. In the dream he woke up on he was trying to clean the blood from his jacket, but it wouldn't come off.

Sitting up, he swung his feet to the floor. Still in his underwear, he was cold and thirsty. The room was chilly.

He felt more pain sitting up than he did lying down. But he was going to pay it no mind. He needed a drink. And he didn't have but about a dollar and thirty cents. He got his good clean jacket out of the closet, the one with the red turned-up collar. Put it on. Got it for three dollars at Salvation Army store up on Sixty-third next door to Sid Feinstein's Pawnshop. They had good clothes there because they picked up things from rich white folks out in places like Wilmette, Wheaton, and Elgin.

The bloody jacket was on the floor by his ratty armchair. Under the sink he found one of those big supermarket paper sacks. He opened it, sat it on the floor. Took the coat and rolled it tight as it'd go then stuffed it in the bag.

He got himself a jar of water at the tap and drank it down in one swallow, shivering, his teeth chattering.

He smelled under his arms. Funky. His mouth tasted like dogshit. Cold as it was, he knew he needed a bath. But the water never got really hot, just sort of warm, if you ran it a long, long time. And if you ran it a long, long time Mister Johnson came knocking on the door saying what's the matter, your water faucet stuck on *on*.

Man turned the water on in the tub and let it run till it started getting warm then he put the stopper in and let it go on running. Fuck Mister Johnson. This wasn't his building anyway. He was just some Uncle Tom nigger for some white slumlord who probably lived out in Wilmette somewhere. When it was nearly full Man stuck his finger in to test it. Just lukewarm.

He couldn't stand being nasty, smelling bad. Took off his clothes and got in. It felt cold to the touch, but he forced himself and stood on his knees, so he wouldn't get his bandages wet—but they got wet anyway. Then he took up the little piece of soap he had left of the bar he bought two weeks ago.

Closed his eyes. Remembered how Aunt Ida used to wash his back. Himself sitting in the bathtub. He'd never seen a bathtub before he had to go stay with her and Uncle Sam in Atlanta. In Lexington they took their baths in a big washtub, same kind Mama used to wash clothes in. Just sat in there and when it came time to get their hair rinsed somebody dumped a bucket of water over their heads. But this was a cityfied true bathtub. Aunt Ida washing his back was one of the first great pleasures of life. He felt special, like somebody loved him. He'd left home because he and his daddy couldn't get along. Actually, they sent him to live with Aunt Ida, Mama's older and only sister. Aunt Ida was the first grown-up to treat him like he was a human being. She talked with him about all kinds of things. He remembered sitting at the kitchen table with her when Uncle Sam was at work or gone out barrel-housing. She'd fix Man a cup of something, apple cider maybe. Tea sometimes. And she'd put her dimpled elbows on the table and smile across at him and say something like, "When you grow up, Freddy, you be good to your wife." And he remembered thinking: I didn't even know I was gon grow up, let lone have a wife. Aunt Ida was the first grown-up to talk straight with him about sex, too. She caught him spying on her through the bathroom keyhole. She came out and said, "Freddy, I knowed you was there peeping. Now, listen, if you so curious about what a woman's body look like let me show you a picture." She took down this big encyclopedia-type book she kept up on a little shelf with the Bible and a cookbook and she put it on the kitchen table and opened it and kept turning the pages till she come to this drawing. "See here, Freddy," she said. "It say 'The Human Female Body.' This here is what a woman looks like. These here is her breasts she nurses the baby with. This is her pee-pee hole. Babies come out there too." Then she said, "It's not polite to peep through a keyhole when somebody in the bathroom. Now promise me you won't never do it again." He felt so shamed he couldn't look at her. But he promised. She kissed his head and hugged him. Said: "Don't be sad. It was just natural curiosity." He didn't know what that meant but it sounded alright. At least he wasn't going to hell for his sin. He loved Mama but he never liked her much. Aunt Ida he loved and liked.

The only thing she ever did that bothered him happened when he was twelve with not much time left to be with them. There was talk of sending him back to Lexington because Aunt Ida had asthma and was sick with other kinds of things, female troubles they called it, and couldn't take care of him much anymore. She used to bribe him. That's what he didn't like. She'd say, "If you scrub the floor, Freddy, I'll make sure you gets some valuable things of mine when I die." He didn't mind so much scrubbing the floor, but he didn't like the way she was trying to get him to do it. And he told her. Told her he didn't want nothing from her. But she still went on saying things like that. He reckoned she thought she was being nice to him. But Sunday his daddy, Quincy, came down from Lexington on the bus and took him back. Seemed like not long after that Aunt Ida died from asthma. They said she couldn't breathe anymore. And for years he remembered trying to figure out how somebody just stopped breathing. And she never did leave him nothing. He didn't think there was anything to leave. Never expected it. Didn't want nothing from her but her love. And that was gone.

Anyway, he finished his bath and got out, dried on the only towel of the three they had that Cleo hadn't taken.

He put on some clean underwear, his pants, and a clean shirt, put on his shoes, put on his jacket, and picked up the bag with the bloody jacket. Figured he'd just drop it in the trash can out by the side of the house.

When he got out there, he saw the overflowing can, with garbage stacked on the ground around it. And a rat shot down alongside the building as he walked back there. He thought, well, he wouldn't add to the mess. He'd just take the jacket and drop it in one of those street cans somewhere or maybe somebody else's can if he could find one not too full.

On the way up to Sixty-third he kept glancing to the side of each building but the only cans he saw were full or behind locked gates.

At the corner of Sixty-third there was a city can. He took the top off, but the damned thing was full, full of all kinds of junk—soft drink bottles, a canvas shoe, a snuff can, a rotten comic book, a bunch of crumpled-up cork, an empty paint can, the leg of a child's rocker, half a doll's head, candy wrappers, greasy wax paper, a barbecue box, a brassiere. He sat the bag on top anyway and started pushing down, forcing it in.

In mid-motion he felt somebody touch him on the shoulder. His body gave an involuntary jerk and then he turned around. It was Lizard, grinning. "What you doing, Big Boy? Can't stay out of trouble?"

Man stood there with his mouth open. Said, "I didn't think putting something in a garbage can was gainst the law."

"What I say is against the law is against the law. These city cans ain't for you to bring your garbage from home. I should run you in for this."

Man took the bag out and held it at his side.

"Okay. Once again, luck is with you. But you gonna keep trying me until your ass will be mine."

Walking away, Man headed west. Thinking: That's what you think.

He heard Lizard call after him, "Merry Christmas, Big Boy. Try to stay out of trouble."

He had forgotten it was Christmas Day.

Looking back at Lizard, Man saw the police car at the curb parked in front of a closed liquor store. Which reminded him how badly he needed a drink. Lizard's buddy Bullfrog was sitting at the wheel. He waved to Man and smiled.

Man stopped at a greasy spoon called Aunt Sally's Café on Sixty-third near South Parkway. The place smelled of stale bacon grease and mildew. The waitress said Merry Christmas to him and he said it back. He set the bag on the floor beside him at the counter, ordered a bowl of bean soup, and started eating without thinking about it or tasting it. Folks up and down the counter talking policy on Christmas day. The whole café talking policy. An old man with ears like a rabbit's next to him was grumping at the old woman sitting at the counter beside him. He told her if he'd followed his own mind, he'd have bet on Four-Eleven-Forty-four and not on her Seven-Eleven-Twenty-two. The waitress said she hit the numbers for two hundred dollars last year playing her dream from the dream book.

Man finished his soup, paid, and started out. The old man called him back. "Son, you forgot yo bag." Man shrugged, picked it up, and walked back into the cold, blinding, daylight.

He started walking, thinking he'd save his money and put it toward a taste later on. It was around noon and cold. Not many people out. He kept walking.

But he got tired, the pain in his thighs and chest started talking to him so he waved down a jitney, crawled in, set his bag on the floor beside him, thinking, Hotdoggit, I'm gonna leave the jacket right here, just hop out like I forgot it, and gon never see it again.

A big woman taking up most of the back seat called out to the driver, "Driver, now there ain't but so much room back here. You don't needs to be picking up nobody else till you gets rid of some of these peoples you already got." And the crowded cab of folk laughed as the car shot on down South Parkway. Man was sitting backwards facing the big caramel complected woman all dressed up in a blue brocade suit and coat with a fox collar. On her lap, she was balancing a stack of Christmas presents.

Man was hoping Solly had a bottle of whiskey. But lately Solly had been buying cheap sweet wine. Man liked bourbon when he could get it. But it didn't make no never-mind today. He'd drink sweet wine if he had to, nasty as it was it would do the job. But Solly might have some whiskey. And Man knew that Solly enjoyed drinking with him as much as he liked drinking with Solly. Solly needed some comfort, somebody to talk to, his drinking buddy. Solomon Thigpen, best blues guitar picker north of the Mason-Dixon Line.

The jitney pulled over to the curb at Thirty-fifth. Man handed the driver the coins then hopped out and started running. He could hear the big lady calling him, but he acted like he didn't hear her, just kept going.

Boogie, man, boogie,
Boogie all night long,
I say, boogie, man, boogie.
Boogie all night long.
You better make tracks and don't look back.
Make you some long tracks, man, and don't look back.
Boogie, man, boogie,
Boogie all night long.
I say boogie, man, boogie.
Boogie all night long.

Solly's lady Holly came to the door, laughing, and said, "I hear you knocking but you can't come in. Merry Christmas, Fred." She was always joking with him like that, saying things like that, like he was not welcome or something. The apartment had a toasty smell. He looked at her. She was good to look at, regal, dark brown–skinned lady with a strong face, wide forehead, high cheekbones like an Indian's, a quick smile, a full heart-shaped mouth. She was a real dignified lady. Never smoked or drank. And never nagged Solly for his bad habits. Lucky dog, that Solly. Got a woman what puts up with all his shit. Man liked her fine with Solly but he couldn't imagine himself with her. Not his type. Too easygoing, too soft-spoken. He liked himself a woman with fire. One that had a mind to talk back. Hard to get along with but he'd hate having one like Holly, the quiet, smiling, gentle type, taking everything, good and bad.

Man laughed and said, "Holly it too early in the morning for yo mess."

"It's afternoon, Fred. Come on in. He's in there on the couch hugging his guitar." One of those pearl-inlaid Epiphone Deluxe babies. As he followed her in he thought that nigger probably sleeps with that fucking guitar.

And there was Solly, a little guy compared to Man. A bit lighter complected than Man himself, Solly must have weighed a hundred and fifty wet. Man was two hundred pounds most of the time, sometimes he dropped down to one-eighty but those were the times when he was running lean and working too hard to love Cleo right and to enjoy life. Solly was lying down on his back with the guitar resting on his stomach. When Man walked in he just turned his head sideways and looked at him and started grinning.

"Hope you brought a bottle," Solly said.

Man laughed. "Me? I was hoping *you* had one."

Man stood there, grinning, looking down at him.

Holly went by past the little puny Christmas tree they had over near the table and on into the bedroom. There was an open box under the tree and a pink playsuit for a small child spread out on the floor on the wrapping paper from the box.

Man sat down in the armchair. One of the springs was pushing out the back, so it wasn't very comfortable leaning back. With his elbows on his knees, he leaned forward, looking at Solly. "What you gon do, Solly? Just lay there? Don't you want a taste?"

"Yeah, but I ain't got no money." Solly looked at him like he thought Man might surprise him and say, Come on nigger, I got some money, let's go get mellow. Man'd done that to him a few times. Then again, one time when he hit the numbers he was right out front with his bread. Said, "Let's go get a setup!" And that was the time Man wrote *Policy Number Blues,* right on the bar napkin, beating out the rhythm on the bartop. But he never wrote down music notes because he didn't know how. It was just all in his head. He wrote down the words and he knew how the melody was supposed to go. He and Solly sang the song to the bartender. She thought they were crazy:

Hey, bartender lady, pick up the bottle and pour.
I say bartender lady please get yo bottle and pour.
I put all my dough, this morning, on forty-four.
Oh, Lord this morning, my wife, she gave me hell.
I say, this morning my wife, she gave me hell.
Forty-four didn't come in, it never rang a bell.
So, bartender lady, pour me another double shot.
Ease my conk-buster, pour me another double shot.
Tomorrow I may be sleeping in a vacant lot.

But Man said, "How bout—" then he stopped, still grinning, and pointed, jabbing his finger in the direction of the bedroom.

Solly shook his head. "She spent it all on Christmas."

Holly had a job as a nurse's aide at Cook County Hospital. He knew she'd been paid Friday two days ago. Holly wasn't like Cleo. She'd give Solly money for liquor if she had it. Sometimes Man and Solly were long time between slaves—not music jobs, music jobs they loved—and Holly would come through and get Solly through such times when he didn't have any money coming in. And she never nagged him and never tried to make him feel bad. Cleo wasn't like that. He loved Cleo but she wouldn't take any shit off him. She never thought he had any kind of right to just do his music and not work a slave for a living.

Man first saw Solly in Washington Park playing his guitar with an old beat-up straw hat on the ground in front of him. Had a dollar and some change in it just to encourage people to contribute. That was last year, 19 and 48, nearly a year and a half—last summer. Solly was just out of the service, though he never saw no action over there in Germany. He was in a colored company that went in after the war ended.

Solly's guitar made this beautiful sound, made you want to dance. Fact is folks were jitterbugging to his guitar right out there on the tough, worn-down, brown grass. Must have been some kind of holiday, maybe Fourth of July. But lots of folks—children and grown-ups—were there hopping around him and grinning and carrying on. Man had his harmonica in his pocket. You never know. And he was itching to get in on the fun too. But he didn't know the thing Solly was doing. It was one of them fast numbers, a little too fast for Man, but he paid attention to it for a few minutes, caught the rhythm, and picked it up on his harmonica. Many times he did that. Open your door, I ain't no stranger, honey. Got into the deep blue sea. Did some hoodoo spells.

That day they collected a whole bunch of money and went and got drunk as two skunks. Had a lot of fun. Hung out together from then on. They used to go out on the street corner, anywhere where there were lots of folks. Lots of times, Man took his sax and blew. Switched to the harmonica. But mostly he did the singing and Solly did the picking. Sometimes Solly would borrow a violin or he'd be switching back and forth from the guitar to the violin. One time he got hold of a bass fiddle and went to town on it.

People were funny though. Sometimes Man and Solly could play on a corner for three, four hours and nobody dropped a penny in the hat. Then other times they'd almost fill up the hat with nickels and dimes. That way it'd take a long time to get enough to buy even a half pint. But his wife, Cleo, never did approve of him playing in the streets. Bullfrog in mud. Said it was lowlife, showed no self-respect. Holly never said anything like that.

. . . .

Anyway, sometimes he envied Solly for having such an understanding lady. But he didn't believe Holly spent all her money on Christmas. Not Holly. She was too practical to spend all her money on one thing, not even on the kid for

Christmas. There was only one present under the tree. He was just starting again to feel the pain from the buckshots. He figured the liquor would take the edge off.

"Come on," Solly said, sitting up and putting his guitar down on the couch. "I know where I can get some money. Let's go."

Solly went in the bedroom and Man waited for him at the door, then Solly came back and they were ready to hit the wind, and Man said, "You know, it don't seem like Christmas Day to me. How bout you?"

"Just another day."

Man started singing, "Just another day . . ." Going down the hallway toward the front door he said, "By the way, I got shot last night." He looked at Solly, waiting for what he knew was coming.

"You what?"

Outside, walking along South Parkway, Man said, "The nigger Cleo with shot me."

Solly laughed. "Then how come you ain't dead, nigger?" He looked like he was waiting for Man to say he was just kidding.

"I'm serious, nigger. That nigger shot me—with buckshots. They didn't hurt much but he did try to kill me. That a fact. He coulda, too. Coulda put out my lights. Coulda hurt me had the nigger hit me the right way, cept the window was open just a little bit and the glass caught most of it."

"Manfred, you better start from the beginning."

"I went over there."

"You what—?"

"Yeah. I know I said I wouldn't."

"That ain't all you said, nigger. You said you never wanted to see Cleo again. Glad she was gone. You was the one spose to be happy to be free again."

"I know, I know. But last night, shit. I got to thinking bout last Christmas Eve and how happy me and Cleo was with the baby just six months old. Something got into me. I got drunk."

"That ain't nothing new."

"I got drunk, went over there, climbed up on the fire scape. Trying to open the window when he shot me. I heard Cleo scream."

"Police come?"

Man told Solly how he walked to the hospital and got himself treated and about his little trip with the police back to the reverend's place.

"And here you is walking around free. Man, you know the cops coulda throwed yo ass in jail and dropped the key in Lake Michigan. Now what you gon do?"

"I been thinking bout going out to Omaha to see my sister, maybe stay with her for a few months. I been talking with her on the phone. Getting to know her. I ain't seed her since I was about fifteen. If I hang around this town no telling when I might go off again and head over there."

"Omaha, huh?" Solly shook his head.

"She say they got a great blues place out there. She already told the owner bout me. Sound like I could go right out and start. Weekends, you know."

"Omaha? Omaha, Nebraska? Who do I know in Omaha? Knew a drummer once from Omaha. Boy by the name of Greg Wakely. Just came here on a visit, trying to get a band started. Mean drummer too. Talk about talking drums! The cat could beat the fuck out of some skin." Solly stopped and turned to him. They were standing at the curb waiting for a red light. "Listen, this old gal we going to see probably don't like liquor and drinking, so be cool. I'm just gon borry a few bucks off her. I ain't never dicked her or nothing."

"You talking about Cindy?"

"Naw. Me and Cindy broke off. Her daughter hate me. I got tired of putting up with that bullshit. This woman I met when I was working as a temp out at the stockyards. She in Bacon. A wrapper for Swift. Estelle. She a older lady but she still real fine. Live up on Forty-third and Calumet. You wanna walk?"

"Naw, man. Let's take a jitney. I got enough for a jitney."

"Okay. Better stop here in this booth and call her first. Don't wanna go there and get turnt away."

CHAPTER 5

"Yall come on in," she said, holding her apartment door open. "Merry Christmas." She was this big fat yellow woman, looked kind of like Lady Day, big strong chin and a straight nose, except Estelle had those dimples that gave off a sweetness and you knew she was a kindhearted woman.

They said Merry Christmas to her.

Solly introduced them to each other.

Man took off his cap and unbuttoned his jacket. So did Solly. Estelle took their jackets and hung them there on her coatrack. Man stuffed his cap in one of the pockets of his jacket.

Estelle, her big fine self, stepped out in front of them and walked down the hall leading them into her little dark living room. She didn't have a Christmas tree or nothing. Man looked at her and wondered. He was already writing himself a song about her—

Oh, mama, mama,
Won't you go tell Estelle I'm in jail,
Oh, mama, sweet mama,
Won't you tell Estelle I'm in jail,
If she don't come for me by night,
I'm gon be shot by candlelight.

"Have a seat, gentlemen. I don't have a tree this year. I said to myself a tree just too much trouble. Just me by myself now. No man, no children. Just me. No point in a tree just for one person. Can I get you something? Coffee, tea, whiskey? I got some eggnog in the frigerator. I made it myself."

They sat down on the couch and she stood in front of them just grinning.

Man looked at Solly and smiled. How lucky could they be? He smiled back. Man thought he was going to blow the whole thing and laugh.

But Solly said, "That mighty nice of you Estelle but I gon just take a little whiskey in a separate glass. My partner here take the same."

She looked at Man with surprise. "You sure you don't want eggnog with your whiskey, Mister Banks?"

"Naw—" Man waved his hand. "Soils the freshness, the crispness. You know. But I'll be pleased to have some of that eggnog in a separate glass. I bet it real good."

While her back was turned and she was at the icebox fixing their eggnog he and Solly gave each other a quiet five.

When Estelle came back she was carrying two water glasses full of this eggnog mess and handed them to them. "I'll bring the whiskey in a minute but first I just want to see what you think of my eggnog."

She sat down in the armchair facing the couch and looked at them like they were children about to drink fresh milk. Man needed the whiskey real bad. These were some hard times. And this was not funny. He gave Solly a look and saw that he was going to drink a little bit of it so Man did too. He took a swallow and it was really good. Right then for the first time in twenty-four hours Man knew how hungry he still was. The soup hadn't helped much. He was hungry as a mule that's been plowing from cain't-see to cain't-see. Still, hungry or not hungry, he didn't want to put out the fire before it started.

"My, my, Miss Estelle, this is mighty fine eggnog you done put together here. Your own formula?"

"Sure is. Handed down in my family from my great-grandmother to my grandmother to my mother and me. Alabama wisdom." She laughed, showing them her big pretty teeth like rows of white corn all even and smooth. She was a great-looking woman. Man gazed at her and thought: Yeah, this here is a mighty fine upstanding woman.

Then Solly said, "This would be a nice chaser with the whiskey."

She jumped up like somebody goosed her. "Oh, yes. I forgot. The whiskey. It's Old Crow. Is that okay?"

"Yes, ma'am. No bird like Dirty Bird," Man said, grinning at her, then giving Solly a sly wink. Beats Jim Crow. Crow Jane, Crow Jane. Man ribbed Solly but Solly kept a straight face. Now Solly, he knew how to control himself. He was really good when he wanted to be.

She brought the whiskey in short glasses, about an inch in each. Man took the first sip and felt the burning liquor go down like fire. He was happy as a hog wallowing in shit. Happy as a Mississippi frog sitting on a log. His eyes opened. He took a deep breath and took another swallow. Two more hits and his would be gone too. But he needed the kick. And if he took it slowly he wasn't about to get the sock.

Solly crossed his legs and Estelle sat back down facing them. She was watching them with that big pretty smile. "What kinda of work you do, Mister Banks?"

"I'm a musician."

"Oh, how nice. Like Mister Thigpen. I was so impressed when Mister Thigpen invited me to hear him play at that place down on Thirty-first and Cottage—"

"What place? When?" Man stretched his eyes.

Solly took a swallow of his whiskey and frowned. "You know. I tolt you about it. Place called Ease On In Tavern."

"Oh, I know that joint."

"Mister Thigpen played with such feeling I was really stirred up."

Mann ribbed him. "What you play, Solly?"

Estelle spoke up first, "He played *All I Got Belongs to You* and *St. Louis Blues* and *Baby Please Don't Go* and that funny one. What was the title, Mister Thigpen?"

"*Got a Gal in Town with Her Mouth Chock Full of Gold.* I took requests too. It was one of them sentimental nights. Folks had me playing things like *What Can I Say After I Say I'm Sorry* and *Sleepy Time Gal.* Man, be glad you wont there."

Alright. Man took him a sip of his whiskey.

"This is mighty good whiskey, Miss Estelle." Man took another swallow and finished it. "Sure is good. But quite naturally it's going to be good if it's Dirty Bird."

She smiled a little bit and he could tell she was getting nervous. "You haven't drunk your eggnog, Mister Banks."

"I was working at it." He was hoping she'd ask him if he wanted more whiskey. But she was watching Solly now, just looking and grinning. Then Solly finished his whiskey too. He smacked his lips.

"Would you gentlemen like some more whiskey?"

They looked at each other as if they were giving the thought serious consideration. Being gentlemen they didn't want to overdo anything. They knew how to be polite. They kept looking into each other's eyes, measuring the thought seriously. Then Man nodded to Solly and he turned to Miss Estelle and gave her a big smile. "What the hell, it Christmas. Folks is spose to have a good time. Right? Sure. Give us some mo. Nothing wrong with relaxing a little bit."

Man could tell it wasn't the answer she wanted to hear but she got up, took their glasses anyway, and reluctantly walked over again to her little kitchen area and took the bottle down from the cabinet again and poured again, this time less than an inch worth of booze into each glass. They were watching her. When they saw her being stingy with the stuff, Man figured Solly was thinking the same thing he was thinking. Solly would have to hit on her for some bread. Christmas, but that didn't make no never-mind: they could go to one of those bootleg joints and cop a bottle. Such places were all over the South Side.

She brought the whiskey over to them. "Yall still ain't drunk your eggnog much. You don't like it, do you?"

Man said, "I likes it, I likes it, Miss Estelle. It mighty fine eggnog. See—" He took another sip, held it on his tongue, hog-tied against swallowing. Then he had to swallow before he could talk. "See. I drink it down. It real good stuff." Then Man put the glass back on the sidetable and took a quick sip of the whiskey.

She was looking seriously at Solly. Just standing there with her hands on her hips. "Mister Thigpen, are you going to drink yours?"

"Sure am. Here go. Down the hatchet. See." And he put away about half the eggnog, sighed, and put the glass down.

Man was about to crack up, knowing Solly had put a damper on his high just to please her. Poor innocent nice lady she was. And they were a couple of crab lice to be treating her like this. She deserved better.

She sat herself down again and said, "So, what you gentlemen up to this Christmas Day?"

"Oh," said Solly, "we just out strolling and thought we'd pay you a visit. Have to stop in on a few other friends too. You know how it is. Christmas and all." He drained his whiskey from the glass. "That remind me. I done left my wallet at home. Estelle, can you lay a nickel on me, just till next week?"

"What?" She looked puzzled.

"Borry me five dollars till next week?" Solly said.

Estelle caught her breath and held it and Man watched her bosom swelling. It was some big bosom poking out there, held without breathing.

Man caught himself holding his own breath. Waiting.

And Solly too. He could tell. Grinning but holding his breath.

Then she grinned and said, "Sure, Mister Thigpen. Let me get my purse." And she got up and went into the next room and came back with a five-dollar bill, and waving it like it was wet and she wanted to dry it, she then waved it in front of his nose and said, "Here you are, sir."

"Thank you, Estelle." He stood up.

Man drained his whiskey glass and got up too.

Solly stuffed the money in his pocket and followed her to the door where she took their coats off the coatrack. "Well," he said, "it sure was nice seeing you again, Estelle. I'll call you next week before I come."

They got into their coats and said Merry Christmas again and she said Merry Christmas again too and that was that.

. . . .

Man and Solly knew this bootleg joint where they always had a good supply on Sundays and holidays. Over on Thirty-first and State, State where the trucks travel night and day, rumbling along carrying all that stuff people use from city to city, passing through Chicago. This bootlegger, little dude with a big salt-and-pepper gray beard by the name of Professor DuBois Canon. He wasn't any real professor. Folks called him that because he had the chemistry of whiskey-making down to a T. And he talked with them big words. Had three women living with him. Miranda, brown. Sandy, yellow. Vada, black. Spose to be sleeping with all three.

Man and Solly walked down and over there. It wasn't that far.

Apartment in one of those old, old buildings on the west side of State, so dark and dingy you could fall down in the hallway and break your neck. Ground floor. They knocked. They knew the steps. Somebody inside would look through the peephole before opening the door. Man could tell by the "Who is it?" that it was Miranda.

"Manfred and Solly. Is the professor in?"

She opened the door. You could see right away down this long hallway that there was a lot going on in there. The professor always had a bunch of drunks hanging around, sometimes passed out on the floor. Man had been in some low-down places but the professor's place took the cake.

Miranda was smoking a cigarette as she led them down the hall to the living room. Real dark in there, all through the place. The professor was sitting behind a desk in his usual way. Somebody on the radio singing *All I Want for*

Christmas Is My Two Front Teeth. Six or seven drunk jokers were in one corner watching some kind of Christmas special on television. It was just starting, and the announcer said they were going to have on a whole lot of stars—Bing Crosby, Sid Caesar, Imogene Coca, the Billy Williams Quartet, and Liberace. Some old drunk joker said, "Perry Como sing *White Christmas* better than Bing Crosby." Somebody else said, "Fuck naw, nigger!"

Around the room were small groups here and there smoking and arguing about one thing and another. Room full a smoke. Smelled of white lightning.

Sandy, the yellow one, came over to meet Solly and Man. "What can we do for you gentlemen?" She was smoking her cigarette in one a those long holders you see Bette Davis with in the movies.

Man showed her his pretty teeth. We here to do business with the professor. Want a fifth of lightning. Best you got. Want yo special discount price too." He laughed.

"I got your special discount price, motherfucker," Sandy said. "You pay three-fifty just like everybody else." She laughed like one of those hyenas.

The professor waved them over.

Man had to step over a drunk to get to the desk. Sometimes Man didn't have any sympathy for drunks. Himself included.

Solly—bless his respect for all God's children—walked around the poor man on the floor.

Professor DuBois Canon took the cigar out of his mouth, reached across the desk, and shook Solly's hand then Man's. "Nice to see you boys. Let's see how green your money is."

Solly took out the nickel and handed it to the professor. Solly said, "Do us right, now, professor."

The professor reached under the desk and came up with a fifth of white lightning and handed it to Solly.

Solly held it up to the light, what little light there was. Man looked too and it looked good to him, nice and clear.

"Here you go, Solly," said the professor, handing him a dollar-fifty change. Solly took it and stuffed the money in his pocket.

The minute Solly had the bottle in his hand here came three jokers from the crowd in front of the television.

Miranda called out from across the room, "You drunk niggers leave them boys alone."

Drunk nigger number one had a harelip.

Drunk nigger number two had one eye.

Drunk nigger number three had yellow teeth, two missing in the front.

Number one had slobber running down his chin. All three smelled bad. "Hey, man, hey," the slobbering one said, reaching for Solly's shoulder. "I'm your friend, ain't I? How about a little taste for a friend?"

"No dice, my friend," said Solly.

"Well that's all right, motherfucker, if you wanna be like that, fuck you motherfucker. Fuck you and yo mama in the asshole. You got that?" the drunk nigger said.

Drunk nigger number two said, "Yeah. Who you think you is anyway? It's Christmas. Don't you love your fellow man?"

Drunk nigger number three said, "Yall leave the nigger lone. You heard him. He don't want to give you niggers none of his liquor."

The professor said, "None of that in here, Tucker," speaking to drunk nigger number one. "That goes for you too, Huff, and you, Jenkins. Leave the customer alone. Go watch Lassie."

"Fuck you too, professor," said drunk nigger number one.

"You want me to throw you out of here?"

All right. That got their attention. They wandered back toward the television group, muttering to themselves, "Motherfucking nigger . . ."

The professor said, "I do believe mankind is declining, boys. Still, I try to keep an optimistic view, though, of my fellow man. But this sort of riffraff—" he pointed at the drunk niggers, "makes it difficult."

One of the drunk niggers said, "You think you still the mayor of Chicago."

The professor took the misuse well. He ignored the drunk nigger. Looked at Man and Solly. Said, "Three years ago, when I was advisor to Mayor Kelly, one day I said to him, 'Ed, what are you going to do about this city—two to three hundred murders a year, two thousand assaults, three to four thousand robberies.' And the mayor shook his head. Said, "Well, Professor DuBois, look at it this way: It could be a lot worse. We're not at war anymore. Troops still overseas, sure, but they're coming home. Chicago boys coming home. There was more killing over there than Chicago ever had.' The mayor went on to say he thought Mister Truman was doing a fine job in the White House. Eisenhower, he said, doesn't believe there will be a third world war. I said to the mayor, 'Ed, the colored folks fought in that war and the boys are coming back here and they still can't vote places in the South and there aren't any decent jobs. You could make a difference here in Chicago, Ed. I told him just like that. You know what he said? He said, 'We're doing all we can to improve the economy. Why, I got a theory. A project like the Dearborn Street–Milwaukee Avenue subway—which they just finished—will create all kinds of new jobs for everybody. The airport too is big business now,' he said. 'The way I see it, Professor, we got a lot to be grateful for.' I just looked at him and said, 'Well, Ed, those things may be a sign of progress, and a few things to be thankful for, but as long as one man tries to establish his dignity by stepping on another's face, then we're getting nowhere. Lynch mobs are tolerated in the South just like they were back in the 1880s. Factory bosses refuse to provide safe and fair working conditions for workers up here. They tell them just being white is enough. They don't need any other advantage. It's a plot against them, Ed. People use many ways to humiliate, degrade, and destroy one another. And, of course, when you humiliate and degrade a person long enough, he may soon start believing he deserves it. And he'll start doing it to himself.' Ed Kelly gave me this funny look and just walked away. But I never held back my thoughts when I was advising him—"

Vada came over. "Is the professor telling you boys lies about working for the mayor again?"

The professor said, "They are not lies, Vada. Not everyone in this world is a skeptic, like you."

Then Vada looked over at the drunk jokers. She grinned. She was real pretty. "You boys having trouble with them clowns there?"

"Naw. Nothing we can't handle," Man said. "We was just leaving."

"Well, Merry Christmas to you both."

· ·

In the hallway, just before they stepped outside, Solly screwed the top off and took a hit then passed it to Man. It burned real nice going down. Man shuddered, shaking his shoulders. Said, "Yes, indeed!" He was happy. "Professor something else, ain't he?" Man handed Solly the bottle.

Solly laughed. "Sure is." He took a slug. "You got your monica?"

"Always."

"We can go over to my place and celebrate Christmas. Get some music going. Holly like that. Play something she like."

"Sound good to me."

· ·

Walking back they kept stopping for a taste. Stopped in front of the Catholic school on Michigan for a taste. Man hit it and handed it to Solly. He said: "You ever feel you just ramming yo head gainst a iron wall trying to get somewhere with yo music in this town?"

"Hell yeah," said Solly. "Too many goddamn blues guitar players in Chicago."

"It like Mister Lee say, this the mecca of the blues. They told me *that* down in N'Orleans. Fact is, that why I come up here. Everybody kept saying Chicago where it happening, go to Chicago, go to Chicago, N'Orleans a thing of the past."

"And you been here, what, four years?"

"Got here summer 19 and 46 and still ain't got nowhere. And I know I'm good. It ain't that I ain't good."

"You good, nigger." Solly laughed. "I can tell you that. And I ain't no expert. But—"

"Yeah, but there is a whole lot of other blues singers in this here town just as good."

"And better."

"I don't know bout no better, now."

Solly laughed. "How long you hanged out in N'Orleans?"

"Oh, man, let me see. I left Atlanna right round the time the war ended, in the wintertime that year. Everybody was saying go to N'Orleans, that where you can get work as a singer, go to N'Orleans. So I went to N'Orleans and never got nothing but handouts. Peanuts!"

Solly said, "N'Orleans and Chicago big towns. It hard to get anybody to pay any tention to you in a big town."

Man said, "I know. That why I gon go where I can be a big fish in a small pond."

"What you mean?"

"I got a lot of reasons to get out Chicago."

"So, Omaha, huh?"

"Yeah, Omaha. You know, it hit me: I coulda lost my life last night. I'm gon get outta this town while I can."

Solly didn't say anything.

"Solly, you ought to come on out with me. Debbie say they like the blues in that town. In a place like Omaha we wouldn't have so much competition."

"I got a family, man. But it sound good though." Solly handed him back the bottle.

"Move your family with you." Man hit it and handed it back. "We could turn that town out with soulful sounds."

"Yeah, yeah." Solly took a swig, wiped his mouth. "Here."

"Think about it, Solly. We can get a fresh start." Chugalugged one more time. Man held it out to him.

Solly waved it away. Man put it in his jacket pocket.

"You need a fresh start. I don't need no fresh start. But, say, what about Cleo? You give up on her?"

"Naw. Love that woman, man—"

"I know you do, nigger—"

"But I know I ain't about to get her back by pulling some drunk-ass trick like I did last night. I got to walk straight fore I can fly."

Looking at Man, Solly laughed nervously.

"I ain't lying," Man said. No question about it, he knew what he had to do now.

Solly wiped his mouth and his hand trembled.

A few moments later Man said, "This stuff all right but sho wish it was some good Dirty Bird." Then he started singing—

The jailer gave me whiskey,
The jailer gave me tea.
I say the jailer gave me whiskey,
The jailer gave me tea.
The jailer gave me everything but the key.

And Solly cackled at the ditty, saying, "You is a case, a real honest-to-goodness born case."

. . . .

They stopped again at the corner of Indiana for a taste. Man was happy. Good liquor and a good friend. It was like he hadn't even been shot and his life wasn't getting away from him.

When they got back Holly had company. Sherry, girl from upstairs who was about Holly's age. She was nice-looking, kind of gypsy-looking with a sexy mole that Man liked though he knew she painted it on her cheek right there by her mouth. And she had these great big blinking eyes like everything was new to her. She had a kid too, a boy, a year older than Annabel. Sherry was on welfare.

Annabel was sitting on the floor playing with her Christmas present, a pink doll with blue eyes.

Sherry didn't want a drink. "No, thank you," she said with a smile.

Man knew Holly wouldn't touch the stuff.

Solly got his guitar, got two glasses and poured himself and Man some joy juice, then settled back in the armchair.

Sherry said, "Guess I better get back upstairs. Andy going to wake up soon."

"Naw," Man said. "Stick around. I'll sing you a song. Just for fun. It Christmas, lady. How they say?—Be of good spirit."

Holly laughed, then Sherry kind of laughed too. She sat back down.

Man pulled a kitchen chair over and sat next to Solly, took out his harmonica, put his glass on the floor between his legs. He warmed up a little bit on the harmonica.

Solly tested his strings. "What we gon do?" he said.

"Whatever comes natural." Man started patting his foot. Held the harmonica with both hands. He hit the middle register, moved on up higher and higher. Breathing smoothly for more action, keeping control of the flow of air. Letting it come nice and easy. Now and then he held his nose, to get the breathing stronger. Now he hit a low note, and a lower one. Real soft-like. No spit. He never spat in the harmonica. No, sir. Said to Solly: "Ready?"

"Follow you."

Solly said, "Les go!" And Man cut loose with—

I'm so sorry to tell you,
So sorry to have to tell you,
Yo mama Miss Sadie is a bald-headed lady.
Yeah, yo mama Miss Sadie is a bald-headed lady.
I hates to talk about yo mama, Miss Sadie.
I sho hates to talk about yo mama, Miss Sadie.
But you leave me nothing else to choose,
You leave me nothing else to choose.
She got hair growing on her feets
So long she can't wear no shoes.

Sherry and Holly were falling out, cracking up.

Man was thinking now this is the way to live. This was better than driving one of them big old pimp roadhog fishtail diamond-dusted decorated Cadillacs with black-out tape on the windows, silver hubcaps, and tail fins long as cannons, better than drinking good liquor and smoking Cuban cigars, maybe even better than most belly-grinding. Times like this he knew why he and Solly became friends. Why they stuck together. The music. Nothing but the music. They came alive in and lived in the music like pollen lived in a flower. And he remembered how they seemed to just understand this the first day they met. Understood it without talking about it. It was a recognition warm and big as a bowling alley. What they shared was always there. They could be together for days without talking and it was as though they were still telling each other all kinds of things. Man with his harmonica or voice and Solly with his guitar, a guitar with such a pretty sound you could've put a pleated skirt on it and some fool would have wanted to marry it.

Now Little Annabel got up and wobbled over to her mama and climbed up on her lap and sat there just looking at her daddy and Man. Didn't crack a smile. She was like that.

So, Man wouldn't have to stop, Holly came over and filled his glass again. Bless her heart. . . .

From

One Flesh

CHAPTER 9

A day or two later, John made up his mind. "I've met a woman I'm in love with her name is Susie Chang she's Chinese-American," he said all in one breath.

His mother said, "That's nice. Is she from China?"

"No, Mom, she was born in San Francisco." He was sitting at his little kitchen table with the phone to his face. "She doesn't even speak Chinese."

"Isn't that odd?"

"What? No, Mom, it's not odd. I don't speak Swahili and I'm part African."

"You're no African!" she said.

He stored this comment away in his percolating mind to reflect on later. An image of his mother, in her armchair, reading the magazine *Race Traitor* flashed before him. "We were talking about Susie."

"I heard you . . ."

Unable to hold off, he was wondering what a "happy whole person" was likely to look like—on the outside, at least. Like Yab-Yum—father and mother embraced in the coital posture?

His mother again said, "I heard you. She's Chinese."

"She's an American. I really like her. I'm thinking about asking her to move in with me."

"Why would you do that? Shouldn't you just date for a while and see how it goes? Why rush into it?"

"I'm not rushing. I met her two weeks ago."

"It is true, God made the world in seven days, but I think people need a little more time, Johnny."

"God?"

"How does Susan feel about moving in with you?"

"It's Susie. I didn't ask her yet. I'm just thinking about it. I might not ask. She might not want to do it. Her parents—"

"Have you met her parents?"

"No. They live in San Francisco."

"Johnny, you have to be careful, you know."

"What do you mean?"

"I hear that the Chinese are not very receptive to—"

"Ah, Mom, there you go."

"I'm only telling you to be careful. I don't want your feelings hurt. The Chinese are very traditional people. Aren't they?"

"What d'you mean by traditional, Mom?"

"You know what I mean. Daughters are supposed—"

"Okay, okay." He looked at the ceiling. This was the response he'd anticipated and feared. Venomous light and shadows of serpents moved across the ceiling in rhythmic patterns, reflected from the glass top on the coffee table in front of the couch.

"How did you meet? What does she do? You haven't told me anything about her except her name."

The third degree. He looked up in the studio at the big filthy windows looking out on Greene and thought what this city needs is a good hard rain to come and wash the grime out into the Atlantic.

"She's a poet. She writes poetry." And he suddenly remembered, the day before, over the phone, Susie had read a fragment of a poem she was working on:

John's body is a practical argument
with his own destiny.
Can he leave it at will?

And his mother was saying, "Where did you meet? She must have a job."

"She came to the opening at the gallery."

"Is she going back to San Francisco soon, or is she living in New York?"

"Mom, she works for a publishing company here."

"That's nice, maybe they'll publish some of her poetry."

"Sure," he said cynically. "Have you heard anything from Dad?"

"Don't change the subject, Johnny. You know your dad's life and mine never cross. How old is your friend—what's her name?"

"Susie. She's twenty-three, a mature twenty-three. She's an adult."

"I don't doubt it, Johnny, honey, but you, do you know what you're doing?"

"Mom, nothing is happening. Not yet. It's not like I'm asking this girl to marry me."

"Woman. You just said she's a mature woman: don't call her a girl. But listen. Asking her to live with you is, is—"

"Is what—?"

"Have you thought about what will happen when her parents call up? There are all kinds of things to think about, John. You don't just rush into something like—"

"I will cross those bridges, Mom. *If* I ask her, I said *if.* I wish I hadn't mentioned it. It was just an idea."

"All I'm saying is think, show some forethought. If you're going to invite somebody to live with you, no matter who it is, think about what it means."

"You mean stuff like sharing the rent?" He gazed down at the greenish-white tabletop, thinking for the first time how much it was like the color of the crucifixion thorn tree, and its abstract patterns were also like the leaves of that tree. He said, "I hadn't thought about asking her to pay any rent."

"Why not? She might want to. She has a job. Maybe she values her independence. Did you ever consider that? And besides, there are other things involving money such as—"

"I know, sharing expenses."

"That's right. Sharing living space with somebody is not something to take lightly."

"Is that why you'd rather be alone?" The minute the words were out he regretted them and feared he'd hit an open nerve, transgressed, stumbled into the wrong corridor.

"I've considered taking in a roommate, but you don't know my situation. You've been gone a long time, John."

John? She called him "John" when she was unhappy with him. Always had. "Not that long," he said.

"Oh, yes, you've been gone a long time, honey."

"Yeah, I guess so, but it doesn't seem that long." John? "How's the weather there this summer?"

"Today wasn't bad," his mother said. "The breeze from the lake has been pretty strong this morning. I did my shopping early though, just in case, so I could be in if it turns hot in the afternoon."

"By the way, Mom, I had a good talk with Dad. He kind of opened up to me, told me about his childhood, and what it's like being a doctor."

"That's nice, Johnny. I'm glad to hear it. You called him?"

"Yes, I did."

"Well, I'm delighted," she said.

Suddenly he was determined to hang up. "Listen, Mom, I'd better go."

This was one of those conversations with his mother that turned out to be like trying to handle a thorny rosebush without gloves.

"Let me know what happens with Susan. And call me more often."

"Okay." He closed his eyes, listening to her, and saw a cathedral rising out of mist.

"How's your painting?"

"Okay. Gotta go, Mom."

After talking with his mother, John felt sad and impulsively dialed his father's home number, thinking he'd get his machine, knowing his father was at the hospital or in his office. This way John could leave a quick message just to say hello. He was still feeling good about the previous conversation with his father and wanted to keep the sense of contact alive.

But no such luck. John's father, the Honorable Dr. James Monroe Canoe himself, answered the phone in a voice calm and low as a sleepy nightingale's."

And like a fool John blurted out, "Oh, I didn't expect to get you. Thought I'd get your machine."

His father's chuckle was strained. "No, it's me in person. How are you, Johnny?"

"I'm okay. How are you?"

"Busy as usual," his father said with a sigh.

John didn't respond for fear he'd say something in anger, something he'd regret.

"Something on your mind, Johnny?"

"No, just wondering how you were doing."

John's father sighed again. "Actually, this is the first day of my vacation."

"Oh, yeah? Going anywhere interesting?" He couldn't keep the resentment out of his tone.

"Della booked us on one of those Caribbean tours—the Bahamas or Jamaica. I don't know. We leave tomorrow."

"How long?"

"I don't know, Johnny, maybe a week, but I don't want to talk about myself—"

An invading image: a giant angelfish vagina in which the whole body of the mating male is contained, and the male has John's face.

"Tell me about you. Last time all I did was talk about myself. What've you been up to? How's the art going?"

"Art?" John was being difficult. He couldn't help it. He resented the impatient tone of his father's voice.

"Your painting," his father said. "I never know what to say to you about your painting."

"What can you say? The painting is going fine. I'm not teaching summer school this summer."

Once again, he was feeling angry about the gratitude he felt for all his father had done for him, all the comfort he'd made available to him all his life, gratitude for this huge, well-located studio in which he now sat.

"I wish I could paint," his father said.

John ignored the comment. He said, "Uh, I wanted to talk with you about something, Dad."

There. He'd said it.

And he heard the tone of his own voice shift. He knew his father heard it too.

"What is it, Johnny?"

"I met a young woman I like."

"Oh?"

"I really like her a lot," John said, while lines of Susie's poetry came riding across the ridges of his mind—

I locate
with my fingertips
the place in you
where my flesh thought
it would remain forever,
and where we trust
a shared path

"Tell me about her," his father said with the patience of a Sunday school lector addressing a five-year-old.

In some ways, it was easier for him to talk with his father than his mother. Was it that there wasn't as much emotionally invested? Sometimes with his mother the emotions got all the skin peeled off. As a small child, he remembered his father in a rage, but in recent years the image of him in John's mind was one as calm as an old painting of a midnight railway station long abandoned and quietly covered with snow. John felt his father respected his right to be a separate, fully grown-up person. He both liked that and hated his father for it, hated the distance it implied, hated his father because he couldn't help feeling that the respect stemmed from a lack of interest, from his father's inability to love him.

John was stalling.

His father said, "If you don't want to tell me about her, why did you bring it up?"

"There's not that much to tell."

"You care about her. What's her name?"

"Susie Chang."

"Susie Chang? Is she Chinese?"

"She's Chinese."

"New York born?"

"No, San Francisco."

"Oh, West Coast, huh."

John held his breath. His father didn't sound all that interested. *I can tell.* A certain level of boredom in his voice.

"I bet she's very pretty."

You would think that—

"She is good-looking."

"What is she like?"

What am *I* like?
My eyes are two white stones
extracted from the belly of a fish.

"What d'you mean?"

"You know, personality, background."

He wasn't sure how to answer his father's question. "Uh, she's very American, but, you know, she comes from a pretty traditional family, from what I understand. I've only known her for a couple of weeks."

"Well, Johnny, I'm delighted to hear that you've met a girl you like."

"Are you?"

"Sure I am." His father hesitated. "Are you by any chance asking me about women—asking for advice?"

"I don't understand what you mean," John said.

"You know, son to father, father to son—men talking about women."

"I don't think I was going to do that, but if you've got any advice about women you want to give me—" Suddenly John laughed. It was an awkward laugh—full of stutter and hesitation.

"I probably don't know any more about women generally than you do. And there's always the danger of generalizing. It all comes down to personality and temperament, you know. Gender is a very small part of it. I mean, what aspect of women are we talking about? If we're talking about women!"

"How do you know when the right woman comes along?"

John's father laughed. "That's a tough one. You may be asking the wrong person. But I do know you can't generalize. I don't believe such myths as the popular notion that American women, for example, geld their husbands and castrate their sons. Oh, I know the feminists have caused a lot of consciousness-raising, but we're far from where we need to be in terms of gender equity." John's father stopped. "As for the right woman, you're the only one who can answer that, and it may take you a long time, but I hope not."

John took a deep breath and let it out into the phone. He watched the shiny surface of the mouthpiece turn cloudy.

"Is something on your mind, Johnny? I've got a lot to do. Got to pack. Make some calls."

"You're too busy to talk with me?"

"Aren't we talking now?" His father sounded defensive.

John felt he had learned lately how to put his father on the hot plate and make him percolate. "You never want to talk seriously with me, do you?"

"Of course, I do. You sound angry." A defensive edge creeping into his tone.

Half the time when John talked with his father, they sounded to him like two lovers at the end of a bad relationship, both with worn-out hearts.

"I guess I am angry."

"I know you are. Johnny, the past can't be changed. All we can do is try to make the future better."

"I know. I try to control my anger—and I do love you."

There! He'd said it—for the first time in a long long time.

And he listened to the pregnant silence on his father's end.

"I love you too," his father finally said in a voice on the low end of the scale. "And I do understand your pain. Believe me. I didn't grow up without a father, but I might as well have."

John couldn't think of anything acceptable to say.

Then his father said, "Do you need anything?"

That had always been his father's way of asking if John needed money. He was thirty-three now and had a good job and his father still asked him if he needed money. A rage inside John lifted like an atomic cloud and spread. His father had always tried to fix things by throwing money at him. He said, "No, thanks, I don't need anything."

His father had finality in his voice now. "I'll call you when we get back."

"Have fun," John said, trying to sound lighthearted but feeling tense and not amused.

. . . .

John took the canvas he'd been working on off the easel and put a fresh one up. He tried to remember a moment with his father when he felt totally sympathetic toward him. It happened two years before John's parents separated and divorced. He was seven and it was just before Christmas. This episode later became one of the grimmer family stories. He and his mother and father walked into an exclusive lady's shop on Michigan Avenue. In the window—which was decorated with twinkling Christmas lights and silver angel hair—the doctor had already seen a lady's tan leather coat with a stylish high collar. John's father had decided to buy it as a Christmas present for his wife, but wanting to make sure it fit exactly right, he was bringing John's mother to try it on. They entered the shop and a salesman in a suit said good afternoon but not with a smile. The doctor pointed out the coat he was interested in buying. John's mother tried it on and liked it. When the coat was all wrapped up and ready, John's father took out his checkbook. Immediately the salesman held up his hand like a traffic cop to oncoming traffic. He said payment had to be cash or in the form of a cashier's check. John, his father, and his mother retreated a few steps from the counter. John himself instantly felt embarrassed. The shop smelled of expensive silk scarves and kimonos, leather capes and leather boots, smelled of wealth. John's mother—red in the face with anger—whispered to John's father, "Give *me* the checkbook." They stepped back up to the counter and, now pulling her husband's checkbook from her own purse, she told the man that she would pay. The man said fine. John's mother wrote out the check, signed it with her name—both their names were on the check—and handed it to the salesman. He looked at the check carefully then put it into the cash drawer beneath the cash tray. And the deal was done.

CHAPTER 21

John and Susie were now back in their room at the Juliana. They had walked back without exchanging any words. The spitting image of a death-defying, defensive female superstar plotting her next move, Susie sat on the bed with her arms folded across her breasts, and with her knees up and feet flat on the bed. Her gaze was unbroken, almost grim. It was aimed at and stopped by the wall next to the bathroom, the entrance to which was four or five feet from the foot of the bed. The red message light on the phone was blinking like a radio signal from far away.

Hands in pockets, John slumped in one of the armchairs. "I'm sorry," he said, gazing at her.

"About what?" Her eyebrows arched.

"I wanted—" he started and stopped, thinking about his simplistic notion of Chinatown before he met Susie, which consisted mainly of Chinese food—the great stir-fries, the soups, and the noodle dishes. Chinese dancing dragons. Pagodas. Fortune cookies. Fortune calendars with animal signs. Kung Fu movies. "I wanted to see Chinatown."

"Oh, that." She waved away the apology. "It's not your fault. I told him we were going to get married."

"You what? Why?" John leaped from the chair.

"You don't know my family. Chinese people are strange. They respect marriage, any institution, law, rule." Her laugh was cynical. "Never mind that 90 percent of the Chinese people in this country wouldn't be here if they had respected immigration laws too."

John was thinking, *But, why did you lie to your father?*

Susie said, "We respect the laws when we're not breaking them. We're just like everybody else. Anyway, we have to get married right away." She laughed louder now. "Don't worry, just kidding."

Gritting his teeth, John gazed at her, wondering what it would be like married to her, a poet, a feminist, a young woman who believed with all her heart in life, liberty, and the pursuit of poetry, a "model minority," an all-American, dimpled, smiling girl with a difference.

"He did say I should bring you to meet Mama."

"You're kidding."

"No." She didn't crack a smile. "I was surprised. I told him we were engaged, planning on getting married, and he waited a long time before he said anything, then he said I should bring you to meet Mama tonight, after they close, bring you to the home."

John sat down again, leaning forward, elbows on knees. "You're not kidding? Howd' you feel about it?"

"I was surprised. I don't like it. It's not like them. Plus, I lied. And I don't know how to get out of it." Her frown suggested the quandary she felt.

"So, we'll go. What harm can it do?" He got up again and sat on the side of the bed and touched her knee. "Besides, I'm proposing right now." He felt himself beginning to smile. "Susie, would you be my wife?"

"Get outta here!" she said, slapping his thigh. "You're not serious." She was wearing her hair sexy-loose and parted in the middle, so that as she leaned forward—as she was now doing—the hair covered about a third of the side of her face.

But he was serious. Wasn't he? He thought he was. And now he wanted to make sure she knew it. But if he was really serious, there was a lot to think about. Marriage, like bringing a child into the world, was a profoundly serious act. What would his mother say? And his father—what would his father say? How would he and Susie negotiate their life together? Would they continue to live in the studio? If so, how long? Wasn't the studio really mostly his space? How soon would they be able to afford an apartment without selling the studio? "I couldn't be more serious. Seriously!" He paused. "Of course, we'll get an apartment. It's unfair for you to have to live in my studio."

"Whoa! Slow down, you're going to fast," Susie said, waving her hands in front of her. Then in a quiet voice, she said, "Listen, John, don't propose marriage if you don't mean it, just because of my father." She jerked her head back, tossing her long hair from her face.

"Your father has nothing to do with it. It's something I've been thinking about for a long time," he said, aware that if he had thought about proposing marriage it hadn't been on any conscious level. "But you haven't answered my question."

"You mean will I marry you?"

"Yes," he whispered.

She touched his cheek as though it were made of gossamer.

"Sure, I would marry you, but maybe I'm not the person you think I am."

"What does that mean?"

Pulling back, she now folded her hands around her knees. "I don't know," she said, with a worried, distracted look.

"Who else could you be but yourself?"

She smiled, looking at him. "So, we can say we're engaged, huh?" An excited light danced in her dark eyes. She released her knees.

"Sure, but what if your parents don't approve?"

"Listen, when it comes to me, my family has been going down The River of Denial for a long, long time. This would just be one more thing." She tossed her hand over her shoulder as though throwing something away.

"But your father sounds like he might be ready to accept the situation."

She waved away John's comment. He's just giving in, at best. It doesn't mean he accepts. They've probably decided it's dumb to cut off all contact with their only daughter. But they see me only in relation to themselves, as little daughter." She sighed. "My family, in a way, is the least of it. It's the world that's the problem. People gaping at us everywhere we go."

John frowned. "The world has never been completely safe for anybody," he said, feeling wise. "We have to choose our places. In New York, we don't have as much of a problem below Fourteenth Street."

"That's true," she said, smiling. She laughed. An image of New York Chinatown with its electric lights burning in bright daylight shadow-danced across his memory, and there in that hot and stale-smelling café was the bewildered face of Uncle Charlie clouded with cigarette smoke. It was almost inconceivable that this man he couldn't even talk to might become his uncle-in-law. "It's true as long as we stay out of Chinatown," Susie added.

"I didn't see people there staring at us. Not like here." He looked at the blinking phone. "That's probably Yuen."

Wetting her lips with the flick of her tongue, Susie reached over and picked up the telephone.

Three gentle knocks at the door. John got up and opened it and was surprised to see that Yuen looked different from the way he'd imagined. Yuen, handsome, in a blue cotton pullover and jeans, had black silky shoulder-length hair. He gave John a big, easy smile, saying, "Hi," as he held his right hand out to shake. John returned the greeting and shook with the young man who might soon be his brother-in-law, and they introduced themselves to each other. In his left hand, Yuen carried a manila envelope.

"Hey, Sis," he said. Susie and Yuen then embraced awkwardly as John closed the door.

"We ran into Baba," Susie said with the kind of sigh that might be forced from her body had she been wearing a tight bodice.

"Yeah, I know," Yuen said, laughing easily, going to the armchair and sitting down. He dropped the manila envelope on the breakfast table. "Good for 'em! Chinese parents need to wake up. We're entering a new century! This is America! This is the modern world! We're in The Age of Information! So are you going over?"

Questioningly, Susie looked at John. "I guess so," she said hesitantly, almost timidly.

"Sure, we are," said John, sitting in a slump in the chair by the bathroom door with knees apart and arms resting loosely across his thighs.

"Why don't you come with us?" Susie said to her brother. Waiting for him to respond, her eyes grew large with expectation.

"I have to pick up Shirley. Tonight, we're supposed to do something." He rubbed his face and shook his head. In that moment he was a teenager, trying to appear jaded and cool.

"Ah, Yuen, please. I need you as a buffer," Susie said, stamping her feet, and going to his side, touching his shoulder. "Please! Pretty please!"

His face held a self-satisfied grin for a second, then he said, "I didn't think I'd see you again so soon."

"You never know," she said, turning abruptly from him, and going again to sit on the side of the bed. She sat facing her brother. "Where're the trust papers you want me to sign?"

"Right here," Yuen said, picking up the manila envelope and shaking it at her. "By the way, I got something I need to talk with you about."

"I can go downstairs for a cup of coffee," John said, leaning forward.

"Oh, no, I didn't mean—"

Susie said, "What's this about, the trust?" She took the envelope.

"No, something else."

She gave him the impatient look of an older sister trying to come to terms with a younger, unruly brother.

"Oh, hell, I'll just tell you. This is America! Shirley is pregnant. We're going to get married."

Susie's eyes stretched. Then she laughed. "Baba and Mama know?"

"Not yet." He looked guilty.

"Oh, boy," Susie said, shaking her head. "You're the dream of their life, and—"

"Don't give me that crap, Susie. You know you've always been the favorite. It broke their hearts when you left."

"That's a lie and you know it, Yuen! You're the favorite!"

"Okay, let's not argue," he said, holding up his hands.

"How far gone is she?"

"Couple of months."

"Too late," she said.

"I know. We thought we might just go off and get married somewhere like in Reno. Tell 'em later."

Susie laughed. "Maybe you and Shirley can do something to make the baby stay in there two months longer."

Watching Yuen, John chuckled. He was charmed by the lightness in Yuen's personality.

"Sure, sure," Yuen said, "and come out looking like Rosemary's Baby."

Susie now looked at the envelope in her hand, sat down on the side of the bed, and opened it on her lap.

While Susie was reading, Yuen, nervously twitching, grinned at John. "So, what kinda of work do you do?"

"Teach high school, art."

"That sounds pretty cool. Summers off. Huh?"

John nodded his head. "Yeah, it's not bad. Susie tells me you're studying business administration at Berkeley."

"Finished."

"That's right," John said. "Finished." He took a deep breath and let it out. "Subject I don't know much about."

As Yuen laughed, Susie finally looked up, saying, "Yuen, I can't sign this."

John leapt to his feet. "I'll be right back. I forgot something." Heading for the door, his gaze was upon Susie's troubled face.

At the same time, Yuen flew out of his seat toward his sister.

But Susie was now looking away from her brother at John. "Where are you going?"

"Downstairs." And he stood now with his left hand on the doorknob.

Behind him, he heard Yuen say, "Why not? Why can't you sign it?"

"I just can't. It's not fair."

Stepping out into the hallway, John closed the door gently behind himself.

. . . .

Moments later, John walked through the bright lobby, past a few men and women sitting together on a bench near the entranceway, probably waiting to be driven to the airport.

Two-thirds of the way through the lobby, glancing at a man in a blue business suit, leaning against a wall, with a payphone to his face, John remembered that the last time he'd spoken with his mother before coming out here she had given him the telephone number of her niece, his cousin Daryl Garrett, whose name was now Daryl Garrett-Meldon. Daryl had recently moved with her husband, Luke Meldon, a stockbroker, and their infant girl, Lucinda, to San Francisco. John's mother had asked him to call Daryl, just to say hello, to do something "unselfish" for a change. But John wasn't yet sure if he wanted, or had the nerve, to call.

Then the man in the blue business suit hung up, and impulsively, John walked over to the phone. He stood there searching through his wallet for the scrap of paper he'd written Daryl's number on. When he found it, he put coins in, then dialed Daryl's number. When a young woman's voice said, "Hello," John almost hung up, but he finally said, "Daryl Meldon? This is John, John Canoe, your Aunt Laura's son. You know, from Evanston?"

His stomach felt tight and his hands were sweating.

"Oh, hi. Aunt Laura said you might call. You're in San Francisco?"

"Yes, but just for a brief time." He didn't want her to propose getting together. "Mom wanted me to call to break—" he abruptly stopped speaking.

Daryl laughed. "To break the ice?"

"I wasn't going to say that," he said. Forever the visual thinker, Daryl's voice gave him the image of a rain tree with golden flowers in long clusters. John continued, "By the way, congratulations on your marriage and the newborn."

"Oh, thank you. She's a darling. We'd all love to meet you, John. Can you come over? Maybe you could come and have dinner with Luke and me? Or we could go to a restaurant."

He forced sadness into his voice. "Oh, I'm sorry. I wish I had time, but this is really a quickie trip."

"I understand. I know what it's like to be on a tight schedule."

"Maybe next time," John said, half wishing he'd said yes, now feeling a growing sense of curiosity about this pleasant-sounding young woman. The photograph of her he remembered best was one taken when she was graduating from high school. She was a pretty girl with a clear complexion, dimples, and light brown hair.

"Can you give me your phone number, I mean, in New York? Luke goes to New York a lot. One of these times when Lucinda is older, I'll probably come with him. Maybe we can get together then."

He hesitated—as though the left hemisphere of his brain had suddenly stopped working—but saw no polite way out of it. "Sure," said John, and slowly recited his phone number into the mouthpiece.

"Thanks!" Daryl said. "I'm so delighted you called. You know you're the big famous mystery in this crazy family."

"Whatd' you mean?"

"A successful artist nobody has ever met."

Well, my dear, thought John, *nobody in your family wanted to even believe I existed until recently. Now, I'm supposed to jump with joy and embrace everybody?* But he said nothing.

Daryl said, "I don't think I've even seen a photograph of you. Would you send me one?"

Somehow the request seemed odd to John, but knowing that it really wasn't, and that it might even be a propitious thing to do, he said, "Sure."

"And I'll send you pictures of us and the baby. Okay?"

"Sure," John said slowly, hoping his bewilderment was not in his tone.

They then exchanged addresses.

"Daryl, I've gotta go. I'm sorry."

"Sure, but this is so great," said Daryl, those golden flowers moving in the summer breeze. "I'll let you go now. Thanks so much for calling, John."

"Oh, sure! Take care."

"Bye-bye," Daryl chirped. "Stay in touch."

. . . .

Night air felt good on his face as he headed downhill, past the church, toward Grant. He felt a deep silence in himself. Daryl sounded like a nice person. He wished he had been friendlier. Well, at least he'd made the call. If she ever came to New York, he'd treat her well. After all, she was his first cousin, and the first person on his mother's side of the family he'd ever even exchanged words with.

As he walked, he thought now about Susie. Leaving when he did was the right thing. Family matters were family matters. The silence he felt was peaceful yet problematic. Noisy cars, trucks, and buses sped down Bush, overhead and all around him were sounds, yet he felt enclosed in his own personal silence. What was noise anyway? He remembered the music—classical, jazz, blues—he worked by. He remembered some time ago coming to the conclusion that there was no such thing as silence. You got disorganized or organized noise. In front of the language school near the corner he stopped, trying to decide if it was too soon to go back.

He suddenly had a headache. He looked up and noticed an elderly white woman standing at the display window of the language school, gazing at him. In a flash, just as he looked quickly away, he saw her smile, and also saw her disappointed frown when he had not returned her smile. When he was sure she was not looking, he glanced back at her, but she was now staring down at an information poster on display in the window. No doubt a nice lady. She didn't deserve his rudeness.

Organ music was coming from the church, and when he was adjacent to its stairway, he looked up and saw an oblong of golden light pouring from inside. John climbed the steps to take a look. After all, it was a Catholic church. The doors were open, and at the entryway, he looked in, feeling as though he'd been here before. The golden interior light fell in complex patterns, from both electric sources and burning candles, with parallelograms of it all around the altar.

John heard clearly the voice of the priest. "Blessed are the poor in spirit, for theirs is the Kingdom of Heaven. Blessed are they which are persecuted for righteousness' sake, for theirs is the Kingdom of Heaven." John was trembling and felt strangely excited. His stomach was upset. And after a brief silence, that clear voice again. "Whosoever shall smite thee on the right cheek, turn to him the other also. Love your enemies, bless them that curse you, do good to them that hate you, and pray for them which despitefully use you, and persecute you." The priest's voice was beginning to have a calming effect on him. Now the priest was saying, "Be ye therefore perfect, even as your Father which is in Heaven is perfect."

Then, just inches from where he stood, John noticed a scraped, bloody, rotting hand emerging from the wall by the door, a wall black as coal. The hand was extended with the forefinger out, furiously emotional, as if to beckon to him. The sight chilled him to the core. Forcing his eyes away, he gazed in at the sprinkling of people on their knees before the altar and sitting in seats, praying. Organ music, possibly a recording, suddenly started. He tore his eyes away from this scene to see the hand again, but it was gone. No question about it, his right hemisphere was definitely right now in charge.

He ran down the steps, and as he walked the short distance back up to the hotel entrance, he told himself he had no reason to suddenly find it impossible to live with his visions and demons. After all, he'd been freely living with them all his life. Freely? *Freely?* Had he ever truly felt free? And what was freedom anyway? Once upon a time, when he was very little in size, he'd thought he was free to do what the white boys in his neighborhood and at school did. His mother, he thought, had to have been responsible for some of his innocence. It had taken him far too long to develop good black survival defenses.

Entering the lobby, he noticed that the people who were waiting on the bench a little while earlier were now gone, and new people were all about—some standing, some sitting, some at the front desk, checking in or checking out. A black man and a white woman, obviously together, were checking in. John noticed that nobody was eyeballing them. Had this moment in this lobby been in Evanston, twenty years earlier, all eyes would have been upon them. As John stood at the elevator door waiting, he noticed a white man walk over to the black man. The two men spoke, smiling. The black man extended his hand to the white man, offering to shake hands. John watched closely. The white man flinched, glared at the black man's hand, then reluctantly stuck his own out toward the black man. They shook hands without breaking eye contact or surrendering their smiles. John smiled to himself. How often had he himself been in the delicate position of both men?

In the elevator, going up, John happened to be standing between two white women, with a white man behind him. It was like being at the perfume counter in Macy's. The women were drenched in the stuff. He almost laughed at the situation, it was so normal. Yes, normal. The people around him in the elevator were acting normal, not looking at him, watching the dial, waiting to get off, keeping their eyes averted. All very normal. John self-consciously fixed his face with a slight, private smile.

Rather than using his key, he knocked, heard Susie respond, "Yes? Who's there?" And he told her. Then, when she swung the door open, standing framed by the doorway and with the windows behind her, she was a brightness at the center of something dark, dark, dark.

At the same time, John could see right away that Yuen had gone.

CHAPTER 22

Susie said, "My parents are usually home by ten or ten-thirty. The cooks close up."

John checked his watch. It was now ten-thirty-five. On Grant Avenue, John and Susie were walking past Washington Street to see if the Chang family restaurant was closed. Chinatown was still aglow with lighted shop fronts and busy and noisy as the narrow sidewalks crowded with tourists. The lights were arrangements of angels dancing in astral unison. Buddha and Buddhism were nowhere in sight. Shop owners stood in doorways trying to encourage business. You could almost see their brain waves floating out to the passersby. American to the core, thought John. Breastfed on the dollar sign. The central nervous system of Chinatown was not in the circular shape of the mandala or the *pa-kwa*. Even the area itself was oblong like the dollar bill.

Looking through the plate glass of the restaurant into the dim light, John saw a boy placing chairs upside down on tables, and beyond him, in what was probably the kitchen, he saw two men dressed like cooks, one standing with arms folded across his chest, listening to the other talk.

Susie said, "Okay, looks like my parents are home. That's Gary, the boy stacking chairs, and the two cooks back there, Wayne and Joe."

John felt something pulling at his pants leg, and turning around, he saw an infant reaching over from his stroller, doing the yanking. John glanced quickly at the man—probably the father—pushing the stroller. He seemed friendly enough. At the moment the father was in an impasse due to the mob on the sidewalk. To the baby, John said, "Pretty strong grip you got there, young man." And the father, appreciating the humor, smiled. Looking up into John's face, the baby said, "Goo goo." Then the baby and father were gone. John smiled. Maybe that statement, "goo goo," summed up the human condition.

When John and Susie reached the building, dark and shabby and leaning against the one next to it, one block over from Grant, near the corner of Wentworth, John looked at the address, 744 Washington Street. The street smelled of decay and garbage.

He and Susie paused in front, and she pointed up at the orange lighted windows of her parents' apartment on the second floor. "The lights are on," Susie said. "They're home." John felt nervous. The ground floor was a closed produce warehouse called Fong & Kwong Food Company. Despite the brown darkness of Wentworth and Washington, going into such deep darkness as the hallway offered so soon after Grant Avenue's crowded, noisy, busy, neon brightness, the hallway was almost tunnel dark. Antenna-less, flashlight-less, John and Susie started climbing the unseen steps in bear-cave darkness, and Susie said, "The hall light burned out." Presumably, John thought, to let him know that this darkness was not normal.

Reaching the second-floor landing, John saw a thin, horizontal, brightly shimmering orange-blue strip of light showing under the door. It was surrounded by a frame of black-brown darkness that also contained Susie and himself—as ghosts with goose-flesh. At least that's how he felt—and graceless as a rhinoceros.

They were now standing outside Susie's parents' apartment door and Susie—though she had a key—had just knocked three times. They waited. Even a short wait was hard to handle when your stomach had taken you with it and dived to the bottom of the daydreaming sea. It was like being stuck in traffic surrounded by crocodiles driving the other cars. Cranial dew dried up real fast.

John gazed at the light from under the door shining on the tips of his ox-blood shoes.

After a long while, Susie knocked again. This time harder. John heard television noise inside. He hoped the patron saint of dark hallways and stairways was with them. If no such saint existed, perhaps St. Gregory, patron saint of desperate situations, might pinch-hit.

Susie was in a foul mood. John didn't know the details at this point, but he assumed that she and her brother had had a violent disagreement about the terms of the trust. Why did they call it "trust"? Who said trust was a plant of slow growth? True, trust, between brother and sister, in human affairs, was important. John understood trust to be like the faith of Catholics. On the other hand, didn't *contract* in German mean "mistrust"? With these thoughts he was trying to distract himself, to contain, control, his nervousness.

"Who—?"

"Baba, it's me, Susie!" She paused. "John and me!"

"Okay okay," Mr. Chang said impatiently. They heard him unbolting the door.

John became aware that he was holding his breath, then forced himself to breathe normally. *St. Gregory, where are you?*

Finally, the door opened into the apartment on a dimly lighted hallway, and Susie's father stood facing them. The faint smell of mothballs came out of the apartment. Framed by the doorway, Mr. Chang seemed larger, a different color, a deeper hue of oxide. He was not smiling. Behind him, John saw a small woman he took to be Susie's mother. Darker than the father, yellowish-brown in complexion, she was dressed in a simple faded cotton print dress, and she was holding the palm of her right hand against her cheek and terror was in her dolphin eyes. Leaning sideways, she was looking around her husband to get a glimpse of her daughter and John in the doorway.

"Sorry, Susie, this no good. We can't have this."

"What do you mean, Baba?"

With eyes closed, he shook his head. "You come in, but you friend—" he shook his head. "You mama heart—"

"But Baba, you invited us here!" Susie shouted in his face.

"Sorry," he said, looking at the floor. "You come in but he go 'way. Okay?"

"No, it's not okay, Baba." Susie was becoming hysterical.

Susie's mother said something in Chinese, and Wei-han, her father, turned halfway around and responded in Chinese, then turned back to John and his daughter. Again, he said, "You mama sick. Too much confusion."

"If John can't come in, then I don't want to." Her voice was choked.

"You come in, see you mama," he said, glancing up from watching the floor, to catch her reaction. "Be good Chinese daughter. This not the way you raised. You come in."

"No!" shouted Susie, turning away.

John had already stepped away from the door and was waiting for Susie at the edge of the landing. Through a hall window, the neon lights outside on the street were blinking blue and red, blue and red.

Susie was sobbing now as she stumbled into John, and his arm went around her. They were two drunk dancers falling deliberately into a graceless stumble.

Behind them, he heard her father slam the door. The sound echoed and reverberated throughout the dark hallway. Susie was making convulsive sounds and holding her breastbone.

John held her arm, leading her down the dark stairway, out into the relatively lighter but dark street. They immediately started walking toward the glare of the neon lights and were soon caught up in the thicket of the crowd on Grant Avenue. Susie was still weeping. On Susie's right side, John walked beside her with his arm still around her, still leading her, as she stumbled along with her face down and using her left hand like the bill of a cap to shield her eyes. He'd never before seen her so upset, in such obvious pain. Along the way, John refused to pay any attention to the many people looking at them, and he managed to steer Susie through the thicket of oncoming bodies without a collision.

Between sobs, Susie said, "I refuse to be their little submissive nothing!" Sob. "I refuse to choose between Chinese and American." Sob. "I'm both!" Sob. "I refuse to let them do this to me!" Sob. "I have options!" Sob. "Do they think they can choose a husband for me?" Sob. "This is not China!" Sob. "This is America!" Sob.

. . . .

By the time they reached Bush, Susie had almost stopped crying but was still agitated and sniffling. As she and John turned to climb the hill to the hotel, she said, "I can't stand going through that bright lobby right now. Let's get in the car and go."

"Go where?"

"Anyplace! Out to the Marina in Berkeley."

They walked on past the hotel up the hill, crossed Stockton, and, in the next block, came to the garage. Inside, a family—father, mother, a small boy, and a small girl—were waiting by the office for an attendant to bring up their car. John asked one of the two remaining attendants for his car, and the young man shot away to get it. While the boy and girl staged a dog and pony show, running around on the concrete driveway, the mother gave Susie very sympathetic glances and glared at John as though he were the culprit.

Fifteen minutes or so later, John was driving east on Bush, headed for the Oakland Bay Bridge, with Susie giving directions. Her voice was thick with mucus, but she was no longer crying. He drove through the financial district with its sleeping buildings. This was bank and business heaven. "You're looking for Market," Susie said hoarsely.

Night driving was never fun. People wearing dark clothes and crossing on the wrong light sometimes stepped out in front of your car. But John was being extra careful, resisting the glare of street lights. Plus, it was hard driving in a strange city, even with good directions.

John was curious about what had happened to cause Susie's father to change from his earlier show of goodwill, and he wanted to know what had happened between Susie and her brother over the matter of the trust, but now was not the time to ask. Later.

Connecting with Market, John drove past the giant glittering Bank of America. He took Market all the way out to Beale, then swung right on Beale, and soon joined the dense traffic headed for the bridge. Driving this new Camry through these night streets was like being an improvisational cursor or spec of light moving with irreverent whimsy through a stream-of-consciousness color field. He was straining to find his way, watching out for unexpected red lights or people suddenly in his headlights.

They were on the bridge now. She was gazing out at the night sky in the direction of San Pablo Bay. Stars were up there but he couldn't see them from here. *Gulliver travels on*. John drove on, keeping quiet, waiting for Susie's directions. "When we come off the bridge turn left. You're going to take East Shore along the Marina."

Slowing down, John felt like he now had the hang of it. When they came to University Avenue, he automatically turned west, and in a couple of minutes they were in the Marina on Marina Boulevard, driving slowly toward the water, past a woman in a flimsy white gown on horseback galloping along a stretch of grass. Lady Godiva on the move.

In a couple of minutes, John saw a sign for parking, and he turned off and found a lot. Three or four other cars were already parked with their lights off.

Couples were in them doing things or just looking at the lights of San Francisco. John came to a stop and parked facing west, with the nose of the Toyota pointing toward the city, a good distance from any other car. He rolled down the window on his side. The night air smelled weedy and mossy. It had taken about twenty, twenty-five minutes to get here. "There is the bridge," Susie said, with a note of forced cheerfulness in her voice.

John looked at the bridge, dim in the far distance, and saw the traffic, like a line of lightning bugs, crawling across it. Human beings on the go! The sight was more lonely than a coyote's howl, more beautiful than a valley full of crimson flowers in the summer.

Susie's hands were folded in her lap. He reached over and covered her hands with one of his. This was a difficult and precious moment.

"I love you," she whispered in a voice still hoarse with pain.

He leaned over, and they kissed. Her trembling lips were salty.

Then, for a while, they sat there in silence. Crickets were talking sex. Irregular streaks of light like those in atako wood were strung across the dark blue sky. His part of that silence filled the car like a nakedness and joined the night all around them. John thought he could smell the whole Pacific Ocean now and, despite the night's smell of weediness and mossiness, the ocean itself smelled of sea fennel and bitter ash.

With her eyes closed, chin up, sitting up straight, with her head back against the headrest, Susie sighed the sigh of bitter memory. "Life is too hard," she finally said. "Everything I do turns out to be a piece of shit." She started crying again softly, crying the cry of a small child trying to comfort her grief-stricken self with her own tears.

"That's not true, Susie. It's not your doing."

"Then whose is it?" She blew her nose with a tissue.

He didn't want to say what he was really thinking at that moment. He understood, or thought he understood, why they were sitting here now, first in gloomy and sad silence, and now exchanging painful and remorseful words. It was because he was not Chinese or white. Either probably would have been acceptable to Susie's parents. Chinese no doubt was preferable, but short of that, only white was acceptable. Or was it *because* he was a black man?

John said, "You warned me about your parents."

"I guess I got my hopes up when Baba invited us home."

"That's understandable. But such a complete about-face. What d'you think happened?"

"He got back to the restaurant and told my mother, and she hit the ceiling, probably started weeping. She knows how to turn on the tears."

"Then she changed his mind?"

"All the time. She runs everything. He only thinks he's making the decisions." She looked at him. "I'm hungry."

"What happened with Yuen?"

She clucked. "Stupid trust!"

"Did you sign it?"

"Hell, no! It gives him control over my parents' entire estate, including what they're leaving me. I just know my mother is behind this whole thing. As if my father isn't bad enough with the boy-first stuff."

"I'm hungry, too. Maybe we can get something to eat out here. I noticed a couple of motel restaurants back there at the turn."

"Lots of them out here." She was gazing through the windshield, probably at the Golden Gate Bridge and the tiny ant-like lights crawling across it.

"Maybe you should call your mom and try to talk to her."

"And say what?" Susie looked at him again. "It's impossible to talk to her. I've tried for twenty-three years."

"But the fact that your dad thought it was okay to invite me must mean there's hope—"

She shook her head no. "Half the time, he doesn't know what he thinks. One day it's good to be American, next day better to be Chinese. This week the only good thing about Chinese culture is the food. Next week, you better observe all Chinese holidays or else. Confucius this month, George Washington the next. He's hopeless. Aren't you hungry?"

"Let's drive around and see what we can find." John started the car, backed out, and drove along in the direction he'd taken in. The drive was circular, and they could see, without getting out, the lighted signs for fairly upscale restaurants. There were restaurants and motels all along the way, but the first one they checked out was closing and the second one was already closed.

The third one was the Ashby Restaurant attached to the Marina Inn right on the shore. It was open. John parked. He and Susie walked through the lobby and down a long hall. They went past a row of about a dozen card tables with convention displays on them. It was a convention to help young people get started in business. Nobody was in sight. At the end of the hallway was the entrance to the restaurant. John and Susie sauntered into the rather classy-looking restaurant; and she stood alongside the reception booth.

They could see the place was big and empty except for two people over by the black windows, a woman in a wheelchair with a young man who may have been her son. Sage and coffee were in the air. In daylight, those black windows would have been blue with sky and water and a profusion of seagulls, schooners, sailboats, motorboats, and yachts rocking gently in the breeze. After five minutes, a young woman showed up. Her name tag said Rosemary Kennard, Hostess. Rosemary was wearing a silk white blouse and a synthetic blue skirt, probably uniform, and she was also wearing a smile that wore out about twelve hours before. Rosemary said, "Just in time. We're closing pretty soon. Window seat?" Yes, they wanted to sit by one of the big black windows. The receptionist, even before she'd finished her question—had gathered up two large cardboard menus from the rack on the side of the reception stand and said, "This way, please."

Halfway through a dinner of grilled Portobello mushroom sandwiches with red onions, lettuce, tomato, pickles, Susie said, "Let's see if we can get a room here."

"Tonight? We'd have to pay for today at the Juliana anyway."

"Well, let's sleep there tonight and book a room here for tomorrow night. I don't want my family to know where I am, and we've got three more nights here. I want to just try to relax and enjoy it as much as possible."

"Sure," he said. "But what are you going to do about Yuen?"

"Fuck Yuen. That's what he was trying to do to me."

John sipped his white wine slowly and kept his eyes on her face. Well, at least, she was no longer weeping. Her anger was familiar. She was nearly her usual self again—pushing and pounding at several different fortress walls at the same time.

They finished eating and drank more wine and gazed through the black window for a while, then paid the waiter, left a tip, and walked back up the hall and into the quiet hotel lobby, where the desk clerk, a young man with a baby face and brown hair, told them the only room available was one starting tomorrow night. Taking out his wallet, John handed the clerk his Visa card. "We're leaving Monday morning." The clerk nodded, and John took the plastic key handed him.

On the way to the room, in a passageway, he smelled myrtle grass and Devil's Dung. To find the room, they had to walk to the end of the building and climb one flight of steps to the second floor. Inside, Susie pushed the light switch. The room was grand, with a sitting area, a dining area, a bar with a refrigerator behind it, and the bedroom was upstairs. Curtains covered one whole side of the wall. They were drawn now, but John and Susie peeked around them and saw dimly the Berkeley Marina out there with its profusion of boats and, looking up the line of the Marina Inn itself, they saw the windows of the Ashby. This was pretty amazing for the money.

When they got back to the Juliana, there was a message from Yuen to call him. Susie made a face.

"Go ahead," John said, "call him. Maybe he's going to change the trust. Maybe it's about something else."

A while later, undressed down to his underwear, John stretched out on the white sheet of the bed, with the television on, but mute. He was watching Susie. She picked up the phone, got an outside line, dialed, and waited. "Yuen? It's me. He told you, huh? Well, he invited us, then rudely told John he couldn't come in. That's what he said. It was the most humiliating experience of my life. You bet I know how they are! That's the problem! I know only too well! But there's no excuse! What's the matter with them? Will they never get their minds out of the past and live in the present? They're acting like the white people act! What? I know they're victims, too! That's the other part of my point. Their generation never got out of Chinatown. They were confined there. And they confined themselves. No, you're wrong. Introversion, my foot! There are limits to keeping a low profile. I don't want to fight, either. I'm just returning your call. Is that why you called? If you and Baba want it that way, you can just take my name out of the trust all together. No! I don't want my name in it! I don't need any money from their deaths! Yours either! No! I'm doing just fine. Yes, he's here. Here? Baba, coming here? You're kidding. No, he hasn't called. Okay. I'd better hang up. Bye!" When Susie hung up she looked at John and said, "Yuen says my father wants to have a man-to-man talk with you."

"A man-to-man—?" John sat up. Briefly, he glanced down at his naked body and saw himself self-consciously for the first time in a long, long while. It hadn't been too long ago that he thought of himself as a boy, but now he was a man. A grown man. His father and his mother treated him as such. It wasn't easy staying grown up. Sometimes one's mind fell back into being a child, with all of the insecurities and doubts of childhood. But this body was the man Mr. Chang now—suddenly and unexpectedly—wanted to have a so-called man-to-man talk with. Halfway up, John was still gazing at Susie in astonishment. Again, he said, "A man-to-man talk?"

"Yes. Whatever that means."

John laughed. He swung his legs off the bed and the moment his feet hit the floor, the telephone rang. Susie picked up. "Yes, Baba. Yes. I don't understand, but if you say so. Yes, John is here. Okay, I'll ask him." She covered the mouthpiece, and, looking at John, said, "My father wants to come over here and have a man-to-man talk with you."

John shrugged. "Fine," he said. "Tell him I'll meet him in the lobby."

Susie looked skeptical as she spoke into the mouthpiece, "He'll be waiting for you in the lobby, Baba. Good-bye." She hung up and said, "He'll be here in no time. He walks fast for a little old man with short legs."

"I'm dressing now."

When Mr. Wei-han Chang entered the lobby, it was five minutes to one. John was sitting in a dark red armchair, reading a news story about gay rights on the front page of the *Chronicle.* John stood up to meet him. The lobby was empty except for the desk clerk who had buzzed Mr. Chang in.

Cautiously, John didn't extend a hand in greeting, nor did Mr. Chang. But John kept a steady watch for any possible sign of friendliness as the old man approached.

"We can sit here and talk, if you like," John said, turning and holding a limp hand toward the chair next to the one he'd been sitting in.

"Okay okay," said Mr. Chang impatiently, waving his hand, then sitting down slowly while holding the arms of the chair.

They were sitting side by side now, facing—across the room—the opposite wall, against which stood a long table on which sat bowls of apples, pears, bananas, and oranges. Both men were silent. For John, it was like waiting at a thousand-year-long planetary stoplight way out somewhere in the untelescoped, star-studded universe. His heart would stop beating before the silence ended.

While waiting for the old man to speak, out of the sides of his eyes, John glanced at Mr. Chang. He could see the man in profile. He was a frail and gentle-looking man with large black eyes. His back was slightly bent. John thought that he probably looked a lot older than he really was.

Then Susie's father cleared his throat and said, "Chinese daughter is very special to Chinese family." He wasn't looking at John as he started to speak. His gaze was focused somewhere on the carpet in front of them. "In America you may not know very much about Chinese custom. But Chinese people not all time like American." Now he looked at John and smiled, and Mr. Chang suddenly seemed boyish and charming, showing teeth too large for his face.

John nodded in agreement.

"When I first come to America, 1964, young Chinese people in uproar, Berkeley students in Chinatown too making lot of racket. Stirring up things. All about International Hotel. These developers want to tear it down, build new building. But Chinese young people and Berkeley students stand up for rights of bachelors. You know? That where they live, in International Hotel. Old Chinese man, no wife, maybe wife in old country, long, long time ago, but not now. So, I come to America and first thing I see is fighting in Chinatown. So,

I say to myself, which country I come to? Is this America, Land of Opportunity, Home of Brave, Golden Mountain, Land of Milk and Honey? Fight go on for nine long years, then they tear down building anyway. So, you see, noise and racket for nothing. Then I read in newspaper about death of Chairman Mao. After death of Chairman Mao, after liberation of China, after normalization, more and more Chinese people come to America for opportunity make money, not to fight about building stand or come down. They come just like I come. I come this country for better life . . ."

As Mr. Chang was talking, John was amazed by the old man's ability to actually be present with his voice only, and at the same time to seem absent in every other way. Although Mr. Chang was talking to John, John had the feeling that Susie's father was merely muttering to himself. It made John himself feel totally absent. It was like watching somebody on television, a character you could not speak to, who, if you spoke, would never hear you.

" . . . and we never had problem," Mr. Chang was saying, "Susie grow up in this Chinatown. She was little girl in pretty good Chinatown. She got everything nice we give her. Not like in old days when little Chinese children work hard all day, or back when only Chinese man live here to work, stay in *gong si fong* like International Hotel, and stay in they own club with just man from they own place in China, just doing like they told to do, not understand Americans, who say, Me first, me, me. Because in the old day, before, after earthquake, Chinese man didn't go out of Chinatown for nothing. Except maybe to pick up laundry. Indian and Mexican woman charge white man big money to do laundry, but not Chinese, so Chinese be laundry boy for white people. Cost white man little bit less."

And John remembered his history professor telling the class that in 1870 in Mississippi, black ex-slaves, now sharecroppers, were reluctantly doing the work because of unfair plantation wages. They knew they were being used. They knew the sharecropping system was designed to keep them in debt to the ex-slaveholder. In that same year, the plantation owner brought in hundreds of Chinese men from the West Coast to do the work and thereby set an example. They were scabs. The planters wanted to show the blacks that the farm work could be done fast and efficiently and for less than the blacks were getting. In that same year in the textile factories of Massachusetts, bosses transported from the West Coast Chinese men in desperate need of work to set the same kind of example for disgruntled Irish workers. These events, the professor said, gave rise to the idea of the Chinese as the "model minority."

Mr. Chang was still talking. "Susie had good life. Pretty girls run for Miss Chinatown now. And she belong in Chinatown . . ."

And John was thinking he could hear Susie saying, "But I'm two persons, in a way, one Chinese and his daughter, and the other, as American as apple pie and pizza, not his daughter at all." And John remembered Susie at some point saying how much she hated the smells of Chinatown—live fish, rot of sewage, garbage in the streets, and the *pu-tong* mess that poor people ate.

And Mr. Chang was saying, "It's not like when Chinese woman come they make clothes on sewing machine, sew all time, summer clothes in winter, winter clothes in summer. Nobody understand Chinese man speak English on telephone back then, so Chinatown got own telephone company, China Five. Five Cantonese dialect." He held up five fingers. "Got operator who speak English and all five Cantonese. Somebody in jewelry store in Jackson Street want to talk to somebody over on California Street or Broadway, in little China, they go through right operator who understand. Hard times back then. Tong wars. Immigration people keep Chinese people in detention long time. Immigration man say he look for hookworms, but he torture while looking. All kind of thing go on. We pay lot to become American. Nobody used to talk about it, but now everybody know. Long before my time, in 1906 the fire from earthquake burn birth record of all people. After that, Chinese people could say they born here and nobody can check to see if they tell true. That was in old day before immigration law change. We all now legal citizen. Chinatown is good place now. This place where Susie grow up. Chinese New Year big thing in Chinatown. Big business for all San Francisco. Chinese people save money. Bank of Canton full of Chinese account. This year it come February nineteenth. Chinatown got Historical Society. Chinatown got English center. Old Chinese lady go practice tai chi in gym. No cat house anymore. Chinatown got own politicians. This many church—three. No more Mr. Crocker. Chinatown got own Chinatown newspaper, three or four—one from Formosa—I mean, Taiwan—and one from Hong Kong. Too many to remember. Chinatown my daughter life. All kind of people from all over Asia live in Chinatown now since 1965. But back then, Chinese man had not even nice park to sit in, no nice restaurant like today, just work in laundry, maybe little gambling, you know, and how they say, shit work." He grinned and glanced at John. "I come over at good time. Chinese girl, to marry, they send over all the time for man by that time. The way they do, they select girl from man village in China, and they send girl oversea to be wife. My uncle before me live through bad time. Had to listen to white boy sing 'So-long, so-long, how long you gonna be gone,' like voice of girl, Ming Toy, back home in China, and white boy laugh at my uncle because he Chinese. We don't like remember bad times. Don't talk much about them. Uncle dead now. But back then soldier boy come to Chinatown for good time. See stripper.

This about 1942. They say, 'Be glad you not no Jap.' Call him 'China boy,' do this, do that, 'China boy.' And his father before him remember bad time—only work laundry work, no women. Couldn't touch white woman. Just they dirty clothes. Some Chinese man in old day work up in Napa and Sonoma to pick grape. That was back in time, but after time Chinese man put down rail track all over. Chinese ancestor been here since Gold Rush day. No woman though. Girl and woman place at home. They come later. They used to stay in China. After they change immigration law, Chinese man send for wife and daughter. Now son and daughter shame to hear us speak English. After all we do for them, make better life in America."

John suddenly blurted out, "Susie?"

For half a second, Mr. Chang looked puzzled, but sternly refused to make eye contact with John. Then he said, "but we got better life in America now. Chinatown good place. I raise my son, my daughter in Chinatown. Some people say no, Chinatown no good place to raise son and daughter. But I say Chinatown best place because they know they Chinese and not just American. In Chinatown we celebrate Chinese holiday like New Year. Like carnival, you know. Everybody happy. Give gift. Firecracker pop. Bright colors. People greet on street, they say good wish-thought for New Year. Ten days, New Year happy-time. This kind of Chinese life my daughter Susie know when she little girl. This make her Chinese girl." At this point, Mr. Chang stopped and looked at John, this time for a longer time than ever before. "When she was little girl, she was good Chinese girl, then she went 'way to college, and something bad happen. Her mama always use say, 'Susie, you good Chinese daughter.' But up there in Davis everything go stop. She go in with wrong crowd. We say why you don't date Chinese boy. She say Chinese boy too dull, Chinese boy just like Chinese father." He touched his head. "Something go wrong in head. Her mama work hard all time to make sure she be good Chinese girl, sew her dress so she look pretty. But no, she go 'way to Davis and she shame of dress her mama make her. We help her buy car in Davis. We send her to Chinese school just like my son, Chinese school right there on Stockton. Something go wrong. She want to wear American clothes. She want to date Negro boy." He glanced at John. "We want to raise her to be good Chinese lady, but no, she want to be girlfriend to Negro boy. No good."

Again John saw the old man glance his way.

"We try bring her back to her own way as Chinese life. I work hard. First come to this country I sleep in *gong si fong* like International Hotel and work any kind of job they give me, in Chinatown, out of Chinatown. Anything. Work and save, work and save. Now I own my own restaurant, from hard work. I was happy man. Good wife. Good son. But not happy now. Bad daughter."

John wanted to say something but he couldn't find the words. He felt ill at ease.

Mr. Chang looked at him fully now for the first time. "You marry my daughter?"

"Yes, sir. I'd like to marry your daughter."

"But she Chinese girl, you not Chinese. You not white. I don't know what you. Maybe you Negro."

"I'm African American, mixed race."

"You African race?"

"African American," John said as gently and patiently as possible.

"African *in* America," Mr. Chang said thoughtfully. "Chinese girl should marry Chinese boy. If not Chinese boy, maybe white boy, but not African boy."

"I would like your blessing, sir," John said, "but we are going to marry anyway, with or without it."

"You marry my daughter even when I say no?"

"Yes, sir."

"This not right way." Mr. Chang touched his own chest with the five fingers and thumb of his right hand. "We Chinese people. We have Chinese way. My daughter Chinese girl, not African girl." He shook his head angrily.

John just looked helplessly and sympathetically at the old man but couldn't find anything to say in response. And it was just as well, because Mr. Chang paused only for a comma of a moment after the word "girl," and was now going on again about how important it was for a Chinese girl to stay Chinese.

"Susie ancestors same ancestors as all Chinese ancestor. You think we be Chinese now if first *Gew-hock* come to San Francisco turned his back on Chinese way? First Chinese come here in 1848 from Guandong, looking for gold, like everybody. But no gold. So then what? Work Crocker railroad, work Central Pacific, cross country, trying to beat other guy, the Union Pacific. Go without nice thing to make better life. Live in small crowded apartment. Do laundry, make clothes. These people Susie ancestor. You see what I mean?"

John said, "No."

This time, Mr. Chang didn't show the slightest bit of impatience. Instead, he said, "Girl baby not always bad luck. Chinese people think girl baby bad luck. In China bad luck-girl baby get ashes poked in her mouth. Susie no bad luck for my family. No little-money daughter. Her mama teach her to cook and sew. To care for her brother. To respect her parents. We teach her that. To obey. We love her. Proud of her. Want her to be good Chinese girl. Long, long time ago, little girl in China got the foot tie—" as Mr. Chang spoke, he made, with his right hand, a wrapping motion. "But China modern way now. Woman free in China. Women work in pottery factory, in silk factory, in ceramic factory. Woman do all sort of thing in China—interpreter, tour guide, you name it. Make pretty good money. Woman go university now in China. In China, woman equal man now day. In America, Chinese girl free, like American girl. But this no mean Chinese girl don't have still be Chinese. If Chinese girl stop be Chinese she nothing, nobody. She lose self."

And John was thinking, *But couldn't the Chinese girl assert her right to be somebody new, somebody different, couldn't she create her own identity, and insist that the world validate it? Wasn't that possible? Even with this father? Why not? Why on earth not?* And with these new questions crossing John's mind, he himself felt suddenly stronger, more hopeful.

Yet, feeling uneasy and restless for the conversation to end, John began to grind his teeth while squeezing his knuckles. Taking advantage of a pause in Mr. Chang's monologue, John said, "So you can't give us your blessing, then, Mr. Chang?"

"What?"

"Susie and I are engaged, we're going to marry. Will you bless the marriage?"

Mr. Chang pointed at John's chest and shook his head negatively. "I no bless marriage."

John stood up. "It was nice meeting you, Mr. Chang."

Looking suddenly bewildered, Mr. Chang too stood up. "You go back to New York now?"

"Soon."

Mr. Chang looked at him with desperate hope in his eyes now and said, "You speak Chinese?"

"No," John said.

"Susie went to Chinese school, but she no learn Chinese good. She marry you she forget she Chinese."

"I doubt it, sir," John said, suddenly aware that the old man smelled clean as a freshly mopped marble entryway. "Good-bye, Mr. Chang."

But Susie's father said nothing in response. . . .

PART TWO

SHORT STORIES

My Mother and Mitch

He was just somebody who had dialed the wrong number. This is how it started, and I wasn't concerned about it. Not at first. I don't even remember if I was there when he first called, but I do, all these many years later, remember my mother on the phone speaking to him in her best quiet voice, trying to sound as ladylike as she knew how.

She had these different voices for talking to different people on different occasions. I could tell by my mother's proper voice that this man was somebody she wanted to make a good impression on, a man she thought she might like to know. This was back when my mother was still a young woman, divorced but still young enough to believe that she was not completely finished with men. She was a skeptic from the beginning; I knew that even then. But some part of her thought the right man might come along some day.

I don't know exactly what it was about him that attracted her though. People are too mysterious to know that well. I know that now and I must have been smart enough not to wonder too hard about it back then.

Since I remember hearing her tell him her name, she must not have given it out right off the bat when he first called. She was a city woman with a child and had developed an alertness to danger. One thing you didn't do was to give your name to a stranger on the phone. You never knew who to trust in a city like Chicago. The place was full of crazy people and criminals.

She said, "My name is *Mrs.* Jayne Anderson." I can still hear her laying the emphasis on the Mrs., although she had been separated from my father twelve years when this man dialed her number by accident.

Mitch Kibbs was the name he gave her. I guess he must have told her who he was the very first time, just after he apologized for calling her by mistake. I can't remember who he was trying to call. He must have told her, and she must have told me but it's gone now. I think they must have talked a pretty good while that first time. The first thing that I remember about him was that he lived with his sister who was older than he. The next thing was that he was very old. He must have been fifty and to me at fifteen that was deep into age.

If my mother was old at thirty-five, fifty was ancient. Then the other thing about him was that he was white.

They'd talked five or six times, I think, before he came out and said he was white; but she knew it before he told her. I think he made this claim only after he started suspecting he might not be talking to another white person. But the thing was he didn't know for sure she was black. I was at home lying on the couch pretending to read a magazine when I heard her say, "I am a colored lady." Those were her words exactly. She placed the emphasis on "lady."

I had never known my mother to date any white men. She would hang up from talking with him and she and I would sit at the kitchen table and she would tell me what he had said. They were telling each other the bits and pieces of their lives, listening to each other, feeling their way as they talked. She spoke slowly, remembering all the details. I watched her scowl, and the way her eyes narrowed, as she puzzled over his confessions as she told me, in her own words, about them. She was especially puzzled about his reaction to her confession about being colored.

That night she looked across at me, with that fearful look that was hers alone, and said, "Tommy, I doubt if he will ever call back. Not after tonight. He didn't know. You know that."

Feeling grown-up, because she was treating me that way, I said, "I wouldn't be so sure."

But he called back soon after that.

I was curious about her interest in this particular white man, so I always listened carefully. I was a little bit scared too because I suspected he might be some kind of maniac or pervert. I had no good reason to fear such a thing except that I thought it strange that anybody could spend as much time as he, and my mother, did talking on the phone without any desire for human contact. She had never had a telephone relationship before; and at that time, all I knew about telephone relationships was that they were insane and conducted by people who probably needed to be put away. This meant that I also had the sad feeling that my mother was a bit crazy too. But more important than these fearful fantasies, I thought I was witnessing a change in my mother. It seemed important, and I didn't want to misunderstand it or miss the point of it. I tried to look on the bright side, which was what my mother always said I should try to do.

He certainly didn't sound dangerous. Two or three times I myself answered the phone when he called, and he always said, "Hello, Tommy, this is Mitch. May I speak to your mother?" And I always said, "Sure, just a minute." He never asked me how I was doing or anything like that, and I never had anything special to say to him.

After he had been calling for over a month, I sort of lost interest in hearing about their talk. But she went right on telling me what he said. I was a polite boy, so I listened despite the fact that I had decided that Mitch Kibbs, and his ancient sister, Temple Erikson, were crazy, but harmless. My poor mother was lonely. That was all. I had it all figured out. He wasn't an ax murderer who was going to sneak up on her one evening when she was coming home from her job at the office and split her open from the top down. We were always hearing about things like this, so I knew it wasn't impossible.

My interest would pick up occasionally. I was especially interested in what happened the first time my mother herself made the call to his house. She told me that Temple Erikson answered the phone. Mother and I were eating dinner when she started talking about Temple Erikson.

"She's a little off in the head," Mother said.

I didn't say anything, but it confirmed my suspicion. What surprised me was my mother's ability to recognize it. "What'd she say?"

"She rattled on about the Wild West," said Mother. "And about the Indians and having to hide in a barrel or something like that. She said Indians were shooting arrows at them, and she was just a little girl who hid in a barrel."

I thought about this. "Maybe she lived out West when she was little, you know? She must be a hundred by now. That would make her the right age."

"Oh, come now, Tommy!" Mother laughed. "What she said was she married when she was fourteen, married this Erikson fellow. As near as I could figure out, he must have been a leather tanner; but seems he also hunted fur and sold it to make a living. She never had a child."

"None of that sounds crazy." I was disappointed.

"She was talking crazy, though."

"How so?"

"She thinks Indians are coming back to attack the house any day now. She says things like Erikson was still living; like he was just off there in the next room, taking a nap. One of the first things Mitch told me was that his sister and he moved in together after her husband died; and that was twenty years ago."

"How did the husband die?"

She finished chewing her peas first. "He was kicked in the head by a horse. Bled to death."

I burst out laughing because the image was so bright in my mind, and I couldn't help myself. My pretty mother had a sense of humor even when she didn't mean to show it.

She chewed her peas in a ladylike manner. This was long before she lost her teeth. Sitting there across the table from her, I knew I loved her, and needed her, and I knew she loved and needed me. I did not yet fear that she needed me too much. She had a lot of anger in her too. Men had hurt her bad. And one day I was going to be a man.

When I laughed my mother said, "You shouldn't laugh at misfortune, Tommy." But she had this silly grin on her face; and it caused me to laugh again. I think now I must have been a bit hysterical from the anxiety I had been living with all those weeks, while she was telling me about the telephone conversations that I wanted to hear about only part of the time.

It was dark outside; and I got up when I finished my dinner and went to the window and looked down at the streetlights glowing in the wet pavement. I said, "I bet he's out there right now, hiding in the shadows, watching our window."

"Who?" Her eyes grew large.

She was easily frightened. I knew this, and I was being devilish, and deliberately trying to scare her.

"You know, Mister Kibbs."

She looked relieved. "No, he's not. He's not like that. He's a little strange but not a pervert."

"How'd you know?"

By the look she gave me I knew now that I had thrown doubt into her and she wasn't handling it well. She didn't try to answer me. She finished her small, dry pork chop, and the last of her bright green peas, and reached over and took up my plate and sat it into her own.

She took the dishes to the sink, turned on the hot and cold water so that warm water gushed out of the single faucet, causing the pipe to clang, and she started washing the dishes. "You have a vivid imagination," was all she said.

I grabbed the dishcloth and started drying the first plate she placed in the rack to drain. "Even so, you don't know this man. You've never even seen him. Aren't you curious about what he looks like?"

"I know what he looks like."

"How?"

"He sent me a picture of himself and one of Temple."

I gave her a look. She had been holding out on me. I knew he was crazy now. Was he so ugly she hadn't wanted me to see the picture? "Can I see the pictures?"

"Sure." She dried her hands on the cloth I was holding, then took her cigarettes out of her dress pocket, and knocked one from the pack, and stuck it between her thin pale lips. I watched her light it and fan the smoke and squint her eyes. She said, "You have to promise not to laugh."

That did it. I started laughing again and couldn't stop. Then she started laughing too, because I was bent over double, standing there at the sink, with this image in my mind of some old guy who looked like the Creeper. But I knew she couldn't read my mind, so she had to be laughing at me laughing. She was still young enough to be silly with me like a kid.

Then she brought out two pictures, one of him and the other of his sister. She put them down side by side on the table. "Make sure your hands are dry."

I took off my glasses and bent down to the one of the man first, so I could see up close, as I stood there wiping my hands on the dishcloth. It was one of those studio pictures where somebody posed him in a three-quarter view. He had his unruly hair and eyebrows pasted down and you could tell he was fresh out of the bath, and his white shirt was starched hard. He was holding his scrubbed face with effort toward where the photographer told him to look, which was too much into the direction of the best light. Beneath the forced smile, he was frowning with discomfort. There was something else. It was something like defeat or simple tiredness in his pose, and you could see it best in the heavy lids of his large blank eyes. He looked out of that face at the world with what remained of his self-confidence and trust in the world. His shaggy presence said that it was all worthwhile, and maybe even in some way he would not ever understand, also important. I understood all of that even then but would never have been able to put my reading of him into words like these.

Then I looked at the woman. She was an old hawk. Her skin was badly wrinkled like the skin of ancient Indians I'd seen in photographs and westerns. There was something like a smile coming out of her face; but it had come out sort of sideways and made her look silly. But the main thing about her was that she looked very mean. On second thought, to give her the benefit of the doubt, I can say it might have been just plain hardness from having a hard life. She was wearing a black iron-stiff dress, buttoned up to her dickey, which was ironically dainty and tight around her gooseneck.

All I said was, "They're *so* old." I don't know what else I thought as I looked up at my mother, who was leaning over my shoulder, looking at the pictures too, as though she had never seen them before, as though she was trying to see them through my eyes.

"You're just young, Tommy. Everybody's old to you. They're not so old. To me, he looks lonely."

I looked again at him and thought I saw what she meant.

· ·

I put the dishes away, and she took the photographs back, and we didn't talk any more that night about Mitch and Temple. We watched our black-and-white television screen, which showed us Red Skelton acting silly for laughs. So, we laughed at him.

Before it was over, I fell asleep on the couch, and my mother woke me when she turned off the television. "You should go to bed, Tommy."

I stood up and stretched. "I have a science paper to write."

"Get up early and write it," she said, putting out her cigarette.

. . . .

"He wants me to meet him someplace," my mother said.

She had just finished talking with him and was standing by the telephone. It was close to dinnertime. I'd been home from school since three-thirty, and she'd been in from work by then for a good hour. She'd just hung up from the shortest conversation she'd ever had with him.

I had wondered why they never wanted to meet; then I stopped wondering and felt glad they hadn't. Now, I was afraid, afraid for her, for myself, for the poor old man in the picture. Why did we have to go through with this crazy thing?

"I told him I needed to talk with you about it first," she said. "I told him I'd call him back."

I was standing there in front of her, looking at her. She was a scared little girl with wild eyes dancing in her head, unable to make up her own mind. I sensed her fear. I resented her for the mess she had gotten herself in. I also resented her for needing my consent. I knew she wanted me to say go, go to him, meet him somewhere. I could tell. She was too curious not to want to go. I suddenly thought that he might be a millionaire, and that she would marry him, and he might eventually die and leave her his fortune. But there was the sister. She was in the way. And from the looks of her she would pass herself off as one of the living for at least another hundred years or so. So I gave up that fantasy.

"Well, why don't you tell him you'll meet him at the hamburger café on Wentworth? We can eat dinner there."

"We?"

"Sure. I'll just sit at the counter like I don't know you. But I've got to be there to protect you."

"I see."

"Then you can walk in alone. I'll already be there eating a cheeseburger and fries. He'll come in and see you waiting for him alone at a table."

"No, I'll sit at the counter too," she said.

"Okay. You sit at the counter too."

"What time should I tell him?"

I looked at my Timex. It was six. I knew they lived on the West Side; and that meant it would take him at least an hour by bus and a half hour by car. He probably didn't have a car. I was hungry though and had already set my mind on eating a cheeseburger, rather than macaroni and cheese out of the box.

"Tell him seven-thirty."

"Okay."

I went to my room. I didn't want to hear her talking to him in her soft whispering voice. I had stopped listening some time before. I looked at the notes for homework and felt sick in the stomach at the thought of having to write that late science paper.

A few minutes later my mother came in and said, "Okay. It's all set." She sat down on the side of my bed and folded her pale hands in her lap. "What should I wear?"

"Wear your green dress and the brown shoes."

"You like that dress, don't you?"

"I like that one and the black one with the yellow at the top. It's classical."

"You mean classy."

"Whatever I mean." I felt really grown-up that night.

"Here, Tommy, take this." She handed me a ten-dollar bill she had been hiding in her right hand. "Don't spend it all. Buy your burger and fries and keep the rest just to have. If you spend it all in that hamburger place, I'm going to deduct it from your allowance next week."

When I got there I changed my mind about the counter. I took a table by myself.

A cheeseburger, fries, and a Coca-Cola cost me three dollars.

I was eating my cheeseburger and fries and watching the revolving door. The café was noisy with shouts, cackling, giggles, and verbal warfare. The waitress, Miss Azibo, was in a bad mood. She had set my hamburger plate down like it was burning her hand.

I kept my eye on the door. Every time somebody came in I looked up; every time somebody left, I looked up. I finished my cheeseburger even before my mother got there, and, ignoring her warning, I ordered another, and another Coca-Cola to go with it. I figured I could eat two or three cheeseburgers and still have some money left over.

Then my mother came in like a bright light into a dingy room. I think she must have been the most beautiful woman who ever entered that place, and it was her first time coming in there. She had always been something of a snob, and did not believe in places like this. I knew she had agreed to meet Mister Kibbs here just because she believed in my right to the cheeseburger, and this place had the best in the neighborhood.

I watched her walk ladylike to the counter and ease herself up on the stool and sit there with her back arched. People in that place didn't walk or sit like that. She was acting classy and everybody turned to look at her. I looked around at the faces, and a lot of women had these real mean sneering looks like somebody had broke wind.

She didn't know any of these people, and they didn't know her. Some of them may have known her by sight, and me too, but that was about all the contact we had with this part of the neighborhood. Besides, we hardly ever ate out. When we did, we usually ate Chinese or at the rib place.

I sipped my Coke and watched Miss Azibo place a cup of coffee before my mother on the counter. She was a coffee freak; she always was; all day long, long into the night, cigarettes and coffee, in a continuous cycle. I grew up with her that way. The harsh smells are still in my memory. When she picked up the cup with a dainty finger sticking out just so, I heard a big fat woman, at a table in front of mine, say to the big fat woman at the table with her that my mother was a snooty bitch. The other woman said, "Yeah. She must think she's white. What's she doing in here anyway?"

. . . .

Mister Kibbs came in about twenty minutes after my mother, and I watched him stop and stand just inside the revolving doors. He stood to the side. He looked a lot younger than in the picture. He was stooped a bit though, and he wasn't dressed like a millionaire, which disappointed me. But he was clean. He was wearing a necktie, and a clean white shirt, and a suit that looked like it was about two hundred years old; but one, no doubt, made of the best wool. Although it was fall, he looked overdressed for the season. He looked like a man who hadn't been out in the daylight in a long while. He was nervous, I could tell. Everybody was looking at him. Rarely did white people come in here.

Then he went to my mother like he knew she had to be the person he had come in to see. He sat himself up on the stool beside her and leaned forward with his elbows on the counter and looked in her face.

She looked back in that timid way of hers. But she wasn't timid. It was an act and part of her ladylike posture. She used it when she needed it.

He ordered something to eat, and my mother ordered too. I don't remember what. They talked and talked. I sat there eating, and protecting her, till I spent the whole ten dollars. Even as I ran out of money, I knew she would forgive me. She had always forgiven me on special occasions. This was one for sure.

She never told me what they talked about in the café, and I never asked, but everything that happened after that meeting went toward the finishing off of the affair my mother was having with Mitch Kibbs. He called her later that night. I was in my room, working on that dumb science paper, when the phone rang, and I could hear her speaking to him in that ladylike way. It was not the way she talked to me. I was different. She didn't need to impress me. I was her son. But I couldn't hear what she was saying and didn't want to.

Mister Kibbs called the next evening too. But eventually the calls were fewer and fewer till he no longer called.

My mother and I went on living as we had before he called the wrong number. And after a while, we never talked about him or his sister again.

Chicago Heat

Hello? Mama? It's me, Floyce. Me and Hank just got back from the courthouse. You won't believe it. Something terrible has happened. They kept Harley. And it looks like my husband is dead. The police was just here and they took my husband out of here all covered up on a stretcher. They asked me and Hank all kinds of questions. And we have to go to the police station tomorrow morning because I got to sign some piece of paper. But, Mama, we didn't even know Medwin was dead. After the trial we drove home like that with him sitting up in the front seat, kind of all slumped over but still sitting up. And I could've sworn he was just sleeping. And you know, sometimes I have trouble waking him up. He just won't wake up. And I thought this was just another one of them times. 'Cause Medwin was messing up! You know, I told you before that Medwin had been abusing his medication lately, and it wasn't the first time he had passed out and come back hours later. So, that's why we thought he was passed out again. But he had to have died while we were in the courthouse. Can you imagine that? Sitting out there in that hot car all that time in this Chicago heat just 'cause he didn't want to see Vernon. And August in Chicago, as you know, is hell. He wouldn't even come in to Harley's trial. But I guess he didn't have any love to lose on Harley or Hank, for that matter, the way they treated that poor man. It was like Medwin and Hank had never been friends. And you remember it was Hank who introduced me to Medwin while they were in recovery in the VA hospital. When was that? Already nearly ten years ago. My, how time flies. And you know, Hank brought Medwin home with him, playing on my sympathy, with all this mess about the poor man didn't have no place to live. Hank kept saying did we want to see his friend, Medwin, homeless, out in the streets? And knowing I had a sympathetic heart! So, there was Medwin staying with us. Hank's friend, but a man almost my own age! And, you know, you remember, at first it was all right because it was just Hank and Medwin being friends and sitting around in the front room, watching television all day, and taking their medication and drinking beer. But when Medwin come justa noticing me and everything, reaching out and touching me when I walked by, no, boy, no way, Hank didn't go for that. Not with his mother! Not his friend and his mother! He couldn't handle it. But you know, Mama, love is strange, a strange thing. You can't stop it. Once it starts it just gets its own fire and keeps spreading. And there wasn't nothing Hank could do. He's my son and everything and I love him, but he sure did show his ass. I tell you, Mama, that boy gave me a hard time. Did I say boy? Shoot! Hank was a grown man! Grown as he would ever be. Hank was a grown, grown man! And is a grown man. And there ain't no way you can tell me he didn't know what he was doing, so evil and all, abusing Medwin, calling him poor white trash. You remember. I told you about it back then. It got so bad I had to put the boy out of the house two or three times. He got to going off his head, talking about how he was going to kill Medwin. I tell you about the time I had to pull that boy off Medwin? Trying to choke him to death. Right across the bed! And poor Medwin was just lying there, gasping for his life, all red in the face. Mama, it was something terrible. And you know my own health started failing me back then. That was the beginning of my downfall, my trouble. I was always healthy before then. You know that. Went to work every day of my life. Never missed a day. But the stress and the strain my son put me through for the last few years has just about killed me, Mama. I myself now have to take medication. Me! I never took medicine in my life before all this mess. The doctor got me on three different kinds of pills. Gave me all kinds of tests. Now they are trying to say I got something called schizophrenia. Well, I know you know more about this sort of stuff than I do. Well, yes, I take the medicine. They say it's supposed to calm me down, keep things from getting on my nerves. But I have to take all kinds of other little pills too. I don't know what most of them are for. But, Mama, I tell you, I'm not going to let these boys kill me. No, no way! They just about finished me off but I'm not going to let them put me in my grave. And Hank himself is so sad about his brother. But you know, Mama, Hank ain't much better off. He just sits around moping. Won't do nothing but watch television and sleep. Ever since he got out of the Marines, ever since he got back from duty in Germany, that boy ain't been the same. You'd think he saw action or something and got—what do you call it?—combat fatigue or shell-shocked. And now his younger brother, his baby brother, oh Lord! Harley's in prison just 'cause he got mixed up in the wrong crowd, running around with dope dealers and now they got him for first-degree murder. But I believe Harley, Mama; I believe he wasn't holding the gun. He's just that stupid. Stupid enough to be out there with a bunch of losers, not holding the gun, and end up being the one they nail. You told me yourself you believe these other boys, Kelley and Pablo, had the gun. And I know you're right. He's got a very gentle, very kind heart. But since the police can't find the gun, they can't prove anything. Now, you know they told the police they drove out to the lake and threw the gun in the lake; but Harley told me they didn't do that. They still got the gun hid somewhere. What? Oh, yeah. That's why I called you. Isn't it? Well, it's all just so shocking and new to me I can't get my thoughts straight, Mama. Let's see. What happened in court? What happened with Medwin? Like I said, well, first of all, Medwin didn't want to go into the court building because Vernon, the father of my sons, was there. And Vernon took a full day off from his job at the Stockyards to be in court with his son. Good gracious! But, Mama, Vernon is still handsome. You know I still have feelings for him? You can laugh if you want to but it's true. Yeah, I know. I know I'm too old for this kind of foolishness. But honey, believe me, I kept looking across the courtroom at Vernon. Even with the gray hair, he looks great. I said to myself, Go on, Vernon, with your fine self. But seriously, Mama, I guess it's like they say. You never get over your first love. And you see that's why Medwin didn't want to come into the courthouse. He got this thing about Vernon; what Vernon used to mean to me, Vernon being the father of my boys. And I mean, they were always reminding him he was just Hank's used-to-be friend and not a stepfather to them. They refused him as a stepfather. And they told him he better not think of himself as their stepfather. And calling him names! It was a shame, Mama. I tell you. Anyway, that's why Medwin didn't go in. He said he'd just sit there in the car and wait for us. But you see, he didn't know, we didn't know, the case would drag on all day into the afternoon. You know, starting out at nine in the morning, like it did, we thought it would be over before noon. Then it looked like it was going so slow. We went in there, Hank and me, my sister and brother, their kids, all of us were there, all of us. By the way, Vernon said his mother, asked about you, asked about your heart condition. I told him to tell her you're doing as well as can be expected at your age. I'm glad you didn't try to come to the courthouse. Your heart couldn't have stood it. But that place was packed. There were people I didn't know; people came out of curiosity, I guess. Who? Oh, yes. The clerk's whole family was there. That's right, Valora. Yes, his name was Gilroy. You heard it on TV. His wife, Ella, they call her; she was there, and she was called up to take the stand. And, you know, Mama, I swear I don't even remember much of what she was saying except she kept going on and on about what a wonderful, generous man her husband was. She said he always tried to help street kids like these boys who killed him. She called my son a street kid. And she cried too. And Harley's criminal friends, Pablo and Kelley, were there, in custody, but they were not on trial, just there as witnesses. They're supposed to be having separate trials. And you know, I told you before that I thought Angelo Passano, Harley's lawyer, was really great. He did the best he could, but it was a hard case. That judge—what's his name, some sort of old funny-sounding name? Judge Yurek Tancik—he was dead-set against Harley from the beginning. The only thinking I know now that Angelo did wrong was advising Harley to waive his right to take the stand. That was a terrible mistake. Harley might be free this afternoon, instead of sitting in Cook County Jail, if he had told the jury what had happened. But I don't blame Angelo. Angelo did what he thought was right. He trusted the jury. And Harley trusted Angelo. He followed Angelo's advice! Told the judge he didn't want to testify! Huh? Oh, the prosecutor's name was Dan Creaver. Same one they had at the pretrial hearing. Remember? Now, you know, I sat there all morning and half the afternoon listening to this Creaver arguing to put my son away and listening to Angelo defending my son's innocence—and I tell you, Mama, that prosecutor did not make any sense, not to me. I mean I don't see how the jury bought his line. He just didn't present a story that added up to anything like the basis for some conviction. That's what Hank said. And I believe him. And Hank, you know, has studied them law books. He's read up on a lot of things. Hank has a good mind on him, but he just won't do nothing with it. Anyway, after hearing Angelo and Creaver we thought surely that jury would say not guilty and let Harley walk out of there. But instead they said, "We find the defendant guilty as charged." And then the judge turned to the police officer standing by the exit, and in this calm voice, like he was bored half to death, said, "Officer, take the prisoner into custody, please." And I almost died. Mama, I tell you, my heart stopped. And it still ain't started beating right again yet. But, anyway, that judge—before you knew it—he was calling the next case. The sentence won't be till a couple weeks from now. You see, all these Chicago prosecutors want is to get some kind of conviction, set their books clear, honey! They don't care nothing about justice. It's like Hank says, all they want is a conviction. Hank says once you get caught in the Chicago criminal justice system, charged with something—anything!—your ass is mud. If you're black you can forget it. Your life is just about over. That's what Hank says all the time. Huh? What'd you say, Mama? Oh, yes. Isn't that something? Dying like that. Just up and dying! Dying in the heat. And us driving home with him sitting up like he was still alive.

Bourbon for Breakfast

A tall, big-boned woman, with a gray sweater thrown across her curved shoulders, comes toward her with her hand extended.

They shake. Edna thinks her own hand in the woman's looks like a child's.

The big woman says, "Edna Nowell? Yes, I thought so. Thanks for agreeing to meet me here in Philly. Sorry I wasn't able to fly you up here or meet you in the capitol. You know my mother lives in Seattle? You'd have to move out there."

"I understand, Mrs. Stevens."

"Call me Ann."

"Ann it will be. The ad was very clear about that. Let me also say that I think you were wise to run your ad in a national medical journal, and to ask for written responses, and résumés rather than phone calls. So many people use local newspapers for such matters. That would seem to severely limit choices."

"Yes. And thank you. And your résumé is upstairs in my room. I was just going over it before you arrived. How was your drive up?"

"Fine. And yours from Norristown?"

"Except for having to dodge the trucks, not bad." Miss Stevens sighs and looks down at Edna. "Well, I don't know about you, Miss Nowell, but I never like to fight the early crowd for breakfast. Any objections to waiting till later?"

"Not at all."

Without saying anything, Ann Stevens starts walking and Edna walks with her, and they end up standing in front of the elevators. All the while, Ann Stevens is talking, saying she read Edna's résumé and was impressed. "Were you *really* born in the South? You don't have a southern accent?"

"Yes, Atlanta."

One of the elevators comes down from the third floor, and the brass plated iron door opens. The lighted cubical with soft music is empty, and they step in. Ann Stevens presses the gold star on the little pink button for the fourth floor and the door closes. They stand with their backs to the wall; Edna is looking up while Ann Stevens is looking down. Edna is thinking, the blazer would have been better, the blazer and the black-and-white dotted halter with the fitted bodice.

Out of the corners of Edna's eyes she can see Ann Stevens is looking up at the circular display of floors listed. Now they step out onto the fourth floor and start down the hallway. Ann Stevens is saying, "It's not that I don't appreciate your work record, you've certainly had the training and experience, but—" She stops, mouth open.

They stop in front of Ann Stevens's door. Oh, God, thinks Edna, don't start like that and not finish the thought. Standing behind Ann, Edna quickly checks her phone. No calls; thank goodness!

As Ann Stevens opens her room door she glances back at Edna. For the flicker of a moment Edna wonders if her hair is neat, if any dead skin might be on the tip of her nose, or worse something visible hanging from just inside.

Ann Stevens glances slightly down and away from Edna as the door opens and she says, "It's just that I don't *understand* why you worked at three different jobs in one year. I must admit *that* worries me a bit. So, you see, it's not the *work* itself. I suspect that you are a competent nurse, and that my mother would get expert attention in your care."

"My patients died," Edna says suddenly, abruptly, and with too much anger; then trying to soften it, she smiles and says, "They *just* died. But they were seriously ill."

"Yes, terminal," says Ann.

"I don't use the word terminal, Mrs. Stevens. No human being, in my opinion, is ever terminal."

They are now inside the doorway.

Ann Stevens's eyes stretch a tiny bit as she gazes into Edna's face. Edna looks back but refuses to hold the gaze.

. . . .

In the room, which is dark and smells vaguely of an unmade bed, Ann Stevens throws the light switch rather than opening the drapes. And Edna's bewilderment increases. She wants the heavy red drapes open. Let in the January light! It's morning! Air out this room!

"Come on in," Ann Stevens says, as she walks over to a round table flanked by two armchairs. "Have a seat. Here's a glass. Let's have a drink."

And Edna suddenly wants to duck, as if somebody has just thrown something at her. A drink this early in the morning! And an image of her father down in the kitchen in the pantry nipping and smacking his lips before anybody else is up. Now she notices a half-finished fifth of Jack Daniels on the table. Is Ann Stevens serious about drinking hard liquor before lunch? If so, why does she need company to do it? Or is this a test?

Two glasses are on the table. Ann Stevens pours liquor into each glass.

Edna sits down across from Ann Stevens and they are both within the light's area of radiance. They are facing each other across the table.

And Edna is thinking, What if I tell the truth, that I don't drink, wouldn't I be better off, or would I offend? She feels a generous surge of insecurity.

Ann Stevens pushes one of the glasses toward Edna and picks up the other. Edna watches her take the first sip. "Aaaa, that's good stuff. Hope you like bourbon. Deba drinks bourbon, you know."

"Deba?"

"Oh, sorry. Everybody calls Mother Deba."

Edna suddenly feels trapped by the new information: *Deba drinks bourbon, you know.* Could this mean she'd be dealing with a drunk invalid day after day? Somebody who is falling down in her bedchamber, crawling about in her own vomit, peeing anywhere? Maybe this is not the job she wants after all. Or does Ann Stevens mean that her mother is a sociable drinker, one who drinks the golden liquid, bourbon, only occasionally in the polite company of others. Or does Ann mean that her mother has a tiny nip before or after dinner, or at bedtime, producing nothing noticeable in her behavior?

She decides Ann's not faking it, she seriously wants to drink bourbon before breakfast and that's her business; but the thought of having to take one sip of the stuff makes her sick. Will Ursula "Deba" Stevens want from her more than nursing care? Will she also expect a drinking partner?

Ann Stevens closes her eyes as she takes another sip. Her whole upper body seems to relax. "Miss Nowell, I should tell you, Deba has very special needs in a nurse." She puts down her glass. "The previous permanent nurse didn't work out because she didn't well enough understand those needs. Mother needs somebody who isn't squeamish about a bedpan, a nurse who knows how to treat bedsores and enuresis. You *do* know what enuresis is, don't you, Miss Nowell?"

"Of course." Involuntarily, Edna suddenly reaches for the glass of bourbon, brings it halfway to her mouth. She catches a whiff of it, and then puts the glass down. She wonders if Ann Stevens's mother will have thickening of the middle muscular layer of her bladder tissue, thickening around her urethral opening. Can't urinate and can't hold it. Poor woman, her last patient, Mrs. Wellington, in Silver Spring, had an awful bladder problem. "Most elderly patients, Miss Stevens, wet the bed if they are not supplied with a bedpan or diapers. By the way, when I spoke with your mother last week, she mentioned the analgesics she's on."

"Oh, yes. Hypothetically speaking, if you were tending her you'd make sure she takes *only* aspirin, no codeine, no matter what she would say." Nervously, Ann Stevens picks up her glass.

Edna slowly crosses her legs. "One thing is not clear to me, Miss Stevens. Does your mother have any serious illness?"

Ann Stevens laughs. "Not unless you count old age as a serious illness. Oh, but she has a touch of arthritis in her fingers."

"But no heart trouble?"

"No heart trouble as such. She's felt some numbness in her lips and down her left arm, and occasionally she feels a heavy dull pain in her jaw and neck, but—"

"Sounds like angina. But her doctor has never characterized these symptoms as heart trouble?"

"Hey, wait a minute," says Ann Stevens, "who's interviewing *who,* here?" Her laugh is short and stiff and staccato.

Edna blinks. "Sorry." She sits back.

"No problem. I understand. You need to know what you're getting into. And we need to know *you*. Mother did have an operation five years ago for pancreatitis."

"And she *drinks*?"

"Oh, not much. Doctor Winford says a shot or two a day won't hurt her. She has such little pleasure in life. The whisky makes her happy. Doctor Winford is a dear, dear man. Been Deba's doctor for thirty years."

Edna takes a tiny piece of notepaper from her purse. "Am I correct in understanding that she doesn't go outside the house anymore?"

"That's correct. Oh, she'll go to the back porch in the summer but not down into the yard. She goes out only when the van comes to take her to the clinic or the hospital for tests. Are you having second thoughts?"

"Pardon me? Oh, not at all. Only trying to get the full picture. When I saw your ad in the journal, I had no idea what was involved; then when I spoke with your mother last week, I learned only so much."

"*So*, this interview is turning out to be as useful to you as it is to us." Ann Stevens leans back against the back of her armchair. "But tell me, Miss Nowell, about your personal interests, habits, things like that. Your résumé tells me everything I need to know about you, professionally. And it's an impressive record, excellent letters of recommendation. But since you would be *living* with my mother, I think I have a right to know a few things about you."

"You certainly do. On my days off I like to go to the movies. But I'm also interested in ancient medicine, so I spend a lot of time at the library reading."

"Ancient medicine?"

"Yes, it's sort of a hobby of mine. I've read the *Tacuinum Sanitatis.* It's a Middle Ages handbook on health and well-being. You know, the tacuinums of various cities such as Paris and Vienna, Rouen, and Rome. It was based on the Taqwim. I'm interested in medieval manuscripts, primarily. I'm especially interested in those relating to the health problems of women. I've been to Sicily to study some of them. I've filled ten notebooks with folk prescriptions. They're fun to read."

Ann Stevens's eyes stretch. "I hope you're not one of these, uh . . . people who is into herbal medicine and all of that mind-over-matter stuff." Here, she seems to catch herself, but it's too late. She says, "I mean, you do believe in *modern* medicine?"

Edna feels her anger rise as she struggles to hide it. She keeps eye contact with Ann Stevens. "Miss Stevens, in my profession as a nurse, I follow the advice of the patient's doctor. Folk medicine is strictly a hobby of mine; but for your information, there's a lot of wisdom in the ways of the ancient world, especially in medicinal remedies for human and animal ailments."

"Such as?"

"Well, we certainly know the curative effects of certain teas and things like mint and dill and marjoram and anise. Don't we?"

Ann Stevens lifts the glass to her mouth. "And alcohol. Don't forget alcohol."

"Even alcohol had its place." Edna suddenly feels foolish. This is *not* the conversation she came here to have. "Miss Stevens, you mentioned bedsores. Does your mother suffer from very *severe* bedsores?"

"Yes, and to be perfectly frank with you, she spends entirely too much time in bed. I hassle her, the doctor hassles her, her sister calls her from Canada and hassles her; we all hassle her about it and it does no good. So, anybody going into that house to nurse her should be aware that it's a problem. She's getting weaker and weaker. And there are people over a hundred walking around, even jogging every day, living active lives." Ann Stevens tries to smile. "Miss Nowell, if you are hired for this job, I hope you can get my mother out of her bed, get her back into life."

"Has she had any therapy?"

"Oh, yes, physical and mental. But you see, she's very set in her ways, very determined to have her way. You know the type."

"Yes, my own mother, for example."

And delightful laughter suddenly bursts from the two women; and Edna suddenly feels as though some sort of stern barrier between them has just been dispelled.

"You know, I have a feeling," says Ann Stevens. "It's just a feeling—"

"Yes?"

"A feeling that you and Deba might actually get along, that she might *like* you. You're proper and conservative, studious and soft-spoken. She likes soft-spoken women. I must admit I had reservation about hiring a colored lady. But not after meeting you. And besides, had you not told me over the phone, I would not have known it by meeting you face-to-face. So, if you're interested in the job, Miss Nowell, why, I think you can consider it yours."

Now, Edna thinks, here comes the hard part. She knows she is no longer so sure she wants the job. Something feels wrong about the whole situation. She certainly feels she knows the temperaments of old people, but Mrs. Ursula Stevens is still too much of a mystery for her. Edna feels she needs to know more. "Well, I appreciate your confidence in me, Miss Stevens, and I certainly will *consider*—"

"Consider? You mean you came up here unsure about whether or not you want the job?"

"Not exactly. But I do feel I need to know more. I mean, just to be sure I'm the right nurse for your mother."

Now she can see that Ann Stevens has suddenly grown stiff with indignation. With her thin wet lips pressed tightly together, she's suddenly glaring at Edna. But, so far, she's speechless. Finally, Ann Stevens says, "Just what is it that you need to know, Miss Nowell?"

"Well, let's see." She opens her hand and the notepaper is still there. "I need to know the type of insurance your mother holds. I never take a private position without such information. Also who comes and goes at the house. Then there's the question of my living quarters. Your mother wasn't very clear about that."

"I see, I see." Ann Stevens reaches for the bottle of bourbon and pours herself about an inch and a half, and then she says, "Mother has Blue Cross. She was on my father's policy up till his death seven years ago and it's continued. Now what else did you want to know?"

"About my room. How is the house arranged?"

"Your room would be off the kitchen and you'd have your own bath. The laundry room is behind the kitchen. There's a washer and a dryer. Oh, yes, Mother has a cat, Lilly. Feeding and caring for Lilly would also be your job."

"May I ask who's taking care of Mrs. Stevens now?"

"A temporary nurse. How much time do you need, Miss Nowell, to make up your mind?" Ann Stevens lifts the bourbon to her mouth and drinks, this time without closing her eyes.

For the first time Edna lifts her own glass and takes the tiniest sip of the harsh liquor. Immediately she suspects it is a mistake because she sees something change in Ann Stevens's face. Edna closes her eyes for the hair of a second as the liquid slides down, burning all the way to the pit of her empty stomach.

This is the first time she's ever tasted this stuff. And she starts coughing. "Excuse me," she says. If she had barnacles, they would now be standing high on her back. "Tastes like something you'd put in a car."

Ann Stevens smiles. "You don't drink, do you?"

"I've been known to sip a glass of wine on occasion, usually in some restaurant with dinner."

"Your résumé says—" Ann Stevens picks it up, "ah, age thirty-three but nothing about marriage. Were you ever married? I guess what I want to know is, will you be dating, that is, men?"

Edna sighs, quickly closing and opening her eyes like an impatient child. "I wouldn't rule it out, Miss Stevens, but I can assure you that I'd *never* bring any man into your mother's house, if that's what you're concerned about. But there's another matter I wanted to ask about, a very important one. Money."

"Oh, yes, salary," says Ann Stevens. "Deba told me what your last job paid. But you didn't live with this—uh, what's her name, Wellington? Did you?"

"No, I didn't."

"In Washington, DC, that may be a perfectly normal salary, Miss Nowell, but out in Seattle, it would be a bit much, especially if you were getting free room and board."

"I see. Then perhaps you can tell me the salary you have in mind . . . ?"

"Mother and I were in the ballpark of about half of that."

Edna's eyebrows lift. "I see. Is that firm? Non-negotiable?"

"We couldn't afford any more; not with my salary and her pension and inheritance, the pittance that they are. But you know, Miss Nowell, the cost of living is so much cheaper out there, *so* much cheaper."

"Yes, I thought of that." Edna looks at her wristwatch. "My goodness, it's late!"

"Yes, it is," says Ann Stevens, glancing at her own wristwatch. "I suppose we should go down. We can have an early lunch!"

Ten minutes later at a table for two in the plush hotel restaurant, by a long trough with well-maintained ivy, Ann Stevens immediately orders the wine waiter to bring a bottle of excellent French Cabernet Sauvignon. In the background Edna heard Ravel's "Bolero," much distorted by the clicking of knives and forks and the hum of polite voices.

The waiter comes. They order.

The food comes quickly, and they start eating now to the rhythm of Strauss's "Emperor's Waltz."

Ann Stevens, who is still acting remarkably sober after so much bourbon, says, "Are you still interested now that you know the salary?" She cuts into her steak.

Edna looks up from the remains of her own steak. "Yes, I think so, although I need time to consider it."

"How much time?"

"I can let you know in a week."

"A *week*?" says Ann Stevens, raising her voice. "Why so long? Are you interviewing elsewhere?"

Edna forks a smidgen of steak into her mouth and slowly chews it till her tongue is satisfied that it's ready to swallow. "No, I'm not considering any other job. In fact, I was wondering if you might not be interviewing other nurses."

She seems to almost duck from Edna's words. "We did get about a dozen responses to the ad. You're the first to be interviewed. I haven't given anyone else reason to hope. Your credentials—Howard University Hospital and the University of Maryland—were so much more impressive than the rest."

The waiter turns up again at this moment and says, "Is everything okay?" They reassure him and he goes away and comes back immediately with a colorful dessert menu but they say no.

. . . .

Edna walks Ann Stevens back to the elevator doors where they stop. Edna's watch tells her it's twelve-thirty. Not a bad time of the day to get out of the city to the highway, to drive back to the District. It will be dark when she gets home. And her roommate, Tanya, a nurse from Russia, will be dying of curiosity; anxious to hear what happened; desperate to know if she'll have to start the painful process of looking for another roommate. Edna knows that Tanya dreads the thought of her, Edna, moving.

Now standing at the elevator doors, in a tired voice, Ann Stevens says, "I wasn't going to tell you this, but I might as well. There are two other candidates for the position. I don't like them." As she glances at Edna suddenly, she looks exhausted. "Frankly, I like you. My mother would like you. I hope you take the job."

"Thank you, Miss Stevens, for being honest with me. And thank you for lunch." Edna is extending her right hand to Ann Stevens.

The other woman takes the hand and shakes it. "So, I'll hear from you in a week?" Meanwhile, Ann Stevens's cell phone chimes. With an apology, she quickly turns it off.

"I'll try to make it sooner, if I can," Edna says. She doesn't mean to sound so mysterious. It's just coming out this way. And she feels the awkwardness of her own smile.

They shake hands and for a moment they engage in an eye-to-eye staring contest. And if she's measuring Edna, Edna is also measuring her.

But Ann Stevens blinks first. And as far as Edna is concerned, that does it. Without changing her pleasant expression, Edna makes up her mind at that very moment.

Victoria

It was a cold Monday morning, in November, with nothing above Chicago but a thick grayness that passed for a sky. The view from Victoria Fouche's large living room bay window looking out onto South Parkway showed an occasional car going by north or south; but mostly what Victoria saw were the women walking by going to the bus stop, half a block north of her white stone house.

She stretched and contracted her fingers, trying to free herself of the stiffness that, lately, lasted most of the day. Arthritis! She had three vacant rooms in the basement she felt she needed to rent, and the ad in the *Chicago Defender*, Saturday, so far, hadn't brought hordes rushing to her door. People passing by on the street, unless they were looking for such a sign, didn't notice her *For Rent* sign in the upper left corner of her bay window.

Also, for three days now, Victoria's beloved dog, Baby, had not come home. Victoria tried to remember exactly the last moment she saw Baby. As nearly as she could remember, she last saw Baby Friday afternoon around three. She was going down the front steps.

Baby was an old, overweight, black mixed breed—mostly Lab—who could barely walk. It was unlike Baby to wander off like this. She was old in dog years, sixteen, and it had been at least six or seven years since she'd gone off on an adventure. Victoria feared the worst. Normally, on a morning like this, Baby would be resting on the porch right at the edge, watching the people and the cars going by. The mornings, and the rest of the last three days, hadn't been right without Baby.

Victoria felt all she had left was Baby, her house, and her hats. She sold the hats—they *were* for sale—and she rented out every crevice of her house she could get away with.

This morning, two years after the end of the Second World War, in her normal way, she sat in her parlor window surrounded by an array of bright and fancy hats—hats made for her by a talented hat maker, Mrs. Sarah Mae Jackson, in Atlanta, Georgia. Mrs. Jackson's cut was 50 percent. Had it not been for the hats, and Victoria's age, she might have been taken for an 1890s New Orleans prostitute, at the window, soliciting customers by tapping on the window with a quarter.

Actually, in her younger days she *had* been a New Orleans Creole prostitute, who, with a quarter, tapped on the window to attract male passersby. She never talked about it to anybody nowadays; and although she remembered the times with a sense of loss—it may have been her lost youth she was lamenting—she, at the same time, knew in her bosom that they were mean, and often brutal, dishonest, and desperate times.

Now, in the bay window, with a cup of coffee sitting on the window ledge, Victoria watched for neighborhood women, not men; and when she saw a likely candidate, using the edge of a quarter (or, when she didn't have a quarter handy, her wedding ring), she tapped on the window to attract the female passerby. And she knew most of the women, either on sight or by name. Some of them took the bus to the north side to do house cleaning. One was a manicurist at the Metropolitan Barbershop. Others worked in factories. They knew her too—knew her as the hat lady with the stone house on South Parkway across from the Ritz Hotel and Lounge, where jazz musicians played late into the night, giving the neighborhood a warm and happy—even cozy—feeling. It reminded Victoria of New Orleans.

But Victoria, this morning, was also waiting for Chaucer. He'd promised last Thursday that he would stop by this morning to finish the plumbing work on the sink in the basement apartment, so she could rent it out.

None of the rooms in the house, with the exception of Victoria's own bedroom, were bigger than a large closet, and everybody, with the exception of those in the basement, had to come through Victoria's living room to enter or leave. Victoria herself both liked and disliked this arrangement. On the one hand she could keep her eye on everybody—make sure nothing unacceptable was going on—and on the other, she was annoyed by the constant intrusion, the foot traffic, kids running in and out, leaving the front door open.

But in a way, she'd come to think of some of these people as family. Regina Ashe, with her two kids, Luke and Willa Mae, moved in only a year and a half ago, but already Victoria thought of Regina as a friend.

On her way to work, Regina, who was passing for white on the job, had told Victoria that Luke was staying home sick today and to make sure he didn't try to go outside and play. He was supposed to stay upstairs in bed.

Victoria thought about Regina passing and smiled. Funny how a colored person can tell but the white folks can't. She remembered going into Carson's and seeing Regina behind the jewelry counter. She smiled and winked at her and kept walking.

. . . .

Now Victoria sat there waiting and watching, feeling unusually excited, despite her depression over Baby. She didn't know why but she just had a feeling she was going to get lucky this morning and sell a hat. She was feeling this way when she spotted one of her oldest neighbors, Mrs. Ruby Louise Young. Mrs. Young had to be in her sixties, yet she got on that bus, come rain or shine, and rode up north to clean house once a week for the same white family she'd been with for the last fifteen years.

The moment she saw Mrs. Young, all bundled in her shabby gray coat, Victoria tapped three rapid times on the glass, this time with her wedding ring. Mrs. Young was stepping along briskly, in her nurse-type low heels, walking faster and looking livelier than lots of folks twenty years younger than she. Victoria fingered for her to come in.

Victoria watched Mrs. Young climb the steps, holding onto the black iron railing, till she gained the porch.

When Victoria opened the door for Mrs. Young, Regina's boy, Luke, slipped by Victoria and went out with a bag of garbage. She noticed him and didn't notice him because she was so focused on Mrs. Young. "Come on in, Ruby," said Victoria.

"Victoria, I'm late for work, honey. What is it?"

"It'll take just a minute. Just one minute. I just got this new shipment in Friday." She closed the door and took Mrs. Young by her coat sleeve and literally pulled her through the living room over to the parlor window, where the hats were spread out on the parlor bench.

Victoria picked up a silly looking yellow hat that looked like an upside-down bird's nest with a black veil attached to it. Victoria was saying, " . . . And the minute I saw it, I just knew it was you. It was just made for you, Ruby, girl."

She was holding it out in front of the flustered Mrs. Young. "Here," Victoria said, "Try it on. Wear it to work! Go on! Keep it! Just see if you like it! I know it is perfect for you. Go on, put it on."

Reluctantly, Mrs. Young took the hat in one hand and pulled her wool cap off with the other.

Victoria pulled her over to the wall mirror in the foyer. "Here," she said, "let me turn on the light here, so you can see." And she hit the button and pushed Mrs. Young closer to the mirror and under the ceiling light. "Isn't it a darling? I think you just look *darling* in that hat."

Mrs. Young looked critically in the mirror, at herself, turning her head from side to side, saying, "Victoria, now you know I ain't got no time to be trying on no hat this morning. I'll come back when—"

"Sure, sure," snapped Victoria, "just take it with you. I'm sure you'll love it."

"Victoria, now you know I can't wear no hat like this to work." Mrs. Young screwed up her face, looking at her old friend. "It's pretty but sho ain't gon keep my ears warm." And she carefully lifted the hat off and handed it back to Victoria.

But Victoria would not take it. Instead, she said, "Let me give you a bag. I'll put it in a bag for you. Don't you like it?"

"It's—"

"You'll like it. You just have to give yourself a chance, Ruby, girl. You have to wear it. Take it home and keep it for a few days."

"I can't take it to work, Victoria. Here, you take it back, and let me get out of here. I've already missed my bus."

"Then you'll pick it up on your way home?"

Mrs. Young was headed for the door. "Maybe. Let me think about it, Victoria." She reached for the doorknob. "I'm not sure I like it very—"

Victoria blurted out, "By the way, Ruby, you haven't by any chance seen my dog Baby down your way, have you?"

Mrs. Young shook her head. "I've got to go."

"It's darling on you, I'm telling you."

But Mrs. Young was out the door now and going down the steps.

. . . .

Victoria was sick and frustrated as she closed the door and returned to the parlor bench. The hat was just right for Ruby Young. She just needed to give herself a chance with it. Not just any woman could wear a hat that looked like an upside-down bird's nest. Victoria smiled faintly as she refocused on the street, touching her hair, making sure all the strands were in place. It was a habit she'd picked up years before when she was turning tricks in New Orleans, before her marriage to James, a porter on the railroad. She just had a feeling about it. James was probably dead by now. With his drinking and gambling, he wasn't cut out to last long.

She turned and looked over at the clock on the wall in the foyer, alongside the mirror she had forced Mrs. Young to inspect the hat in. It was eight-fifteen and Chaucer had said he'd be here between seven-thirty and eight. Always operating on CP-time. That was Chaucer. A wonder he'd done so well with his little plumbing business all these years. But then again people always needed plumbers, so they were pretty much at his mercy, which meant he could call the shots.

. . . .

She got up and went back to the kitchen to get another cup of coffee. Polly, in her big cage, said, "Polly want a cracker, Polly want a cracker." Sometimes when Baby was out of the house, Victoria let Polly out, so she could wander around through the house just to exercise. And as Victoria poured coffee into her cup, she heard Luke's voice out in the backyard shouting, "It's Baby! Miss Fouche! It's your dog, Baby! Better come, quick!"

She climbed down the steps, holding onto the railing, and walked around the house as quickly as her old legs could carry her.

In the backyard she saw Luke down on his knees, looking under the house.

"What is it, Luke?" She could hardly catch her breath.

"It's Baby! She's under there! She's not moving! I called her but she wouldn't come out."

"Oh, my God," said Victoria with her hand over her mouth. "Crawl under there, Luke, and pull her out."

Luke flopped to his belly and started crawling under the house.

"Be careful," Victoria said, "if she's sick, she might bite you."

Luke crawled under the house; and a moment later he backed out, pulling the stiff body of Baby by one of her back legs.

"Oh, my God," said Victoria. "She's dead. Baby is dead. Oh, my God. Oh, Luke, what am I going to do? Oh, my God!"

Luke said, "We'll have to have a funeral."

"Oh, my God; yes, we'll have to have a funeral."

Sketch

Morning, on the terrace. I can hear Jean Baptiste Quenin crooning "Veilleur de toutes les nuits." Radio in the kitchen. Middle of February. New Grumbacher French Portable easel out here on the terrace. A sketchpad against my lap. A particular pen. A particular brush. Things changed.

Things continue to change. Here, we are somewhere else, knotted, unknotted, and the wallpaper, the sky, everything is different. If this is doppelganger-time, you are not my uncle, not my brother, not my Other, but me. I can't capture you in lines. We live in the spasm of each other's sagging lives. While shopping at the old market today I saw you look suspiciously at me (in a mirror) the same way you looked suspiciously at the onions, the red fish, the aged cheese. How are we sleeping these days? Orthodox or paradox? I'm the ox but I'm also the bull.

My wife? She's in there, in the cool house, sitting up in bed reading a magazine, no, reading a novel. We have a particular morning ritual. We donate time to thoughts like clouds, they linger over our heads, mackerel-sky-stuff, then I'm up and the coffee is going, and she's up too. But this morning, she's hanging out in bed, coffee at bedside. Marie-Paule Belle singing "Les Petits Paletlins." Is that really our kitchen radio or the neighbor's?

Running out of things to sketch? View from café-bar at corner of rue Alphonse Karr and rue de la Liberte. Quick action of people walking. Juxtaposition. Traffic jam. Noise into the clashing of lines. The rue de la Liberte traffic is hectic with honking and fumes, shouting hot, shouting cold. Four figures of the left hand. Flower spikes!

The view from the mall with its potted tropical shrubbery at Palais de Quency against the gray of the old apartment buildings. Concentrate on this. Where are all my Arab friends this morning? Insults floating over their heads—no grass grows under foot—like scripture in a Negro church. *Une negresse morte,* or should I say dead soldiers? But my Arab friends don't drink red wine and empty bottles are as taboo as, uh, *sheygget* (disgusting!) to Berhane, my friend from North Africa, born to a Jewish mother, which is all that counts, so they count him in high places. A firebrand. Son of sorrow. To Berhane. I'm as clear as Running Water, so he never calls me *shokher*, no sir.

But the question arises: What else is there to draw here? I've done the faces—spirited, noble, valorous, comely, harmonious, brightly, lily-like, hospitable, fair, helmeted, feminine, animated, veiled, pleasant, blooming, wise, and unwise—and though I know there are still endless uncharted faces, all different, damsel and gazelle, I'm sagging like a palm tree with face-boredom.

So go home. What's home? Whose home?

At the end of February. A bar across the street from Hall du Voyage. The crowd is younger here. Motorbikes crowding the curb. British music, French kids, jukebox screams. Yet, moderation, moderation. The Russian with his coffee at the back table. Tatiana in apron. Sidonia in the doorway. Tara coming in with a shoebox under arm. My sketchpad on table. My hand waiting for a jewel, a sea, a prosperous moment, the tip-off for the right motif. A thick forest of ideas floating just out of reach. Outside, a double-parked delivery truck. That's good enough for the moment but move fast. Girl with white mane blocks view. (So, stick her in!)

The lycee crowd, this. View of street construction crew and trip hammer, drill-noise creating gems of terror, rosemary-throbbings. But any of this could be anywhere, in the City of Light or the Eternal City. Nice is nice. I nickname it Salty, Reborn, Without Fault, The Happy Peaceful Place, Patrician Nymph of Ageless Lust, Opal. Café across from Hotel Vendome on Pastorelli? Orange plastic chairs, white metal tables. This is the right stuff, the honored model, no, ideal model, the archetypal—simple things. Metal tables. Chairs.

Sit here as in a dream house, dazed but alive as Mars. Sketch the Arab street sweeper washing and sweeping the sidewalk with fire hydrant water, cleaning the street of its unending string of dog turds and piss.

Keep the hand moving. Care not to knock over the coffee. Two francs, not three. An old woman in a third-floor window as she opens her shutters with a bang. Her eyes connect with mine; she draws back as though slapped. Rebellion-face, a face belonging to Bitterness, to the Ill-Tempered Kingdom. Seventy different meanings for such a face, Mary, Mary, quite contrary. Touch it with a laurel, cast it in a battle, under a lime tree or keep it with the barren, the diseased. Find the right motif to move with the hand, as now the voice of Catherine Ferry singing "Bonjour, Bonjour," in the spirit of Roman goddess of spring or the Serpent of Light.

Even this late in February, this cozy, translucent, ceramic-white sunlight, multicolored sunlight pours down in the nickname of Joy, on my sketchpad. And page after page, I am filling it. Fulfilling it, like a promised oath. A name, a bond, a lilac in a meadow. Before leaving for Old Town, I do this: My Wife Sunbathing, her bra beside her on the towel.

Sitting with Coffee. Artist with Coffee and Sketchpad.

Across from the Palais du Justice where the fisherman parked his pushcart. Early, old shoppers trudging into rue du Marche. Three young girls skittering by in *les jambierres* and shiny boots. Ambulances from Saint-Roch Hospital. Delivery boy unloading bottled water.

Along Jean Medicin. Panoramic. Like a staircase of tinsel sweethearts, complex crisscrossing, and violent black-and-white, red-and-white forces—sound, light, supplanted, protected by its own wild goat-spirit, its vine-like network reaching out from some absolute Wrathful but Gracious Sanity.

Along the Promenade. A medley of TV antennas over on the roofs of the big hotels, roosting pigeons. Winter sky, winter light, February strife, unsurpassed. Skyline, bathers, strollers, supplanted strollers, supplanted bathers, supplanted delivery boys. Thirst. A burst of rain shoots down from the splendid sky with its hedgerow-shaped clouds out over the sea.

Run across the wide, wide boulevard. Brightness and simplicity follow me all the days of my uncluttered life.

Pivot, enter a small street. I wear a mask of comfort, pass doors I will never knock on, draped windows through which other lives peer in the same wonderment I have known since the beginning of Human Time. Clothes strung on short lines drying between buildings not more than ten feet apart. The Palais parking lot and the big clock in the beige bell tower. I've done that before, done it from three different angles. Rushing walkers under umbrellas and snug in raincoats. How come I didn't know? Two women talking Dali.

. . . .

Brazzerie le Liberte. A seat at the bar. Overhearing a conversation, in French, of course. He wanted her to do this unmentionable act with another woman and himself. She got sick of the whole affair. Nothing to sketch in such a Post-Modernist moment. It's a verbal corridor leading to an architectural disaster, partitions of pain and staircases of desire, gifts, and habitation, the archer's arm stretched. The gap.

. . . .

Sunday morning. Walking along rue Patorelli. At Gubernatis, stop. A cloudy day. Strange, powerful forces at work. Keep moving. Something is bound to give. You're onto something, something like you've never captured before. I can taste it, hear it. It's flourishing, animating me. I know for the first time I was never a Tower Dweller, always an earth-level observer of the Mighty Moment, the Silent Splash. Cross Square Dominique Durandy. A river crosser, this ancient resolution. Even today the mood as Crosser remains that of a wolf or a raven. There is resolution in crossing. Firmly I cross Square Dominique Durandy!

Cross and enter a crowd. Crowd gathered around philatelists huddled over their precious, beautiful stamps. In each tiny stamp I am somewhere different, on a carpet flying over India, in a California gold rush, on a Mediterranean island, a dairy farm, a homestead, with a prince, gazing into the eye of a conqueror.

* * *

These stamps Teutonic and Anglo-Saxon gaze back, occasional disquisitions of brilliant design—in fern green, mosaics, in gold, in stairway blues, in nineteenth-century Bordeaux reds. Wonderment stamped, stilled, held down with ink. Clustered narrowly, spinning in the spacious eye. And seagulls coming overhead from the slap of the sea, circling, nosy, checking us out.

I'm looking slowly, looking. And when there's this much already accomplished, when you see its Power even in miniature, it's hard to raise the rooftop from inspiration, so let it soar, to give Nature undivided attention or to take it. So, you move on. Wading, as one who moves homeward, a full sketchpad under arm, the known plot of What Comes Next already thick with afterthought.

Innocence

Nydia and I are watching television when a news bulletin comes on saying that somebody just shot a government official in Los Angeles. The official was making a speech. A "suspect" was seized on the spot. The suspect says he is innocent despite the fact that the cameras caught him in the act. So many televised deaths lately, I am too numbed to react. A further loss of spirit is what I feel.

I wake up in a sweat. It's one fifteen and Nydia is still not home. I get up and go to the kitchen for a glass of water. I check my email. Nothing but unwanted crap!

In the living room I sit on the couch to drink the water. While sipping water, I turn around and look out the window at the dark city with its sprinkle of lights scattered across my vision.

Then I glance down at the street. The cars, lined bumper to bumper, are dark and silent. Then I notice the burning red tip of a cigarette glowing in the car just below on the other side. I stare at the red spot till I make out the figure of a man sitting at the steering wheel. Beneath the glowing cigarette something seems to be bobbing. I stare at the area till it becomes clear. It's somebody's head moving up and down.

I get the binoculars from the closet and, standing on my knees on the couch, focus them. This is perverse, but what the hell. I can now see the moving head clearly. It's a woman.

When she lifts her face the streetlight catches it. My heart seems to come to a full rest and moves up into my throat. I refuse to believe what I am seeing.

At that moment the door on the driver's side opens. I had not seen him approach, but another man in shadows opens the door and I can see the streetlight glowing on the barrel of his silver pistol. He pulls the trigger. I am surprised by how faint the sound is. Then it comes again. Then two times more. He closes the door back, turns, and—still a shadow—hurries down the street back toward Eighth.

Had the gunman not arrived, what would have happened?

Possibly this: I watch till the woman finishes. She kisses the man on the mouth. They talk for another five or seven minutes, then she climbs out of the car, checks the contents of her purse, glances up and down the street before crossing over to this side. While crossing she glances up at this window but, obviously, she can't see anything.

Then, I think, possibly it is Nydia. And she comes in and we have this conversation:

"I saw you," I tell her while she is taking off her clothes.

She looks shocked then tries to appear calm. "What did you see?"

"I saw what you were doing in the car."

She waves me away. "There you go again with your jealousy."

"I got the binoculars."

"How *low* can you stoop?"

But if it was Nydia then I had to be the gunman. I am not ready to be the gunman.

....

The morning TV news has the story: two bodies, a woman's and a man's, each shot through the head, found in a parked car in the Village off Eighth Street. What a relief! What sadness!

....

This is early Sunday morning. We're in the living room. I'm standing, looking down at Nydia.

"I'm leaving," I say. I'm surprised to hear myself say this. I realize at this moment how desperately unhappy I am, how desperately unhappy Nydia must be. I have no idea where I'm going.

She says nothing to my announcement. She is sitting slumped over on the couch. She begins to cry.

"You keep the apartment, if you want it." Apartments are hard to find in New York and I feel like I'm being very generous.

She stops sobbing and says, "Who gave you the right to judge?"

....

I'm in California. I answer the phone. It's Nydia. I don't remember giving her my new number. Could I have called her at a moment of weakness in the middle of the night? "Hi! Just want you to know I'm on my way to California," she says. "I'm not going to let you dump me." She hangs up.

....

Before I know it, Nydia is walking beside me on Fisherman's Wharf. Her request. We've had lunch and this morning I had my feet measured at the sandal shop. Now, at three, we should be able to pick up my sandals.

She looks different, better. I wonder why I left her. What was it about her that bothered me so? Oh, yes. I didn't love her. Or was it that I shot her and her lover and had to get out of town? Need I say anything about the quality of my memory?

The sandal shop is crowded so we have to wait a whole hour before the guy can go to the back to see if they are ready.

I have a little green convertible MG now. With the sandals in a plastic bag, we hop in and head for the hills. "I love it out here," says Nydia. "Let me drive."

I get out and walk around to the passenger side. She climbs over the stick. She blushes and giggles when she notices me watching.

I get her going in the right direction and once she's got it, she hits the gas; in fact, she scares me. The cops out here don't play that shit. Anybody black or in a sports car already has a highway patrol demerit—driving while black.

Surely enough, we're pulled over and as the officer writes the ticket I keep my mouth shut. I figure it's the only way to stay alive when you're in this situation.

. . . .

My new house is far back behind a swirl of palms.

We get out and while walking up the long flagstone path to the deck stairs, a stranger waves and calls out, "Hi! Didn't mean to startle you. I'm your neighbor. I'm Maxwell. My house is over the hill there. You can't see it from here." He's holding out his hand.

We shake. He's a healthy brown—that kind of brown California white men love to sport.

I tell him my name and say, "This is Nydia Wilson, from New York." He holds her little hand a moment longer than is polite. I can see Nydia gets the message. Whether or not she wants it I can't tell.

I unlock the house. "Can I get you something, Maxwell, a drink?"

While I work in the morning, Nydia goes for long walks on the beach. This morning, two weeks after her arrival, I can't get anything started so I decide to go catch up with her, to walk with her.

I set out across the sand following the tracks of her tennis shoes. They seem unusually far back from the edge of the water, which isn't especially dangerous-looking this morning.

Then the prints cut back away from the ocean up a dune and over it. I follow. At the top, I see what must be Maxwell's house, a modest one with bay windows and a wrap-around deck perched on stilts.

No Nydia yet in sight.

You already know what's coming. I walk on down the sand and up to the house. In the front yard I stop. All is silent except for the sound of sea gulls and the distant beat of the ocean. I shudder as I walk up onto the porch.

Just as I am about to knock I hear a loud gasp from inside. I think oh well, why should I be surprised. Another gasp, a whimper, a moan, all punctuated by grunts.

I start to go back across the sand but once I'm in the yard I decide to make sure. I tip alongside the house and look into the first window. This is a crime, I know. A dining room. I walk around a pile of debris to the next window. A pantry. Then the kitchen. There! On the kitchen floor Maxwell and Nydia making those noises. Need I say more?

I refuse to watch.

I turn to leave but then a muffled scream pulls me back. I look again, and I realize I am seeing a man killing a woman. I am witnessing a crime—murder! The woman is not Nydia. She's pink, not brown. But the man is Maxwell. He has a kitchen knife and he is driving it repeatedly into the woman's upper body. She is beginning to make fewer sounds.

Running back across the sand, I see Nydia strolling along the beach. I catch up. I know she has a cell phone. But I'm too out of breath by the time I reach her to tell her what I want. I want her to call the police but I can't get the words out.

They simply won't come. Nydia reacts to my distress by holding me in her arms. I weep with the pain of my distress. She begs me to tell her what's wrong, but I can't.

Back at the house, feeling calmer, I call the police and spill my guts.

Nydia and I gaze out the window toward Maxwell's house, waiting.

Three hours later three policemen come to my door and say, "You imagined the whole thing. Mr. Maxwell is fine. No one was murdered. No blood is on his kitchen floor."

Before leaving they give me a warning about trespassing on my neighbor's property. "If it happens again, Maxwell will file charges."

. . . .

Now that Nydia is back in New York, I am alone here again, and winter is coming. But it is not as before when I was unaware that another house was just over the hill. Oh, I knew a house was over there, but I didn't know about it. Now it is a sinister house of uncertainty. And anyway, how can I trust the police?

When I walk on the beach—wearing my heavy sweater—in the afternoon, I am apprehensive. I dread coming face-to-face with my neighbor Maxwell. How can I be sure he is so innocent? How can I be sure I am so innocent?

Five Years Ago

It was Labor Day, September 2, a Monday, five years ago, and I was twenty-seven years old and about to bring my forty-four-year-old mother and my forty-four-year-old father together for the first time in my adult life. All my life I had daydreamed about this moment, wondered if it would ever happen, and now that it was about to happen, I was so emotional, I was almost out of control. The night before, my father had flown into Chicago from Boston, where he worked as a real estate broker. I drove down to his mother's on Fifty-fifth and Indiana Avenue to pick him up. Mother Zoe—that's what I call his mother, my grandmother—was sitting at the kitchen table with her cup of coffee when I knocked on the back door; and there was my father—whom I hadn't seen but once before—two years earlier when he came back to Chicago, that time, I think, because a brokers' convention was being held in Chicago. He was slender and brown and handsome and wore a beard and was smiling at me as I came in. Apparently ready to go, he was already holding a tan summer jacket across his arm. I blushed and felt something like a current of electricity shoot through my body as I simply lowered my head, hiding my joy, and walked straight over to him and slid my arms under his and around his body—which fitted mine nicely—and hugged him for all I was worth. I knew I was going to cry. Tears were already rimming my eyes. All it would take was a blink. And I wanted my face over his shoulder, so I'd be looking out the kitchen window, my back to Mother Zoe, when the tears came. But it didn't help and finally it didn't matter. I not only cried but, also, I sobbed, sobbed with joy and pain and love for this man I'd dreamed of and fearfully wondered about all my life. And here he was. Two years before, I had expected him to appear suddenly bigger than life, but when I came into Mother Zoe's house that time and saw him sitting at the dining room table with his mother, with his elbows on the table, he seemed so small, so fragile, so frail, compared to the giant I'd imagined. He was just a flesh and blood human being, a man, and one not especially imposing, just an ordinary man. But this time I didn't rush to him and hug him. I was too confused, too scared. He stood up and came to me and hugged me, put his arms around me and kissed my forehead. And, yes, this time, too, I cried. I cried but I pulled away in embarrassment, pulled back and went and sat down beside Mother Zoe, who patted me on my thigh. I was wearing jeans. I remember. Jeans and a blouse! And my curly hair was pulled back. I hadn't known how to dress for him. Before going down to Mother Zoe's, I'd tried on four different dresses and six pairs of jeans and told my husband, Austin, "If my father can't accept me in jeans, then, then—" but I couldn't finish the sentence. And I remember my husband—who, by the way, is ten years older than my father—saying, "Don't worry. He'll be happy to see you." But, you know, I was never quite sure that he was. Something about him seemed guarded. I'm still talking about that first time two years before. Sure, he hugged me but it was a stiff hug. Maybe he was nervous, too. Maybe it was simply that he didn't know what to expect and was maybe even a little bit scared of me. Yes, that's what I felt. Felt that he was scared of me. After all he hadn't seen me since, since . . . . Well, actually, I don't think he ever saw me after I was two or three years old. And I don't remember him at all. I know from what Mother told me. They took him to court, you know. Tried to force him to marry or support her. But my mother, Pandora, was only sixteen. And my father, Barry Stanton, was exactly sixteen, too. Both of them still in high school! Messing around, they got me. And got themselves in a world of trouble. In fact, Mother got thrown out of school and Father joined the army. Mother's family said he ran away from his responsibility. That's the way they saw it. But I was talking about that first time seeing him and comparing it to seeing him this time. And this time I just walked right over to him and put my arms around him and he didn't feel like a stranger anymore. And I had gotten this fantasy version of him, this giant of a man, down to size. I was just hugging my father, just a normal human being, a man, and a handsome man with a face like mine. I could see myself in his face. Looking into his eyes, in a wonderfully strange way, gave me myself in a new way for the first time. I felt so close to him it was almost terrifying. When I hugged him, I felt his heart beating against my breast and I held him close just to continue feeling his rhythm. Tears running down my cheeks, sobbing! I held him long and hard. But I started shaking and I pulled back and said, "I'm sorry, I'm sorry—" but I couldn't bring myself to call him Daddy or Father. I also couldn't call him Barry, just plain Barry. I didn't know what to call him. Anyway, the plan was he'd have breakfast, no, brunch, with Pandora—his old high school girlfriend—and my husband, Austin, and my sister Yvette, and my six-year-old daughter, Octavia, and me. Mother Zoe was still in her bathrobe, with her gray hair kind of standing out every whichaway. And just as we were leaving, Winona came down the hall into the kitchen and said, "Now, Ophelia, when are you bringing Barry back? You know we got plans for this afternoon?" And something in Winona's tone offended me but

I held back and refused to lash out although I wanted to. He was *my* father. I had spent twenty-seven years without him and here was his sister—who grew up with him, who had visited him more than once in Boston—telling me to cut my time with him short, to bring him back, not to hog his time. I got so pissed I could have screamed but I didn't. I just looked at Winona standing there in her bathrobe with the corners of her big pretty mouth turned up like she was expecting me to give her trouble. And Mother Zoe jumped in and said, "That's right. And I sure hope you aren't planning to have your mother over there. I told you not to invite her. Didn't I?" And I couldn't remember Mother Zoe making such a request or demand till she said, "Remember, I said, just you and Barry; a quiet brunch together with you and your husband and your daughter; to just get to know your father." Then I remembered but I hadn't taken her words to imply that Mother wasn't to be invited. And anyway, what was this thing about, anyway? Mother Zoe hated my mother from the beginning; from the time she came home from work unexpectedly and caught Mother and her son making love on the couch. Mother told me all about it. Mother Zoe drove her out, shouting at her, calling her a whore, a tramp, a cheap little bitch. No woman, Mother said, was ever good enough for Mother Zoe's son. Mother said she thought he would turn into a faggot—her word—the situation was so bad. But why now all these years later did I have to be the victim of this shit, the victim of these ill feelings that existed between Mother Zoe and sixteen-year-old Pandora Lowell years ago? Why did the mess present itself just when I wanted more than anything in the world to bring my mother and father together and feel, for the first time, like I had a real family? So, I didn't say anything. I just nodded. I assured Winona I'd get her brother back before noon. And my father and I left. Octavia was waiting in the car in the back seat. And while we drove south—I live at Ninety-fifth and Yates—I had the warmest feeling listening to my father talking with my daughter. He was asking her about her school, about what she liked to do, and being the smart kid she was, she kept telling him about a spelling contest she'd just won, and about her winning in the girl's footrace, and about her great math scores. They seemed to hit it off better this time than they had the first time when she was four. Back then she wasn't really that interested in him. But now she had a great curiosity because she had been made to feel his importance to her. Some kids had grandfathers, others didn't. In a way, it had become very important to her in the last year or so to have a grandfather. Having one—at least at her school, Martin R. Delany School, the best private school on the South Side—was a status symbol, especially since so many kids there don't. In fact, I had encouraged her to write to him in Boston and she did send three or four letters, but he answered only once, and only with a postcard. I had to reassure her that her grandfather loved her—though I didn't believe it, didn't even believe he loved me, his own daughter—and that he was simply too busy to spare time to write often. Anyway, when we got to the house my sister, Yvette, was in the kitchen working on the muffins. She makes great blueberry muffins. We could smell them the minute I turned off the motor and the smell got stronger as we walked up the back walkway from the garage, and while crossing the patio, I slid my arm around my father's waist and hugged him to me. My father, I thought, my father, here with me. And I quickly kissed his cheek. And the minute we stepped up onto the back porch there was Mother sitting in one of the straw chairs waiting. And I thought of Mother Zoe and her warning and all I could hope was that my father would not tell. This was the moment. I had brought these two together for the first time since they were teenagers. I think the last time they saw each other was in a courtroom. When they both were not yet eighteen; and Mother was trying to get some money out of him, just before he joined the army and disappeared. But this was the big moment now. The one I had waited for. This was my moment. The three of us stood there. Octavia walked between us into the house and into the kitchen, following the smell of blueberry muffins. I watched my father and mother just looking at each other, looking fearfully. There was a distance of about five feet between them. He was trying to smile. God only knows what he was thinking. He didn't look happy to see her. In fact, he seemed a bit irritated. And she was giving him this cynical sideways look like she can get. It's a half sneer. I've seen it all my life. Then she did something she no doubt thought was a smile, but it really didn't come out right. It was more a grimace. But she sort-of slung her string bean of a body over to him and in a split second I thought she was going to hug him, thought he was going to respond by hugging her, but that's not what happened. She grabbed his beard and tugged at it forcefully, yanked it back and forth, and her mouth was twisted in an agonizing grin; and her eyes were blazing with contempt, though she was trying to laugh and to be playful. I'm sure she meant the gesture to be playful but it didn't come off that way at all. She yanked him too hard and he frowned and stepped back a couple of paces, pulling away from her. And she was saying, "What is this crap on your face?" And he was beginning to sneer. I saw just the edge of his canine. An almost imperceptible shudder moved through his face—his cheeks and his chin especially, and his eyes, like hers blazed. And I wondered why I myself was feeling so elated, so up, so complete—for the first time—and why at the same time everything was obviously going wrong. These two people, I could see, should never have been brought together. Not only did they not like each other, they held contempt for each other. And though I had known that to be the case, I hadn't wanted to know it.

And it gave me, for the first time in my life, a clear sense of the emotional foundation of my life. But even then, sensing this, I didn't want to face it, didn't want the full sense of it to reach my conscience. So I ignored it; pretended the hostility between them was not serious, not important, that, in fact, there was something deeper that held them together and that something was me, my presence in the world. Like it or not, I was their link. And I wanted them to like it. Oh, I so desperately wanted them to like it. So, grabbing Mother by the sleeve and my father by the elbow, I pulled them toward the kitchen, saying, "Come on, let's see what's cooking." And in the kitchen, there was my sister and my husband and my daughter. My sister turned around from the stove as I introduced her to my father, Barry Stanton, and she reached out, smiling, and shook his hand. Yvette is a very pretty girl, with bright red full lips, and yellowish green eyes. She's tall and slender with naturally reddish hair. (People say we look alike. It's because we both look like Mother; who also has red hair.) My sister was twenty-three then. And men were after her like crazy. In fact, she said, "I invited Robert over for brunch. Hope you guys don't mind." And though I resented the liberty she'd taken, I held back saying anything. Then my husband, Austin, standing in the doorway watching my father meet my sister, was smiling. Austin is such an elegant gentleman. He was nearing retirement, early retirement at that time. He was fifty-five and had been head of his own law firm, Tate, Jones and Bedford, on Seventy-third and Cottage Grove, for the last fifteen years. He was now financially secure and wanted to stop work, so he could go fishing when he felt like it, so he could be with his young daughter more and with me, too. Although he and I hadn't been getting along all that well lately, I still respected and liked him. He was like a father to me. In fact, it's true he had raised me, in a way. Taught me a lot! As he put it, he had made a "lady" out of me, sent me to law school and given me a comfortable middle-class life in a good South Side neighborhood. I now had a position in his firm and I was holding my own. And after passing the bar last year I defended my first client in a civil case, a woman fighting for child support. I was saying, "Austin Tate, my husband, meet Barry Stanton, my father," and I sounded awkward, but the moment seemed grand to me and I felt that a certain formality was needed. Now, my husband and my father were shaking hands and gazing into each other's eyes with tentative kindness. And at least their meeting was going well. Then Austin said, "Welcome to our home. How does it feel to be back in Chicago?" And my father was saying something but I was no longer listening to him because Yvette was having an emergency with the omelets she was making, breaking eggs into a big enamel bowl, she'd come across a bad egg, and she'd cried out as though bitten by a snake or as though she'd burned her hand on a hot stove; and I turned to her to help. And Mother all this time stood in the doorway between the kitchen and the back porch watching, I sensed, with a lingering though slight expression of contempt. And Octavia ran her finger around in the blueberry batter bowl, then, with her eyes closed in bliss, licked the finger. And I said, "By the way, we're eating out on the patio. It's nice out there this time of morning. You guys go on out," I said with a wave of the hand, "and get started. I want to get my camera and show my father my office." And I took him by the hand and pulled him up the hall, then up the narrow stair to the second floor, where Austin's and my and Octavia's bedrooms were. And I led him into my little study at the back of the house, a place I was proud of. My law diploma was framed on the wall over my desk and I wanted him to see it. But I wasn't planning to point his nose in that direction. Yet I did stand with my back to my desk—my camera was there on the desk—and took my father by both of his hands and pulled him to me, so that he would be facing—over my shoulders—the vivid evidence of my accomplishment. Three things I was proud of: this degree, my career, and my daughter. And I wanted my father to admire me for those three accomplishments. So, I pulled him against my belly and put my arms around him and held him close so that our bodies were breathing together. Thinking back on that moment I know it was a strange thing to have done, but I felt so close to him; I needed to be so close to him; and I wanted him to feel what I was feeling. Touching him this way was the only way I knew how to reach him. Then I kissed him, fully on the mouth and forced my tongue into his mouth, kissed him the way I kissed my husband, kissed him deeply, so deeply he would have to feel how passionately I loved him, how deeply I felt for him, how much he meant to me. I held his head with one hand and held his back with the other; I lifted my stomach toward him and pressed harder and harder, and I felt him respond, felt his whole body come alive in my arms. Then I slowly let him go and nodded toward my diploma, and said, "See? I earned that all by myself?" And he took his glasses out of his jacket pocket and put them on and read the words, actually read the words, read them slowly, then he said, "I'm very proud of you, Ophelia." And I squeezed his hand. Then he said, "We have so much to talk about. I wish there was time—" And I said, "Now that we've found each other, there will be endless time. I want to know everything, everything you've ever felt and done, *everything*." And while he looked a little embarrassed by my passion, I picked up my camera and pulled him by the hand and we went downstairs and out to the patio where the others had gathered around the long table. Robert, Yvette's boyfriend, had arrived. Robert was tall like Yvette, and good-looking with curly hair. He was standing there by Yvette at the table as she set out the plates. Mother and Octavia were helping at the other end. After I introduced Robert and my father, Yvette and I brought out the various platters of eggs and bacon and muffins and, following us, Octavia brought out the jam tray and other miscellaneous condiments. Then Mother went in and got the pitcher of orange juice. Now Austin was in his natural place, at the head of the table. I sat down to his right, my usual place, and when I saw my father beginning to sit between Robert and Octavia, I said, "Oh, no you don't." And I patted the seat next to me. "You're sitting right here next to me." And everybody laughed, and he came over and sat down beside me. Then I said, "Let's all hold hands." I took my father's hand and my husband's hand. We all held hands and closed our eyes. Then Austin said grace, a short, and to-the-point prayer of gratitude. I glanced at Mother down the table and she was looking cheerier than before as she reached for the muffins and held them in front of Octavia, saying, "Just take one at a time, now. Don't let your eyes be bigger than your stomach." And I remembered her saying those same words to me when I was a child and I had to choke back resentment. One thing I dreaded was her influence on Octavia. I felt that in many ways she had given me an unnecessarily hard time, had often struck me in rage for minor things, and had nagged me constantly when I was growing up. I felt in myself a tendency to treat Octavia this way and I was on guard all the time against the tendency. I meant to break the cycle. This was all the more reason why I was leery of Mother's presence around Octavia. Anyway, this was a happy moment and I wasn't going to let anything spoil it. I had put the camera down at the end of the table. "Robert, do me a favor. Please take a picture of my father and me together here like this at the table?" And I could see everybody glancing at me, understanding my eagerness, and sympathizing with me. I was acting frantic, acting like I thought he was going to suddenly disappear, and I'd never see him again. And the fear wasn't unfounded. So, Robert, a sweetie, got the camera and stood up and went into a crouch and snapped the picture as I leaned closer to my father, my face cheek-to-cheek with his. Later, after brunch, we took more pictures. And before I knew it, it was eleven-thirty and I shouted, "Oh, Winona's going to kill me! We've got to get you back!" So I ran inside, grabbed my purse and car keys while my father shook hands with Austin and Mother and Robert and kissed my sister on the cheek. Octavia hopped in the back seat and we drove back down to Fifty-fifth and Indiana Avenue. Octavia waited in the car. And we walked into Mother Zoe's kitchen exactly at five minutes to twelve. Both Mother Zoe and Winona were dressed now, and both were sitting at the kitchen table smoking cigarettes and drinking instant coffee. Giving me this severe look, her crazy look, the first thing Mother Zoe said to her son was, "You have a nice time?" And he said, "Yes, very nice." And she wanted to know who else was there. And my heart stopped. I tell you, my heart literally stopped because I had forgotten her concern. I started to say something but couldn't. Then my father said, "Oh, just Ophelia's sister and her boyfriend." And the relief I felt was obvious, maybe too obvious. I'd been holding my breath; then I let it go. And it was then, for the first time, that I thought to ask my father how long he was planning to stay, and he said, "I'm leaving in the morning, Ophelia. I've got to get back. I have an important transaction coming up. I'm representing both the buyer and the seller this time and it's a very sensitive situation. But I'm coming back when I can stay longer. Okay?" But all I heard was him saying he had to leave, and it caused something in me to cave in and I couldn't hide my feelings. With all my might I tried not to start crying and shaking. Somehow, I'd thought he would be around at least a week. At *least*! I sighed and said, "Can I take you to the airport?" But Winona answered for him, saying, "That's all right, Ophelia. I've already asked for the morning off, so I can drive him out to O'Hare." And I said, "Oh, I see. Then I guess this is the last time I'll see you, at least for a while. Huh?" I could feel the tears coming up again and I didn't want Winona and Mother Zoe to see me cry again so I said, "Come out to the car with me and say goodbye to Octavia. Okay?" And he followed me back out the back door, down through the backyard, out the gate, to the curb where Octavia was sitting at the wheel pretending to drive. By now I was shaking all over and tears were running down my cheeks and I didn't give a damn who knew it. I was miserable. He squatted down by the car door and spoke softly to Octavia for a minute or so, then stood up and I grabbed him and hugged him. I know I was being dramatic, too melodramatic. But I couldn't help it. It was how I felt. I didn't know how to feel or be any other way. I held him like it was the last time I would ever see him. And, like I said, that was five years ago.

PART THREE

ESSAYS

Icarus Crashes and Rises from His Own Ashes

The short story "Flying Home" is an important contribution to American literature not only because it defies convention and succeeds in terms of style, technique, and its use of aspects of Negro culture but also because it is the stuff of fine literature. I always enjoy reading the story; and although its subject matter and themes are not joyous, it leaves me feeling good, enriched, better about the promise of humanity.

The story also succeeds in exploring Negro consciousness and what is often called racial conflict in the Deep South without being didactic. And perhaps most important, "Flying Home" also succeeds in its use of folklore and myth. Folklore and myth blend in as intrinsic parts of the story.

The story is set in Alabama in the 1940s near Tuskegee Institute, where, at that time, Ralph Ellison was a music student. There was in fact an air school at Tuskegee like the one described in the story. The air school was established by the War Department in response to complaints about discrimination against black men in pilot training. Here black pilots were being trained for the war, yet few would ever see combat. Most black soldiers were placed in service companies. So, in a sense, Todd, the young Negro pilot in the story, is an anomaly—and he thinks of himself and is seen as such.

The subject matter of "Flying Home" is simple: a conversation takes place between an old black man and a young black man in a field where the young man's airplane has crashed. The themes are powerful and universal: crisis, ambition, shame, pride, racism, redemption, recovery, and deliverance.

The myth of flying has long roots in African American culture. In the folklore there are many examples of characters flying away from earthly troubles. The legacies of these myths found their way into the literature. Two examples are the 1930s Broadway play *All God's Children* and Toni Morrison's novel *Song of Solomon.*

"Flying Home" is both a complex and a very simple story involving just a few characters: the protagonist, Todd, a young Negro pilot; Jefferson, an old

Negro sharecropper; Jefferson's grandson, Teddy; Todd's mother; his girlfriend; Dabney Graves, a mean-spirited old white man who owns the land Todd's plane has crashed on; and Jefferson's ox, Old Ned. Only Todd, Jefferson, and Teddy are central to the action.

The story starts out in the voice of a third-person-limited narrator for the first ten pages. Then Ellison switches to first person for a brief time to cover the material set in Todd's past having to do with his mother and girlfriend as well as the lurking terror of the KKK. At first glance these five pages seem to be a conventional flashback. Ellison then switches back to third person for two pages to end the story. This is something that in creative writing workshops students are often told not to do.

Flashbacks are difficult things to handle because they interrupt the flow, but Ellison has managed to transform this flashback into an interesting story within the frame of the larger story. In fact this frame holds many such little stories.

Ellison makes expert use of myth as part of the compositional scheme for his story. Perhaps the most apparent one is the story of Icarus and his father Daedalus. The correlation between Todd's fall and the fall of Icarus is obvious without being corny. Icarus, after all, is flying to escape bondage on Crete. Some readers might find a parallel between King Minos of Crete and Dabney Graves, and another one between Jefferson and Daedalus—especially since Jefferson tells a story of flying in Heaven. And in a way Todd's effort to fly is an escape from the bondage of racism.

Other analogies and prototypes are possible. The phoenix is certainly one possible model for Jefferson's story of dying and going to Heaven. It may be a conscious motif for the image of the bloody buzzard flying up out of the carcass of the dead horse. It is also a useful model for Todd's story itself.

The phoenix is essentially a mythical bird about the size of a buzzard. It's found in many cultures and countries—Turkey, Persia, China, and Egypt—and in the folklore the legend usually has it that when the phoenix saw death approaching, it made itself a nest of special aromatic woods and resins. The bird's story is essentially a re-creation myth that attempts to explain why life continues. Out in the open sun the bird sat calmly in its deathbed. When the sun reached its full intensity the nest caught fire and flames shot up, burning both the nest and bird to ashes. Then out of its own ashes another phoenix rose. In some cultures the new bird comes up out of the marrow of the dead bird.

The Christian version signifies a belief in life after death and a belief in eternal life. It is easy to see how the phoenix would have great appeal for Ellison, and why it is such an appropriate model for a young man who falls from the sky and is finally lifted up, both physically and mentally, and returned to his culture. Todd is renewed and given a new sense of life.

In psychological terms the bird represents our own inner private phoenix, which enables us to survive all the little deaths we encounter each day. This is just another way of talking about getting through one's problems, which are, as James Baldwin often said, always coming.

The two biblical prototypes for "Flying Home" are the Fall from Grace and the Prodigal Son. I see more of a correlation between the Prodigal Son and "Flying Home" than between the Fall and Ellison's story.

In relation to "Flying Home" the Fall has its connections but they are limited. The Fall of man and woman has to do with the birth of the Christian Devil, or evil. It's a myth that tries to explain how evil came into the world. It is one of the early Israelite doctrines describing the temptation and transgression of the so-called first man and first woman and how—to put it simply—they messed up and got kicked out of the Garden of Eden. It essentially expresses a longing for and a speculation about a state of primordial existence before human self-consciousness, or should we say, full-consciousness. Todd in a sense does come out of a state of deadness into one of consciousness through his contact with old Jefferson. But to carry the analogy beyond this point into a moral area of sin and redemption would imply that it was wrong for Todd to be flying in the first place. To do so would echo Booker T. Washington's advice to the Negro: start where you are with what you have. In other words, go slowly; do not push forward too quickly.

The Adam and Eve story also attempts to make clear why we die and why it is necessary to work, and perhaps the most striking thing about the myth is its attempt to show why women must be subjected to men. The often overlooked and most important implication is that human beings gained self-consciousness and intelligence through an act of defiant disobedience. The story makes no attempt to explain Original Sin, just as Todd's story makes no attempt to justify why he is a pilot in a culture that does not want him to be one.

But the Prodigal Son is more accessible as a prototype. In the New Testament, Christ tells the story of the Prodigal Son, a story of a young man who, after going out into the world and squandering his share of the family fortune, is accepted back into the bosom of the family by his father. The father forgives him for his foolishness. But here again to carry the analogy too far and to believe that Ellison meant to suggest this analogy, would be to imply that Todd should not have attempted to fly. It is likely that Ellison was aware of not only T. S. Eliot—whose poetry he was studying at Tuskegee—but James Weldon Johnson's poem "Prodigal Son," which uses the biblical story as a model. Given the fact that Ellison was so well read, he may have also been aware of the many Sea Island legends of prodigal sons actually flying—airplanes, that is—back home after much misadventure in the world beyond.

"Not a machine," Todd says of the airplane, "a suit of clothes you wear.... It's the only dignity I have." One of the values of Jefferson's talk with Todd is that he comes to realize that the crashed airplane is not necessarily his only viable source of dignity. Until now he has used the aircraft as an extension of himself.

When the buzzard hits the windshield, causing Todd to lose control of the aircraft, Todd thinks: "It had been as though he had flown into a storm of blackness." The coming-home aspect of this thought is obvious. And it is the incident of the buzzard that triggers Jefferson's highly relevant story of the horse and the buzzard, which may be seen to represent death. Todd's symbolic death and rebirth, culturally speaking, is not without "loathing," but alongside the loathing he also feels admiration for the buzzard he sees flying so gracefully in his world of the sky.

Jefferson's grandson, Teddy, calls the buzzards "jimcrows." The name is significant in that it is an upfront reference to the Jim Crow laws put in place during Reconstruction. These laws made life almost as bad as it was during slavery. They legalized segregation between people of noticeable African descent and people known to be white. The name Jim Crow comes from a racist minstrel song of the latter part of the nineteenth century. The laws were not struck down until the 1950s, about a decade after "Flying Home" was written. So the existence of Jim Crow laws in the context of the story makes Teddy's play on the term all the more important.

The buzzard itself occupies a central role in African American historical culture. Jefferson's buzzard story also echoes the famous 1940s song "Straighten Up and Fly Right," sung by Nat King Cole. In that story a buzzard takes a monkey for a ride up in the sky: "The buzzard took the monkey for a ride in the air / The buzzard said everything was on the square."

There is another notion connecting Todd and the buzzard. Jefferson is teasing Todd about the possibility that he might get shot down—mistaken for a crow. The implication here is, for a black man, you are flying too high. Much of what Jefferson says echoes the grandfather's deathbed oath in *Invisible Man.* In both cases, it is a mixed message. On the one hand, Jefferson is proud of Todd, proud to see him up there in the sky, like a white boy, flying a big metal bird; but on the other, he is fearful for him, fearful that he is not conscious enough of the restrictions white men have placed around his life.

Todd also briefly thinks of himself in symbolic terms as a buzzard: "Maybe we are a bunch of buzzards feeding on a dead horse, but we can hope to be eagles, can't we?" The buzzard tends to fly higher than most other birds, but part of the symbolic lesson here is that even the buzzard has to come down to earth to feed. And the moral of the Negro fable Jefferson tells about the horse and the buzzard is that in basic matters we are all on the same level, no matter how high and mighty we may feel we are in relation to others. And the hope of being an eagle, in the end, is a reality as Todd is lifted out of his fallen state.

When in America we speak of race we often mean culture. Even before reflecting on his own fallen condition, when Todd regains consciousness his first thought has to do with skin color or race. Are the faces looking down at him black or white? In this context race is implied by color yet Ellison knew perhaps better than most American writers of the period that skin color had only a relative relationship with the culture of race in America. Ellison was once speaking at a university and said to the gathering of students: all of you white kids are part colored and all of you black kids are part white. And the students seemed to understand the essential truth of the statement. Classification by race is perhaps the most fatal and tragic flaw in America. Ellison has Todd respond the way he does because Ellison understood this tragedy.

Yet "Flying Home" is ultimately not about race. Todd looks toward Jefferson and the boy "realizing and doubting at once that only they could release him from his overpowering sense of isolation." Isolation, then, is certainly one of the great themes of the story. It is an inner isolation earned at the expense of Todd's quest for dignity, his need to be respected, even honored. While in this quest Todd is "poised between two poles of fear and hatred," which makes his actions and thoughts ambiguous and ironic. This is deeply ironic, and there is nothing unusual about irony in African American life or literature. Irony is the cornerstone of African American life. The seeds of what Todd feels and needs at the end of the story were present at the beginning when he observes: "The closer I spin toward the earth . . . the blacker I become." Todd's fall from the sky in the beginning of the story is itself ironic—ironic because it brings him into himself, into his history, into his culture. When Jefferson and Teddy finally lift Todd onto the stretcher, he is lifted culturally and spiritually. He becomes that dark bird gliding into the sun "like a bird of flaming gold."

“Thanks for the Lunch, Baby.”

Clarence Major Has Lunch with James Baldwin

It’s hard to believe but after thirty-one years, I’m once again back in Nice, France. I taught here from 1981 till 1983. This time my stay will be brief.

Back then, my old friend James Baldwin was living a short distance away, in Saint-Paul-de-Vence.

Today, as I step out of the blazing sunshine into the cool Restaurant Tolentini (Jimmy’s favorite restaurant in all of Nice), I see that Jimmy has already arrived for our lunch. There he is again, with that famous, wide-open smile.

I haven’t seen Jimmy since that last dinner party at my apartment in 1983. That was fun, but I am especially fond of my memory of the little impromptu gathering Jimmy, my wife, Pamela, a few other friends, and I had after the formal ceremony when the university here awarded Jimmy an honorary doctorate.

Jimmy stands as I approach our table and, I don’t know what I was expecting, but I’m surprised to see that he looks exactly the same as when I last saw him. In his fancy blue dress shirt, black slacks, and black loafers, he looks especially happy and well. His bright smile always lands me in a good mood. We embrace.

He says, “Hey, baby! Good to see you! The years have treated you well.” This is pure Jimmy. He calls everybody he likes “baby.” He puts out his cigarette in the ashtray on our table.

I say, “Hey, Jimmy!”

We sit facing each other.

It’s great to see Jimmy looking so well. Let’s face it, he never had an easy time of it. He preached in a Harlem storefront church from the age of fourteen to seventeen, then as a young man, he moved downtown to the Village, where life was difficult. Finding work was not easy. When he was lucky, he worked as a waiter.

But he was broke a good deal of the time. Sometimes he slept on rooftops. This was the late 1940s, when legal segregation still existed. Restaurants, for example, routinely refused to serve black people and public schools were legally segregated by race.

So, in 1948, Jimmy left New York with forty dollars in his pocket. He'd reached his breaking point. And by now he also knew he was a writer and was determined to prove it to the world. A lot has changed since those days: the Supreme Court's ruling on *Brown v. Board of Education* in 1954, the Civil Rights Act of 1964, and the Voting Rights Act of 1965. But a lot also hasn't changed.

Jimmy moved to Paris, to a hotel, but broke and alone, unable to speak the language, he was very, very lonely. Paris was no immediate panacea. Soon, he was ill. He had no money to pay for doctors or his hotel bill. Rather than putting him out, the elderly Corsican woman who owned the hotel nursed him back to health for three months. This man was a survivor.

And now, here we are at Restaurant Tolentini. Jimmy knew the maître d', Maurice, for many years. Maurice is an elegant middle-aged Frenchman with patrician manners. He doesn't miss a beat. You can tell that this restaurant is his ship and he's its captain. Meanwhile, the background music is Mozart's *Magic Flute*. As always, I feel comfortable and pampered here.

Restaurant Tolentini is airy and plush inside. The white marble-paved floor is shot through with streaks of green and purple. The restaurant has lots of red velvet drapery, and the tables and chairs are all of highly polished dark oak, with matching red velvet upholstery.

The elaborate crystal chandeliers above us are aglitter with soft light. The wallpaper shows an eighteenth-century outdoors festival with plenty of food and frolicking. The napkins are embossed with the restaurant's name. The railings are gold chrome.

To the left of us there's a big long fish tank on the far wall with a variety of native Mediterranean fish: goby, mullet, skate, blackhead, dory, sardinella, and bass, all swimming around and around in their own private universe. It's lighted like a ship at night, at sea.

The din of voices is rich and low, speaking proper French. We may be in Provence, but this restaurant is no place for provincial rubes.

Maurice strokes his little black moustache.

Jimmy says, "Maurice, this is Clarence Major, a good friend of mine, and a fine writer. He taught here at the university back in the 1980s."

Maurice says, "It's a pleasure to meet you, Monsieur Major."

We're in seats by the window, with a full view of the lush, blooming garden. Maurice places menus before us. He fills our water glasses, leaving the carafe of water on the table.

Maurice says, "Puis-je vous commencer avec des refraichissements?"

"Yes," says Jimmy and we order an excellent dry Sauvignon Blanc. Maurice returns with the bottle and expertly uncorks it, pouring a tiny bit in each of our glasses for our approval.

Jimmy sips, I sip. He nods his approval and so do I. Dry and slightly sweet, it's an excellent wine. Maurice pours more wine into each glass, bows slightly, then in English, says, "We're not so busy right now, so today, I will be your waiter. It's always a pleasure to serve you, Monsieur Baldwin."

Maurice bows slightly and leaves.

"Are you still teaching at the University of California at Davis?" Jimmy asks me.

"No, I'm retired from teaching. I'm writing and painting full time now."

"I remember when you were teaching here. I remember you telling me about your students, many of them from North Africa, how smart they were, and how much you were learning from them. Teaching is always better when you too are learning. We had some good times back then. You finished your novel *My Amputations* here in Nice, didn't you?"

"That's right, and I wrote it on a manual typewriter. Hard to imagine nowadays, after so many years of working on a computer, how I ever managed to write novels back then on a manual typewriter."

"I still write in longhand," says Jimmy, leaving me to quietly wonder just *where* and *how* he did this.

"There's a lot to be said for the tactile assurance of longhand. You're in touch with each word on a more intimate basis," I tell him.

Jimmy says, "That's true." He pauses for a sip of wine. "Listen! Things everywhere have changed a lot; not just the widespread use of computers and mobile phones. For example, a lot of European countries are turning against foreigners. Think of all the terrorist killings. I'm sure you've seen it all on TV. They've been rampant in Paris and many of the other major cities of Europe. Over here you never know where the next disaster will happen. It keeps everyone on edge."

Jimmy sighs and shakes his head, then continues. "It's depressing: the frequent police killings of unarmed black men, the constant antigay killings, the school shootings, with hundreds of kids dead, the rise of so many new hate groups. The growing mania of the gun culture in America; and, of all people, Donald Trump as president. Don't think I don't follow what's going on."

"I'm sure you do, Jimmy." I pause. "What about gay marriage now being legal?"

Jimmy says, "That's a good thing. It surprised me. If it had happened years ago, I would have taken advantage of it." He drinks his wine. "Seems every time something positive happens in America there's a negative counteraction."

"Such as positive Obama then Trump?"

"Yes, excellent example. It's the same old backlash every time."

"And were you surprised to see the country elect a black president?"

"Shocked! I admit, I never thought such a thing could ever happen. Most Americans truly believe race is a real thing. But I tell you, Obama will go down in history as one of our best presidents, certainly one of our most intelligent."

"I agree."

Jimmy picks up his menu. "Maybe we should order, huh? What looks good to you?"

I pick up the menu, scanning it. "Remember, Jimmy, lunch is on me."

"Okay, baby." Jimmy says, "Why don't we just order a lot of good stuff and share it?"

"I like that idea."

For appetizers we decide on tapenade with olives, garlic, anchovies, and capers and onion tarts. For the two main courses we select bouillabaisse and lobster with Fettuccine Alfredo and fresh green beans in butter. Our two desserts are a ripe fig dish with fresh feta and petite tomatoes and socca crepes, with whipped cream and almonds.

Maurice returns and we order.

Jimmy goes on. "As I was saying, things back in your country look grim.

I say, "There's all kinds of delusional thinking. A disturbing number of people in America, for example, don't believe in climate change, don't believe we've messed up the atmosphere of our planet."

Jimmy says, "I know. It's sad. Do we *all* have to perish before they see the light?"

"Did you hear about the Bush administration's response to Hurricane Sandy?"

"Sure did: depressing and shameful."

I say, "I found it depressing that Congress refused to work with President Obama for the good of the country, even when they agreed with what he wanted to do. They started out saying they wanted him to fail."

Jimmy smiles. "Baby, you have to keep the faith, you know that."

"Yes, I do know that. And I try, I try."

"You know, Clarence, I've said it many times, my country was America and I still love my country, and for that reason I reserve the right to criticize it."

"As well you should. You always felt that it's the business of the writer to disturb the peace."

I'm looking at Jimmy. After all these years I still think of him as a mentor, a big brother and a father figure, but long before I knew him as a person, I knew him as an ideal writer, and as such, he was for me a beacon and a mainstay.

"I remember one time when I was living here, Jimmy, you left for one of your visits to the States; and at the same time, I also left France. I went to Africa on a lecture tour with stops in Liberia, Ghana, Ivory Coast, and Algeria."

"I remember that. When you came back you told me all about that trip. It reminded me of my first trip to Africa. I wrote an article about it for the *New Yorker*. I had conflicting feelings. I knew I was not returning home. Africa was the land of my ancestors but America was my home."

I say, "That's what I felt, too."

At this point, Maurice brings out our appetizers and refills our water and wine glasses. There is a pause in our conversation while we enjoy our appetizers.

When we are done with the appetizers, the main course arrives, and Jimmy and I eat for a while still without talking, just enjoying the food (now the frisky, playful *Eine Kleine Nachtmusik*), Tolentini's ambience and atmosphere, and of course, each other's company.

Then Jimmy says, "What're you working on these days?"

"A novel."

"Is it going well?"

I say, "Yes, except that I have to keep stopping to do other things such as take out the garbage, make dinner, and write an essay for a magazine or a foreword to a book I like, you name it. It's life."

Jimmy says, "I remember writing my first novel and discovering, in each paragraph, things I really didn't want to a face, but something in me was driving me to face those hidden realities anyway and I discovered things about myself by writing that book; I discovered not so much who I *was* at the time but who I was *not*. A lot of it I improvised."

"I hear you."

I notice Maurice across the room, watching us, waiting for his cue.

"Jimmy, your fiction is realistic, it's true, but when I read your novels I can see how you were improvising every step of the way, like a jazz musician riffing. The ostinato is there. The repeated chord is there. There is a pattern to your prose. How is *that* not improvisation?"

"Sure, but in the end you hide all of that to let the story rise to the surface. That is the important thing. The story! If you leave your workings, your improvisations, on the surface, you are likely to be bored, and if it bores you, it's going to bore your reader."

"'Touché!" I tell Jimmy.

"I've stopped writing things and torn them up because they bored me. Sometimes it was the story, other times, the writing. But I knew there was no point in going on." I pause and take a sip of wine. "I got serious about writing when I was quite young; so over time I've learned a lot by practice and by instinct. I've learned to trust my gut feelings and to rely on them to drive what I've learned about technique."

Jimmy says, "Good! As you know, my father's death was a turning point for me. That was the moment I got really serious about focusing all my energy on writing, on making a career of it. At that point I was now the male head of my family and I was not going to let them down. And more importantly I was not going to let *myself* down."

"I hear you."

Maurice places our desserts before us. To the sound of the "Finale Molto Allegro" in Mozart's Symphony No. 41, C-Major. We stop talking and dive into them with unapologetic brio.

When they've been ravaged, Maurice returns and asks, "How was your lunch, gentlemen?"

Jimmy beams. "As usual, Maurice, everything was delicious; and *you* were splendid."

I say, "Absolutely delicious!"

"Merci, messieurs!" He says, "Would you like a little digestive drink?"

"I'm up for it, how about you, Clarence?"

"Sure. How about cognac?"

Jimmy says, "Cognac is an excellent choice."

Maurice says, "Cognac it is."

Maurice leaves us, and sends a busboy to clear away the dishes, then delivers our cognac. Jimmy and I linger another half hour over it, enjoying the moment, the music, and our friendship.

When it's time, I fish out my credit card and pay.

"Thanks for the lunch, baby."

"Any time, Jimmy. I feel so lucky that we could get together and talk again."

"I will always be here, baby. Never forget that."

I excuse myself to visit the restroom, but when I return, Jimmy has vanished. What will never leave me, however, is that spectacular smile.

Richard Wright

The Long Hallucination

The story of Richard Wright's career, perhaps more than that of any other black American writer, not only illustrates the high and low points such an author can reach, in terms of his work and how it is received, but also dramatizes sharply the general problems of an independent career in writing. I will examine here the activities of Wright's writing career and some aspects of his personal life and the works he produced, and touch on correlations among these aspects in the hope of achieving not only a better understanding of his life as a writer but also with the suggestion of what such a life means for a black writer in a culture that is largely white.

When the novel *Native Son* was published in 1940, it sold out in all the bookstores in Manhattan within three hours. It became an overnight bestseller. The author, Richard Wright, became a prominent figure in American literature.

Who was he and what was he really like? "His voice was light and even rather sweet," James Baldwin says in *Nobody Knows My Name.* Most of the bare facts are well known. In *Black Boy,* one of the greatest autobiographies ever written, Wright told the tragic story of his childhood in the South. When he was born in Mississippi on September 4, 1908, his mother, Ella, was determined that her son would not grow up to become just another dirt farmer like his father, Nathaniel Wright. It seems reasonably safe to assume though, that she never once dreamed that he would ever become the world-famous figure he became, particularly since her initial reaction to his first published short story, "The Voodoo of Hell's Half-Acre," was negative.

I often wondered about that story. Of it he writes in *Black Boy:* "It resolved itself into a plot about a villain who wanted a widow's home. It was crudely atmospheric, emotional, intuitively psychological, and stemmed from pure feeling." This does not sound like a very bad premise for writing fiction, though apparently Wright later thought so.

The story was published in the *Southern Register,* the local Negro newspaper in a town where Richard, his brother Alan, and his mother Ella, now separated from her husband, were living with Richard's grandmother, Margaret Wilson. Margaret Wilson was a very religious and superstitious woman. Hearing of the story, she called Richard and asked him if it was a true story. It was not, he told her. Then it was a lie, she said. As a lie, Grandmama Wilson continued, it was surely the work of the Devil! The Devil had certainly got into Richard! Ella, his mother, took the untrue story to be a sign of a lack of seriousness. She worried about her son. She told Richard, "You won't be able to get a job if you let people think that you're weak-minded."

Wright met opposition to his early efforts not only within his family but also outside. One day he was doing an odd job for a white woman in her home when she asked him what he wanted to become when he grew up. A writer, he told her. The woman was shocked and warned him that no colored boy could ever become a writer. She told him to set his heart on something more practical.

Referring to this time in his life he wrote, "In me was shaping a yearning for a kind of consciousness, a mode of being that the way of life about me had said could not be, must not be, and upon which the penalty of death had been placed." So in a sense his will to change was the root of his hope and survival. He would run away to the North. He would try to come to terms with his own heritage, understand its implications, and find a means to a better life.

Wright arrived in Chicago on a freezing day in December 1927. The city seemed unreal to him and he was soon disappointed. But he would not go back.

While living with his Aunt Maggie, one of his mother's sisters, he worked in a delicatessen and later at the post office. Before long, his mother and brother joined them. During these days he began the long and painful struggle to teach himself to write. He turned out many crude stories and poems and, on the side, read everything he could get his hands on. A self-conscious Negro boy with a southern accent, he had no social life—he couldn't even dance.

One year passed into another but time did not kill Wright's desire to master his chosen craft and art. In the most wretched kind of poverty, no longer working at the post office, he took a job sweeping the streets and continued to read and write after work into the wee hours. Eventually the family went on welfare and through their caseworker, Mary Wirth, Wright got his first break. In addition to finding a better job for him, she persuaded her husband, Dr. Wirth, a well-known sociologist at the University of Chicago, to give the young, beginning writer a list of books to read. Naturally, he read them all and was hungry for more. Meanwhile, also thanks to Mary Wirth, Wright became publicity agent for the local Federal Theater Project, a government-sponsored cultural project to help with the theatrical unemployment problem during the Depression. While the people in the theater group wanted to see staged plays showing the "sweet" side of black life, Wright argued with them; he felt that the bitter hardship of black life should be presented on stage. This belief would influence his later work.

When Mary Wirth was promoted to chief social worker of the Seventh Chicago Works Progress Administration, she secured for Wright a job as a professional writer in another WPA program. He became manager of essays for the Illinois Writers' Project. Meanwhile he was listening to the political speeches being made in Washington Park, and he soon started attending Communist meetings at the John Reed Club. It seemed to him that, at last, he had found a means of revolutionary expression in which the Negro experience could find new value and a new role. Soon after, his poems began to appear in various magazines that supported Communist ideas, and in 1932 he officially joined the John Reed Club. He met people there who later became characters in his books. Eventually he became the club's executive secretary.

Always a very serious and honest man, Wright believed that this social philosophy would make a new and better life possible for *his* people, black people. He now wanted to show in his stories how Communism could relieve black suffering.

Accepting the position of Harlem editor of the *Daily Worker*, Wright moved to New York in the spring of 1937 at the age of twenty-nine. He liked New York but still felt closer to Chicago and continued to write about his experiences there and in the South. In his new job he met many new people. One of them was a nineteen-year-old boy from Oklahoma named Ralph Ellison, who had come to see Wright because he had read some of his poems and liked them. In school Ellison had majored in music but was also interested in writing. Fifteen years later he would become established as one of the United States' outstanding writers when his book *Invisible Man* won the National Book Award.

During the late 1930s Wright assembled a collection of his stories and entered it in a contest sponsored by the Federal Writers' Project. Nobel Prize author Sinclair Lewis was one of the judges. Wright's work won the top prize of $500. Before long Wright's earnings from his work were enough to support him. *Uncle Tom's Children*, the prize-winning collection of stories, was published in a special edition by the Federal Writers' Project. Even better, Harper & Brothers offered Wright a contract to publish the book for the general public; the author would receive 15½ percent of the wholesale price of each copy sold and $1,300 as an advance on expected royalties. Wright accepted.

Meanwhile Wright was working on *Native Son* while living in a one-room apartment of a friend in Bedford-Stuyvesant, Brooklyn. At about this time he met the ballet dancer, Dhima Meadman, who later became his first wife; it was also at this time that he met Ellen Poplar, a social worker, who would later become his second wife.

Uncle Tom's Children had made Wright famous. It was a bestseller and he was making more money than ever before. He was also working harder than ever trying to finish *Native Son.* When the book was published in 1940 by Harper, it was an overnight smash success and Wright's name was inserted on the "Wall of Fame" at the New York World's Fair that year. More money than he had dreamed possible swelled his bank account. *Native Son* was a Book-of-the-Month Club selection, bought for $9,380. Yet Richard Wright remained calm. Already he was quietly working on a new novel.

With Paul Green, Wright wrote a dramatic version of *Native Son.* It appeared on Broadway, starring Canada Lee as Bigger Thomas. Bigger is seen as a "bad nigger." In the play, as in the novel, he kills a white girl accidentally and out of fear; then to hide his deed he stuffs her body into a furnace. Obviously, from this point there is no way for Bigger to turn back. But he feels suddenly alive for the first time in his life. The crime liberates him (whereas in Theodore Dreiser's novel, *Sister Carrie,* the white hero's crime ultimately leads him to destruction, inwardly as well as outwardly). When Bigger tells his colored girlfriend what he has done, she becomes afraid of him, so he kills her too and begins his flight from the police. He is captured and brought to trial and is defended by a Communist lawyer. Bigger is no longer just the shadow of a person. He *is* somebody! He *feels* important. He is *seen.* People look directly *at* him. Bigger goes proudly to the electric chair to die at the hands of a society that condemned him from birth.

The year 1941 was also the year that Wright's book *12 Million Black Voices: A Folk History of the Negro in the United States* was published. Illustrated with photographs, it is a long poetic essay that deals with black life in both the South and the North.

Although Wright was having great success in his work, his marriage to Dhima Meadman was failing, and the novel he was writing, "Little Sister," was also doomed to failure. It was rejected by Harper and remains unpublished; this was a great disappointment to Wright.

After divorcing Dhima, Wright married Ellen Poplar in March 1941, and in April 1942 their first daughter, Julia, was born. Wright was a proud thirty-three-year-old father.

Two years later he left the Communist Party, which he had joined back in 1934. During recent years his relations with Party bosses had become strained. Many of them had strongly disliked *Native Son.* More important, Wright had come to believe that the Party meant to *use* Negroes for its own purposes.

He had joined it in good faith and for a long time believed that they meant to make a new and better life for everybody. But then all his life Wright had had faith in some bigger and better ideas of life. In Mississippi his family was Seventh Day Adventist. He had been taught through that religion that earthly life wasn't a person's *actual* life, that the *real* life of a person came *after* death. It was a religion that few Negroes in the South followed, and this fact had made Wright feel even more an outsider. The other boys and girls he knew were usually Baptists or Methodists. But Seventh Day Adventism was what he had been taught and it was what he believed as a child. It said, in effect, that *someday in the future* the suffering would stop and everything would be good for black people—for all people.

In a way, the Communist Party's plans for the future had made the same sort of promise to Wright. It was painful for Wright to have to give up one dream after another.

Before Harper published Wright's famous autobiography, *Black Boy,* in 1945, his editor asked Wright to cut the last third of the book, the chapters about his Chicago and New York experiences, saying the cutting was necessary because of the wartime paper shortage. But Wright didn't believe that was the reason; a lot of the section cut dealt with Wright's activities as a Communist. Even before publication date *Black Boy* became a bestseller. The sales figure was 30,000 copies. The success of the book, naturally, added considerably to Wright's fame in the United States and in other countries where it was in translation. Of course, the reactions were not all favorable. An outraged senator from Mississippi rose up on the floor of the senate and said the book was a "blasted lie." No bookseller in Mississippi would sell the book.

In the spring of 1946 the French government invited Wright and his family to visit its country. The Wrights liked France and enjoyed their stay there. The following year they moved to Paris permanently. There, in January 1949, their second daughter, Rachel, was born.

In France Wright made many friends, many of them among the French writers known as existentialists. While the "rootlessness" of the existentialist philosophy was formally a European experience, Wright found it contained much meaning for him as a black man.

By 1953, Wright had finished what is in my opinion one of his best novels. He called it *The Outsider.* It concerns Cross Damon, an intelligent black man who manages to switch identities with a dead man after a train wreck. The people he knew now think he is dead and Cross sees this as an ideal chance to escape his past and his troubles. Cross leaves Chicago for New York but troubles, rather than staying behind, follow and mount in intensity. In the end he realizes that he cannot escape who and what he really is.

The book was not a success. In the United States *The Outsider* had an advance sale of 13,500 copies, not very promising compared to his earlier sales. Wright's popularity had waned since 1945. During this time the United States' wartime friendship with the Soviet Union had ended, and those who had belonged to the Communist Party were being branded by many as traitors. Senator Joseph McCarthy had started his witch hunt for Communists and Communist sympathizers in the government, using the tactics of wild claims and unfounded charges. McCarthyism created fear of any connection with Communism, even of books written by Communists. And though Wright had quit the Party before the end of the war, it was still well known that he had been a Party member. As a result, many American readers stayed away from his books and a large number of libraries removed *Native Son* and *Black Boy* from their shelves in response to pressures from McCarthy's supporters.

In Europe, however, *The Outsider* sold quite well. In fact, some European critics considered it the most important novel to emerge from an American experience.

In *The Outsider,* Wright tried to probe beyond the social context of race into the "human condition," to put it one way, and in his next fictional effort, *Savage Holiday,* he gave up the category of race altogether. A gripping novel, *Savage Holiday* was rejected by Harper. Wright eventually sold it, however, to Avon, a paperback publisher, who gave him a $2,000 advance. As a paperback original it went almost unnoticed in the United States, but in Europe, it was translated into German, Italian, Dutch, and French and the book sold quite well.

At this point Wright turned his attention to a kind of book new to him. The first one was about West Africa's Gold Coast (now Ghana). He called it *Black Power: A Record of Reactions in a Land of Pathos.* It is the reflections, sharp and sensitive, of a black American on his first contact with Africa. It was published in 1954 by Harper but it sold poorly. By this time, Wright's bank account was very low, and he had to continue to work to earn a living. He obtained an advance of $3,000 from Harper to visit Spain and to write a book about its people and their lives.

To Wright the Spanish seemed more primitive than the Africans. Though of African descent, in Africa Wright had found the African mind rather strange. He was forced to realize how much an American—or at least how little an African—he actually was. Wright had difficulty relating to the Africans' emotions and thoughts. In Spain he felt a similar distance between himself and the

Spanish. But he felt that Spain, unlike Africa, was not moving toward the future, was not a growing society.

While working on the book, which he called *Pagan Spain,* Wright continued to take deep stock of himself. Aware of many of his own prejudices, he worked to overcome them. He meant to see and write about Spain as honestly as he could. It was in *Pagan Spain* that Wright said: "I have no race except that which is forced on me. I have no country except that to which I'm obliged to belong. I have no traditions."

While working on the manuscript of *Pagan Spain,* Wright read in the newspapers about the world's first Asian African conference, to be held in Indonesia. The idea excited Wright—he felt he had to attend. He put aside his unfinished book and flew to Djakarta. There he talked with local Asians as well as many of the delegates from other countries. He wrote about this experience in *The Color Curtain*. There, as in *Pagan Spain,* Wright's new vision of himself and the world continued to show itself. "Color," he wrote, "is not my country. . . . I am opposed to all racial definitions."

The Color Curtain was rejected by Harper, and World Publishing Company published it in 1956, the year in which Harper brought out *Pagan Spain.* After this Wright finally broke all ties with Harper. He turned to Doubleday & Company. To them he submitted an outline of his novel *The Long Dream,* and a contract with an advance of $6,000 was signed. At this time he also put together for Doubleday a thin volume of his essays and speeches, titled *White Man, Listen!,* which went by almost unnoticed by general readers. Meanwhile, neither *Pagan Spain* nor *The Color Curtain* was selling very well.

The Long Dream appeared in bookstores in 1958. It is the story of Fishbelly, a black boy growing up in Jackson, Mississippi. Not a "bad nigger" like Bigger Thomas nor an intellectual like Cross Damon, Fishbelly is middle class. His father, Tyree, an undertaker, is murdered by racist cops and local businessmen. To escape the fate of his father, Fishbelly flees to the North. He then heads for France. In this story Wright returns to the theme found in his earliest short stories and in *Native Son*: to be black in the United States, particularly in the South, is a very fearful and tragic situation.

The actor Anthony Quinn was deeply moved by the book. He helped Wright with advice toward a stage production and Quinn himself, a white man, was anxious to play the role of Tyree. Three years later a good Broadway production of *The Long Dream* became a reality—but without Quinn. Cheryl Crawford, its producer, felt she couldn't afford the lowest salary Quinn would accept—$3,000 per week.

In spite of many discouragements, Wright did not give up. He still believed in himself and in what he had to say. All his life he had dreamed that things could get better. They *would* get better. Although his recent books had not done well, he finished a sequel to *The Long Dream* and called it *Island of Hallucination.* It tells of Fishbelly's adventures in Paris among Afro-American spies. The book was rejected by Doubleday, however, and this was one more great disappointment for Wright, who began to wonder if his writing career was over. Short of money and his daughters nearing college age, he considered teaching to make a living. He was not in the best of health, however. He was fifty years old, and not nearly as strong physically as in the past. It exhausted him too greatly to work the long stretches he had managed previously.

Meanwhile, his oldest daughter entered Cambridge University in England, and his wife Ellen and their youngest daughter took up residence in England. Wright, for mysterious and unknown reasons, was denied the right to remain in England. Even close friends in the British government could not help him.

So, in another apartment in Paris, on rue Regis on the Left Bank, Wright brooded, staring out the window. He wrote hundreds of haiku poems, a form of poetry he had become fascinated by while in Indonesia. He was unhappy and he missed his family. Nevertheless, he put together *Eight Men,* the first collection of his short stories since *Uncle Tom's Children.* However, the book did not appear until after his death. Wright's health remained poor. He was being treated by Dr. Valadimir Schwartzmann, an expert on tropical diseases, for what was at first thought to be an "amoebic infection." It was believed that he had picked up this infection while in Africa in 1953. But he never recovered, and information on the cause of his death is conflicting. Wright was in bed, in a clinic for a checkup. It was near eleven o'clock when the nurse saw his signal. Just as she got to him, she saw him die—with a smile on his face.

Painting and Poetry

Poets almost inevitably reflect painterly ideas and ideals, and methods and processes in their work. Painters too almost inevitably reflect the principles of poetry—metaphor, narrative, symbolism, and so forth.

At a conference at Washington University in St. Louis in 1997, on the relationship between poetry and painting, Derek Walcott said: "When we look at paintings that do not attempt to mimic the page, but make something more than just calligraphy, there is an echo that goes with that painting. The echo need not be the linear representation of an idea, like a piece of prose, or fiction painted, or even a poem painted, but some other echo that it creates."

This observation is related to the German poet Rainer Maria Rilke's point in *Letters on Cézanne* that a great painting looks back at you with a life of its own. It does not have sound or smell but through a kind of "echo" of the senses (all of them), it speaks with its own life.

Our memory of what we've seen, heard, smelled, tasted, and felt is actively involved in looking at a painting just as those same senses are actively involved in understanding a poem we hear read or we read on the page silently.

The South African writer, Breyten Breytenbach, at that same conference, makes a somewhat similar point about painting, "In painting . . . there are echoes created, allusions, references, and repetitions, and these go into creating a sense of moving forward, of changing. What one sees becomes something else; there's something else behind it. It unleashes a certain movement, this pattern-making, this repetition."

In several letters van Gogh writes that he sees no differences between literature and painting. He was a very writerly painter, and a very painterly writer, a writer of letters. He spent as much time writing and reading as painting. He read poetry and he read fiction. And he thought long and hard about both in relation to painting.

French painter Camille Pissarro also wrote many letters to one of his sons. Although there was no conscious effort to explore the relationship between painting and poetry, he certainly implied that he was doing so often in what he said about the act of painting. For example, when of painting he said, "Do not define too closely the outlines," one is reminded of how poetry works: allusion, metaphor, simile, and so forth. These tropes are avenues to "not defining too closely."

Pissarro also says something poets have always instinctively followed, "Don't precede according to rules and principles, but paint what you observe and feel. Paint generously and unhesitatingly.... For it is best not to lose the first impression." The great poets have always mastered the rules then gone beyond them. We would not have a Walt Whitman, as we know him, had he not broken all rules of writing poetry. Whitman opened up the line and created a new kind of poetry, as big as America.

French poet and philosopher Paul Valery's description of the modern dance when refocused also might well serve as a description of the essence of painting or poetry: "The same limbs constructing, deconstructing and reconstructing shapes, or movements responding to equal or harmonic intervals, form an ornament of duration, just as the repetition of motifs in space, or their symmetry, forms the ornament of extent." Valery wrote this in 1938 while reflecting on a painting of a ballet dance by Degas.

Finally, there are many ways in which painting and poetry are alike but there has to be at least a few ways in which they are not alike.

In "Notes on Painting and Awareness" (2006) painter Louis le Brocquy writes, "The human body is a constantly recurring theme of both poet and painter, but their two arts—each a whole continent of consciousness—do not touch directly... at any point. They have no common Fortier, no bridge other than their shared state of aesthetic awareness."

But there are problems with this observation. Le Brocquy goes too far. Poetry after all, like painting, is about process and discovery. Le Brocquy, later in the same essay, makes the point very well (and does so without any conscious contradiction): "Discoveries are made—such as they are—while painting. The painting itself dictates." This is precisely the poet's experience as well. Still, although he has a difficult time outlining them, Le Brocquy senses some differences between the making of poetry and the making of paintings.

The main way they are *not* alike is this: Painting is primarily spatial, and poetry is primarily temporal and conceptual. They can, however, be seen as parallel activities. But ultimately words in a poem are not going to achieve the same effect on our senses as paint strokes on canvas. By the same token, paint strokes on a canvas cannot add up to the kind of impression we get from words in a poem. There are limits. And there are boundaries set by the nature of the media.

A Meditation on Kenneth Patchen's Painted Poems

Kingdoms and Utopias

While in my teens in the mid-1950s in Chicago, I discovered Kenneth Patchen through reading an essay titled "Patchen: Man of Anger and Light," by Henry Miller. This was before Miller's *Tropic of Cancer* was available in the States. I had already read all of Miller's New Directions books. Once I discovered Patchen, I read everything of his I could find. And in doing so discovered the inner world of the man's passionate feelings and thoughts. They gave me an anchor.

In that essay on Patchen, Miller says, "The first thing one would remark on meeting Kenneth Patchen is that he is the living symbol of protest." Miller describes Patchen as "Tender and Ruthless at the same time." He also describes him as a man of justice and truth.

William Butler Yeats says, "Man can embody truth but he cannot know it." And so it is with Kenneth Patchen's painted poems. They are objects of truth, vibrantly expressive, tactile objects set in the world as *acts* of truth. Patchen once said, "To recognize truth it is only necessary to recognize each other." Again, Henry Miller: "Patchen stands out, a herald of peace and truth, endowed with invincible heart and integrity. No one can read him without being influenced in his own life and work."

His first book, *Before the Brave* (1936), was a collection of poems. My favorite books among his early works are the self-published third book, *The Journal of Albion Moonlight* (1941), a work of prose with drawings, *The Dark Kingdom* (1943), and *Sleepers Awake* (1946). I discovered later the painted poems, but *Cloth of the Tempest* (1943), because it contained poems *and* drawings, had already given me a first glimpse of Patchen's graphic work that he would more fully explore later in the painted poems and the painted books.

Over the years readers and critics have tended to compare the quality of Patchen's early works with the later works, usually finding one or the other superior. My argument here is that the early prose books, the early drawings and the poetry speak directly—in an unbroken voice—to the painted poems done after 1959 and vice versa.

In his last interview, Patchen said, "I don't consider myself a painter." Nevertheless, most of the painted poems were done in the 1960s, done in the little house at the end of Palo Alto's Sierra Court. He and his wife, Miriam, lived there till his death in 1972. The images in the painted poems are indeed—as Patchen maintains—things that extend words.

In other words, the painted images work as allegorical words. In *Kenneth Patchen: An Exhibition of Painted Poems,* edited by William E. Mullane (Pig and Iron Press, 1989), Patchen is quoted as follows, "I think of myself as someone who has used the medium of painting in an attempt to extend—give an extra dimension to—the medium of words. There is always . . . between words and the meaning of words, an area which is not to be penetrated . . . the region of magic, the place of the priestly interpreter of nature, the man who identifies himself with all things and with all beings, and who suffers and exalts with all of these. . . . I think that the mystery of life will ring in the work, and when it rings most strongly, truly and honestly, it will ring with a sense of mystery . . . of wonder, childlike wonder . . . a sense of identification with everything that lived."

Speaking of the painted poems, in a 1969 Corcoran Gallery exhibition catalogue, Miriam said the figurative creatures are "visual-structured creatures. . . . Despite saying he is not a 'painter' . . . Patchen has been acclaimed by many leading artists and galleries as a powerful force in the art world. Everywhere his influence is to be seen."

In the picture poem, "What Shall We Do Without Us," these words are both the title and part of the poem. On one side, against a background of gray-blue, is a face with cat-ears, cat-eyes, a nose, a mouth, and bird-legs. It carries a smaller face perched on the left side of its head. On the other side is a small figure, more human-like, with a big head, big eyes, and two legs.

The point here is one that Patchen often makes:

Everyman is me,
I am his brother.
I am everyman
and he is in and of me.
This is my faith,
my strength
my deepest hope,
and my only belief.

I am reminded of Patchen's limerick-like poem, "I Went to the City" (from *Doubleheader*, 1966, and recorded to jazz in collaboration with Allyn Ferguson, on El Records, 2008). In it are these lines:

> Yes, I went to the city,
> And there I did bitterly cry,
> Men out of touch with the earth
> And with never a glance to the sky.

This recited poem shows commitment to the serious issues of life, and at the same time, gives expression to joy. A poem like this also seems to me to speak out of that same passion that made the early works with drawings, such as *The Journal of Albion Moonlight*, *Cloth of the Tempest*, and *Sleepers Awake* so strong.

In the same—but more bitterly ironic—spirit is the painted poem, "I Am the Ghost." It is set against a bright yellow background. There is a tadpole-shaped figure with a red body spotted all over with white dots. He stands facing the viewer with large yellow eyes and a white nose. To his left is a transparent cat. The free verse message of the painted poem is, "I am the Ghost of Chief Mountain-Lyin' (Since Everyone-Else-Is) I wedded pretty Red Wing and if you don't believe it, right down there's our daughter, Bob [referring to the transparent cat]." To the left of the figure the Ghost continues, "Lucky you made no deposit on the country—just throw it away when you're finished."

In the late fifties when I first read *The Journal of Albion Moonlight* reflexive fiction was new to me. Perhaps you can imagine how I—an aspiring painter and writer—responded to the shocking and refreshing quality of the following:

> Carol wants me to write a novel: "You've met so many interesting people," she tells me.
>
> "Very good, there was a young man and he could never get his hands on enough women. That's a novel."
>
> "There was an idiot and he became God. That's the same novel. I can't possibly think of any others."
>
> "It is rather pleasant to be the author of two such excellent novels. The critics are divided in their opinions. One lot believes that they should be shorter, another not, that they should be a mite longer. I rather prefer short critics to long ones. I like critics with tan shoes—look nicer, I think" (41).

This passage generates the same humor and magical quality one finds in the painted poems. Patchen's prose can't be separated from his poetry and his poetry can't be separated from his prose. When I finished Patchen's *The Journal of Albion Moonlight,* I had to go for a long walk just to collect myself. Miller had the same reaction. With the appearance of *Moonlight,* Miller says it "opened up a vein unique in English literature."

In the same irreverent spirit—and a play on *Little Red Riding Hood*—is "Come Now My Child." It is a magical tale that is also set against a bright yellow background. Two black-brown figures are placed one above the other. A tiny figure in a dress is in our lower right corner. Although the lower figure actually faces the girl, it seems to me that the upper figure is the speaker if only because I can see his mouth. He says, "Come now my child, if we were planning to harm you, do you think we'd be lurking here beside the path in the very darkest part of the forest?"

What the viewer loves about these works—both the early ones like *The Journal of Albion Moonlight* and the later painted poems—is Patchen's ability to wed seriousness and humor seamlessly in almost every sentence. In his last interview, conducted by Charles S. Maden and published by Capra Press, Patchen said, "I have . . . done a great deal of graphic work . . . very often my writing with pen is interrupted by my writing with brush, but I think of both as writing."

Patchen's title, *Sleepers Awake,* echoes J. S. Bach's Cantata 140. In this, Patchen's most ambitious novel, he uses a vast array of techniques and critiques the book as he writes it. His words are often graphic designs engineered to drive home the urgency of his argument. It's a fragmented and strident pastiche of prophecy and poetry, prose and political argument—and much more. This is a reminder of Patchen's *Sleepers Awake*:

> The old man—I'll bet your life's a mess—The old man lifted the cover off the box and everybody started to cry. By damn that was a sad thing. You have to understand that it takes a pretty good story to stand up against the fact that there never was anything but one story since the world began.
>
> A lousy story. A story of how the whole business doesn't make sense.
> The facts—
> You live. You die.
> And nothing ever comes very near you.

And later in the book:

SEVEN BEAUTIFUL THINGS
MADE MORE BEAUTIFUL BY APPEARING
IN THIS WAY

1. A tree in a flower.

4. Sleeping girl.

3. Colt and huge red stones. . . .

In Patchen's picture poem, "All at Once," four yellow oxide figures, tinted slightly green, loom against a gray background. Three figures are placed at the bottom with a larger winged one in flight above. And in white, these words: "All at once is what eternity is." Here again we hear that same philosophical voice, at times lamenting the plight of humanity. And, at other times, attempting to give direction and meaning to life. It's the same varied voice we hear in the poetry recordings Patchen made between 1957 and 1959 to jazz with various jazz musicians.

"An Interview with the Floating Man" is also set against a bright yellow background. There are three figures, one large penguin-like figure, a blue man-like figure, and a parrot-like figure, facing left. In part, the message is: "But if you see no hope at all, isn't it sort of . . . well, a lie—all your talk about how human beings must love one another?"

These painted poems spring from a definite aesthetic and a definite social context. They evolved in a uniquely American context. Miller talks of Patchen's early years in Ohio, where he was born: "The hours he sacrificed in the steel mills . . . served to fan his hatred for a society in which inequality, injustice and intolerance form the foundation of life." But Patchen would soon discover a way to harness that anger into art.

His publisher, James Laughlin, in a postscript to the posthumously published collection of painted poems, *What Shall We Do Without Us* (1984), said, "[Patchen] spoke out constantly against war, and it was this, perhaps, more than anything else in his writing, which made him such a hero to the young."

In "A Letter to God," Patchen writes, "I am . . . conscious of another being in myself." This sounds very much like Blake in one of his moments of passionate God-inspired inspirations. Blake too made painted poems. Patchen, also like Blake, cries out to God. Each has his unique vision of God. In a way, the painted poems too cry out to God. Patchen's God seems to have a mortal presence. "He" is somebody you can talk to, even criticize.

In "Letter," Patchen says, "Come down God and continue your fight." The painted poems, like the "Letter," are driven by lofty artistic and spiritual concerns. Patchen is always aiming for art and often for utopia. And he keeps his eyes on the achievements of the past.

Those experimental poets and painters who came before him certainly influenced him. And some of his contemporaries also influenced him. One sees in Patchen's painted poems the influence of Dadaism, Surrealism, Expressionism, Art Brut, Cobra, African art, Oceania art, comic strips, and the Free Figuration movement.

Patchen certainly was aware of the innovations of the then recent past and those then presently going on in Europe. I say this because when I look at Patchen's painted poems I think of Rouault, Paul Klee, and Joan Miro. With them, as with Patchen, spontaneity is the key. It is certainly the key to Patchen's painted poems. Klee once talked about the importance of children's drawings and the drawings of the insane. Somewhere in one of his interviews Patchen too talks about the importance of getting back to child-like innocence in his art.

Spontaneity also underscores the social passion of the painted poems. In "O Take Heart My Brothers," the social issue is rendered with the ease of spontaneity:

> O Take heart my brothers
> Even now . . . with every Leader & every resource & every strategy
> of every nation on Earth
> arrayed against Her—Even now
> O even Now!
> my Brothers
> Life is in no danger
> of losing the argument!
> —for after all . . . (As will be shown) She has only to change the subject

These words are drawn (not written, *drawn*) around two figures: one bird-like and the other an odd-looking V-shaped figure with gigantic eyes. The colors are dark, brooding, gray, and blue.

But Miller also asserts that Patchen made "no pretense of being a painter or illustrator." Nevertheless, like Picasso, Miller says Patchen, in the early New York days, exposes himself to "every influence."

Miller calls him a "snorting dragon." But the snorting dragon is also a "gentle prince" who suffers over the "slightest cruelty or injustice" done to anyone. Miller says Patchen is at that time "a tender soul, who soon learned to envelope himself in a mantle of brim-fire in order to protect his sensitive skin." Largely self-educated, Patchen's sensitive nature made him a loner who read the great writers and studied the great artists.

And just as Patchen was influenced by this experience he himself influenced many poets and artists who came after him. Whether or not direct lines of influence can be traced from Patchen's work of the 1930s, 1940s, and 1950s to the painters and poets of the 1960s and 1970s (who were reacting to Minimalism and Conceptual Art) observation shows us that Patchen's work anticipates theirs just as Blake (without intending to) anticipates the Romantics. Patchen was certainly a forerunner to artists like Crash, Basquiat, Haring, and Scharf.

Also, it's interesting that while Patchen was developing his free way of painting and writing, in Europe artists like Karl Appel, Constant, Corneille, Christian Dotremont, Asger Jorn, and Joseph Noiret were developing along similar lines. Like Patchen, they too self-consciously referred to primitive art and children's drawings as motif.

Also, like Patchen, they were politically minded. After all, early in his career, and because of his early political poetry, Patchen was typecast as a Proletariat poet. However, he refused to identify with any ideology. He was convinced he was making socially conscious art, not overt polemics.

Through his art, Patchen speaks for the rights of victims of injustice, for the poor, for the working class, for the outcast, for minorities, for women. Even in his despair Patchen is hopeful for humanity, hopeful for justice. In his painted poems, subject matter and themes are rather consistently about all of the above. But Patchen is first and foremost about love. Of Patchen, Miller says, "It's always because we love that we are rebellious; it takes a great deal of love to give a damn one way or another what happens."

Using a virtuoso palette and a virtuoso vocabulary Patchen weaves together, with lyrical harmony, magical images and rhythmic words. Both involve how we relate, or fail to relate, to each other and how we care or fail to care for one another.

Patchen depends on a succession of associations to decorate and nail home his aesthetics and social and political messages. The painted poems are really like illuminated texts forecasting the dangers we face as a people. They also remind us of what is most important—love and each other. At the same time, they tell us how ugly and how beautiful we are.

He creates mythical birds and beautiful strange animals that speak to us of these matters. In "There Are Not Many Kingdoms Left," Patchen writes, "Away from this kingdom, from this last undefiled / place, I would keep our government, our civilization, and all / other spirit-forsaken and corrupt institutions." He gives us hopeful messages of peace in a time of war in a quiet and passionate voice and in quiet colors and in loud colors and in Veronese greens and in Rubens reds.

His passionate anger at corruption sometimes takes over as in "Eve of St. Agony or the Middleclass Was Sitting on Its Fat," when he shouts,

Man-dirt and stomachs that the sea unloads; rockets
of quick lice crawling inland, planting their damn flags,
putting their malethings in any hole that will stand still,
yapping bloody murder while they slice off each other's heads
spewing themselves around, priesting, whoring, lording
it over little guys

Patchen's approach is one of uninhibited and vigorous creativity. He works with overt emotion and subjective symbolism. He creates a serious, yet playful, visual universe. In addition to images already mentioned, he uses a lyrical concert of signs and symbols to underscore his message. With a passionate eye and a caring heart, his technique, his style, his form is honest. As stated earlier, his compositions are infused with a child-like innocence as convincing as Picasso or Dubuffet or Rouault.

Finally, Patchen's painted poems stay with you. The figures—though not quite like anything we can identify—and the words (beautiful and hopeful) stay with us because somehow we recognize the feelings and thoughts of a human being giving expression to that inner area of ourselves that we have not been able to articulate. This is why Kenneth Patchen remains important. It is also why, in years to come, readers and critics will continue to argue over which period of Patchen's work is the highest point of his achievement.

Reaching and Leaving the Point

At a certain point early in my development as a writer who also paints, I made a conscious decision to try to understand on some sort of personal, if eccentric, level the essential, technical aspects of writing and painting.

I came to this decision because I had been feeling like somebody from a remote tribal village who had accidentally learned to drive a car. I could make the car move but I had no idea *why* it moved.

To begin my investigation, I tried to imagine the earliest humans just beginning to stand upright and to look about. I thought that at *that* point a sense of space—different from the one likely generated by searching the earth's floor for food—might have begun to evolve.

While other animals were still looking down more often than not, early humans (and related primates) might well—at least occasionally—bend their necks and gaze at the sky. I toyed with the idea that erect posture itself might have led to daydreaming—about aesthetics—or to abstract thought.

I speculated—with Pliny the Elder—that the first paintings were probably line drawings made on the ground, outlining the shadows of real human beings or objects standing upright against the light of the sun. It was possible to go a step further and speculate about how *real* space might have gotten itself transformed into *symbolic space* and how actual size—or near actual sizes—got reduced or enlarged. The next step was the question of an organizing principle.

It didn't take long before I discovered the incredible importance of perspective and point of view. It hit me how important a fact it was that perspective imposes and organizes human thought on what is seen. I came to see perspective as a process through which space is organized just as point of view organizes our perception of direction in a text.

I began to think that since the decline of the tribal belief that the individual or the tribe was the center of the universe, which correlates with the a decline in the concept of the self as a symbol of the ultimate creator, questions of *how* to organize space and time and the objects and experiences—both actual and represented—in them have been in crisis. (More on the nature of this crisis later.)

For me, the real eye-opening revelation was the sudden realization that *real* space, even in tracing a shadow on the ground, could not be transferred to a two-dimensional surface. In other words, all uses of any degree of perspective in painting were based on deception. Three-dimensional space could not be rendered on a two-dimensional surface, not even in isometric terms. The worlds of *temporal* space and of *static* space were perceived in separate intellectual frames.

So, in a similar manner, point of view itself, I thought, had to be some sort of literary sleight-of-hand. Which in part might be what Leonardo da Vinci was getting at when he wrote, "perspective is the bridle and rudder of art."

If deception and sleight-of-hand were problems, they were not the only ones. I soon also came to see how impossible it was to alter the inherent position of the spectator in relation to the object, whether made of paint, stone, or words.

Although the writer or the artist could rotate the position of creation, the spectator or the reader was fairly fixed as a confined viewer watching static convergences. We as spectators came *after* the fact of creation and that was that.

I also discovered that, although perspective had changed over the centuries, according to the needs of the particular culture, it remained essentially a subjective, provisional, abstractionist, and arbitrary organizing device.

If I understood the situation properly, it seemed to me that the question for modern creators was how should space be measured since Newton and Descartes and Costa. Different answers led to the formation of different organizing devices. But an organizing device could be almost anything from a whip to a ruler or a kiss on the cheek.

In the meantime, I felt I needed a kind of metaphor as agent to operate as a research tool, at least part of the way, the way a studio teacher uses a mannequin to direct the drawing of action. I came up with a human figure.

This figure had to be flexible enough to be a character as well. It might be male or female or genderless. Being a product of my particular culture, I arbitrarily called it a "he."

So, there he is.

He, with my permission, is about to create a story with himself as its center.

It's a fictional story and as such I'd like to offer a definition of fiction before his story begins. Blake's *Law Dictionary* says fiction is "An assumption or supposition of law that something which is or may be false is true, or that a state of facts exists which has never really taken place."

I find this legal definition in most ways superior to literary ones because it supports the thesis that if the fiction writer renders the truth of the experience then you have a fresh, new reality; but it also goes further to assert that "a state of facts" exists.

So, what does he need in order to begin?

He already has the factual space.

Very likely the next most important thing he needs is the fact of time to tell his story. Time, for the purposes of his story, might be interchangeable with space, whether it is the space of the printed page or the surface of the canvas.

His story can move in almost any direction but no matter where it moves, the point of view or points of view are going to serve as my main instrument for following his signals.

I move in closely.

As I focus on his face I begin to see the details of his story. What does this face tell me? How old is it? What emotions are held by it and are readable in it? How about his hands? Are these the hands of an office worker or a monk or a dishwasher or a carpenter? Have they ever stroked a kitten or fired a gun or made mud cakes? He needs time to let his story emerge.

In a formal sense he has earned the space and the time from my conception of him and his frame. Both are granted as to a stone, a tree, an idea, a dog, a passion, or merely something that wishes to come into existence, in a new way.

This concept begins from the assumption that everything that exists has, in some form, always existed. The only reason I recognize his story and his landscape has to do with the fact that both have, metaphorically speaking, always existed in me.

As I watch him begin, I become aware of the fact that, as a figure in the landscape I am looking at, he is also an agent of my own inner sense of what is about to happen. I cannot overemphasize this point: what happens to him happens mainly in me as I observe.

In other words, whatever will take place, in a sense, has already taken place in me first. His presence, as agent, is the static evidence of the mobility of my continuous life and its need for continuous proof of its own existence.

Do I then dare believe that *my* landscape—which also needs details of color, lines, smells, sounds, texture, credibility, truth—and the figure in it, groping for a point of view from which to demonstrate his "story," are other than what they seem? Is he a cloak for something else? Is the landscape itself a pretext? What do they have to do with the restless models found in the real world beyond myself?

Let's see. If the figure chooses to move far back into the frame so that he is closer to the vanishing point, what changes take place in *my* perception of this transfer? Have I lost control? Do I, for example, then strain to see him?

I doubt it. I doubt it because he is no longer the subject at the center of the landscape's composition. That construction then becomes more important than he. But what if he is rendered in greater detail than objects in the foreground; in other words, what if he is sharply focused, in the way that a camera might present him with his surroundings becoming hazy?

If he is sharply focused in this manner then surely I must intend to continue to consider him the most important factor in the compositional arrangement.

But without the change of focus, the figure is unmistakably part of the background though, intellectually, I know that he has not actually gotten smaller as he moved into the distance. Visually, knowing this is not so easy. Unlike real life, where (from the point of view of the observer) a man or woman leaves home for work in the morning, and in doing so, seems to get smaller, metaphorically speaking, the figure in my landscape, in his small stages, is actually small.

But in being so, it contains the memory of the relative largeness of its full size. We know that, with the shifting of the perspective or point of view, he can become large again.

Understand that, here, I am not dealing with camera logic. Things seen in the distance are not seen in minute detail. Although I *know* that his detail is seeable, if I move closer; or I may know about it from memory of previous close experience.

But in any case, there he is, far back, and, in this frame, only a stroke or two of the brush, so to speak. Like van Gogh's tiny sower in the wheat field, he is somehow the most significant element in the composition.

You begin to see how crucial it is for me to make an interesting decision about where my focus is, in painterly or literary terms. Under the best conditions, this focus stems from vision and vision depends almost entirely on the thinking process that is fed by surrounding stimulation. Another way of putting it is to think in terms of Kenneth Clark's notion of "moments of heightened perception," which, in his words lead to "the inexplicable."

What Clark is getting at here is, "The flow of accepted associations in which the mind . . . is sometimes interrupted, and we are shocked to realize, for a second, how odd things really are."

And, in a way, one could argue that all the modern art isms—Impressionism, Expressionisms, Surrealism, Dadaism—are responses to that shock, stimulated by moments of focused vision, conjured up out of thought connecting with external stimulation.

A viewer or a reader will ask demanding questions that are not likely to be answered except by the physical bluntness of the canvas itself or by the linguistic elusiveness of the written text. The artist or writer is not likely to always be available to answer questions, assuming he or she could, regarding these shifts.

So, my thesis hangs here within this elusive landscape. Although it appears that anything can happen within it, on its present terms, it is far from my wish to have it open-ended. Because perspective exists only in a closed scheme the elements in the frame are much like those created by Nature in, say, the formation of a leaf. My figure, or character, is therefore the agent of a *constructed* reality, signifying primarily within the context of that closed scheme.

At the same time, I suspect that all attempts to categorize and label his position are arbitrary and limiting. Forms of him, from different angles and at different distances, have existed throughout recorded art history.

Therefore, it is difficult to speak of any period in isolation. Vermeer placed him one way and Philip Pearlstein placed him another. Richard Estes avoided him but used his space as though he had just walked down the subway steps.

Specifically, my figure signifies by the angle of vision *I* impose on him. In the process, as a fictional sign, he attempts to tell me what fiction's focal function always has been, namely, to explore perceived experience in a particular way with a particular effect.

Also, through the signifying angle, I am expected to transform myself into the terms of the experience of language and its particular slant on language-events, language-characters, language-conflict, and so on.

In the same way, when he is guiding me through a visual composition, of draftsmanship or painting, he works with lines and colors as tools for signifying and focusing. Here, too, he seeks to keep me within a frame—although often a pasty or fluid one.

He causes me to conjure up memories of things that are models in my own personal world. The new things of his structure, fixed state, become signs of, and allusions to, a reality that intensify and diversify what is going on within the frame.

But since fiction and painting were not alike in every single aspect, point of view differed in some important ways from perspective. In point of view traditionally we had the familiar first-person protagonist (the *I*, the *me*, the *my*; or second person; and the third person, *he* or *she*.

And the subdivisions proliferated: the unreliable narrator, third-person limited, third-person multiple, third-person omniscient, and so forth. But in poetry and fiction perspective usually referred to *how* things were seen. In painting, perspective had a more complex function.

It seems the most important difference was this: fiction and poetry were essentially *temporal* in nature; it was also sequential and linear, linear because that was how writing worked.

Painterly perspective had many functions but perspective, in perhaps its most important sense, was about *how* the artist chose to *see* and *organize* things within the frame. When I remembered the differences, I thought I could see why I might not always recognize my figure as the agent of essentially the same function though transformed by the particular decisions I made for him in the frame he happened to be part of.

The figure in the landscape is subject is to a continuous crisis of perspective from age to age, just as he has been there in each moment of a similar sequence of crises in point of view.

Nevertheless, in painting, the basics did not often change: three-dimensional objects on a two-dimensional surface played tricks on the eye; objects seemed far or near, objects looked natural or realistic or impressionistic or expressionistic or surrealistic or cubistic or abstracted, and so on.

In other words, an illusion of space and depth were often rendered to pleasing effect. In linear perspective, receding parallel lines traditionally converged at the horizon. But disruptions to the tradition continued; hence, the crisis.

For my purpose, the word "crisis" referred to "the turning point when an affair must soon terminate" (Webster's). Since such turning points were nearly always just passed and others arriving, no wonder my figure in the landscape has such an anxiety-torn expression. In terms of theme, he's in a permanent crisis.

My figure, therefore, feels like the clown who sits on the trick-stool above the tub of water. The minute he feels secure in his position, a new generation of waters or painters comes along and throws innovative balls at the button of cultural assumptions that will trigger his fall.

When he falls—and fall he must—he invariably remerges the same-but-different. This is natural and constant decomposition and rearrangement, much like that found in Nature.

Some of these turning points, I guess, are more important than others. The fall, for my figure at such times, is harder. He gets caught in a revolution. Though we are shocked by the new we are never surprised by its necessary appearance. One of the first signs that something might be a breakthrough innovation is often detected in what is at first perceived to be its *ugliness*.

One obvious turning point, which may have been even more unsettling than all those preceding it, took place around the end of the nineteenth century. It became clear that neither the senses nor the ways by which people sought to express conclusions (drawn from information gathered through them) could be trusted any longer.

The new scientific thinking began to show that not only could language not explain the universe, mathematics—an undoubtedly better tool for doing so—also had its shortcomings. If both language and mathematics had their shortcomings and had failed science, they failed all the art just as miserably.

The presence of historical logic and its authority were surrendered. Intuitive/conceptual thinking (Romanticism and its fallout) was, for the first time in a long while, challenging the power of the rational and the scientific.

It seemed the Age of Reason had finally ended. Following my figure through all of this action, it might be fair to say that he witnessed himself as an agent in the overthrow of the *expositional* in visual art and literature.

In other words, there was a *conscious* effort to avoid object-as-representation and to *scatter* point of view or perspective. My figure was once again in a tribal setting, freed from mimetic commitments. He and his landscape represented nothing but themselves. He could hardly remember the protocol of Classical Realism or even Impressionism.

Around the same time, in painting, Cézanne's own personal turning point—a shift from the old Cyclopean view of space to that of the Binocular—would soon revolutionize pictorial space altogether. In its own way, the discovery was, to the art of painting and drawing, as important as the theory of relativity is to physics.

The mobile axis (or free-style perspective) gained respectability, and users of it paved the way for the emergence of Cubism and Abstract Expressionism, as well as a return to new forms of radically altered Realism. William Carlos Williams and other poets of his generation also put the mobile axis to use as early as the 1920s in poetry.

Rilke talks about Cézanne painting "on the strength of a single contradiction." Although color contrasts were involved, such as blue/orange and green/red, I felt that the contradiction must have roots deeper than in lines or color.

"Contradiction" was perhaps Rilke's way of talking about Cézanne's active use of the mobile axis. Rilke also understood that Cézanne was not primarily interested in representation and therefore was not interested in the lineal demands and illusions made available by Renaissance perspective. Cézanne used patterns of color to achieve perspective, in a manner not unlike the ancient Egyptians' use of patterns of color to emphasize and to minimize certain aspects of pictorial information.

Rilke also refers to a metaphor he calls the "folding of hands" as an example of the relationship between Nature and Art. I didn't trust it much but duality held its attraction. I could find no way to insist that new forms of point of view or perspective were absolutely unconcerned—in the ways they were used—with finding ways to reinforce representation.

I came across a little prose sketch by Robert Walser called "Thoughts on Cézanne," (1929) in which he echoes or predates Rilke's: "the things to which he [Cézanne] gave shape looked back at him as if they had been pleased, and that is how they look at us still."

The insight gained from Rilke's "folding of hands" achieved its goal in that it led me to conclusions Rilke might have flatly disagreed with. I began to think that the modern relationship between Nature and Art was not necessarily like the *double-ness* or mirroring of that image because the image refuses to completely surrender its hold on representation.

Although the image worked for Rilke, it failed as a general model, for me, when I tried to apply it to movements such as Abstract Expressionism in American painting. Too many mutations had brought my figure into a context where the relationship between Nature and Art required a metaphor designed less on *duality* and more on the *non*representational nature of a thing emerging out of its *own* nature.

At a later point in Rilke's evolving aesthetic, a much more flexible method of interpretation presented itself when he made the observation that Cézanne's paintings "so incorruptibly reduced a reality to its color content that *that* reality resumed a new existence in a beyond of color, without any previous memories."

That "color content" and that "new existence" achieved were not separable from the subjective transformations Cézanne imposed on perspective by way of his mobile "motif" (that is to say, Nature) and its relation to the painting as *thing made.*

This gave me more confidence in achieving some sort of understanding of my own about the equivalences between perspective created from the subjective experiences of the painter and the illusions supported by that which he/she observed.

It also occurred to me that, in fiction writing, for example, an equivalency could be found in letters as signs, in words, and in words as signs, in sentences, and in sentences as signs, in paragraphs, and in paragraphs as units of whole verbal structures with particular focus within frames.

Like Cézanne, Rilke himself was in search of "the smallest constituent element as a means of "expressing everything." Without articulating it as such himself, for Cézanne this meant the basic cube. We can see three sides of it.

The important thing about it is that, from the point of view of the observer, it is known to possess three other *unseen* sides. Knowing this is as important to the conceptual birth of a cubistic work as the seeable sides of the cube. In other words, Cubism was about what was *known* as well as about what was seen.

Both Rilke and Cézanne really were after the "intimations of the say-able." What this said to me by example was that point of view and perspective were basic elements, both having beginnings in "the smallest constituent element," in writing and painting and were *engineering* devices aimed at, among other objectives, establishing balance, and *distance*, between model and object created.

But perhaps more important than those balances or distances was the final, ultimate freedom the thing created achieved from the model, served as an entry point where the viewer might experience epiphany—in the Joycean aesthetic sense.

But that was not the whole story.

I was still thinking of Cézanne and Rilke. In the light of their efforts and aesthetics, there was something I can call *symbolic perspective*. The juggling of symbolic perspective and the use of visual metaphor to create works of concrete *thingness* served as its own truth, though often to many first viewers, there seemed to be some sort of fraudulence going on.

In a similar way, early readers of "breakthrough" texts (such as things by Joyce and Stein) felt they were in the presence of a similar kind of fraudulence. It was usually difficult to distinguish the real innovation—especially with so much of both—from the fake, mainly because these creators took a lot of chances. They were "trying for freedom," as Conrad said of his own efforts.

It was hard to know where the metaphor began and the symbol or sign ended. There were times when they were one and times when they were partly or completely separate. Alterations of angles of vision worked in harmony with eclectic uses of nonrational erotic stimuli and emotionalism. I saw this in the works of Bonnard, Picasso, Gauguin, van Gogh, Conrad, and Gertrude Stein.

The foreground and background sometimes had seemingly new and freshly established relationships. Thus Kenneth Clark's "vividness" was achieved. All aspects of the pictorial space magically were equal.

Something that remains a good example of this for me appeared in a short story by Sherwood Anderson called "Death in the Woods." He summarized the *thingness* of the function of angle of vision in eight words: "*A thing so complete has its own beauty*."

Lines and colors have histories. Poillot, for example, thought that it was possible to suggest just about any human emotion or condition through the nature of lines. Zigzag lines were generally associated with unrest or violent emotion, with vehemence (which corresponded with the effects of short sentences and fragments in writing).

And when you remember and compare them to the delicacy of sensuousness of his nudes, you can begin to trust Poillot. In a similar way, in Newtonian color symbolism, each color had specific emotional personality. Green, for example, suggested the terrestrial. Hogarth felt that a curved line was inseparable from the visual sense of beauty. In a subtle sense, I hoped that, for myself, this sort of scientific exploration might be seen as groundwork for the rebirth of my own experiments in symbolism.

I learned that modern symbolism had deep and wide roots, especially in terms of how some of its principles were used to organize space. Linear perspective—which had been the rule since the Renaissance—had lost ground long before Monet and Degas; massive landscapes of the Italian Renaissance did not exactly obey the mathematics of linear perspective. Certainly, by the time van Gogh and Gauguin, Bonnard and Cézanne were working, the rule of linear perspective had fully given way to a conceptual, or symbolic, approach.

In a lecture titled "Moments of Vision" delivered at Oxford in the early fifties, Kenneth Clark made an interesting observation regarding perspective: "Perspective, by which figures of human size could be related to each other in some plausible and measurable system, tended to paralyze the intuitive faculty by which objects are seen with immediate vividness."

This "immediate vividness" was, I concluded, one of the most essential qualities of symbolic or conceptual perspective. It was the same thing Gauguin sought and what he referred to when he talked about "the mysterious center of thought" as the source for painting. Was this then *the* key to symbolism?

Symbolism, as an organizing principle, or form of perspective, I thought, could be approached in many different ways. In an effort to explain the qualities of form, Helen Keller described what she thought a straight line should *feel* like: "It feels, as I suppose it looks, straight—a dull thought drawn out endlessly. It is un-straight lines," she said, "or many straight and curved lines together, that are eloquent to the touch. They appear and disappear, are now deep, now shallow, now broken off or . . . swelling. They rise and sink beneath my fingers, they are full off sudden starts and pauses, and their variety is un-exhaustible and wonderful."

If you could run your fingertips over the narrative spirit of, say, your favorite poem or short story, this sort of reading of the organizing principles might be the results.

My figure on the scene says, "But how is this different from what I experienced in the mosaics and other remains of the Byzantine empire, for example?" In response I say, "What goes around, comes around."

Finally, as I said in the beginning, I believe that the choice of an angle of vision is the most important decision made at the initial stage of a work of art. This decisive moment not only determines those things mentioned earlier in the sketch of the figure in the landscape, but also controls the nature of narrative and allusions, symbols and tone; how the parts connect; conflict and drama, setting and credibility; action and color, pattern and distribution of space and objects; sense of movement, and so on. My stick figure, for my purposes, is the agent of each of these acts at every turn.

What I've tried to suggest, in several different ways, is that the primal model was in my own nature and experience. The way I exist as an active presence in the world is, of course, partly beyond my own control. But as a writer or painter, I am continuously obliged to make decisions regarding every aspect of composition. Happy accidents also happen. Those are lucky moments. The quality of any of those decisions necessarily depends on the clarity and depth of those initial ones I've been talking about.

Necessary Distance

Afterthoughts on Becoming a Writer

People have a tendency to ask a writer, *Why* did you become a writer? *How* did you become a writer? Every writer hears such questions over and over. You ever hear anybody ask a butcher a question like that?

So, what's so special about being a writer? Maybe we are simply fascinated by people who are brave (or foolish) enough to go against—and lucky enough to beat—the odds.

We seem fascinated in the same way by the lives of people in show business, and probably for the same reasons the lives of writers interest us.

It is also always amazing to see someone making a living doing something he or she actually enjoys.

I never seriously tried to deal with these questions till I was asked to write my life story. If my autobiography were going to make sense, I thought I'd better try my best to answer both questions.

So, my speaking on the page to you is, in a way, an effort to answer those questions—for myself and possibly for others. I don't expect to succeed, but here goes.

It seems to me that the impulse to write, the *need* to write, is inseparable from one's educational process—which begins at the beginning and never ends.

In some sort of nonobjective way, I can remember being an infant and some of the things I thought about and touched. I had a sister, but my sister didn't have a brother. I had no self because I was *all* self. Gradually, like any developing kid, I shed my self-centered view of the world: saw myself reflected in my mother's eyes, began to perceive the idea of a self. In a way it was at this point that my research as a writer, and as a painter, began. (For me, the two impulses were always inseparable.) The world was a place of magic, and everything I touched was excruciatingly *new.* Without knowing it, my career had begun.

In his meditation on the art of fiction, *Being and Race,* novelist Charles Johnson writes, "All art points to others with whom the writer argues about what is. . . . He must have models with which to agree . . . or outright oppose

. . . for Nature seems to remain silent." Reading this passage reminds me of Sherwood Anderson's short story "Death in the Woods," in which the narrator retells the story we are reading because his brother, who told it first, hadn't told it the way it was supposed to be told. In a similar way, that early self of mine had already started its long battle with the history of literature and art.

In the early stages of the battle, some very primary things were going on. By this I mean to say that a writer is usually a person who has to learn how to keep his ego—like his virginity—and lose it at the same time. In other words, he becomes a kind of twin of himself. He remains the self-centered infant while transcending him to become the observer of his own experience and, by extension, the observer of a wide range of experience within his cultural domain. Without any rational self-conscious at all, early on, my imagination was fed by the need to invent things. My older cousins taught me how to make my own toys—trucks, cars, houses, and whole cities. We used old skate wheels for tires. Our parents couldn't afford such luxuries as toys; we were lucky if we got new clothes. Watching physical things like the toys we made take shape, I think, showed me some possibilities. (William Carlos Williams said a poem is like a machine. If I understand what he meant, I can see a connection between what I was making at age seven and the poems and stories I tried to write later on.)

Plus, the *newness* of everything—trees, plants, the sky—and the need to define everything, on my own terms, was a given. At my grandparents' farm, my cousins and I climbed trees and named the trees we climbed. Painfully, I watched my uncle slaughter hogs and learned about death. I watched my grandmother gather eggs from the chicken nests and learned about birth. I watched her make lye soap and the clothes we wore. But I didn't fully trust the world I was watching. It seemed too full of danger, even while I dared to explore it and attempt to imprint the evidence of my presence upon it—by making things such as toys or drawing pictures in the sand.

Daydreaming as a necessity in the early disposition of a writer is not a new idea. Whether or not it was necessary in my case, I was a guilty practitioner. I say this because I had an almost mystical attachment to nature. If looked at from my parents' point of view, it was not a good sign. I could examine a leaf for hours or spend hours on my knees watching the way ants lived. Behaving like a lazy kid, I followed the flights and landings of birds with spiritual devotion. The frame of mind that put me through those motions was, later, the same frame of mind from which I tried to write a poem or a story: daydreaming, letting it happen, connecting two or three previously unrelated things, making them mean something—together—entirely new. I was hopeless.

And dreams. In dreams I discovered a self that was going about its business with a mind of its own. I began to watch and wonder. I was amazed by some of the things I had the nerve to dream about. Sex, for example. Or some wonderful, delicious food! One guilty pleasure after another! This other self often invented these wonderful ways for me to actually get something—even a horse once—that I *knew* I wanted, something no one seriously wanted to give me.

At times, waking up was the hard part. Dream activity was all invention, maybe even the rootbeds of all the conscious, willful invention I wanted to take charge of in the hard indifference of daylight. Unlike the daydreams I spent so much time giving myself to, *these* dreams were not under my control. Later, I started trying to write them down, but I discovered it was impossible to capture their specific texture. They had to stay where they were. But I tried to imitate them, to make up stories that *sounded* like them. The pattern of these dreams became a model for the imaginative leaps I wanted to make (and couldn't for a long time!) in my poetry and fiction.

My first novel was twenty-pages long. I was twelve when I wrote it. It was the story of a wild, free-spirited horse leading a herd. Influenced by movies, I thought it would make a terrific film, so I sent it to Hollywood. A man named William Self read it and sent it back with a letter of encouragement. I never forgot his kindness. It was the beginning of a long process of learning to live with rejection—not just rejection slips. And that experience too was necessary as a correlation to the writing process, necessary because one of the most important things I was going to have to learn was *how* to detect my own failures and be the first to reject them.

Was there, then, a particular point when I said *Hey! I'm going to become a writer!* I think there was, but it now seems irrelevant because I must have been evolving toward that conscious moment long, long before I had any idea what was going on. (I was going to have to find my way—with more imperfection than not—through *many* disciplines, such as painting, music, anthropology, history, philosophy, psychology, sociology—before such a consciousness would begin to emerge.)

I think I was in the fifth grade when a girl who sat behind me snuck me a copy of Raymond Radiguet's *Devil in the Flesh*. This was *adult fiction!* And judging from the cover, the book was going to have some good parts. But as it turned out, the *single* good part was the writing itself. I was reading that book one day at home, and about halfway through, I stood up and went crazy with an important discovery: *Writing had a life of its own!* And I soon fell in love with the life of writing, by way of this book—Kay Boyle's translation of Radiguet.

From that moment on, up to about the age of twenty, I set out to discover other books that might challenge my perception forever. Hawthorne's *The*

Scarlett Letter showed me how gracefully a story could be told and how terrifying human affairs—and self-deception within those affairs—can be. Conrad's *Heart of Darkness* caught me in an aesthetic network of magic so powerful I never untangled myself. I then went on to read other nineteenth-century, and even earlier, works by Melville, Baudelaire, Emerson, Dostoyevsky, and the like.

But I always hung on with more comfort to the twentieth century. I read J. D. Salinger's *The Catcher in the Rye* early enough for it to have spoken profoundly and directly to me about what I was feeling and thinking about the adult world at the time that its agony affirmed my faith in life. Richard Wright's *Native Son* was an overwhelming experience, and so was Rimbaud's poetry. But the important thing about these discoveries is that each of them led to Cocteau and other French writers, going back to the nineteenth century. Salinger led me to a discovery of modern and contemporary American fiction—Hemingway, Faulkner, Sherwood Anderson, and on and on. Wright led to Dos Passos, to James T. Farrell, to Jean Toomer, to Chester Himes, to William Gardener Smith, to Ann Petry, to Nella Larsen and other Afro-American writers. Rimbaud led to the discovery of American poetry (which was not so much of a leap as it sounds), to Williams, to Marianne Moore, to Eliot, to cummings. This activity began roughly during the last year of grade school and took on full, focused direction in high school. At the time, none of these writers was being taught in school. I was reading them on my own. In school we had to read O. Henry and Joyce Kilmer.

But during all this time, it was hard to find books that came *alive.* I had to go through hundreds before hitting on the special ones, the ones with the power to shape or reshape perception, to deepen vision, to give me the means to understand myself and other things, to drive away fears and doubts. I found the possibilities of wedding the social and political self to the artistic self in the essays of James Baldwin. Autobiographies such as Billie Holiday's *Lady Sings the Blues* and Mezz Mezzrow's *Really the Blues* were profound reading experiences. These books, and books like them, taught me that even life, with more pain than any one individual had any right to, was still worth spending some time trying to get through—and, like Billie's and Mezz's, with dignity and inventiveness.

Although I was learning to appreciate good writing, I had no command of the language myself. I had the *need* to write well, but that was about all. Only the most sensitive teacher—and there were two or three along the way—was able to detect some talent and imagination in my efforts. Every time I gathered enough courage to dream of writing seriously, the notion ended in frustration, or sometimes despair. Not only did I not have command of the language,

I didn't have the necessary distance on experience to have anything important to say about even the things I knew something about.

I daydreamed about a solution to these problems: I could learn to write and go out and live it up in order to have something to experience. But this solution would take time, and I was not willing to wait. In my sense of urgency, I didn't have that much time.

Meanwhile, there were a few adults I ventured to show my efforts to. One teacher told me I couldn't possibly have written the story I showed her. It was *too good*—which meant that it was a hell of a lot better than I had thought. But rather than gaining more self-confidence, the experience became grounds for the loss of respect for her intelligence. Among the other adults who saw my early works were my mother, who encouraged me as much as her understanding permitted, and a young, college-educated man who was a family friend. He told me I was pretty good.

I was growing up in Chicago, and my life therefore had a particular social shape. The realities I was discovering in books didn't, at first, seem to correspond to the reality around me. At the time, I didn't have enough distance to see the connections.

The fact is, the writerly disposition that was then evolving was shaped not only by my life in Chicago—in the classroom and on the playground—but also during the times I spent alone with books—and anywhere else for that matter. Which is only one way of saying that a writer doesn't always make the most of his or her own decisions about personal vision or outlook.

Jean Paul Sartre in *What Is Literature?* makes the observation that Richard Wright's destiny as a writer was chosen for him by the circumstances of birth and social history. One can go even further and say that it's as difficult to draw the line between where a sensibility is influenced by the world around it and where it asserts its own presence in that world as it is to say whether or not essence precedes existence.

To put it another way, the educational process against which my would-be writerly disposition was taking formation was political. Political because I quickly had to learn how to survive, for example, on the playground. It was not easy because I had an instinctive dislike for violence. But the playground was a place where the dramas of life were acted out. Radiguet's book (and Jean Paul Rossi's *Awakening*, too) had, to some extent, dealt with the same territory. As a microcosm of life, it was no doubt one of the first social locations in which I was forced to observe some of the ways people relate—or don't relate—to each other. Among a number of things, I learned how to survive the pecking order rituals with my wits rather than my fists. This was an area where books and art could not save me. But later on, I was going to see how what I *had* to learn in self-defense carried over to the creative effort.

The classroom, too, was not a place where one wanted to let one's guard down for too long. To be liked and singled out by a teacher often meant getting smashed in the mouth or kicked in the stomach on the playground. If one demonstrated intelligence in school, one could almost certainly expect to hear about it later on the way home. It was simply not cool for boys to be smart in class. A smart boy was a sissy and deserved to get his butt kicked.

I had to be very quiet about my plans to become a writer. I couldn't talk with friends about what I read. I mean, why wasn't I out playing basketball?

All of this, in terms of education (or plans to become a writer), meant that if you wanted to learn anything (or try to write something, for example), you had to do it without *flaunting* what you were doing. Naturally some smart but less willful kids gave in, in the interest of survival; they learned how to fail in order to live in the safety zone of the majority. And for those of us who didn't want to give in, it was hard to keep how well we were doing a secret because the teacher would tell the class who got the best grades.

I was also facing another crisis. If I wanted to write, eventually I had to face an even larger problem—publication. I thought that if I were ever lucky enough to get anything published, say in a school magazine or newspaper, it would be a success I would have to keep quiet about among most of my friends, and certainly around those out to put me in my place. And God forbid that my first published work should be a poem. Only sissies wrote poetry.

But I couldn't go on like that. I remember once breaking down and saying to hell with it. I walked around the school building with a notebook writing down everything I saw, trying to translate the life around me, minute by minute, into words. I must have filled twenty pages with very boring descriptions. A girl I liked, but didn't have the nerve to talk to, saw me. She thought I was doing homework. When I told her what I was up to, she gave me this strange, big-eyed look, then quickly disappeared—forever—from my life.

I now realize that I must have been a difficult student for teachers to understand. At times I was sort of smart, at other times I left a lot to be desired. One teacher thought I might be retarded, another called me a genius. Not knowing what else to do with me, the administrators, in frustration, appointed me art director of the whole school of 8,000 students during my last year.

Why the art director? Actually, my first passion was for painted pictures rather than the realities I discovered in books. Before my first clear memories I was drawing and painting, while the writing started at a time within memory.

So, I think it is important (in the context of "how" and "why," where the writing is concerned) to try to understand what this visual experience has meant for me.

At about the age of twelve, I started taking private art lessons from a South Side painter, Gus Nall. I even won a few prizes. So, confidence in an ability to visually express myself came first. But what I learned from painting, I think, carried over into my writing from the beginning.

My first articulate passion was for the works of Vincent van Gogh. This passion started with a big show of his work that the Art Institute of Chicago hung in the early fifties. There were about a hundred and fifty pieces.

I pushed my way through the crowded galleries, stunned every step of the way. I kept going back. I was not sophisticated enough to know how to articulate for myself what these things were doing to me, but I knew I was profoundly moved. So, on some level, I no doubt did sense the power of the painterliness of the pictures of winding county paths, working peasants, flower gardens, rooftops, and the stillness of a summer day. They really got to me.

Something in me went out to the energy of Vincent's *Sunflowers*, for example. I saw him as one who broke the rules and transcended. Where I came from, no socially well-behaved person ever went out and gathered sunflowers for a vase in the home. No self-respecting grown man spent ten years painting pictures he couldn't sell. On the South Side of Chicago, everything of value had a price tag.

Vincent, then, was at least one important model for my rebellion. The world I grew up in told me that the only proper goals were to make money, get an education, become a productive member of society, go to church, and have a family—pretty much in that order. But I had found my alternative models, and it was too late for that world to get its hooks in me. I wasn't planning to do anything less than the greatest thing I could think of: I wanted to be like van Gogh, like Richard Wright, like Jean Toomer, like Rimbaud, like Bud Powell.

In the meantime, I went home from the van Gogh exhibition and tried to create the same effects from life around me. I drew my stepfather soaking his feet in a pan of water, my older sister braiding my younger sister's hair, the bleak view of rooftops from my bedroom window, my mother in bed sick, anything that struck me as compositionally viable. In this rather haphazard way, I was learning to *see*. I suspect there was a certain music and innocence in Vincent's lines and colors that gave me a foundation for my own attempts at *representing*—first through drawing and painting, and, very soon after, in the poetry I was writing. The first poems I tried to write were strongly imagistic, in the symbolist tradition.

I made thousands of sketches of these sorts of everyday things. I was responding to the things of my world. I had already lived in two or three different worlds: in a southern city (Atlanta); in a rural country setting; and now in Chicago, an urban, brutal, stark setting. We moved a lot—so much so that my sense of place was always changing. Home was where we happened to be. Given this situation, I think the fact that Vincent felt like an alien in his own land (and actually was an alien in France) and that his sense of estrangement carried over emotionally into his work found a strong correlating response in me.

If there were disadvantages in being out of step, there were just as many advantages. I was beginning to engage myself passionately in painting and writing, and this passion would carry me through a lot of difficulties and disappointments simply because I *had* it. I saw many people with no strong interest in *anything*. Too many of them perished for lack of a dream long before I thought possible.

At fourteen, this passionate need to create (and apparently the need to *share* it, too) caused me to try to go public, despite the fact that I knew I was doing something eccentric. One of my uncles ran a printing shop. I gathered up enough confidence in my poetry to pay him ten dollars to print fifty copies of a little booklet of my own poetry. The poems reflect the influence of Rimbaud, van Gogh, and Impressionism generally—even used French words I didn't understand.

Once I had the books in hand, I realized that I didn't know more than three people who might be interested in seeing a copy. I gave one to one of my English teachers. I gave my mother three copies. I gave my best poet friend a copy. I may have also given my art teacher, Mr. Fouche, a copy. And the rest of the edition was stored in a closet. They stayed there till, by chance, a year or two later I discovered how bad the poems were and destroyed the remaining copies.

Shortly after the van Gogh exhibition, the Institute sponsored a large showing of the works of Paul Cézanne, whose work I knew a bit from the few pieces in the permanent collection. I went to the exhibit not so much because I was attracted to Cézanne but because it was there—and I felt that I should appreciate Cézanne. At fifteen that was not easy. And the reasons I found it difficult to appreciate Cézanne as much as I thought I should had to do with, I later learned, my inability to understand at a gut level what he was about, what his *intentions* were. Cézanne's figures looked stiff and ill-proportioned. His landscapes, like his still lifes, seemed made of stone or wood or metal. Everything in Cézanne was unbending, lifeless.

I looked at the apples and oranges on the table and understood their *weight* and how important the *sense* of that weight was in understanding Cézanne's intentions. I wanted to say, yes, it's a great accomplishment. But why couldn't

I *like it?* I was not yet sophisticated enough to realize that all great art—to the unsophisticated viewer—at first appears *ugly,* even repulsive. And I had yet to discover Gertrude Stein in any serious way, to discover her attempts to do with words what Cézanne was doing with lines and color.

It took many years to acquire an appreciation for Cézanne, but doing so, in its way, was as important to my development as a writer as was my passion for van Gogh. But the appreciation started, in its troubled way, with that big show. When I finally saw the working out of the *sculpturing* of a created reality (to paraphrase James Joyce), I experienced a breakthrough. Cézanne appealed to my rational side. I began going to Cézanne for a knowledge of the inner, mechanical foundation of art, and for an example of a self-conscious exploration of composition. All of this effort slowly taught me how to *see* the significant aspects of writing and how they corresponded to those in painting. Discovering how perspective corresponded to point of view was a real high point.

These two painters, van Gogh and Cézanne, were catalysts for me, but there were other painters important for similar reasons: Toulouse-Lautrec, Degas, Bonnard, Cassatt, and Munch for the way they intensely scrutinized private and public moments; Edward Hopper for his ability to invest a view of a house or the interior of a room with a profound sense of mortality; Matisse for his play, his rhythm, his design. I was attracted by the intimacy of the subject matter in their work.

I also had very strong responses to Gauguin. He excited and worried me at the same time. At first, I was suspicious of a European seeking purity among dark people. (I placed D. H. Lawrence in the same category.) Later, I realized Gauguin's story was more complex than that (as was Lawrence's). But more important to me was the fact that Gauguin's paintings used flat, blunt areas of vivid colors. Their sumptuousness drew a profoundly romantic response from me. Not only did I try to paint that way for a period, I also thought I saw the possibility of creating simple, flat images with simple sentences or lines.

For a while I was especially attracted to painters who used paint thickly. Turner's seascapes were incredible. Up close they looked abstract. Utrillo's scenes of Paris, Rouault's bumpy people, Albert Ryder's horrible dreams, Kokoschka's profusion of layered effects—these rekindled feelings that had started with van Gogh. (Years later, I came to appreciate Beckman and Schiele for similar reasons.) To paint that way—expressively, and apparently fast—had a certain appeal. It was just a theory, but worth playing with; in correlation, it might be possible to make words move with that kind of self-apparent urgency, that kind of reflexive brilliance. The expressionistic writers—Lawrence, Mansfield, Joyce, and others—had done it.

I kept moving from one fascination to another. Later, the opposite approach attracted me. The lightness of Picasso's touch was as remarkable as a pelican in flight. If I could make a painting or poem move like that—like the naturalness of walking or sleeping—I would be lucky.

I was easily seduced. I got lost in the dreams of Chagall, in the summer laziness of Monet, in the waves of Winslow Homer, in the blood and passion of Orozco, in the bright, simple designs of Rivera, in the fury of Jackson Pollock, in the struggle of de Kooning, in the selflessness of Vermeer, in the light and shadow of Rembrandt, in the plushness of Rubens, in the fantastic mystery of Bosch, in the power of Michelangelo and Tintoretto, in the incredible sensitivity and intelligence of Leonardo da Vinci, in the earthly dramas of Daumier and Millet. Later on, when I discovered Afro-American art, I got equally caught up in the works of Jacob Lawrence, Archibald Motley, Henry Tanner, Edward Bannister, and others. I was troubled from the beginning by the absence of Afro-American painters, novelists, and poets, generally, whom I might have turned to as models. I was seventeen and on my own before I discovered the *reason* they were absent: The system had hidden them. It was that simple. They had existed since the beginning but were, for well-known reasons, made officially nonexistent.

Although this learning process was a slow and very long one, and I wasn't always conscious of even the things I successfully managed to transfer into my own painting and writing, I can now look back and realize that I must always have been more fascinated by technique than I was by subject matter. The subject of a novel or a painting seemed irrelevant: a nude, a beach scene, a stand of trees, a story of an army officer and a seventeen-year-old girl in a foreign country, a lyrical view of a horrible accident. It didn't matter! What did matter was *how* the painter or storyteller or poet seduced me into the story, into the picture, into the poem.

I guess I also felt the need to submerge myself in the intellectual excitement of an artistic community, but I couldn't find one. Just about every writer I'd ever heard of seemed to have had such nourishment: Hemingway, Stein, and Fitzgerald in Paris among other expatriates. . . . But I was not in touch with any sort of exciting literary or artistic life (outside visits to the Institute) on the South Side. True, I had met a couple of writers—Willard Motley and Frank London Brown—and a few painters—Gus Nall, Archibald Motley, and a couple of others. But I felt pretty isolated. Plus these people were a lot older and didn't seem to have much time to spare. So, I clumsily started my own little magazine—a thing called *Coercion Review*. It became my substitute for an artistic community and, as such, a means of connecting (across the country and even across the ocean) with a larger, cultural world—especially with other writers and poets.

I published the works of writers I corresponded with, and they published mine; in a way, this became our way of *workshopping,* as my students say, our manuscript. When we found something acceptable, it meant (or so we thought) that the particular piece had succeeded. We were wrong more often than not. It was an expensive way to learn what *not* to publish, and how to live with what couldn't be unpublished.

Seeing my work in print increased my awareness of the many problems I still faced in my writing at, say, the age of eighteen. I wrote to William Carlos Williams for help. I also wrote to Langston Hughes. They were generous. (In fact, Williams not only criticized the poetry but also told me of his feelings of despair as a poet.)

Rushing into print was teaching me that I not only needed distance on approach (the selection of point of view, for example) and subject matter *before* starting a work, but I also needed to slow down, to let a manuscript wait, to see if it could stand up under my own developing ability to edit during future readings, when my head would be clear of manuscript birth fumes. As a result, my awareness of what I was doing, of its aesthetic value, increased. I became more selective about what I sent out.

During all this time, I was also listening to music. Critics of Afro-American writing often find reason to compare black writing to black music. Each of my novels, at one time or another, has been compared to either blues songs or jazz compositions. I've never doubted that critics had a right to do this. But what was I to make of the fact that I had also grown up with Tin Pan Alley, bluegrass, *and* European classical music? I loved Chopin and Beethoven.

Something was wrong. It seemed to me that Jack Kerouac, for example, had gotten as many jazz motifs into his work as James Baldwin. At a certain point, when I noticed that critics were beginning to see rhythms of music as a basis for my lines or sentences, to say nothing of content, I backed up and took a closer look. I had to argue, at least with myself, that all of the music I'd loved while growing up found its aesthetic way into my writing—or none of it did.

True, I had been overwhelmingly caught up in the bebop music of Bud Powell when I was a kid—I loved "Un Poco Loco," thought it was the most inventive piece of music I had ever heard, loved all of his original compositions ("Hallucinations," "I Remember Clifford," "Oblivion," "Glass Enclosure," and on and on—and as I said before, I swore by the example of his devotion to his art).

But I soon moved on out, in a natural way, from Powell into an appreciation of the progressive music of other innovators, such as Thelonius Monk,

Lester Young, Sonny Stitt, John Coltrane, Clifford Brown, Miles Davis, Dizzy Gillespie, Charlie Parker, Dexter Gordon, and Ornette Coleman—and, at the same time, I was discovering Jimmy Rushing, Bessie Smith, Billie Holiday, Joe Turner, Dinah Washington—singers from my father's generation and before.

My feeling, on this score, is that Afro-American music generally (along with other types of music I grew up hearing) had a pervasive cultural importance for me. I think I needed to take this assumption into consideration in trying to trace in myself the shape of what I hope has become some sort of sensitivity not only to music but also to poetry, fiction, painting, and the other arts. I've already mentioned the importance of other disciplines—anthropology, history, philosophy, psychology, and sociology—in an attempt to lay some sort of intellectual foundation from which to write. Without going through the long, hopelessly confusing tangle of my own profoundly troubled questing, I think I can sum up what I came away with (as it relates to themes I chose or the themes that chose me) in pretty simple terms.

I remember my excitement when I began to understand cultural patterns. Understanding the nature of kinship—family, clan, tribe—gave me insight into relationships in the context of my own family, community, and country. I was also fascinated to discover, while reading about tribal people, something called a caste system. I immediately realized that I had grown up in communities, both in the South and the North, where one kind of caste system or another was practiced. Being extremely light or extremely dark, for example, often meant being penalized by the community.

Totem practices also fascinated me because I was able to turn from books and see examples in everyday life: There were people who wore good-luck charms and fetishes such as rabbits' feet on keychains. I became aware, in deeper ways, of the significance of ritual and ceremony, and how to recognize examples when I saw them. It was a breakthrough for me to begin to understand *how* cultures (my own included) rationalized their own behavior.

The formation of myths—stories designed to explain why things were as they were—was of deep interest to me. Myths, I discovered, governed the behavior and customs I saw every day, customs concerning matters of birth, death, parents, grandparents, marriage, grief, luck, dances, husband-and-wife relationships, siblings, revenge, joking, adoption, sexual relations, murder, fights, food, toilet training, game playing. You name it.

Reading Freud, and other specialists of the mind, I thought would help me understand better how to make characters more convincing. At the same time, I hoped to get a better insight into myself—which in the long run would also improve my writing. I read Freud's little study of Leonardo da Vinci. I was also interested in gaining a better understanding of the nature of creativity itself.

But even more than that, I was interested in the religious experiences psychologists wrote about. I consciously sought ways to understand religious frenzy and faith in rational terms. I was beginning to think how, as too much nationalism tends to lead to fascism, too much blind religion could be bad for one's mental health. To me, the human mind and the human heart began to look like very, very dangerously nebulous things. But at the same time, I kept on trying to accept the world and its institutions at face value, to understand them on their own terms. After all, who was I to come along and seriously question *everything*? The degree to which I did question was more from innocence than arrogance.

I was actually optimistic because I thought knowledge might lead me somewhere refreshing, might relieve the burden of ignorance. If I could only understand schizophrenia or hysteria, mass brainwashing and charisma, paganism, asceticism, brotherly love. Why did some individuals feel called to preach while others feel overwhelmed with galloping demons? What was the function of dreaming? I skimmed the Kinsey reports and considered monastic life. I read Alan Watts and was a Buddhist for exactly one week.

I liked the gentle way Reich criticized Freud and, in the process, chiseled out his own psychoanalytical principles. If I ever thought psychoanalysis could help me personally, I was not mad enough to think I could afford it. I did notice, though, how writers of fiction, and poets too, from around the turn of the century on, were using the principles of psychoanalysis as a tool for exploring behavior in fiction and poetry. So I gave it a shot. But the real challenge, I soon learned, was to find a way to absorb some of this stuff and at the same time keep the evidence of it out of my own writing.

Yet I kept hoping for some better, more suitable approach to human experience. If a better one existed, I had no idea. But there wasn't much to hold on to in psychoanalysis or psychology, and even less in sociology, where I soon discovered that statistics could be made to prove anything the researcher wanted to prove. If the *very presence* of the researcher was itself a contamination, what hope was there for this thing everybody called objectivity?

While I was able to make these connections between theory and reality, I was still seeking answers to questions I had asked since the beginning—*Who and what am I?*—questions we discover later in life are not so important. Everywhere I turned—to philosophy, to psychology—I was turned back upon myself and left with more questions than I had at the start.

Growing up in America when I did, while aiming to be a writer, was a disturbing experience. (Every generation is sure it is more disturbed than the previous one and less lucky than the forthcoming one.) This troublesome feeling was real, though; it wasn't just growing pains. There was something else, and I knew it. And I finally found part of the explanation. My sense of myself was hampered by my country's sense of itself. My country held an idealistic image of itself that was, in many aspects of its life, vastly different from its actual, unvarnished self. There was severe poverty, ignorance, disease, corruption, racism, sexism, and there was war—all too often undeclared.

But I, as a writer, could not afford the luxury of a vision of my own experience as sentimental as the one suggested by my country (of itself, of me). As I grew up, I was trying to learn how to see through the superficial, and to touch, in my writing, the essence of experience—in all of its possible wonderment, agony, or glory.

Despite the impossibility of complete success, I continue.

I want to be as forthright as possible with these afterthoughts because I know that afterthoughts can never *truly* recapture the moments they try to touch back upon. Each moment, it seems to me, in which a thought occurs has more to do with that moment itself than with anything in the past. This, to my way of thinking, turns out to be more positive than negative, because it supports the continuous nature of life, and that of art, too. The creative memory, given expression, is no enemy of the past, nor does its self-focus diminish its authority.

A Paris Fantasy Transformed

Paris! Why Paris? Why did I—or any African American artist or writer—go to Paris?

When I was a teenager in the 1950s, African American artists (and writers, dancers, jazz musicians, actors) had already enjoyed a long relationship with Paris. Even before the end of slavery, free mulattos, some of them artists, were traveling to Paris and other parts of Europe. They went for many different reasons. One of the best known of those who went in the nineteenth century was the painter Henry O. Tanner.

In retrospect, I realize that my motives for going to Paris were similar to those of the people who had gone before me. Although they had various personal reasons for settling in Paris, there was a commonality about their motives. Beauford Delaney, for example, in 1951, stopped in Paris on his way to Rome, found there the artistic nourishment he needed, and stayed.

As a young man, I read Richard Wright and James Baldwin, and knew they lived in Paris. Baldwin, who was a good friend of Delaney's, said African Americans went to Paris because "We . . . had presumably put down all formulas and all safety in favor of the chilling unpredictability of experience."

Considering this history, I can now see how I, as a teenager, got focused on a fantasy of Paris as a desirable place to live, paint, and write. I had been lucky enough to win a scholarship to attend the James Nelson Raymond lecture and sketch classes at the Art Institute of Chicago, where, by the way, I spent a lot of time in front of Tanner's "Two Disciples at the Tomb," gazing at the dramatic light on the faces of Peter and John. At the Institute, my earliest fantasies of Paris fed on scenes of the city by French painters—especially those of Maurice Utrillo's views of Montmartre. Paris was the place of so much that interested me. Art! Poetry! Philosophy! I remember at age seventeen struggling through a book by Sartre on Existentialism, understanding perhaps only 20 percent of it.

The presence of Paris was also surprisingly vivid on the South Side of Chicago while I was growing up. The painter Archibald Motley was back from Paris, living in Chicago. We both had paintings in Gayles Gallery on Sixty-third. I admired his cool, gray Paris café and street life paintings. Ex-Parisian jazz singer Lil Armstrong (Louis's first wife) held a kind of Chicago salon for young artists like me. Regularly I also saw Ollie Harrington's funny, humane "Bootsie" cartoons in the black newspapers, sent over from Paris, where he lived. And Josephine Baker used to come over to our neighborhood in Chicago and dance for us on the stage of the Regal Theater at Forty-seventh and South Parkway. She brought with her what I imagined was the glamour of Paris.

But the Paris I fantasized about most often was a Paris of grimy bistros, Toulouse-Lautrec–type dance halls, narrow dark streets, dimly lit bars in Montmartre, small dusty bookshops, the rue des Lombards, the rue Blomet—a nocturnal Paris, a place of outcasts, poets, and artists. Orwell's *Down and Out in Paris and London* gave me a vivid picture of the "solitary half-mad grooves of life" lived in these areas. This was, in a sense, also Henry Miller's postwar Paris.

Definitely not Hemingway's young man "lucky enough to have lived in Paris" before a certain age and therefore able to carry always in my bosom a "moveable feast." I didn't get around to going to Paris till I was thirty-five. By then I had somehow become more visible as a novelist and poet than as a painter, though I was still painting persistently. But on this first trip there, caught up in the endless tourist rounds, my fantasy-Paris was nowhere in sight. My frustration was almost enough to cause me to agree with Virginia Woolf when she wrote, "Paris is a hostile brilliant city."

But subsequent trips showed me Paris was no more hostile than any other big city and considerably more brilliant—and beautiful—as can be seen, for example, in Delaney's street scenes. His impasto technique, whirling expressionistic lines, called to mind van Gogh and the Fauves. I'll never forget a day in 1982, in the South of France in Jimmy Baldwin's home, when I found myself in a room full of Delaney canvases.

Although I also lived and taught, for a year and a half, at the University of Nice (near Jimmy's home), it was in Paris, with all the various trips stitched together as a kind of tapestry, that the real artistic nourishment happened. Because I paint, Paris was a special, symbolic place for me. But as a writer, I found just as much inspiration there.

Paris provided me with some of the same aesthetic energy and freedom that it had always given artists. I went there again and again to connect with that energy. A city that named its streets after artists and writers, not politicians, was my kind of city. A city that had so many art museums and galleries that art seemed part of daily life, in my book, was not an exotic city but a sensible one.

Yet how was I personally rewarded and changed by this real Paris sojourn? While staying in various parts of the city during the eighties, and for an extended period in 1985 in the 11th Arrondissement, near Pere-Lachaise Cemetery,

I came to make a Paris of my own. We Americans were getting seven francs to the dollar, so my wife, Pamela, and I felt we could splurge occasionally, but there were always wonderful things to do for free. Walking through the cemetery and reading the headstones was a chance to touch many who had fed my earlier fantasies—Seurat, Modigliani, Gertrude Stein, Richard Wright himself.

Seeing the difference between my American culture and the French helped reveal who I had been and who I was now becoming. Paradoxically, Paris gave me my national identity, although I hadn't gone there looking for that part of myself.

To be sure, there was as much racism in France as in the States, but in Paris, I was not the target of French racism. As soon as the French discovered I was not an African or Arab from one of their former colonies, I was treated well. This was an ironic and ambiguous position to be in.

All my life, in my own country, I had seen Americans treat Africans and Arabs—people they had no historical ties to—with the same kind of dubious respect. Despite its questionable basis, it was better treatment than black Americans got. The point is, in Paris—as pathetic as it sounds—I *felt American* for the first time, and in a way I had never felt at home.

Plus, Pamela and I found that Parisian life itself—in the way we lived our day-to-day life—was sensible and satisfying. We came to know the neighborhood shopkeepers and vendors, and they us. Like those before us, we had our favorite cafés in our own neighborhood, and the waiters, after a time, didn't need to be told what to bring to the table. I would amuse Pamela by making up stories about other customers or passersby. In my sketchbook, I'd jot down the outline of an interesting face or try to capture the motion of an interesting man or woman walking by. In one such café, off Place de La Reunion, we could sit for hours watching the cat in the window watching the people walking by, or sit in the park across the street and watch the children play. This Paris was far from that grimy rue Blomet Paris, or the dark, mysterious rue des Lombards of my fantasy. It was closer to Renoir's or Degas's Paris.

Venturing beyond the neighborhood, we of course always ran into tourists. Because of them, galleries and museums tended to be crowded. One night, Pamela came up with a plan to get around the problem. The next morning, we rushed off to the Jeu de Paume to be at the front of the line. When the doors opened, instead of doing the first floor with the mob, we shot directly upstairs and had all the great van Goghs to ourselves for almost an hour. Our skipping the first floor confused the guards, and for a while they watched us closely, obviously on the lookout for any further false moves on our part. When the mob hit the second floor, we were ready to go.

The last time Pamela and I were in Paris, one of the first things we did on our last full day was to walk along Quai de Gesvres. It was one of those clear spring mornings that make you happy. We could see Notre-Dame. A tourist boat was moving slowly down river toward the port at Hotel de Ville. From the boat people waved and we waved back.

But, despite the precariousness of my status as a foreigner, I felt consistently good about being in Paris. And I understood what Elizabeth Barrett Browning felt while on her honeymoon there, when she wrote to a friend that she and Robert "were satisfied with the *idea* of Paris."

Rhythm

Talking That Talk

My interest in informal speech is long-standing. I edited two dictionaries of African American "slang," an anecdotal one in 1970, and a scholarly one in 1994. The latter was not an embellishment of the earlier one. The interest stems from two concerns: one, for the richness and the way informal speech nourishes formal speech, and two, for the ways I could possibly use that richness in my own writing.

Slang has never had a consistently good reputation. Often it is characterized as much by arrogance, bigotry, sexism, and self-contempt as by humor, compassion, and wisdom. But it also happens to be the most alive aspect of our language. My goal, at least in part, was to help bring to the language we call slang a better name, a better reputation; and to suggest, by the example of those dictionaries, how intrinsic it is to the quest of human culture to express and to renew itself.

Also, there is the sense that slang is tolerated because, for the most part (in the minds of some critics), it belongs to the young, the youth culture, and there is the sense, or hope, that they will eventually grow out of it, advance to standard speech, which, the official guardians of the culture seem to hope, will signal their acceptance of the status quo. J. L. Dillard makes the point in *Lexicon of Black English* (1977, 17), that the word "slang" itself has caused many people to take lightly or negatively a complex and rich language: "The general public has long associated slang with a transitory stage in the language development of teenagers, soon to be dropped by all except those few who never enter the adult, mainstream world. "Slang" was, for the average American, an exotic language phenomenon primarily for children outside the domain of working language and not ready to be considered seriously."

Kids aside, maybe the case is more pervasive and serious than that. Slang has always been considered, by official watchers of culture, to be a threat not only to "proper" language but to "proper" society as well. Irving Lewis Allen, in his *City in Slang: New York Life and Popular Speech* (1993, 22–23), takes a broader view:

> Around 1850 the word slang, while in English a century earlier, became the accepted term for "illegitimate" and other unconventional speech. Disapproving comment on low speech forms, fueled by class anxieties in the changing city, probably helped establish the word slang in the United States. By 1900 the term had all its present meanings, including that of a vocabulary regarded as below standard and that threatened proper, genteel usages. . . . Street speech . . . expressed the troublesome spirit of the social underside of the industrial city: unconventional, experimental without license, insubordinate, scornful of—or merely careless of—authority. These locutions spread rapidly and began to be noticed, recorded, and deemed something of a social problem.

The way black jazz and blues musicians have been talking, say, since the latter part of the nineteenth century, might be seen as an outstanding example of this rebellion Allen speaks of. In fact, Robert S. Gold, in his introduction to *A Jazz Lexicon* (1964), supports Allen's claim, saying that there is an "essential rebelliousness at the heart of both the music and the speech" (xviii). And I would go so far as to say that *all* alive art is rebellious, and *all* alive speech, slang or otherwise, is rebellious, rebellious in the healthy sense that they challenge the stale and the conventional.

African American slang cuts through logic and arrives at a quick, efficient, interpretive solution to situations and things otherwise difficult to articulate. It serves as a device for articulating every conceivable thing imaginable—the nature of sex, the taste of food, social relationships, life itself, and death. Just as the word "Watergate" explains a vast and complex incident, a word like "bondage" to refer to being "in debt," or a phrase like "jump the broom," to explain that somebody will get married, makes the point quickly with a strong, clear, symbolic gesture, and a sense of vibrant, alive humor.

Black slang is a living, breathing form of expression that changes so quickly no researcher can keep up with it. A word or phrase can come into existence to mean one thing among a limited number of speakers in a particular neighborhood and a block away it might mean something else or be unknown entirely—at least for a while.

One group of speakers—such as a gang, a social club, or even a whole neighborhood—may feel the need for secrecy from another gang, social club, or neighborhood only just around the corner. At this point, when it is most private, this mode of speech thrives and is at its most effective. It is the classic example of a secret tongue. At the same time, both groups will feel the need to maintain a rapidly changing vocabulary unknown to the larger, mainstream culture, known generally or loosely as white America. The need for secrecy is part of the reason for the rapid change.

Since the days of slavery, this secrecy has served as a form of cultural self-defense against exploitation and oppression, constructed out of a combination of language, gesture, body style, and facial expression. In its embryonic stages during slavery, the secrecy was a powerful medium for making sense out of a cruel and strange world. African American slang is a kind of "home talk" in the sense that it was not originally meant for listeners beyond the nest.

As is always the case with informal private talk, it becomes, formally speaking, *informal* language—slang—when it reaches the larger speaking population. In other words, slang is, in a sense, a corruption of the more private forms of informal speech, such as cant, argot, or jargon. This evolution from private to public is natural for the words and phrases strong enough to survive for any considerable length of time.

But once such a transition is made, original meanings are very often lost. For example, "uptight" in the fifties, among the original group of black speakers who created the term, had a specific sexual reference. Once the phrase fell into general use, it took on a psychological meaning, referring to some sort of mental disturbance. This evolution from private to public is not only essential to the vitality at the crux of slang but inevitable. By this I mean African American slang is not only a living language for black speakers but for the whole country, as evidenced by its popularity decade after decade since the beginning of American history. The most recent example of this popularity is rap and hip-hop during the 1980s and the 1990s.

One important aspect of this "aliveness" is its onomatopoeic tendency. How words sound has always interested black speakers. "Zap," "yacky-de-yack," "bop," "bebop," "ticktock," "O-bop-she-bam," "hoochy-coochy," "honkytonk"—have all been popular at one time or another. Perhaps even more than any other type of slang words, onomatopoeic words deliver the pleasure of immediacy—the "sock!" (as in "sock it to me").

In a similar way, the rhyming jargon of black slang gives the same sort of satisfaction—especially for the pleasures of syncopated sound—as do rhyming terms such as Muhammad Ali's "rope-a-dope." Related in form is the language of rap and hip-hop. Rappers and would-be rappers carry on a tradition—just as the break dancing of the eighties followed the flash dancing of the forties—that started with pre-twentieth-century forms of playful, informal African American speech.

Some rap and hip-hop words and phrases will enter the canon, just as in the past hip and jive words such as "dude" and "cool" ended up in general use and in dictionaries.

While a certain vocabulary or idiom might please and serve one generation, it will not necessarily work for the next. Changes in black slang word forms take place continually. It happens when the speakers drop syllables, usually from the end or sometimes from the beginning of a word, such as "Bama" for "Alabama, "cap" for "backcap," "bam" for "bambita," "bro" for "brother," or "head" for "crackhead."

Other changes occur through shifts in the function of African American slang words. A noun, for example, might be used as a verb: "He *boozed* himself to death" or "I *jived* my way to Brooklyn." Black speech is fluid in this way because it remains open to the influences of verbal forces from every conceivable direction.

And it is important to remember that it is anonymous speakers who create and sustain the initial contents and shape of this language. Black social groups across the country are the homes of such anonymous speakers. Their talk draws on many levels of language, and popular culture in general, for its storehouse of words and phrases.

. . . .

Let me return to an earlier point in order to complete the thought. The private talk of an African American gang or social club becomes slang when it reaches the larger African American community or communities. It continues to be slang from that point on as it moves out into the general American speaking public. But African American slang is *not* colloquialism; it is not dialect, not argot, not jargon or cant. Black slang is composed of or involves the use of redundancies, jive, rhyme, nonsense, fad expressions, nicknames, corruptions, onomatopoeia, mispronunciations, and clipped forms.

In this way, the collective verbal force of black speakers throughout the many black communities in America carries on the tradition of renewing the American language while resisting and using it. Yet African American informal speech and slang are quite distinct in many essential ways from common American speech and slang. There is a basic grammatical difference between black speech and American English. Today, in the 1990s, nouns, for example, tend to be repeated within a single sentence along with pronouns as they were 150 years ago. At the same time, the overall shape of African American slang is also influenced, through exchange and conflict, by American English words and phrases that are adjusted to the African forms.

Again, for example, "This guy, he come at me out of nowhere." Or, "The mayor, he done the best he could with an impossible situation." Past, present, and future tenses are often not used in the expected order. No matter the subject, it gets the same verb form. Plurals are employed where in English structure they are not required. Sentences are commonly structured without the "to be" verb forms.

To say it another way, what I am calling African American slang *includes* black dialect. Black speakers generally sound like other speakers of their regions. We know this as dialect. But African American slang, as late as the 1920s, 1930s, and 1940s, was still largely regionalized. If, in the thirties, a southern black speaker of slang came into contact with a northern black speaker of slang, neither one usually had any idea what the other was talking about.

Today, in the nineties, just about every segment of the country is in touch with every other, due to television and radio, air travel and telephones, faxes and computers, so a homogenized form of African American slang has been emerging since the 1950s while dialects seem less altered by extra regional influences.

This makes for a fertile language environment and for even more accelerated change in African American slang. It evolved over the decades best when the social and political atmospheres were most fluid and creative. A social environment that is accommodating is necessary for the evolution of any form of slang. African American communities have been generally receptive to slang, although it has had to evolve in a moral war zone between the secular position of street culture and the sacred position of the sisters and deacons of the black church.

American society generally is receptive to slang. Slang never evolves in isolation. Black slang in particular uses the receptive American atmosphere to its own advantage while creating and maintaining a private language with its own center of gravity, integrity, and shape.

Many of the words and phrases are borrowed from very specific cultural pockets in the country—from the drug scene, prison life, street life, entertainment, and especially the areas of blues and jazz. These categories are important areas upon which black slang draws. They are every bit as essential to the vitality of black slang as is the presence of the mainstream American cultural scene.

This also means that, even when there is relatively little direct outside contact or communication between African Americans and other American social and racial subgroups, cross-fertilization—by way of television or whatever—is essential for the continuation of a private black alternative language—one that is, to some extent, destined to return to the white public arena from which it was borrowed.

So it is useless to ask, "Why an alternative language? Why not *one* American tongue for every ethnic or social group?" Most African Americans, like most Americans of any ethnic group, are skilled in what is called the common American culture—and the American language is the instrument of that culture. Each group's individual cultural identity is essentially established through the bond of its own distinctive expression. As is the case for other subcultures, African Americans are *also* skilled in their own racial culture. Informal speech is part of that culture, and they have many effective uses for informal speech. In daily life there are situations so sensitive or painful that slang often seems the only way to deal with them.

One of the primary functions of this language is its quest to create a coherent cultural construct of positive self-images. Though many of the words and phrases may sound harsh and even obscene to outsiders, the language is essential to the cultural enrichment of African Americans.

Black speakers, in self-mockery, can call each other "nigger" and, in a sense, make null and void racial slurs of white bigots. As James Baldwin often says, "I told you *first*." But the effectiveness of such a strategy, and its long-term psychological benefits, remains open to question. Yet it is a social phenomenon that has significant historical consensus simply by virtue of its long practice.

• •

American English, perhaps more than any other language, has borrowed from other tongues, period. Black slang is a form of black speech and black speech is a form of American English, but in the early stages, say, in the sixteenth century, black speech was still close to its African roots. Such African words and phrases as "okra," "cocacola," "turnip," "jazz," "gorilla," "banana," and "juke" (as in "jukebox"), for example, became common symbols in American English. More important, African American speech and slang have contributed to the ultimate formation of formal American English. And not only through the process of African nonslang words entering the language, but also as slang words and phrases such as "ace boon coon," "Afro," "attitude," "bad," "not," and so on, enter the mainstream formal language. Stuart Berg Flexner, in *I Hear America Talking* (1976, 31), writes: "When we heard America talking, we heard Blacks talking. . . . The 'we' is Black and White. . . . The Blacks have influenced the American language in two major ways: (1) by using many of their native (Black African) words and speech, and (2) by causing, doing, being, influencing things that have had all America talking, often using terms created or popularized by the Black presence and expedience."

There are roughly four areas of African American slang: (1) the early southern rural slang that started during slavery, (2) the slang of the sinner-man/black musicians of the period between 1900 and 1960, (3) street culture slang out of which rap and hip-hop evolved, and (4) working-class slang. All areas are fully represented in this dictionary, from the beginnings of black people in this country to the present.

The point, of course—and it's a pity to have to stress it—is that not all black speech is "street speech." But a surprisingly large number of Americans believe this to be so. "There are now thousands, perhaps millions of black Americans who . . . have limited contact with vernacular black speech," says John Baugh in *Black Street Speech* (1983). "Dialect boundaries therefore don't automatically conform to racial groups. Then collectively, black Americans speak a wide range of dialects, including impeccable standard English" (127).

Not only has there been, historically speaking, geographically determined diversity to African American slang, but the Africans who made up the language out of Portuguese Pidgin, Bantu, and Swahili, primarily, created what was known early on as Plantation Creole. The persistence of Africanisms in the formation of black slang and African American culture generally can be seen as a grand testimony to the strength of the human spirit and to the cultural strength of that polyglot group of Africans dumped, starting in 1619, on this continent to work the land.

But make no mistake, this is not another African language. And I am not pushing the Afrocentric program by spelling out the origins of this language. Black slang is an African language with distant roots in the ancient coastal tribes of central west Africa, as well as, indirectly, in Anglo-Irish culture and elsewhere.

But perhaps more important than any of the above is this: African American speech and slang form is, in a sense, one of the primary cutting edges against which American speech—formal and informal—generally keeps itself alive.

Don, Here Is My Peppermint Striped Shirt

There were a lot of things I didn't understand till I moved to New York. I moved there from the Midwest in 1966. Once I knew certain cultural pockets in the city, I had a frame of reference for understanding, for example, the emotional restraint and the sophistication of Donald Barthelme's fictional world.

Don and I did not meet till the year my second novel, *No*, was published (1973). Faith and Kirk Sale gave a Christmas party that year. They lived downstairs in the same building Don lived, at 113 West Eleventh Street, across the street from Grace Paley (one of his closest friends). Faith was involved with the magazine *Fiction* and had just accepted one of my stories. She invited my girlfriend and me over for the festivities. It wasn't a big crowd, a few people from publishing.

Donald Barthelme was there. He looked like a Mormon in aviator glasses, denim work shirt, and jeans. He was friendly in a subdued way. He was drinking scotch. We talked quietly in a corner for a while, mostly about how much he disliked going up to Buffalo in the cold to teach creative writing.

We also talked about the elegant old prints he was using to illustrate his stories. The prints were in the public domain, he said. He took what he wanted from old medical books and the like. These pictures fascinated me as much as his prose.

I remember thinking: He doesn't look like a man who is about to commit suicide. (A year or two before, somebody had written an article about Barthelme that appeared in the *New York Times Magazine*. Near the end the journalist said that he wouldn't be surprised if Donald Barthelme eventually committed suicide. Well, that journalist's tentative credentials as a reader of the future are permanently shot.)

It was a quiet party. Not much moving around. There was, though, one animated but obnoxious young woman, from publishing, who managed to get Don to take her upstairs to his place so that he could show her something or other—maybe an etching. When they came back half an hour later all the animation had left her face.

Occasionally I ran into Don on the street in the Village. One Monday I saw him near Sixth Avenue. The day before, I had read in the Sunday *Times* a letter he'd written on the matter of a certain young man who had been writing Donald Barthelme stories and publishing them under the name Donald Barthelme.

"Are you going to sue?" This was the beginning of the period when everybody was suing everybody for the slightest offense.

"No," Don said. "I asked him to stop. He said he would. That's good enough for me."

In the summer of 1977, Gotham Book Mart in New York held a book signing for William Burroughs. Penguin had just reissued his 1953 novel, *Junky*, in paperback. Burroughs was upstairs signing copies of the book. The place was crowded as hell and it was hot. People were spilling out onto the sidewalk. We were drinking wine from plastic cups.

I went outside and joined a small group of people sitting on the steps leading down into the store. Don was sitting there with another man. He introduced the gentleman as W. S. Merwin. Although I knew Merwin's work and liked it, he and I didn't have much to say to each other.

What I do remember of that occasion is a conversation Don and I had about the shirt I was wearing.

"That's a very cool-looking shirt, Clarence."

"Thanks. I like it too."

"I wish it were mine. I like the peppermint stripes."

"I'll leave it to you in my will."

Don smiled. He said something else but I don't remember precisely what. It was probably clever. (By the way, in the jacket photograph of his 1986 novel, *Paradise*, Don is wearing a shirt just like mine.)

The next time I ran into Don was in Fort Collins, Colorado, in the winter of 1978. He was there to give a reading at Colorado State University. At the time, I was living in Boulder, Colorado, about an hour away. In the freezing cold, I drove over for the reading and the reception.

He read slowly and carefully, keeping his voice at an even pitch. You had to really listen to the words. The Barthelme humor was there but easy to miss because his voice didn't warn you. He was the straight man delivering the lines of the other Barthelme, the comic.

At the reception we talked about critics, especially the ones who had recently been working on so-called postmodern fiction. Some of those critics had recently written about his work and mine too. Don didn't care much for what they had to say about him although what they said was very positive.

After the formal reception a few students—Yusef Komunyakaa among them, I think—gave a reception for Don in a nearby house where some of them lived. The students knew Barthelme's work: they had plenty of good scotch on hand.

Most of the action was in the kitchen. Don, however, sat quietly on the couch in the living room. He never moved all evening. Once in a while a student would muster up enough courage to go and sit beside him and talk a bit. But it was clear that such conversations were hard to sustain because Don's responses were cryptic. They did keep his glass filled, though.

In the early part of the evening, I hung out mostly in the kitchen where the food was. Later, the host played some very special blues records. At this point I withdrew to a corner. I sipped white wine and listened till eleven-thirty. I dreaded night driving and there was no heat in my car. I shook Don's hand and said good-bye. I said good night to the host. That was the last time I saw Donald Barthelme.

In the fall of 1989, when my wife told me about his death, I felt sadness for the loss of something that had never been. It is the same sadness I feel when I look at the yellowed pages of a book that has been in my life, unread, for more than twenty years.

Rhythm

A Hundred Years of African American Poetry

Why poetry? And, anyway, what is poetry? We need poetry because it speaks to us in terms and rhythms most instinctive to our existence. Poetry has its basis in the very beating of our hearts, in the rhythms of our footfalls as we walk, and in the pattern of our breathing. It is the refinement made of our voices speaking in everyday terms.

Because of the importance of these rhythmic patterns, poetry is always as much about itself as it is about, say, the West Coast, van Gogh, violence, snapshots, paintings, fishing in a creek, riding a bike across a tightrope, being born, prison, slavery, menses, language, jazz, insomnia, self, death, or anything else you can think of.

One of the central things to poetry is metaphor, and there are a variety of metaphors—juxtaposed, past tense, positive, negative, double, triple, multiple, organic, nonorganic, you name it. But its central functions are fairly consistent in all of its mutations: metaphor is about *equivalences*, especially of objects or ideas not commonly seen together or thought to have similarities. Another way of saying this is to say that metaphor seeks to unearth an *assumed sameness* submerged in dissimilar objects or ideas. The implied analogy that metaphor makes between, say, a car and a lemon, is well known. This is the basic business of metaphor.

Of equal importance is voice. In poetry voice can be everything. A poet without a good ear, without a sense of the music in speech, is like a snowstorm without snow. June Jordan grew up listening to the "Black English" of Harlem and Bedford Stuyvesant, Brooklyn, its syntax and grammar, its music, and listening to the "impeccable" jive talk of a favorite uncle who lived upstairs. Rita Dove, as a kid, listened to relatives and neighbors talking on the front porch, to the "women in the kitchen," listened to the pitch of voices at, say, a Fourth of July cookout, hearing the cadence of the speech, doing research without even knowing she was working. Yusef Komunyakaa chose poetry because of the "conciseness, the precision, the imagery, and the music in the lines." Cornelius

Eady says he has an eye and an ear for the "music inside" the poem. He follows the directions that music takes. In a sense, he sees language everywhere: when people are talking, he watches the way their hands move, and the way the light falls, and so on.

But to get back to metaphor: As one of the tropes, metaphor—especially complex metaphor—is a device in which the original object has at least two distinct functions. It not only changes our perception of the *compared object* but also continues to both change and represent *itself*. And metaphor, perhaps more than any other device of poetry, is on the best terms with the natural world while being on equally good terms with the materials (language) out of which poetry is sculpted. In short, poetry is necessary.

....

Again—what do you *do* with poetry? And, anyway, *how* do you do what you do with poetry? The question isn't so much what is going on in the poem, as it is what is going on between you and the poem. You *experience* poetry. If a poem can be taken as a "sonic entity," as Denise Levertov says, then we can read it the way we listen to music. Rita Dove has said: "Poetry connects you to yourself, to the self that doesn't know how to talk or negotiate. We have emotions that we can't really talk about, and they're very strong. . . . I really don't think of poetry as being an intellectual activity. I think of it as a very visceral activity." And this "visceral activity" we call poetry happens in time, the way music is experienced. Ernest Fenollosa said that poetic form is *regular* (like the heartbeat) and that its basic "reality" has to do with its existence in time. And in the case of poetry on the page, we can say too that poetry, like painting, to some degree exists in space. It's both temporal and spatial.

Fenollosa writes: "All arts follow the same law; refined harmony lies in the delicate balance of overtones." Powerful poetry that moves us has to be constructed with language that is in motion and vividly alive. It can fly and "quiver," as D. H. Lawrence felt it should. It can use the "real world" as Hart Crane believed. It can be closed or open in form. It can use breathing as a measuring device, as Charles Olson said. The poet can concentrate on the relationship between the mind and the ear or give more attention to how the poem on the page strikes the eye.

Poetry is a "formal invention" (to use William Carlos Williams's phrase), and as such it is concerned with its own scheme, its design, the physical and tonal shape of language. And when it is most successful, it is composed of *things*—things held together or suspended together with tension and *in*tension. Abstractions, such as ideas, concepts, emotions, or feelings, are also best rendered through the thingness of metaphor. Or as Pound put it in one of his three principles for writing poetry: "Direct treatment of the 'thing' whether subjective or objective." Or Williams: "No ideas but in things" (*Paterson*). Or Williams in an even more precise manner when he said: "A poem is a small (or large) machine made of words" and because of the machinelike *thingness* of poetry "its movement is intrinsic . . . [and has] a physical more than a literary character."

. . . .

Poetry, like myth and slang, may also be closer to our intrinsic natures than we normally think of it being. It can, for example, be enacted in religious terms. Robert Hayden and Derek Walcott come to mind.

Robert Hayden believed poetry, though rendered in concrete terms, has a spiritual basis, that it is the poet's way of responding to the basic abstract questions—birth, death, love, the meaning of life, God, and so forth —that concern "all human beings."

Hayden's interest in the essential mysteries shows throughout his work. Although for him, Nature itself supplied many answers to the less difficult spiritual questions of life, Hayden seems to have reached a certain level of peace in the absence of absolute answers. He came to believe that suffering was essential to salvation, to deliverance, to sanctification.

Walcott, in a similar way, sees the *act* of writing poetry as a form of praying. In an interview, he said:

> I have never separated the writing of poetry from prayer. I have grown up believing it is a vocation, a religious vocation. . . . I imagine that all artists and all writers in that moment before they begin their working day . . . [find that] there is something about it votive and humble and in a sense ritualistic. . . . I mean, it's like the habit of Catholics going into water: you cross yourself before you go in. Any serious attempt to try to do something worthwhile is ritualistic.

Poetry discovered *me* when I was four or five. My mother wrote a poem for me and I had to recite it in church. Soon I was writing my own poems. This was during a time when my primary artistic expression was drawing, usually with crayons. We also called it "coloring." Since my command of the crayon was greater than my command of writing, in a sense, my drawings became my poems. Then at about the age of twelve—while still drawing and now painting with a passion—I seriously (too seriously!) committed myself to writing poetry. The idea was to be a full, rounded Renaissance artist: I would write, paint, compose music, invent things. I had my heroes and da Vinci was among them. Whatever authority I have in this area has its roots in those long-ago naive events.

In 1966, when I was twenty-nine, I published a statement called "Black Criterion," an early articulation of what later became known as the Black Aesthetics Movement. If I was among the first to make such a statement, I was also among the first to turn my back on the straitjacket philosophy of the movement because it represented an ideological prison for the artist. I could not see art's main function as a cultural arm of a political movement—which is what Black Nationalism taught. After all, it was already clear to me that art produced under political direction was pretty bad art. This is not the same thing as saying that I do not believe poetry can be, in the French sense, a means of *engagement*. It certainly can. An example of first-rate political poetry is Robert Hayden's "Middle Passage." It begins:

> Sails flashing to the wind like weapons,
> sharks following the moans the fever and the dying;
> horror the corposant and compass rose.
> Middle Passage:
>   voyage through death
>   to life upon these shores.

In a sense, then, I resolved the confusion in my heart and mind. And in the words of Langston Hughes's famous 1926 essay manifesto, "The Negro Artist and the Racial Mountain": "An artist must be free to choose what he does . . . but he must also never be afraid to do what he might choose." If black people were pleased, Hughes said, fine, if white people were pleased, fine. If they weren't, to hell with them. The way to the universal was through the particular. An old truth."

I found the spirit of Hughes's artistic rebelliousness much more attractive than the military goose-stepping propaganda of sixties Black Nationalism. I came to believe that poets (and writers) should feel free to tap into a deeper truth than the important though not *all-important* social or political aspects of experience.

I wanted to write *and to read* poetry that spoke from the depths of what was most human, from the depths of what we *all* shared, not merely from the levels where our differences could be detected. I wanted political poetry that was organic in its ideas, a political poetry that in no way compromised its own artistic nature.

But can poetry be both political and didactic and at the same time still be art? Among recent African American poets, Audre Lorde, I think, proved that it can. Sonia Sanchez, with her haiku-like style, in her exploration of self in exchange and conflict with community, in her probing of the personal self's relation to the public self, in her search for the higher public good in that public self, in her constant redefining of those selves, especially as female body and spirit, proves that it is possible. Haki R. Madhubuti, too, in his militancy, in his black pride, in his interest in family and culture, in his sociopolitical philosophy of the black community as a self-directed entity, in his interest in the heroic black perspective, I think, proves that it can be done. Jayne Cortez, with her improvisational free form, in her struggle to define the black female in the context of family, class, body, spirit, and moral self, proves that it's possible to focus on these social issues—as well as drug addiction, persecution, rape, war, sexism, racism—and create poems that stand on their own as works of solid art.

In other words, certainly by 1970, I firmly believed that political or social issues were legitimate subject matter. I saw my way clearly from there. I suspect my background as a painter compelled me to *see* language, almost as a plastic form, see it in a *direct* way—the way a painter confronts color and lines before visual narrative can become an issue—as the raw material of poetry-making, and to find a sense of urgency at this level rather than, say, in message.

Just now, in looking again at that little "essay," I noticed a key element—something I still believe, something that obviously came from a deeper place in me than most of what that essay represents—at its core: "A work of art, a poem, can be a complete 'thing'; it can be alone, not preaching, not trying to change men, and though it might change them, if the men are ready for it, the poem is not reduced in its artistic status. I mean we black poets can write poems of pure creative black energy right here in the white west and make them works of art without falling into the cheap marketplace of bullshit and propaganda. But it is a thin line to stand on."

In 1968—a politically and socially turbulent year—I edited an anthology called *The New Black Poetry* (1969) and wrote a strident introduction, one that, in retrospect, seems perfectly in tune with the hue and cry of that year—a year of infamous assassinations and insurrections on a grand scale. Composed of the works of seventy-six poets, the anthology somehow escaped the most obvious pitfall it faced: all of the poems might have been didactic but, perhaps for the same reason that the essential portion of my little essay escapes being pure propaganda, they are not.

And, in fact, only about 10 percent of the poems fall into that category. I was pleased to notice that even the didactic or propagandistic poems in my anthology are good—not bad—political poems. Many of them are organic *and* engaged at the same time.

A good number of the poets included went on to become "high-profile," highly accomplished poets, such as Audre Lorde, June Jordan (then called June

Meyer), Al Young, Ishmael Reed, Nikki Giovanni, Sonia Sanchez, and Etheridge Knight. (LeRoi Jones [Amiri Baraka] was already famous.) But editing the anthology taught me a lot—about poetry, about the politics of poetry.

. . . .

The teaching (and learning) of poetry has long interested me. I taught my first formal poetry course at City University of New York–Brooklyn College in 1968, when I was thirty-one, under the umbrella of something called the SEEK program. Adrienne Rich was teaching in the same program. We were not *real* college professors—at that time at least—and had been brought in strictly as poets. The anthology I hastily selected and used (hopefully, less hastily) was my first mistake. I've forgotten the title and the editor, although I do remember that she was not a poet but a junior high school teacher in the Bronx. It could not have been worse. Uneven in quality, I came to hate it, and all but abandoned it two-thirds of the way through the course. This threw me back on my own resources, and in the final third of the course there was some noticeable improvement.

But I did learn a couple of things from that initial experience. A good anthology is essential, and the poem, like the short story, is a powerful and useful thing to place before students. They can, as William Carlos Williams indicated, perish from lack of what they will find there.

. . . .

African American literature, formally speaking, is perhaps best known for its vast body of diverse and often brilliant poetry. This has a lot to do with poetry's relationship to music—another cultural form in which black Americans, from the beginning of their presence in this country, have worked joyously. (Autobiographies—including slave narratives—run a close second.)

It's ironic that there were black poets born slaves—Lucy Terry, Jupiter Hammon, Phillis Wheatley—who were writing and publishing their poetry on these shores or in England in the eighteenth century, a time when slave ships were still unloading their captured or purchased cargo to be sold as property. Ironic because the European explanation for slavery was rooted in the Christian belief that Africans were subhuman, incapable of learning anything requiring abstract thinking. The legacies of this belief and that institution linger stormily in the hearts of Americans even now.

Today, in the sophisticated and complex poetry of Rita Dove, Michael Harper, Derek Walcott, Ai, Jay Wright, or Audre Lorde, thematically speaking, tribal or folk elements and the universals are obvious. In fact, such elements are ironically more in evidence in the twentieth century, and especially since the mid-1940s, than in the efforts of Lucy Terry, Jupiter Hammon, or Phillis Wheatley.

Lucy Terry was the first known African slave on these shores to write a poem in English, "Bars Fight" (1746), about an Indian "ambush" in Deerfield, Massachusetts, that same year. The poem describes, among other things, Samuel Allen's resistance and his death. (The bars were a prominent area along the Deerfield River.) The poem first appeared in George Sheldon's essay "Negro Slavery in Old Deerfield" (1893).

But Hammon, of Queens Village, Long Island, was probably the first person of African descent to publish a poem ("An Evening Thought: Salvation by Christ, with Penitential Cries . . . etc.") in English (1760), and Wheatley was the first to publish a collection of verse, *Poems on Various Subjects* (1773).

Both Wheatley and Hammon, slaves with "advantages and privileges"—as Hammon said of himself—were strongly influenced by the Wesley-Whitefield evangelist movement. They wrote the type of sentimental and pious Christian poetry typical of and favored by the Puritans in New England at that time—a point that Thomas Jefferson might have added to his comment about Wheatley's work being "below the dignity of criticism." Better educated than Terry or Hammon, Wheatley's poems show—relatively speaking—a level of technical skill absent in their work.

The period between the 1820s to the end of the Civil War gave rise to black poets who spoke out—though perhaps not always strongly—against slavery. Many of them also looked piously to middle-class gentility, British verse, and European Christianity for models, and only marginally to their own culture and tradition. Poets such as Mary E. Tucker Lambert, George Boyer Vashon, Ann Plato, James Monroe Whitfield, Charles Lewis Reason, Charlotte L. Forten Grimke, Timothy Thomas Fortune, Henrietta Allson Whitman, Alfred Isay Walden, and Elymas Payson Rogers—all considered minor poets—, showed only marginal interest in black folk material.

But then that tradition—the folk—had yet to gain in respectability. The richness and power of it were perhaps too close to be seen clearly. Clergymen and professors, these poets wrote in formal religious terms and too often (like their white counterparts) were formally derivative. They *were* concerned with injustice and war, yes, and spoke out against American hypocrisy, but most of them were also much concerned with making a good impression—with, in effect, proving that "colored" folks were intelligent enough to write verse in the manner of the poets of England.

Then, in 1829, George Moses Horton (1797?–1883?), sometimes called

"The Colored Bard of North Carolina," at about the age of thirty-two, published his first collection, *The Hope of Liberty* (reprinted in 1837 as *Poems by a Slave*), and in that volume we can see the beginnings of a black poet's efforts to break away from the earlier themes. Like the authors of the slave narratives, he too spoke out against slavery and is considered the first *southern* slave to do so in print.

But Paul Laurence Dunbar, the first major African American poet, turned, for sustenance and for models, to the folk tradition more dramatically than any previous poet of African descent. His poetry reflects a wide range of ideas, forms, and habits in African American folk culture. He made use of the spirituals, the storytelling tradition, work songs, sermons, tall tales, the secular and religious blues songs. Yet Dunbar too was cautious about what his work implied and what he said in print. Diplomatic and optimistic at the same time, his was a careful militancy.

While Dunbar's African American contemporaries writing poetry—James Weldon Johnson, Frances Ellen Watkins Harper, James Edwin Campbell, Aaron Belford Thompson, Charles Douglas Clem, Josephine D. Head, James D. Corrothers, James Ephriam McGirth, William Stanley Braithwaite, Daniel Webster Davis, Benjamin T. Tanner, Frank Barbour Coffin, Joseph Seamon Cotter, and Alice Dunbar Nelson, to name a few—reflected some of the same thematic concerns, the same political caution, the same optimism, the same measured social militancy, none of them—with the possible exception of Johnson—equaled him in literary range and power.

While this was a period of accommodationist thinking, it was also the beginning of serious political and social protest. With this newfound confidence, African American poets, whether in terms of dialect or the King's English, began to explore their own folk culture. (Johnson's novel, *The Autobiography of an Ex-Colored Man* [1912], in a sense, is a romantic, if ironic, embracing of the folk tradition in that the protagonist recognizes and admires the richness of it but chooses to turn his back on it.) The embracing of the folk culture was a conscious choice on the part of the poets of this period.

And this conscious choice placed American black poetry firmly in the broadest and oldest context of world poetry—oral and musical—where it remains. As suggested earlier, poetry is, after all, a form of music made out of words. So, a written tradition, based on an oral one, evolved side by side with that continuing oral tradition. But African American literature, again formally speaking, did not evolve this way in isolation. Its developmental pattern correlates with—while maintaining its own distinctive elements—the evolution of various forms of American writing generally.

Yet in this period following the Civil War, black poets (and writers of prose) interested in creating believable, true images of their people and the diverse experiences of those people, were up against a hard wall of public resistance. Remember, this was a time that gave rise to a popular generation of white American writers and poets—many politically to the right, pro-slavery, even reactionary—who worked in what we now call the plantation tradition. These writers—Joel Chandler Harris, Thomas Nelson Page, William John Grayson, Ruth McEnery Stuart, Irwin Russell, Sidney Lanier, and others—developed formulaic images of the ex-slave as buffoon, lazy roustabout, figure of ridicule, mammy, half-wit, criminal, thief, and rapist.

These minstrel and sentimental stereotypes were deeply implanted in the American psyche, not only by way of the stories and poems of these writers, but through the vastly popular traveling minstrel stage and sideshows and newspaper cartoons of the day. The legacy of those stereotypes, a hundred and thirty years later, is still with us—both in popular culture and to some extent in literature.

As the end of the nineteenth century approached, American writing generally—and African American writing in particular—showed signs of breaking away from its absolute dependency on European influences. Walt Whitman was also at work boldly creating and insisting on a *native* art form. The idea of a *formal* native poetry—though still a strange idea—was at least now in the vocabulary. True, even if he and those few who believed as he did didn't have a large tribe of followers.

During this period, Paul Laurence Dunbar's achievement in writing deceptively simple pastoral poetry matches Charles Waddell Chesnutt's in serious literary fiction and Du Bois's in lyrical and analytical nonfiction. (By the way, in terms of form, Dunbar was influenced more by the poetry of Swinburne and Rossetti than by, say, Whitman or even Tennyson.)

Dunbar's dialect verse became better known than some of his more complex and sophisticated poems, of which there were many more and by which he is represented in this anthology. (Dunbar, among other early black poets, is the clear forerunner of the jazz poetry of the sixties, seventies, and eighties, and today's rap and hip-hop poetry.) In a way, it was William Dean Howells's introduction to Dunbar's first commercially published volume, *Lyrics of Lowly Life* (1869), that helped to bring a certain respectability to dialect poetry *by black poets*.

But neither the dialect nor the "straight" poetry earned him much money. He made a modest living into the twentieth century writing novels about white characters. Unlike the dialect poetry of white southern poets such as those mentioned a moment ago, Dunbar's is distinguished by its use of *readable* dialect and believable if not complex—and certainly likable!—characters. (This is not to say that some black poets didn't also write bad dialect poetry: James Edwin Campbell certainly did.)

An early Dunbar poem titled "Sympathy," which appears in *Oak and Ivy* (1893), shows—despite its somewhat insipid nature—the young poet's talent and ability to echo the dialect tradition, but a poem written near the end of that same decade (when Dunbar was not yet thirty and with less than ten years to live) and published under the same title, "Sympathy," is Dunbar at his best. The third stanza reads:

> I know why the caged bird sings, ah me,
> When his wing is bruised and his bosom sore—
> When he beats his bars and he would be free;
> It is not a carol of joy or glee,
> But a prayer that he sends from his heart's core,
> But a plea, that upward to Heaven he flings—
> I know why the caged bird sings!

The greatness of the poem is in its powerful rhythms and in its sophisticated use of sentiment to forge the startling and beautiful image of the caged bird without resorting to maudlin sentimentality.

During the first two decades of the twentieth century the so-called New Negro came into vogue, and for the first time the general public started reading the poetry and prose of African Americans. The Dunbar-Chesnutt-Du Bois-James Weldon Johnson generation of writers became the Old Guard as a group of younger poets—Claude McKay, Countee Cullen, Jean Toomer, Langston Hughes, and others—emerged as the leading poets of what later was called the Harlem Renaissance.

But who were these young upstarts? In terms of poetic form, they were individualistic, but in terms of thematic concerns they—especially Toomer, McKay, and Langston Hughes—shared a great deal.

Toomer's poem "Her Lips Are Copper Wire," for example, is an "imagistic" modernist work as vigorous and original as the best of its period:

> whisper of yellow globes
> gleaming on lamp-posts that sway
> like bootleg licker drinks in the fog
>
> and let your breath be moist against me
> like bright beads on yellow globes

telephone the power-house
that the main wires are insulate

(her words play softly up and down
dewy corridors of billboards)

then with your tongue remove the tape
and press your lips to mine
till they are incandescent

She is, of course, a work of art, one to behold. The poem is about desire that follows a kiss. Here, electrical energy is compared to the energy of the kiss, a kiss like electricity. (Copper wire was used to conduct electricity to the first electric streetlights.) The images of "bright beads on yellow globes" and lampposts in a row form a kind of "corridor" and in the "dew" of night. They and everything else are shrouded in a moist softness. Toomer's poem, like so much of his work, is a celebration of life itself and he insists that energy equals life.

The new poetry was vigorous and often universal in its subject matter and themes; yet it retained much of the sensitivity to racial issues and injustice expressed by the earlier generation. Modernism was in the air, Ezra Pound, T. S. Eliot, e. e. cummings, Amy Lowell, and other key white American poets of the period were self-consciously involved in exploring new forms. They were all—black and white—breathing the same air.

It is often said that Claude McKay's *Harlem Shadows* (1922) signaled the African American shift—at least in poetry—to the self-consciously modern mode, and, at the same time, the beginning of "The New Negro" Movement, better known as the Harlem Renaissance. But McKay's volume published two years earlier, *Spring in New Hampshire and Other Poems,* reflects as much of the same consciousness of the new aesthetic, which insisted that a poem was a lyrical *thing* and not merely a vehicle for ideas.

Despite McKay's aesthetic sophistication as a poet, a considerable number of contemporary critics believe that McKay's poetry lacks originality. On the contrary, McKay's best poetry is every bit as vibrant and fresh as, say, Toomer's. Listen to McKay's "The Tropics in New York":

Bananas ripe and green, and ginger-root,
　　Cocoa in pods and alligator pears,
And tangerines and mangoes and grape fruit,
　　Fit for the highest prize at parish fairs,
Set in the window, bringing memories
　　Of fruit-trees laden by low-singing rills,

And dewy dawns, and mystical blue skies
In benediction over nun-like hills.

My eyes grew dim, and I could no more gaze;
A wave longing through my body swept,
And, hungry for the old, familiar ways,
I turned aside and bowed my head and wept.

The poem conjures up, in vivid images of the Caribbean, specifically Jamaica, the familiar paradox of being compelled to be far from one's beloved home, a paradox often expressed in McKay's work. The autobiographical short story "Truant" (*Gingertown*, 1932), in part deals with this subject in great detail. The paradox is based not only on the poet's nostalgic love for the green hills of Jamaica, juxtaposed with his attraction to the great steel and asphalt world of the city, but also on the struggle between the moral and social demands made by the city and the relative "freedom" suggested by the simpler way of life in a tropical setting.

In other words, and, in a more subtle sense, the struggle for the poet is between life and art—and the hungry poet wants both. In an untitled poem in that same short story, McKay describes the cities of the northeastern United States "Where factories grow like jungle trees, / Yielding new harvest for the world" (159). And McKay, in the prose text, continues the thought: "The steel-framed poetry of cities did not crowd out but rather intensified in him the singing memories of his village life." The point was, of course: "He loved both, the one complimenting the other."

These poets, Jean Toomer, Langston Hughes, Claude McKay, and Arna Bontemps, in matters of technique and form, as I said before, aligned themselves with the modernist movement—as expressed by, say, William Carlos Williams. Like Williams, Hughes especially was interested in unearthing a native tongue, an American idiom, speaking his poetry in that tongue. This is Langston Hughes's poem "Cross" (1925):

My old man's a white old man
And my old mother's black.
If I ever cursed my white old man
I take my curses back.

If I ever cursed my black old mother
And wished she were in hell,
I'm sorry for that evil wish
And now I wish her well.

My old man died in a fine big house.
My ma died in a shack.
I wonder where I'm gonna die,
Being neither white nor black?

The poem achieves its "sonic" power and complexity through repetition of certain words: "old," "man," "curse," "black," "white," "shack," "hell," and "well."

Thematically on one level about anger and forgiveness, on another it ultimately explores a full network of profound social and philosophical issues. Each quatrain, for example, advances the racial paradox of a complex fate, especially when one considers the social context in which the dilemma occurs: a racist society. The social context operates here as a subtext. In certain other cultures and to varying degrees, the so-called racial color aspects might cause bewilderment, but in terms of the class issues raised by the speaker, the poem would be understood universally. Each of us, it seems to say, has some type of "cross" to bear. "Color" as it relates to a mixed-race person's identity is an issue, yes, but coupled with it, inseparable from it, is the equally urgent issue of mortality: "I wonder where I'm gonna die."

Many of the other prominent black poets of this period—especially Countee Cullen and James Weldon Johnson—were largely influenced by the conservative technical tradition (sometimes called the academic tradition) handed down in British verse by Shelly, Byron, and Keats, and carried on (and also then newly redefined, incidentally) by such white American poets as Allen Tate.

Cullen's "ear" for the music of language was as good as the best. This is the opening couplet from "Leaves": "One, two and three, / Dead leaves drift from a tree." Despite the fact that he paid little attention to the American idiom, and held fast to the European Romantic tradition of poetic language to the point of being a bit out of step at best and old fashioned at worst, Cullen has to be seen as a serious poet of considerable accomplishments in this period called the Harlem Renaissance.

In a way, Bontemps, though, might be closer to another kind of modernist, Wallace Stevens, than to William Carlos Williams, in that he was interested in looking deeply into the meaning of life and making complex philosophical connections. Never fully appreciated as a poet by the reading public, Bontemps, in my opinion, was a poet of great breadth and depth who has been denied credit for his brilliant accomplishments. In the first stanza of his visionary "Close Your Eyes," listen to the sharp, clear voice, see the dramatically etched image of the idealized landscape, the gate, the woodman, the hill:

Go through the gates with closed eyes.
Stand erect and let your black face front the west.
Drop the axe and leave the timber where it lies;
a woodman on the hill must have his rest.

That this modernist movement carried the name Harlem in its title was of course only symbolic, and, as many have suggested, maybe even natural, because New York City was and is perhaps the greatest artistic and cultural center in the States. In his introduction to *The New Negro* (1968), Alain Locke—a professor at Howard University in Washington, D.C., and an important historical scholar of the moment—attempted to refocus the "New Negro" in the quickly evolving context of the modern world taking shape after the First World War. He said:

> The New Negro must be seen in the perspective of a New World, and especially of a New America. Europe seething in a dozen centers with emergent nationalities, Palestine full of a renascent Judaism—these are no more alive with the progressive forces of our era than the quickened centers of the lives of black folk. America seeking a new expansion and artistic maturity, trying to create a new kind of an American literature, a national art, and national music implies a Negro-American culture seeking the same satisfactions and objectives. Separate as it may be in color and substance, the culture of the Negro is a pattern integral with the times and with its cultural setting.

Locke went on to say that "Negro life" was "finding a new soul. There is a fresh spiritual and cultural refocusing." He saw a renewal of "race-spirit" and great creativity that "profoundly sets itself apart." He called what he saw "the Negro Renaissance."

. . . .

Then, in 1929, publishers and other supporters of the movement, with tight budgets resulting from the world economic crisis, turned away. The public attention given the Harlem Renaissance started winding down from that point onward. By the mid-thirties many of the poets (fiction writers, painters, sculptors, playwrights, actors, musicians, and other artists associated with the movement) were starved for attention.

In African American literature, the period between the late thirties and the early sixties, sometimes called the "protest" period, which correlated with hard times in America, is best known for its black prose writers such as Richard Wright, Chester Himes, Ann Petry, Dorothy West, Ralph Ellison, and later, James Baldwin. But, as quiet as it was and still is kept, some of the finest black poets—Gwendolyn Brooks, Margaret Walker, Sterling Brown, Robert Hayden—the culture had produced up till that point were at work. These poets were users of the folk culture in either rural or urban settings.

Take Gwendolyn Brooks. Using a modernist aesthetic, and in poems variously about racism, sexism, and classism, Brooks explored social problems, poverty, social justice, black rage, and pain. Her setting has often been Chicago's South Side—in the forties known as the Black Belt or Black Metropolis. Brooks called it Bronzeville and focused on the relationship between the individual and the community. In graceful line after graceful line, in a powerful performative voice, she took the reader into bleak kitchenettes and into the crowded streets. From "Kitchenette Building": "We are things of dry hours and the involuntary plan, / Grayed in, and gray. . . ." But her work has always been about a great deal more—about love, about other locations. The first six lines of "Strong Men, Riding Horses":

Strong Men, riding horses. In the West
On a range five hundred miles. A Thousand. Reaching
From dawn to sunset. Rested blue to orange.
From a hope to crying. Except that Strong Men are
Desert-eyed. Except that Strong Men are
Pasted to stars already . . .

The poem relies on an interplay of sound and color that evokes powerful images of a way of life vastly different from that lived by most people on the South Side of Chicago, as the rest of the poem demonstrates.

While Gwendolyn Brooks explored primarily African American urban folk culture, Sterling A. Brown, using the folk idiom or rural black speech, investigated the rural culture and the possibilities of dialect poetry. An expert in the folklore of his culture, Brown was interested in the so-called low-down people and found the Depression years a ripe source of subject matter. He believed in what was then called "the common man." The models for his poems were work songs, blues, and spirituals. Among his many themes were the early-twentieth-century relationship between the town and the city, the effect of the railroad on individual and community life, the interplay between black people and white people, and so on. This is the first stanza of "Foreclosure":

Father Missouri takes his own.
These are the fields he loaned them,
Out of heart's fullness, gratuitously;

Here are the banks he built up for his children,
Here are the fields, rich fertile silt.

Consider Hayden, too, for example. Hayden, without question, is a major American poet whose gift is large and whose understanding of the craft matches that of, say, Bud Powell in jazz, Romare Bearden in painting. This is from "Names":

Once they were sticks and stones
I feared would break my bones:
Four Eyes. And worse.
Old Four Eyes fled
to safety in the danger zones
Tom Swift and Kubla Khan traversed.

Here, the poet looks back at the "names" he was called as a child, revisits the pain caused by the cruelty of other children, and remembered retreating into the "safety in the danger zones" of books, the magical world of literature.

. . . .

We tend to associate poets with the periods in which they came into prominence, and in a way that is often unfair. Such poets as Arna Bontemps and Langston Hughes were still writing and producing some of their best works, and, in fact, reinventing their public personas through these works, in the new contexts of the fifties and sixties.

Then there are really fine poets not as widely known who have worked for several decades—from the fifties through the eighties and longer—such as Pinkie Gordon Lane, Norman Henry Pritchard II, Lebert Bethune, Ed Roberson, Conyus, Russell Atkins, and Gloria Oden, to name just a few, without proper recognition. This is the first stanza of Oden's "The Carousel":

An empty carousel in a deserted park
rides me round and round,
from end to beginning,
like the tail that drives the dog.

There is no way to miss the beauty and energy of such an image. It comes at you full force.

Pritchard and Atkins, on the other hand, occupy a special place in the ranks of African American poets working in the sixties and seventies. Both might be described as "concrete" poets, but that word doesn't really do them justice. You could just as well call them "cubist" poets. I think of Bach when I read Atkins.

I think of early Picasso when I read Pritchard. The point is, they make the presence of the poem on the page as significant as the poem's meanings and sounds. This is Atkins's "Probability and Birds in the Yard":

> The probability in the yard is this:
> The rodent keeps the cat close by;
> The cat would sharp the bird;
> the bird would waft to the water—
> if he does he has but his times before,
> whichever one he is. He's surely marked.
>
> The cat is variable;
> the rodent becomes the death of the bird
> which we love
>   dogs are random

And Pritchard, like an abstract expressionist at times, like a cubist at other times: this is "Burnt Sienna":

> Trust thrust first tinder kindling grown
> the maple gave rust air its bark
> and ample and plain
> fair orange orb
> sworn to that sea line stretching bare
> courteous and neat
> still gleaming meekly weaned
> by some awesome twilight rise
> beyond be gone
> the nameless colored yarn

But it was not till the sixties, during the Civil Rights Movement, that the general poetry-reading public—sparked by the loud clamor of many people fighting for freedom from racism, sexism, war, and for justice—started reading and listening to African American poetry again. Poets born in the thirties had come of age—Derek Walcott, Etheridge Knight, Gerald Barrax, Audre Lorde, Sonia Sanchez, Jay Wright, Colleen J. McElroy, Jayne Cortez, Norman Henry Pritchard II, Ed Roberson, Amiri Baraka, and others of the period tried to give lyrical expression to the complex personal, social, and political issues before them.

This is Baraka (when he was still LeRoi Jones) at his best with "For Hettie":

My Wife is left-handed.
Which implies a fierce de-
termination. A complete other
worldliness. it's WEIRD baby
the way some folks
are always trying to be different.

But then, she's been a bohemian
all her life . . . black stockings,
refusing to take orders. I sit
patiently, trying to tell her
what's right. TAKE THAT DAMN
PENCIL OUTTA THAT HAND. YOU'RE
RITING BACKWARDS. & such. But
to no avail. & it shows
in her work. Left-handed coffee
left-handed eggs: when she comes
in at night . . . it's her left hand
offered for me to kiss. damn.

& now her belly droops over the seat.
They say it's a child. But
I ain't quite so sure.

This is a love poem sung by a man in love with his wife in her ninth month, in love with her for her "fierce determination." The baby is late. The wonderfully and playfully sardonic tone is fresh, immediate, and refreshing. Left-handedness here is a metaphor for the wife's rebellion against convention. She's "a bohemian," she's even planning natural childbirth at a time—the fifties—when it was rare in the States. Hettie Jones, LeRoi Jones's first wife, in her autobiography *How I Became Hettie Jones* (1990), writes, "What I prized in myself he loved most."

These were the days when poets started singing and chanting their poetry before audiences, putting it on record. In an article of mine, called "The Explosion of Black Poetry," which appeared in *Essence* as the sixties pushed into the early seventies, I tried to map some of this excitement, calling it "a great explosion." Rap, in a sense, has been one outgrowth of that explosion.

From the late seventies through the mid-nineties, African American poetry—along with American poetry generally—despite the conservative political climate, continued to regain its good health. New voices of poets born in the forties—Ellease Southerland, Quincy Troupe, Sherley Anne Williams, Calvin Forbes, Marilyn Nelson Waniek, Nathaniel Mackey, Christopher Gilbert, and others—emerged or gained prominence for the first time. A richness and universality of theme and technical maturity were present in much of the work. Waniek, for example, was not afraid to explore the much treaded territory of the traditional ballad and to come up with refreshing results. Here is the opening quatrain of "The Ballad of Aunt Geneva":

> Geneva was the wild one.
> Geneva was a tart.
> Geneva met a blue-eyed boy
> and gave away her heart.

It was as though the new generation had learned from the mistakes of excessive didacticism of many of those who came of age in the sixties and early seventies. Another example is found in the opening lines of Christopher Gilbert's "Kite-flying":

> June at Truro Beach the joyous bathers,
> specs of jewel fallen along the sand.
> Walking near them there is this polarity—
> their lives the way stars hold the sky . . .

. . . .

Adding the younger poets of this period—Lucinda Roy, Karen Mitchell, Michael S. Weaver, Cornelius Eady, Patricia Smith, Lenard D. Moore, Carl Phillips, Thomas Sayers Ellis, Elizabeth Alexander, Kevin Young, C. S. Giscombe, and others—to the list makes the nineties look like another renaissance, one bolstered by the proliferation of technology into an outburst of diverse creativity many times greater than the first one in the twenties.

Two examples of their voices: C. S. Giscombe and Lucinda Roy.

C. S. Giscombe's cryptic "note-taking" style—echoing Paul Blackburn, Gary Snyder, and Robert Creeley in some ways—is concise, unpredictable, odd, and, at times, vividly beautiful, as seen in the lines from "(1980)":

> In the dream I became 2 men my age
> & we confronted the old man
> who'd been K's lover once who
> wanted her back he sd
> on whose land she still lived
>
> but that one of us was black, the other "of mixed blood"

Such lines move as intricately woven patterns, indeed, just like the candid language of risky dreams, moving from the emotional depths of the most private places to places post-personal yet not quite public, making the journey with elegance and urgency as they attempt to render a hard-won "self" in line-by-line breath, with no frills.

Three lines from "Suffering the Sea Change: All My Pretty Ones," by Lucinda Roy:

> What isn't water in us must be bone;
> what isn't weeping must be what remains
> when weeping's done.

Three lines of precision, intensity, understanding, power, and beauty.

Giscombe's, Roy's, and the other voices of this newest generation of poets are as individual and as rooted in the culture as I imagine it's possible to be in this day and age of internationalism and multiculturalism. Their voices are constructed out of intense cultural and artistic conflict and cross-fertilization. This, for example, is Michael S. Weaver's last stanza in "My Father's Geography":

> *At a phone looking to Africa over the Mediterranean,*
> *I called my father, and, missing me, he said,*
> *"You almost home boy. Go on cross that sea!"*

"Go on cross that sea," indeed.

. . . .

In African American poetry, there were many seas to cross and there are many seas yet to cross—most of them at home, on these shores. In 1931, James Weldon Johnson wrote a new preface to his 1922 classic anthology *The Book of American Negro Poetry.* Near the end of that introduction Johnson wrote, "I do not wish to be understood to hold any theory that they [Negro poets] should limit themselves to Negro themes; the sooner they are able to write American poetry spontaneously, the better" (42). That, as it turns out, is a domestic "sea" that African American poets have now clearly crossed.

At the end of Johnson's long preface, he wrote: "Much ground has been covered, but more will yet be covered. It is this side of prophesy to declare that undeniable creative genius of the Negro is destined to make a distinctive and valuable contribution to American poetry."

Struga '75

I was invited to Yugoslavia because Galway Kinnell once gave my name, by mail, to Meto Jovanovski in Yugoslavia. Meto was planning to translate American poetry for a Macedonian anthology. This was in October 1973 when Galway and I were teaching at Sarah Lawrence. Meto recommended that Yugoslavia's International Poetry Festival invite me as the official U.S. representative. I was first invited in 1974 but was unable to accept the invitation. During the spring of 1975, while I was participating in the visiting writer's program at Columbia University, William Jay Smith, its acting director, told me about his trip to Yugoslavia for the festival in 1974. His description excited my imagination. At the same time an invitation to participate in the 1975 Yugoslavian festival arrived. Traveling expenses would cost more than a thousand dollars. The festival would handle expenses while I was there, but the problem was how to pay for transportation. Bill Smith contacted some people he knew in the State Department and thereby sparked the interest that finally caused the U.S. government to sponsor my trip. Technically this was called a "cultural grant."

Someone suggested that, during a time when President Leopold Sedar Senghor of Senegal was to receive an important literary prize at the festival, it would be politically hip for the United States to have a black poet there. I don't know the motives of the State Department, but I do think I know the motives of the Yugoslavs: they were not racial.

The first official meeting of the participants took place at eleven the morning after our arrival at the Bristol Hotel, about twenty minutes by bus from the Metropol. The Bristol was in Struga. Gathered around a table in the meeting room were Meteja Matevski, the festival's president, several vice presidents, and the director, Jovan Strezovski. The meeting was brief: a few words of welcome, some hints as to what was to come, some theory.

Then we all went out on the terrace for lunch.

Here, in a relaxed atmosphere, we began to meet people. Herbert Kuhner, an American, introduced himself. Kuhner lived in Austria and said he supported himself by doing translations. He also said he was a poet and fiction writer who had attended many of these festivals. I ordered a bottle of good Holland beer and my wife, Sharyn, had coffee. One of Senghor's press agents joined us. He had lived in the United States for some years and we exchanged a few impressions. Very soon we were talking with a wide variety of poets: Fatty Said from Egypt, who reminded me in manner and appearance of Calvin Hernton, from America; tall, handsome, quiet Saadi Yousif from Iraq, who also wrote short stories; E. M. De Melo Castro, a friendly, bearded, and plump young man from Portugal, one of their leading young poets; Waldo Leyva Portal from Cuba; Lassi Nummi and his wife from Finland; Hans van de Waarsenburg from the Netherlands, who had a head of long, silky blond hair and a thick beard. His girlfriend or wife, Riet, was with him; she was beautiful; there was the big Viking, Kjell-Erik Vindtorn, from Norway; and Frank De Crits and Eddy von Vliet, both of Belgium; Sergio Macias, originally from Chile, was presently from the Instituto Latinoamerica in Rostock; Homero Aridjis, with his warm smile, originally from Mexico, was presently from The Hague where he was serving as cultural attaché in the Mexican Embassy.

After supper at the Metropol, we all went to the official opening of the festival at the House of Poetry in Struga. The ritual lighting of the festival fires in front of the building had already taken place earlier in the day.

Our books were carefully displayed in the exhibition hall. Hundreds stood inspecting them. Guards watched to make sure no one touched them. We could inspect the covers of books by Castro, Nummi, Vindtorn, Macias, Vliet, De Crits, Waarsenburg, Portal, Yousif, and Fatty Said. If a guard happened to turn his back, of course we got a brief chance to open them. Senghor's books occupied the center of the exhibition. His press agents were there already though President Senghor himself was still in Belgrade talking politics with President Tito. Senghor would arrive tomorrow afternoon. This whole affair, the entire festival, was in honor and memory of the Yugoslav poet Ivo Andrić, a Nobel Prize winner.

From the English program notes we knew vaguely what was happening: Jovan Strezovski made the introductory remarks, opening the ceremony; then the readings; then, the language of all people—a concert performed by the Macedonian Philharmonic Orchestra conducted by Pero Petrovski.

Scene: the next morning, Bristol Hotel. I was in the Symposium Room listening to speeches translated through earphones. Sharyn was doing the same thing next to me. Young Yugoslav poet Tomaž Šalamun came in. He reminded me that I'd promised him I'd allow him to interview me before the television camera for Television Skopje. I excused myself and Tomaž and I went out to the terrace where they had the camera all set. For twenty minutes we discussed poetry, fiction, form, technique, language.

After the morning symposium, Sharyn and I sat on the patio under a bright canopy talking with one of Senghor's press secretaries. The radio and television people were still busy interviewing various foreign visitors. The lake was calm and light blue, with long streaks of yellow light rippling across it. Above, in an otherwise clear sky, a few clouds drifted out toward the distant mountains of Albania. A Macedonian newspaper reporter introduced himself, and with Sharyn's help, speaking French, asked me a few questions about my work and American literature in general. (The next morning we discovered I was grossly misquoted—made to say many contradictory things that supported the reporter's political views of America.)

Later. Outside the House of Poetry, Sharyn and I were catching fresh air, night air. Inside, Yugoslavs were still reading and reciting their poems. We'd already listened to over an hour's worth of it. Presently, we saw Kjell-Erik approaching us. He too felt restless, so the three of us went along the river walkway, rubbing shoulders with hundreds of people out for a night stroll; at the bridge, we crossed and went down the other side till we came to an outdoor café. We took a table and ordered beer. Sharyn had campari. Kjell-Erik was telling us of his adventures in New Orleans, where he once stopped while working a fishing boat, when Homero, Eddy von Vliet, and Frank joined us. In a somewhat smug manner we talked about the shortcomings of the present festival, its lack of effective organization, then, perhaps feeling guilty, we outlined its virtues, even mentioning how valuable its lack of organization was in the long run.

This was also the night I met Meto Jovanovski for the first time. He reminded me that he and I had corresponded, and that Galway Kinnell had put us in touch with each other. Meto was brought over to us by two American college students, Paul and Nelljean. Both were aspiring poets working on MFAs at a university in one of the southern states.

Later that night, on what was officially called "Night Without Punctuation," there was a party for the participants at the Bristol's café. This was the 29th. After a vegetarian dinner, Sharyn and I joined friends at one of the crowded tables near the stage, where a local band was making loud, brassy music. Already seated at the table were Hans and Riet, Homero, Frank, Eddy, and Kjell-Erik. We all watched Kjell-Erik line up about seven tiny glasses of very sweet wine and drink them all without stopping. I ordered dry white wine and turned to watch the people on the floor, who had begun to dance holding hands and forming a long line, moving snakelike between the tables. They were singing and jumping about awkwardly and having a lot of fun. An African poet went up to the microphone and recited a powerfully revolutionary poem full of chants and barks, and everybody cheered and laughed, which was not the right response. The poem was also wrong for the occasion, but it didn't matter. A woman from Belgium, a well-known poet, kept coming over to our table, pulling at my arm trying to get me to go up and read one of my poems. To demonstrate how easy it was, she took the microphone and yelled one of her own poems into it, and people screamed with joy. Then somebody else read a slow poem and nobody paid any attention. Then Homero decided to do it and nobody noticed or listened, and when he returned to his seat he said, "It was a very bad idea." He seemed hurt but it passed quickly, and we all drank to the festival and to poetry.

Very late, back at the Metropol: We ran into Castro, Waldo, and Sergio and invited them up to our room, where I had a large bottle of white wine. The bar had closed. So we sat on our balcony and drank and laughed and talked and looked up at the starlit night sky. There was something joyous yet lonely in our spirit. We needed to comfort each other. Later Fatty came up bringing signed copies of his own books. He stayed on after the others left and teased me about having been married more than once. In his country a man could marry as many women as he could afford but he could never divorce. He told us about his work as a newspaper writer. His poetry collections were read widely in schools in Egypt.

On this exciting night, Leopold Sedar Senghor had quietly arrived. From the balcony we could see the cars of his motorcade parked in the darkness of the parking lot.

August 30! Morning before the big day! Save Cvetanovski (Yugoslav translator of Faulkner) presented me with translated copies of my two poems, "Blind Old Woman" and "Form," which I would read the following night at the Central Manifestation of the Festival, where Senghor would read and also receive the Golden Wreath. The Macedonian versions of the poems were simply for my own record. An actress had also received copies. I would read the poems in their original English.

After breakfast we went for the usual morning symposium. Predrag Matvejevic, a very popular figure at the festival, was speaking on Yugoslavia's literature of rebellion and resistance.

When Matvejevic finished, an Oriya Indian poet, Sitakant Mahapatra, spoke on the problems and joys he had encountered while translating primitive Oriya poetry for the four anthologies of it he had published in his country. Mahapatra, author of three separate volumes of his own poetry, generally dismissed "self-indulgent" trends in European literature, strongly insisting on a functional art, giving the example of the tribal poetry of the Oriya as a fine example of useful art. I sat there listening and wondering. Surely it was a matter of definition. He mentioned Rimbaud, surprised at how a brilliant poet such as

Rimbaud could be so self-indulgent. I finally decided that the art of Mahapatra's primitive communities was probably no more useful to the Oriya than Rimbaud was to the French, which is to say they each were extremely useful, though in different ways. Even the most self-indulgent art—if it's art—is useful.

Mahapatra and another Indian poet, K. Ayyappa Paniker, joined Sharyn and me for lunch at the Metropol. We talked out some of these ideas and I discovered we didn't really disagree as much as I thought we might. We talked about reality. Later, Paniker gave me a copy of the Indian magazine *Chitram*, in which he had published an article. In it he wrote, "I know what reality is. It is what I imagine to be real. And art at its most sublime is the creation of that reality." Repeat: *the creation of that reality.* My own ideas coming back at me. A nonrepresentational art. It was the position, years ago, that Senghor had also taken when defending the flexibility of African languages as a medium for poetry. It is the position the innovative fiction writers in America take: art is an extension of reality, not a mirror image of it. As such, it has spiritual, emotional, psychological, and utilitarian functions.

That night there was a concert in an ancient church, Saint Sophie, held in honor of Senghor. Senghor sat stiffly through the entire occasion. Then he and his entourage marched out under the glare of clicking cameras and bright lights. Following this we all went to a special dinner party, also in Senghor's honor, and sitting at our table were our usual friends, plus quite a few others. One was a top official of the festival who had not especially liked the idea of Senghor getting the Golden Wreath. Apparently, the prize for Senghor had been pushed by the former ambassador to Senegal, who also happened to be Senghor's Macedonian translator.

There were more than 150 official guests from 25 countries, including Greece, France, Russia, and Hungary. There were hundreds of officials, members of the press, unofficial visitors, and friends of the festival. On the morning of August 31, about a fourth of us were transported by yacht to the area of Saint Naum's Monastery on the shores of Lake Ohrid, where we all unloaded, ate, and drank lots of wine. We danced folk dances to the quaint music of little old men standing erect under weeping willows playing violins too loudly. Of our group I was the first to join the Yugoslavs in their dance, then Nelljean took my hand, then Sharyn, then Kjell-Erik and Castro and Homero—everybody, I think, joined in, dancing around in a fantastic circle and singing and yelling.

Soon Senghor and his party joined us and the dancing stopped. The music became more formal. But a good feeling was still in the air despite so many uniformed guards and bodyguards standing at the edges of the area. Senghor, at one point, stood up from the table they had set for him under a willow. He said something kind about the occasion and the festival in general. Then, with his party and his beautiful French wife at his side, he started out. At this point, the president of the festival grabbed my hand and pushed it into Senghor's, and we, in this way, found ourselves shaking hands and smiling at each other. In French the president explained who I was, and Senghor immediately spoke in English, saying he admired black American poets and was looking forward to hearing me read. Sharyn and Senghor then shook hands and exchanged greetings. We stepped back, and others pushed toward him.

After Senghor left the picnic area, the fun started again. The dancing and the wine drinking and the music. Long tables with stacks of chicken, steaks, pork chops, salad greens, tomatoes, cheese, potato salad, and fresh fruit lined the edges of the area. As soon as the tables ran low, members of the catering service would haul out more. Someone had a large book with clear pages. He was going about asking various guests to sign their names or write something in his book, perhaps a poem. Somebody gave me a pen and I closed my eyes, held my face toward the sky. People crowded around me, apparently watching my face, my closed eyes, then the page. Without looking I drew a picture of myself: it was expressionistic. Wow! They liked it. Were amazed. The owner of the book was delighted. Another person was circulating with a scrapbook of photographs he had taken of many of the official guests, asking them to sign their own pictures. A woman from Radio Skopje cornered me and reminded me that I had promised her a radio interview.

We found a quiet corner. To make a long story short, this is what I said in answer to her questions: The goal of literature is to operate as an extension of life. What did I think of literature that dealt with social revolution? I said it was all right if you could *show* me the message and not tell me *what* to think about it.

On the way back to Metropol I drifted into thoughts of Senghor. Senghor was one of the founders of the cultural theory called *negritude.* A man who'd spent time fighting for France, who'd spent time in a German prison camp. What had he said—"The object does not mean what it represents but what it suggests, what it creates." I closed my eyes, closing out the lake and the countryside and the mountains. A red sky shimmered before me. I felt Sharyn's hand softly curled into my own.

We were going back by bus. Waldo and Sergio sat across from us and were telling Sharyn, in Spanish—they did not speak English—about themselves, and Sharyn was translating everything said, and when I said something to them, she'd translate it, and so on. Castro, who spoke excellent English, was somewhere in the rear. He and Homero had been two friends we had often depended on to help in communicating with Sergio and Waldo. Waldo was a university professor in Santiago, Cuba. Sergio wanted to know the type of poetry I wrote. Castro, on one occasion, took a very long time to explain to Sergio my ideas and ideals in this area. Sergio smiled and said he wrote mostly nature poetry. Now, they were good-naturedly laughing with Sharyn about the "corny" music we had just heard at the picnic and on the previous night at the Bristol. They reminded Sharyn of Latin American friends she had hung out with at City College in New York. Her enthusiasm was generated to me, and though I could not speak well with them in their language nor in my own, I felt close to them and cherished their friendship.

The Central Manifestation of the Struga Poetry Festival is called "Bridges" because it takes place on a bridge. The whole city is brought to a standstill while the entire occasion is televised. There were chairs for special guests alongside the stage facing the river. Possibly seven or eight thousand people lined the river on both sides. Television crewmen and newspaper photographers ran around the outer edges of the stage setting up equipment. Sharyn sat among the special guests. Riet was there, too. Lassi Nummi's wife was also there. Honorary members of the festival also held those seats. We, the poets, were on the stage. Senghor arrived. A huge display of the Golden Wreath decorated the back of the stage. Senghor was introduced and praised for his contribution to literature, then presented the prize. He came up on the stage from the right. He accepted the prize, said a few words in French, then read a poem, an old poem written years ago. I felt someone's elbow in my ribs. "He hasn't written a poem in thirty years!" I tried to keep a straight face.

Fatty's reading was inspired and powerful; then I read, and there was a tremendous ovation. I felt good. Really good. We all read: Waldo, Homero, Hans, Kjell-Erik, Saadi, Nummi. After the affair, Senghor and I talked briefly again while the photographers snapped pictures. I gave him an autographed copy of *The Dark and Feeling* and he was delighted, then signed a copy of his new Yugoslav collection for me. He felt that my reading and my poetry showed great sensitivity. I thanked him. Was happy that he liked the poems I had read.

Later that night, some friends from the American Embassy joined us at the Metropol for a late-night snack. One felt the poem "Form," which appears in *The Syncopated Cakewalk* was the most powerful attack on imperialism he had ever heard. When I explained that it was, in fact, quite literally a poem about language, about *form*, he blushed and said, "I guess I was just reading too much into it."

September 1. Breakfast with Frank and Eddy. Promises to meet again in Skopje at Hotel Grand.

We went downstairs. Homero was sitting in the lobby with his luggage at his knee. He gave us a sleepy smile. Most of our other friends were staying till the end. Tomorrow, the final day of the festival, September 2, some of them were scheduled to read at a theater in Skopje. But I had to get back: I had classes to teach. Homero, too, had to return to The Hague. Not realizing that the airport bus had already gone, we sat there waiting. The desk clerk did not offer any help or ask us any questions. A nervous taxi driver paced back and forth in the lobby. Only two others, a man and a woman, were waiting. What they were waiting for is anybody's guess. Finally, the taxi driver approached us. He wanted to take us to the airport. I waved him away and went outside to look for the bus. No bus. He followed me saying, "Bus gone!" He said this over and over, waving his arms angrily. I kept waving him—and his words—away just as angrily.

Sharyn, Homero, and I finally gave in and took an overpriced taxi to the airport. On arrival, Homero was told that he could not take the flight because he didn't have a ticket. He had only a reservation. It did not mean anything to them. Meanwhile, the morning flight to Belgrade had been delayed because of bad weather at Belgrade. This probably meant we would miss our flight to Frankfurt. As it turned out, we did. And because of the initial screw-up the remainder of the return trip was a nightmare not to be believed.

But once we were home, and I had slept nearly fifteen hours, in despair and exhaustion I lay there in bed knowing that the festival would stay with me as rare and good and important.

Looking at the *Dial*

In May 1880 when, in Chicago, Francis F. Browne started publishing a magazine he called the *Dial*, he was aligning himself with a spiritual and intellectual tradition. Margaret Fuller and Ralph Waldo Emerson edited the first *Dial*, a quarterly, in Boston from 1840 to 1844. They had been interested, among other things, in providing a forum for transcendentalism, broad views of theology, and philosophical investigations. Sixteen years later, in Cincinnati, Rev. Moncure D. Conway attempted to carry on the *Dial* tradition, but his magazine lasted only a year. Browne's *Dial* began as a monthly, and the first issue carried an essay on the original *Dial* by Norman C. Perkins. Browne's employer, General McClurg, published the magazine under the imprint of his house, Jansen, McClurg & Company.

Browne, a printer, had earlier bought stock in the *Western Monthly*, and in 1871 he became the magazine's editor, later changing the title to the *Lakeside Monthly*. This publication folded due to money problems in 1874, and from then until 1879 Browne was without a magazine and in poor health. In 1880, he went to work for McClurg. Browne edited the *Dial* for the company as its house organ until 1892, when he bought it and renamed its publisher the Dial Company. He had already taken on his brother, F. C. Browne, as business manager in 1888, and now he enlisted William Morton Payne and Edward Gilpin as associate editors. With the September 1, 1892, issue the *Dial* became a semimonthly and included the subtitle "A Semi-Monthly Journal of Literary Criticism, Discussion, and Information." The following year, 1893, Browne established Dial Press to print books for writers ("authors' editions or private editions"), although his efforts here were modest.

In the October 16, 1882, issue, Browne wrote that the *Dial* was very proud of its distinguished list of contributors, which included former presidents, professors, scholars, and even the current president of the United States, Chester Arthur (no. 3: 120). Later, in the 1890s, listed among its contributors were Woodrow Wilson, Melville B. Anderson, Frederick J. Turner, Katherine Lee Bates, Joseph Jastrow, H. H. Boysen, W. P. Trent, Richard Henry Stoddard, Fred Lewis Pattee, and Chief Justice Melville W. Fuller.

In 1898 the *Dial* absorbed Herbert S. Stone's *Chap-Book*. Before the merger, Browne's *Dial* was hostile to the experimental works of its day. On the one hand, it found little to praise in the prose of Stephen Crane and leveled negative criticism against Walt Whitman's poetry. On the other hand, it more than once featured the bad poetry of Harriet Monroe. It was editorially queasy and opposed any artistic or intellectual attempt to break with tradition. It took the moral and genteel position when evaluating the worth of American culture. Prior to the merger with the *Dial*, Stone and his assistants, Bliss Carman and Harrison Garfield Rhodes, had published important poets of the day, among them Stephen Crane, W. B. Yeats, and William Vaughn Moody. Among the fiction writers was Thomas Hardy. The spirit of Stone's efforts carried over into the *Dial*. For the first time, because of Stone's interest in experimentation and new writers, the *Dial* showed a variety and aesthetic excitement it had never before possessed. Although Browne had, as late as 1896, told his readers that he had avoided making the magazine physically attractive because he believed that to do so would compromise "the high ideals set for the journal at the start" (no. 20: 348), he nevertheless tolerated two years later a relatively radical change in content brought on by Stone's influence. Generally, Browne ran essays and book reviews. Topics usually had to do with literature, history, or some aspect of culture. Regular departments were "Briefs on New Books," "What's in the Magazines," "Trade Book Lists," and "Topics in Leading Periodicals."

Lucian Cary was editor of the *Dial* from October 1913 until February 1915. Only twenty-eight when he took over, Cary was especially interested in the free verses Harriet Monroe was publishing in her magazine *Poetry*. He also gave more attention to "Recent Fiction" than had Browne. But his taste in fiction was, in retrospect, questionable. Most of the novels he reviewed were of little lasting value, although works by Arnold Bennett, Theodore Dreiser, Louis Couperus, H. G. Wells, and Anatole France were exceptions. Nevertheless, Cary set the magazine on a course toward a position where it would begin to serve the new movements in the arts that had been fermenting in London, Paris, and New York since the turn of the century.

By April 1915, Francis Browne's sons were in charge, Waldo Browne as editor and Herbert S. Browne as president. Frank Luther Mott incorrectly states that Charles Leonard Moore was at this time an associate editor. As editor, Waldo Browne attempted to sustain the publication in the genteel, conservative spirit his father gave it. He brought back William Morton Payne as a contributor as part of this effort, Lucian Cary's influence no doubt being seen as negative. Payne's new presence, as it turned out, was brief. An essay he wrote on German war guilt angered Waldo Browne. Although it was slated for the

September 30, 1915, issue, Browne rejected it, and with the rejection, the relationship ended. In some small way, it signaled Herbert Browne's departure from his father's outlook, although the gesture probably is not strong enough to be characterized as a declaration of independence. In June, Waldo Browne moved the magazine from the fashionable Fine Arts Building (where Margaret Anderson's *Little Review* started in 1914) to the Transportation Building at 608 South Dearborn Street.

After Payne's departure, Edward Everett Hale Jr., who also preferred the consciously polite in literature, wrote the "Recent Fiction" column. For Hale, H. G. Wells was more important than, say, Bernard Shaw. Waldo Browne's sensibility and taste could not have been more compatible with this modest revolt against the so-called vulgar in contemporary literature. Browne was equally closed to what he considered bad taste in painting and the other arts. His *Dial* featured several articles attacking the newer experiments.

However, times were changing, and the *Dial* was losing readers, or certainly not gaining any. After changing it from a semimonthly to a fortnightly in March 1915, the brothers decided to sell. Waldo Browne's last issue was published on July 15, 1916. Yet, perhaps in spite of himself, Browne made the magazine more specifically literary. Political essays and essays on aspects of society and history of the type his father had published were unacceptable. Perhaps Lucian Cary influenced Browne's direction. Certainly, Browne's social consciousness was every bit as active as his father's had been. But it manifested itself in a literary way. He was a liberal who supported the efforts of black people toward full equality. For instance, he published Benjamin Brawley's "The American Negro in Fiction" in the May 11, 1916, issue (no. 60: 445–50). This essay attempts to dispel the stereotypical and propagandistic image of the Negro in contemporary fiction by white American writers. It was a brave position for Browne at a time when taking up the cause of the Negro was unpopular. Browne also had strong feelings about the war. In a review of Romain Rolland's *Above the Battle* in the March 16, 1916, issue, he spoke out firmly against nationalism and in favor of human fraternity.

In 1916, Martyn Johnson purchased the Dial Company from the Brownes. Earlier, Johnson had been involved with the *Trimmed Lamp*. Its editor, Howard Vincent O'Brien, had started the publication, then titled simply *Art*, in October 1912, the same year *Poetry* started, "to keep the art world of Chicago and the West familiar with what was going on in the O'Brien Art Galleries." In March 1914, O'Brien changed the title to the *Trimmed Lamp* and also opened the pages to poetry and criticism of the arts. Johnson convinced the editors of and contributors to the *Trimmed Lamp* to merge their magazine with his. He also managed to obtain the financial help of Mary L. Snow, Laird Bell, and Dr. Clinton Masseck. Johnson's takeover was announced to readers of the *Dial* in August 1916. Johnson was listed as the president, and Masseck was the editor. Masseck's editorship lasted one month.

During this period of upheaval and reorganization, representatives of the old school and the new movements were published. John Gould Fletcher wrote a piece for the January 11, 1917, issue titled "The Secret of Far Eastern Painting" (no. 62: 3–7), in which he called for a turning away from such experiments in Europe as Cubism toward the lessons of natural forms in Japanese and Chinese art. In the same issue, Richard Aldington's "Poet and Painter: A Renaissance Fancy" appeared. One might say Fletcher represented the old and Aldington the new. Among other advocates of the new movements to appear were Van Wyck Brooks, Maxwell Bodenheim, Babette Deutsch, and a young Yale man, Henry Seidel Canby, who would later assist Wilbur Lucius Cross in editing the *Yale Review*. Also included was Amy Lowell. She was, in a sense, the first to get revenge on Waldo Browne's *Dial* with her essay "In Defense of *Vers Libre*," published in August 1916.

Johnson felt completely confident that he had opened his magazine to the spirit and challenge of the contemporary scene. George Bernard Donlin, a graduate of the University of Chicago, was appointed editor, which was announced in the January 25, 1917, issue. In the same column, this statement from the management appeared: "The *Dial* . . . will endeavor to carry on a fruitful tradition . . . to meet the challenge of the new time by reflecting and interpreting its spirit—a spirit freely experimental, skeptical of inherited values, ready to examine old dogmas and to submit afresh its sanctions to the test of experience" (no. 62: 37). Poetry, for the first time in seventeen years, began to appear in the pages of the *Dial*. The Johnson *Dial* on the one hand took issue with Cubism and Futurism, but on the other hand thought Cézanne (the "father" of Cubism) a valid, important experimentalist.

Many persons already involved with Johnson's *Dial* would influence cultural tastes through the *Dial* of the 1920s. Among them were Paul Rosenfeld, Gilbert Seldes, James Sibley Watson, Scofield Thayer, and Randolph Bourne. Bourne died from the flu on December 22, 1918, but he became a source of inspiration for Thayer, the future editor of the *Dial*. Late in 1917, Johnson's *Dial* absorbed the *Seven Arts*, a literary monthly that had been published in New York since October 1916. The *Seven Arts* published D. H. Lawrence, Carl Sandburg, Robert Frost, Bourne, Waldo Frank, Van Wyck Brooks, Sherwood Anderson, Eugene O'Neill, and many other new writers. The prestige the *Seven Arts* brought to the *Dial* was undeniable.

Suffering from tuberculosis, Donlin quit the magazine and moved to the West. For a brief period in 1918 the *Dial* had no editor, but Harold Stearns agreed to act as caretaker and moved from New York to Chicago to take charge. Ironically, the magazine itself moved to New York during July and August, and Stearns, who did not like Chicago, was among many of those happy with the move. The new office opened in an artistically symbolic place—Greenwich Village, at 152 Thirteenth Street.

With the January 11, 1919, issue, Robert Morss Lovett became editor, but the end of Johnson's fortnightly was already in sight. According to S. Foster Damon, Scofield Thayer bought Johnson's magazine in December 1919. The November 29 issue carried notice of Johnson's resignation (no. 67: 486). This same issue announced termination of the entire editorial staff and gave the first public notice that the publication was now owned and managed by Dr. James Sibley Watson Jr., president, with Scofield Thayer as secretary-treasurer and editor. The new owners announced that the magazine would become a monthly. Thayer had already been an associate editor on Johnson's and Donlin's staff. But now, in their fourth issue of April 1920, they declared that the *Dial* "cannot be everything to everybody. It is non-political and has no message for the million" (no. 68: unnumbered opening page). This amounted to a declaration of independence from the past. Thayer, the guiding force, aimed to publish the best creative and critical works available, excluding scientific or sociological essays. He felt that America was stuck in an apathetic, unimaginative state, and in response he would push Bourne's theory of transnationalism, among other ideas.

Although he said politics were out of bounds, before long he used the *Dial* to oppose the activities of the New York Society for the Suppression of Vice, but only because, in his view, it interfered with artistic freedom. (This group brought a lawsuit against Margaret Anderson for publishing an excerpt from James Joyce's *Ulysses*.) Nicholas Joost sees a paradox in the magazine's commitment to both nonpolitical liberalism and pure aesthetics. Although the *Dial* encouraged philosophical argument, it remained stern in its liberal progressive views, in its commitment to aesthetic diversity.

Meanwhile, Thayer, Watson, and Mitchell were publishing the writings of Djuna Barnes, John Dewey, Bertrand Russell, Van Wyck Brooks, Paul Rosenfeld, Sherwood Anderson, e. e. cummings, Marianne Moore, Carl Sandburg, Hart Crane, John Dos Passos, William Carlos Williams, and William Butler Yeats. In 1921, they published T. S. Eliot's "The Waste Land," Ezra Pound's "Cantos," and Thomas Mann's *Death in Venice*. D. H. Lawrence's work, like that of most of those mentioned above, was not then widely known in the United States. In the September 1921 issue, the *Dial* began to publish Lawrence, starting with his story "Adolf." This was followed by the poem "Pomegranate" (March 1921). Excerpts from *Sea and Sardinia* ran in October 1921, and the February 1922 issue carried an excerpt from *Aaron's Rod.* In fact, Lawrence's writings appeared in almost every issue of the *Dial* until June 1925. In 1922, two years after Martyn Johnson gave up on the *Dial,* he made an assessment of Lawrence in a review of *Aaron's Rod* for the *Los Angeles Times* (Sunday), quoted in the *Dial*: Lawrence was "one of the most important [figures] in the entire range of literature." Through the *Dial,* Lawrence reached a larger yet no less sensitive audience than he had previously through Harriet Monroe's *Poetry* and his books published by Thomas Seltzer.

In addition, wonderful and simple line drawings by e. e. cummings and Toulouse-Lautrec were reproduced. Reproductions of Picasso's clowns, Chagall's dream-schemes, Brancusi's sculptures, and the expressionist art of Bosschere, Hunt Diederich, and Maria Uhden appeared. Also included were cartoons by William Gropper, pencil and ink drawings by Beardsley, Gaston Lachaise, Claude Bragdon, Ivan Opffer, Hildegarde Watson, Richard Boix, Adolf Dehn, Diederich, and Max Liebermann, as well as reproductions of woodblock prints by Uhden, Ann Merrimn Peck, and Frans Masereel.

The departments were no less interesting. The *Dial* commonly reviewed books such as Irwing Babbitt's *Rosseau and Romanticism,* Leon Bazalgette's *Walt Whitman: The Man and His Work,* Chekhov's *The Bishop and Other Stories* and *The Cherry Orchard,* Chesterton's *Irish Impressions,* Samuel Langhorne Clemens's *A Double Barrelled Detective Story—Roughing It—A Tramp Abroad,* and new editions of Walt Whitman's *Leaves of Grass.* It focused a keen eye on theater, too. Reviews of *Hamlet, Power of Darkness,* and *Richard the Third,* as well as productions of newer works such as *Clarence and His Lady Friends* appeared. Frequently, in the departments, there was a "Dublin Letter" and one from London.

The *Dial* was now firmly joined in the task of achieving a cultural revolution. Thayer could depend on the quality of art and writing in his pages to help achieve the common goals he shared with Margaret Anderson, editor of the *Little Review,* Gorham B. Munson of *S4N* and *Secession,* Ford Madox Ford of the *Transatlantic Review,* Ezra Pound in London and Paris, Eugene Jolas and Elliot Paul of *transition,* and others committed to the struggle. By maintaining high standards and creating an attractive, appealing magazine, Thayer moved the *Dial* quickly to the forefront and, by 1925, when Marianne Moore replaced him as editor, the magazine had been established as a trend-setter, a cultural institution, and, for some, a work of art itself. The year before Thayer left, the staff reestablished Dial Press.

Marianne Moore continued in the direction set by Thayer and his coeditors and assistants. In 1927, a Dial Award was created, and the first one, announced in the January 1928 issue, was given to Pound. The issue also carried T. S. Eliot's enthusiastic review of Pound's *Personae,* originally published in London in 1909, and drawings by Pound's friend and coeditor of *Blast* (1914–15), Wyndham Lewis. H. D., who had also been close to Pound, had her *Hippolytus Temporizes* reviewed here. This was a very special issue for Pound.

By 1929, when so many cultural forces were squashed by the world economic crisis, the *Dial* had already served its purpose well. Along with the *Little Review* and the other journals of the arts and literature, it had introduced to an astonished world the art of the twentieth century. Unfortunately, the *Dial* was forced to fold because of money problems.

The role the *Dial* played in presenting, preserving, and advancing the new literature is enormous. Any assessment of modern literature in English would be incomplete without an acknowledgment of that role.

Claude McKay

My 1975 Adventure

Claude McKay was born in 1889 in Jamaica and died in 1948 in Chicago. At the time of his death, all ten of his books were out of print. Author of three novels, four books of poems, a collection of short stories, and an autobiography, McKay grew up in rural Jamaica, lived most of his short life in the United States, Europe, and North Africa, in bleak poverty, and died in extreme poverty and ill health. During the worst years of the Depression, McKay was forced to live in an upstate New York shelter for drunks and bums.

Another irony: McKay, better known as a poet, was by far a better novelist. Though it was in the United States that McKay published his books, he was not an American novelist. He was not an English writer, either, though some of his books were printed there. McKay was unquestionably an international writer. Two of his books were translated into Russian during his lifetime but none of his works have been published in his homeland. According to his friend and agent, Carl Cowl, McKay was never fully accepted in Jamaica. And he certainly was not really *involved* in the so-called Harlem Renaissance. It is simply another irony that his book, *Spring in New Hampshire and Other Poems* (1920), should be seen as the thing that kicked off the Harlem Renaissance.

Lately I've given a lot of thought to McKay. I was recently asked to write an introduction to three unpublished McKay manuscripts. They were to be published, but before I could finish my introduction, the project folded. The manuscripts (controlled by Hope McKay Virtue, McKay's daughter, and by Carl Cowl) went, I assume, to another publisher. This was mid-1974. I was left with a pile of notes.

I had reread all of McKay's poems and novels and Wayne Cooper's *The Passion of Claude McKay* (1973). It's the best book ever done on McKay. I met with Carl Cowl, a pleasantly intelligent man, and with Wayne Cooper, a brilliant scholar, somewhat shy, a white southerner living in a black neighborhood in Brooklyn. Cooper was doing some sort of night work in a hospital. His ambition was to collect and publish McKay's letters, but he could not afford to work steadily on the project. Cooper also planned a full-scale biography of the Jamaican writer. I asked him about the possibility of his receiving a grant to hold him while doing his work. He smiled. Apparently, he did not know the right people. My talks with Cowl and Cooper gave me insights and sidelights I would not have otherwise gained.

McKay is probably best known for his poem, "If We Must Die," which Winston Churchill recited at a crucial moment during the war. But *Banana Bottom* (1933), a novel, is McKay's best work. It is set in Jamaica and of his completed fiction, it is the most clearly conceived and imaginatively written. The pace is slow, and, like many good books, it is not easy to read.

Yet I wonder about a McKay novel we will never see. He called it *Color Scheme*. In 1925, William Bardly, his agent at the time, could not sell it because it was too frankly sexual. In a letter to A. A. Schomburg (quoted by Cooper in *Passion*, 26), McKay says of *Color Scheme*, "I make my Negro characters yarn and backbite and fuck like people the world over." McKay eventually destroyed this, his first novel.

Identified as a writer of the so-called low life, McKay wrote about prostitutes and pimps, Pullman car porters, dreamers, revolutionaries, bums, drifters, cabaret good-time folks. Most of these characters were either at odds with or struggling against the concepts of the worlds in which they found themselves.

Stylistically, McKay was no innovator. His poetry was formal and rigidly conventional. His fictional technique showed the influence of more interesting concepts then being explored by D. H. Lawrence, Gertrude Stein, and several French writers of the 1920s. McKay's characters generally felt it better to live a carefree, gutsy, primitive life than to conform; better than to spend one's time a slave to the socially acceptable.

This is demonstrated dramatically in *Romance in Marseilles* (1929–30), one of the unpublished McKay manuscripts. *Romance* is a thin, colorful, and choppy story of a West African black man who has just lost both legs and an Egyptian girl whoring on Marseilles' Quayside or, as McKay says, the Dreamport. It is the Mediterranean Harbor.

As the novel opens we see Lafala briefly in a New York hospital where his legs are being amputated. A crooked lawyer, called the Black Angel, handles Lafala's lawsuit against the shipping company that Lafala is suing for compensation. His position is simple: the company is responsible since ship authorities, after finding Lafala and his pal Babel aboard as stowaways, locked them in a place where Lafala's legs froze and therefore had to be taken off. Lafala is fixed up with artificial legs, the court rules in his favor, and he returns, this time as a ticket paying passenger, to Mediterranean Harbor, where he immediately begins to flaunt his potential settlement wealth. But the fifty thousand dollars is still a long way from his hands.

Right away two whores, Aslima and La Fleur Noire, start vying for his attention. La Fleur Noire doesn't stand a chance because Lafala already has his eyes set on Aslima. The "two wenches" fight like "little rats in the hole." Much of the battle takes place at the rendezvous of the colored colony Café Tout-va-Bien. Rock, an American black, Diup, a Senegalese, Petite Frère, who works at the Domino Café, and Big Blond, a white American (involved homosexually with Petite Frère), are a few of the characters who enter along the sidelines among a dazzling spread of love and drink seekers, drifters and dreamers, pimps and their women, revolutionaries and underdogs. Mostly they dance, fight, laugh, stretch out in the sun, maybe unload a ship for a little extra money with which to buy more Italian Spumanti. Etienne St. Dominique is the local crusader fighting for the rights of the Quayside dwellers.

With a belly full of wine and a light head, Lafala concludes that money is better than sound feet. Plus he is finally sleeping with the girl of his greatest daydream. In fact, he wants to marry her and take her with him to his homeland. Meanwhile, Titian, Aslima's evil-spirited pimp, is growing impatient and is not fully convinced that Aslima is simply holding out for larger gains. Aslima continues to refuse the money that Lafala offers her. Theoretically, she is waiting for the full settlement. She permits Lafala to assume she is with him because she has sincere feelings for him. Cat Row is buzzing with gossip. Lafala plays the flute and remembers dancing the Banana-Split and the Jolly Pig.

Aslima's past rushes into the present. Born a slave in Marrakesh and raised in Moulay Abdallah by "a wise old courtesan," Aslima knows instinctively that Lafala, the cautious one, does not trust her though he wants her. She is waiting to gain his trust as well.

Before Lafala can get his hands on the settlement money, he and Babel are thrown in jail for the crime of stowing away. St. Dominique pulls a few powerful strings and the two pals are set free. Lafala's money is also now clear. Quayside jumps with joy. Folks are dancing and celebrating in the streets. McKay tells us there is a new feeling about and among blacks.

Aslima plans to exploit and abandon Lafala. She also plans to stay with him. Titian resolves her conflict: he kills her.

Thematically and even structurally, *Romance* resembles *Banjo* (1929) minus the intellectual agonizing on political and social matters.

Lafala is based on a real person named Deda. McKay describes him in a letter (in the James Weldon Johnson Collection at Yale) dated January 13, 1928. Deda had been a great dancer much admired by the girls of Vieux Port quarters.

Harlem Glory, the second manuscript, is also a novel. Set in the early 1930s, its central figure is Buster South, a West Indian who lives in Harlem where he divides his time between running numbers, romancing women, and spiritualism. The story opens with Buster in Paris as Policy Queen Millinda Rose's traveling companion. There is a big party at Millinda's. Her secret is she's bankrupt—suddenly. She's the widow of the late, powerful Policy King Red Rose. Before the party ends, Millinda goes to the bathroom and commits suicide. And Buster returns to Harlem alone.

High life on Sugar Hill and the numbers racket seem to be in trouble. Not enough money around. Harlem big shots think that whites—who have most of the money—should be spending more of it in Harlem. Because Buster knows how to deal with whites and how to manipulate blacks, he is considered valuable to the community. This is only one ideological force at work. There are others.

McKay fills the novel with many characters and aspects of Paris and Harlem life. There's a flashback to Red and Millinda's wedding on Sugar Hill; barbershop talk on man-woman relations; the relation of conjure and voodoo to the numbers and how the racket got started; the reader meets, in Paris, impish, light-skinned Lotta Sander; Baron Belchite, from Austria, Prince (black) and Princess (white) Kwakoh Fanti, from West Africa; pushy, middle-class, Afro-American Miss Aschine Palma; Madame Marie Audacem, a high society type; and others.

In Harlem, the impressionistic vision is just as wide. We hear Cleopatra Price testifying; witness Abdul, the revolutionary who dies in the end; we hear Katie, a maid, tell her story; Javan Brown loses his wife to the Glory Savior; Luther Sharpage is the Glory Savior's partner in the formation of the Helping Hand; we get a glimpse of the semi-secret spiritualist chapels of the Glory Soulers, a place of primitive Christian mysticism and African black magic and fetishism; we hear an alarming (and alarmed!) number of male characters referring to something called "the female problem"; there's Larry, the truck driver who goes wild from drinking rubbing alcohol; Baldwin Hatcher, the white journalist and radio personality; Tilli Ashmead, a teacher; Patsinette Smythe, a house decorator; Bibba Prentice, a numbers game controller; Millinda's cook, Charlotte, and Charlotte's husband, Mr. Pointer; on the streets we see leather-coated dudes bopping and twitching in strange ways from the effects of reefer.

McKay takes us into a nickelodeon; we watch people sip hooch and read *The Harlem Nugget*; there's the Big Bang Club on 133rd between Fifth and Lexington; early on the reader meets the Senegalese dancer, Kamassa, and the Afro-American pianist, Pucksur, at Lamour's Cabaret playing "The Peanut Vendor," with a delightful sweetness. And when McKay mentions the magic of Josephine Baker, your reporter must inform you that he knows *exactly* what McKay means, from having held tightly to Miss Baker's hand for the longest moment you can imagine.

Then, it is mainly because of Buster's association with the late Policy Queen that he is in such demand as a manipulator of his own people. Jerry Batty, a businessman, offers Buster a "position," which is refused. Though broke, Buster is respected by such big shots as Spareribs Duke; the Harlem politician Homer Lake; the beautician Gypsy Nilequeen; the Colonel, who runs Neufields (a bar); and by Robert Byrd, the Glory Savior himself, for whom Buster becomes a special right-hand man whose primary job is to drive the glowing white Virgin, Queen Mother, where she wants to be driven. Buster is given a new name by the lofty black Glory Savior. Henceforth he shall be known as Glory Pilgrim Progress. It is while Buster is attempting to romance a young college girl, Oleander Powers (also a Glory Savior follower known variously as Chrystal Water and Glory Chastity), that he discovers that Mother has romantic designs on him.

Buster wastes no time in taking her up on her subtle offer. Before long they are deep into an affair, and Glory Savior is too busy running his spiritual empire to notice. But Oleander is alert and suspicious.

Meanwhile, Omar, the revolutionary, steps in and denounces Glory Savior as an agent of the evil white man whose aim is to get black people to destroy themselves. How? By abstaining from sex. Opal, a former member of Garvey's Universal-Negro-Back-to-Africa movement, turns up as Commander of Omar's yeoman. Omar preaches self-help and pickets white-owned and -operated Harlem businesses demanding jobs for colored. Whiffs of Pan-Africanism are aired. We see the plight of socialism, nationalism, and communism right alongside the spiritual and political exploitation in Harlem. But more distressing than these rip-offs is how closely the picture of Harlem in the 1920s correlates to Harlem today.

Finally, Madame Marie Audace and Lotta Sander return to the United States, bringing news that Aschine Palma has succeeded in taking Prince Fanti from his white bride. Aschine, a plain Afro-American girl, is now a Princess with a kingdom in West Africa.

The book ends with Buster proposing to Oleander. Marriage would make them Glory Prince and Glory Princess!

My Green Hills of Jamaica is the weakest of the three books. It is an autobiographical sketch of McKay's childhood and early adulthood years in Jamaica. The writing is poor in quality. Written near the end of McKay's life, it was obviously more unfinished than *Romance* or *Glory.*

Cedric Dover, an Anglo-Indian, author of *Half Cast* (1937) and *Know This of Race* (1943), asked McKay to do *Green Hills* as part of a projected book Dover had in mind to be called *East Indian, West Indian*. Dover himself would supply the other portion, about his own East Indian childhood. Aside from the fact that Dover and McKay did not share literary, social, or political views, the project never got off the ground.

In *Green Hills* McKay explains how he grew up believing that high culture came first from England, then the rest of Europe, and finally from the United States. (It is also interesting to remember that once McKay left Jamaica, he never returned.)

Claude McKay was a young man of great personal aloofness. His mother appears to have been a woman who expressed great sympathy for people who had experienced misfortune. Many of the stories in *Gingertown* (1932), all of McKay's novels, and many of his essays, and some of his poems deal sympathetically with victims.

McKay grew up singing American Negro spirituals and fully accepting the terms of Jamaica's rigid class and caste system. Yet there is one place in *Green Hills* where the author, self-consciously and proudly, describes how a black judge effectively handles a court case.

Like other little black Britons, McKay played cricket and softball. But the African side of his heritage was present too. He made moonshine dolls. He refers to his father as a real black Scotchman.

The thin manuscript deals mainly with McKay's relation to an elderly eccentric Englishman who encourages McKay to write. The Englishman has an interest in Negro dialect and encourages McKay to use the creole that he speaks in unguarded moments. McKay would rather use the King's English, but reluctantly follows the advice of his patron. The Englishman finances the publication of McKay's first book, *Constab Ballads* (London: Watts, 1912). I took a look at a first edition recently. The format was beautiful but the poems were terrible! It consists of poems McKay wrote while a young constable in Jamaica. McKay did not like the constabulary service. When he left, he spent more time in Spanish Town with his English patrons.

Green Hills does not compare well to McKay's superb autobiography, *A Long Way from Home* (1937), but as a statement on the plastic years of an important international novelist, it is a valuable document.

Reading William Faulkner's *Light in August*

Sometimes William Faulkner's fiction conjures up for me images akin to those found in, say, the paintings of Edvard Munch. Both painter and writer share a particular kind of cold and cold-blooded angst. Munch's 1901 lithograph "Dead Lovers," which depicts a man and a woman lying dead on a stark bed, blood running down from the mattress to the floor, might have served as a jacket illustration for *Light in August* (1932).

Although first read more than twenty years ago, *Light in August* is one of the few novels whose scenes have stayed with me, I think primarily because I find three of the five or six main characters in this complex, third-person narrative—Joe Christmas, Joanna Burden, and Lena Grove—so unforgettable. And they live in my mind as *characters,* not symbols—though they generate much symbolism.

The story of Lena Grove (the fertility implication in the last name is not to be missed) is running side by side with that of Joe Christmas. One of the main surface connections between Joe and Lena is that established by Joe's senile grandmother who, due to confusion, has decided that Lena is Milly (her daughter), Joe's biological mother and the daughter of (her husband) the crazy old Doc Hines, Joe's maternal grandfather. Although Lena and Joe have come to Jefferson, a relatively small Mississippi community, their paths never cross during the several months duration of the novel's action.

Although Joe and Lena never meet, and have no practical reason to, their stories are connected by ironic threads: Lena arrives in town and immediately establishes her presence while Joe has been in Jefferson three years and still has none; because she's pregnant, Lena can be read as a bringer of life, while Joe harbors and carries the blueprint for his own symbolic demise and actual death; Lena is searching for something—fulfillment, a husband?—and Joe is fleeing something—his own invalidated and undefined self. These two are also connected through Joe's bunkmate, Joe Brown, the runaway father of Lena's unborn child.

Joe Christmas doesn't know whether he's black or white in a community where, arguably, being one or the other—where race—matters more than anything else. Joe might be seen as a racialized sacrificial figure, and if looked at in that way, he can be said to represent the main social and moral plight of the Old South, the New South, and perhaps the whole country, past and present. Because of the moral history of his region, Joe can also be seen narrowly in the context of a Puritan system of thought. The same is true of Joanna Burden, the white woman who employs Joe and whom he eventually murders.

Following this line of thought, one could argue, as some critics have, that Joanna Burden carries the burden of liberal guilt for the legacy of slavery. But the irony of her position, in her relation to Joe, is striking, because from Joe's point of view, being either white or black becomes unacceptable. He eventually defies the American pathology of *race naming*, which I believe is one of the primary causes of American racism.

At the same time, Joe is the ultimate force of self-denial. In the beginning, he is the victim of a cruel and vicious misunderstanding. Left as an infant on the doorstep of an orphanage, he begins to grow up, and one day when he's five, he is caught by the dietician eating toothpaste. The act itself becomes a personal legacy he must carry all his life because, rather than punishing him for something he himself felt to be wrong, the dietician instead attempts to buy his silence—incorrectly assuming that the boy has been witness to her clandestine encounter with a man in her room.

In the meantime, the narrative tone and slant seem to suggest that Joe, as a result of the encounter with the dietician, later in life cannot tolerate the idea of food (which can be read as a symbolic rejection of life itself), although he must eat to live. In fact, all the needs of the body and spirit are forces he is at war with. Joe eventually has sex with Joanna Burden, but there seems to be only torment in the guilty passion generated between them.

Intimacy, love, warmth, romance, caring are all totally repulsive to Joe. Early on, his first sexual encounter is with a "Negro" girl in a toolshed. Rebelling against the white South's male custom of initiation into sex by way of the black woman, he attacks the girl and the other white boys who wish to have sex with her. Further, when Joe discovers that women shed blood periodically, he goes out and kills a sheep so that he can bathe his hands in the blood of the lamb, so to speak. This Old Testament ceremony is not Faulkner's only biblical reference. When his foster mother, Mrs. McEachern, washes his feet, the correlation to Christ is obvious. Although Faulkner himself denied that there were any intended biblical analogies, the name Christmas, and Joe's "birth" date—December twenty-fifth—are enough to justify reading the string of correlations as biblical analogies.

Abstinence—from food, sex, and so on—is associated in Joe's mind with masculinity and manhood. From the very beginning, he seems to have a sense of the betrayal and the execution awaiting him in the near future. At one point, Joe could see himself floating away as pure air, a moment that foreshadows his death. By the time he takes up with Joanna his days are numbered. Joe's brief encounter with the Reverend Gail Hightower has already foreshadowed this, as has his relationship with the no-account drifter, Joe Brown (also known as Lucas Burch).

Faulkner's novel can also be read, in its main thrust, as a critique of the moral influence of the Puritans on southern Protestant Christianity. The key voice representing this posture is that of the Reverend Gail Hightower who denounces his fellow townsmen because they cannot "bear" pleasure or "ecstasy." Hightower: "And so why should not their [his neighbors'] religion drive them to crucifixion of themselves and one another?"

Hightower's indictment of southern Puritanism and perversions of Christianity might be seen as Faulkner's most direct rejection of their component mythic stance, fanatical white supremacy. But to believe this one would have to be convinced that Faulkner shared Hightower's position. It's true that Hightower expresses despair in the face of the grim fundamentalist racist community of which he himself—like Faulkner—is part. At the same time, Hightower is the only character who expresses sympathy with and finally pity for Joe. On the other hand, Joanna's interest in Joe cannot be described as purely sympathetic. Also, unlike the third-person narrative voice of the implied author, Hightower refuses to see Joe as a sacrificial figure. It is to his credit that he doesn't, and it is precisely because Joe is *not* a Christ figure (but, hypothetically, in almost any other context, a "regular" human being) that Hightower sympathizes with and feels sorry for him. Gods and saviors don't need the pity of men and women.

The proof of Joe's down to earth humanity is all over the place. In terms of behavior, he is cocky and arrogant. Like so many other uneducated, rural drifters, Joe is suspicious of strangers and is a man of few words. To disguise his own chaos or emptiness, he wears a poker face. The point is, Joe is not solely a freak product of his culture as so many critics have argued: he is easy to locate, and this is Hightower's point, and one of the causes of the minister's despair. Ironically, in terms of a culturally shaped personality, Joe could easily be someone in a lynch mob about to string up a guilty or innocent Negro for sport, just like many of the other "white" young men in Jefferson. The ambiguity of Joe's so-called negative "racial" identity—always there, though at times subtextually—does not alter entirely what he shares culturally with the Puritan Christian community of which he is a product. In fact, I would argue that he has more in common with these people (who would reject him) than he has with what potentially separates him.

On the other hand, Joanna Burden is as deeply subject to the Puritan code as is Joe Christmas, but by nightfall she is, at least on the surface, a whirlwind of sexual passion. Juxtaposed to this activity she begs Joe to pray with her for forgiveness. The two separate acts begin to constitute a ritual. Consequently, Joe begins to hate Joanna as much as he hated his foster mother and Bobbie his first (white) girlfriend. He especially hates those who love or try to love him. They seem to defy or defeat his primary mission, which is both an intricate, common, and intrinsic blending of the will to survive and a drive toward self-destruction. His hatred for women equals his self-hated and his hatred of both white and black people. Both forms of hatred are connected and have the same roots.

Although one might make an argument in favor of the mirroring effects of Joe and Joanna, the case is not especially interesting to me. Of far more interest is the case of how they differ. Although Joe's encounter with Joanna—and her death—show him more about himself (in all of his bleakness) than any other experience with another human being has, he has no way to put the knowledge to use and to change his deterministic outlook and fate. Joanna, on the other hand, has had her fling and now retreats to her harsh, repenting, and repressive way of life, especially now that she has entered what she thinks of as the "change" of life.

The crisis is also intensified if not triggered by Joanna Burden's plan to send Joe to a Negro college—essentially a "normal" school. Although she means well, Joe cannot accept her definition of him as "colored." But her liberalism and the history of her good efforts on behalf of Negros leaves her with no other choice. Given her convictions, it is her personal means to salvation.

Not surprisingly—in theory, at least—together she and Joe find a way to resolve this conflict. So, loaded with guilt still, she comes close to getting Joe to agree to double suicide. After she attempts to shoot him, he lets her have it with a knife. In terms of the novel's plot, this act seals Joe's death-fate even tighter and points the way toward his redemption. In addition to the legal and moral nature of this act of murder, such a plot device as this is given additional grim weight by the sexualized racial history of the region.

Joe's flight, whether or not Faulkner intended it, can be read as an indictment of the southern legal definition of race and color cast, and as an indictment of the racial legacy of the South generally, especially since it is while in flight that Joe achieves a kind of social wisdom, if not a spiritual delivery from his own emptiness and chaos. Essentially, while in flight, Joe has figured out the bogus nature of race itself without fully articulating it as such, and by doing so he comes to make sense of himself, validates himself as he is, and rejects permanently the racial pathology of the country when he decides not to *ever* be white or black.

But given its history and how it uses the myth of race, Joe's country cannot accept his validation of himself as a nonracialized being. With nowhere else to go, and given this insight, for Joe, death will be a form of salvation. But first, as if to test his own resolve, he makes a real and symbolic trek through "white" town, then one through "black" town, and discovers that his mind is not changed. Instead, Joe becomes even more set on his destiny of death as the only way out of the racialized world into which he was born.

Joe finally surrenders in a Negro town after exchanging his shoes for those of a Negro woman. Earlier at Mottstown, he had burst into a Negro church and in the pulpit damned the Christian God the colored folk were busy worshiping. The congregation escapes his wrath unharmed. Although Joe appears here in an aggressive manner, the essential thrust of his aggression is directed both at the abstraction of theology—not at the Negroes themselves, as some critics have argued—and inwardly at his own newly affirmed self—a self that, nevertheless, and in practical terms, has no place yet to *be.*

But it is hard to know for sure Faulkner's position, if any, on any moral point concerning Joe Christmas. Yet there is no question that Faulkner understood his character completely, at least as a southern "type." Joe is so much a product of the Puritan South that he cannot envision any moral judgment but fire-and-brimstone justice—even for himself—and of course, at least in literary terms, this sort of justice is precisely the prescriptive plot device Faulkner needed to open and close the scene of Joe's death.

After being chased and castrated by a mob of white men (perhaps more angry because of Joe's sexual relations with Joanna than because of his killing of her), Joe Christmas, after a long fight, dies on the floor in Reverend Hightower's home. From the reverend's point of view, at the moment of death, Joe's spirit seems to ascend, suggesting that in death he achieves the vindication of divine delivery.

Joe Christmas, then, is in many ways like Melville's Ahab, in that he insists on *his own* final "truth" at any cost. Also, like Ahab, Christmas would rather die than hide behind the safety of a façade—such as *whiteness* or *blackness.* In Joe's case, choosing to be black or white would have meant living the lie of wearing a false mask. So, in the end, he is transformed from the question mark he starts out being, even perhaps transformed from being mainly a local drifter and farmworker, by being made more positive through his own new resolution concerning—and acceptance of—the absence of a racial identity.

In the end, it is not Joe Brown whom Lena finds but the good, simple Byron Bunch, a part-time preacher and millworker, a man of good faith and goodwill. There is, I believe, less uncertainty about the meaning of Lena than there is about Joe. She seems to represent what Faulkner might have described as true Christian virtues, among them love and faith. Faulkner also seems to draw a healthy correlation between Lena and the regenerative seasonal cycles.

At the same time, Lena's future mate, Byron, is Hightower's only real friend. Byron seems to understand how and why Hightower's idealism and abstract approach to life keep him removed from his community in Jefferson. The two men, after all, share an interest in things spiritual. Acting self-consciously as a Christian and a minister, Byron befriends the eccentric, isolated minister the way he might any other unhappy person. He has a way of reaching out to the lost.

It's possible, finally, to find many kinds of symbolic meanings or to draw biblical analogies while exploring *Light in August.* Some critics have seen in the novel the message that suffering is universal, played out in the implied relationship between Joe and Lena as two individual characters who carry different kinds of burdens or crosses. Other critics have seen a struggle between time and space in the way the novel spreads itself out—in a limited way—both temporally and geographically. Still others see Joe and Lena as representing the opposing forces in Nature—though in a way that reaffirms Nature's variables and digressions.

Finally, Faulkner is careful to adjust his third-person points of view to the main characters he happens to be focused on in any given section as he orchestrates the novel. For my money, it is the complexity of Faulkner's points of view, and how that network of *narrowly represented* voices corresponds to, and sets up, a tension with the plot, and its deeply realized characters, that I find so fascinating.

In Search of Rebecca

The hard questions usually have no simple answers. For me, writing stories is the best means of dealing with difficult questions of ethics, morality, and philosophy. In confronting perplexing questions in my fiction and poetry, I've achieved an odd kind of success. Often, I have no idea how to formulate the question, let alone the answer, before I struggle with it through the process of writing. The writing then becomes the avenue into the complex nature of the question itself. If I come out of the process with a clearer sense of the question, and with no answer—which is more often the case than not—I am satisfied. That's the odd success. I stopped, for example, asking, "Is there a God?" by age twenty-one, after which everything, in Gide's words, seemed "downhill."

Finding life's questions is the business of fiction and poetry. But it's impossible to separate the writing from the living and its stories. They are two narrow highways running parallel through an unclear and unpredictable landscape. I write to understand my life, and to understand the lives of people who interest me. My family, for example, interests me. I want to understand what the stories of their lives meant and mean. And we know that great stories can be parables for our own lives. They serve to show us how long we have been at our best, how the patterns of human behavior don't change all that much, and also how long we've been at our worst. Stories lay out for us possibilities for the future.

While recently rereading Genesis, I dwelled for some time on the brief story of Rebecca. I am aware that a small number of African Americans have traditionally claimed ancestry in ancient Israel, tracing their lineage back to one of the twelve tribes. I am also aware of the symbolic importance of Jewish biblical stories to the religious feelings of African slaves in the colonies, and the spirituals they forged from the hardship of their lives. But these two facts didn't concern me when I reread the story of Rebecca.

Her story conjured up for me a seedbed of questions about human behavior that I'd been dealing with both in life and in my fiction. Questions regarding the negative aspects of life, such as selfishness, deceit, pettiness, shrewdness, cruelty, evil, complicity in evildoing, materialism, treachery, naturally interest a writer of fiction. So do questions about the positive, such as obedience, goodness, generosity, kindness, honor, trust, suffering, tactfulness, ambition, devout faith, piousness, scrupulousness, the sense of nobility. Rebecca's life calls to mind each of these traits and tendencies. Her story is a story within stories.

Who, then, is Rebecca? Fixed firmly in the mother-line of the family of Abraham, Rebecca is the daughter of Bethuel and Milcah, sister of Laban, wife of Isaac, mother of Esau and Jacob. She is mentioned only in a few brief episodes of Genesis, and only her burial in Abraham's cave, not even her death, is recorded. But Rebecca's generosity and kindness are demonstrated in the first episode in which she appears. Abraham's servant, Eliezer, on a trip from Canaan to find a wife for Abraham's youngest son, forty-year-old Isaac, meets her at the Padan Aram (Aram-Nahariam/northern Mesopotamia) community well where the family's water is drawn. Though she's wooed with jewelry, it is probably not the glitter of gold that ultimately wins her over. Rebecca's selfless generosity in this scene, where she insists on watering all the camels of Eliezer's caravan, sets the stage for her marriage to Isaac.

Rebecca marries Isaac in his mother's tent (by going to bed with him) and becomes a devoted wife. Later, while the couple is on a trip to Gerar, when Isaac tells the Philistines that Rebecca is his sister to protect her from being seized by them, Rebecca effectively plays the part of sister. She and Isaac both obviously believe in the use of deception in an emergency. Twenty years later she gives birth to twin sons, Esau and Jacob, destined from birth to be in conflict with each other. Esau is a hunter. He's physical. Jacob is spiritual. He's quiet.

Years pass and their father Isaac grows old and blind. One day Rebecca, probably eavesdropping, overhears her husband Isaac telling his eldest son, Esau, that it is time for an important ritual. But first, Esau must bring his father venison. Isaac plans, after the ritual of eating the venison, to bestow, according to Jewish law, the patriarchal blessing of heirship upon his eldest son. Directing the family bloodline was of the utmost importance.

But there seem to be some problems with Esau. Rebecca and her husband believe Esau to be unqualified for a quiet spiritual life of devotion to God and family, the most desirable qualities in a son entrusted to carry on the family birthright. Both parents disapprove of Esau's marriage to a Hittite woman of Canaan. Overhearing the conversation between Isaac and Esau, Rebecca hurries to her youngest and favorite son, Jacob. She convinces him that he must intercede. By pretending to be Esau, Jacob can trick his blind father and receive the irrevocable blessing, becoming heir. She cooks goat meat and gives it to Jacob. He, taking it in to his father, apparently convinces Isaac that he is Esau and receives the blessing.

If Rebecca gambles, she loses, because Jacob retreats to his mother's birthplace to avoid the wrath of his brother, Esau. Jacob is gone for twenty years, during which time his life is miserable. Rebecca's scheme to get the heirship for her favorite son ends, ironically, in her loss of his presence for twenty years. But Jacob marries a woman, Rachel, in the desired family line. It's a bitter victory. And, finally, as the patriarch of his own tribe, Jacob is destined to become the everlasting symbol of the birth of Israel.

Despite the strong symbolism of their stories and the archetypal natures of Rebecca, her husband Isaac, and her twin sons Esau and Jacob, the few brief episodes containing Rebecca herself spoke to me on a profoundly personal level. In some very essential ways, Rebecca reminded me of the hardworking, generous, strong, quietly ambitious, and determined, though relatively powerless, women in my own family, going all the way back to my great-grandmother, Rebecca, on my father's side.

Every time I teach Jean Toomer's story "Becky," I think about this white great-grandmother, Rebecca Lankford. Toomer's story starts, "Becky was the white woman who had two Negro sons. She's dead. . . ." The story takes place in the backwoods of Georgia in, say, the 1880s or 1890s. At the end of the story, Becky's house (built by the black and the white townsfolk) falls in on her, becoming her tomb. In other words, her neighbors' condescension and grudging generosity eventually help to kill her.

My great-grandmother Rebecca Lankford gave birth to my grandmother, Anna Bowling, in 1878 in Oglethorpe County. She brought bastardy charges against William T. Bowling, a young white man, which probably served to save my great grandfather, Stephen Bowling, a black man (born 1861), from death by lynching. Stephen and William no doubt grew up together on the Bowling plantation.

Rebecca was poor and, like the rest of her immediate family, largely uneducated. I can only imagine the pain she endured and the possible deceit she had to exercise to survive a racist social system that doubly condemned her for having a child out of wedlock and for breaking the racial code.

On the black side of my family it is well known that Rebecca lied to the community to save Stephen's life—she even threatened suicide if any harm came to him. The court records of course do not show any of this, only the bastardy charges against a young white man. Rebecca's life is an ironic metaphor for and commentary on the racialized system based on whiteness as privilege that has dogged America since the end of the Colonial period.

Rebecca gave up Anna soon after birth. Anna was cared for by a black woman, Edith Jackson, till her grandmother (my great-great-grandmother)

Harriet Bowling (born a slave in 1833 on Thornberry Bowling's plantation) took charge of her at about age six, adopting her legally a few years later.

Like Rebecca of Genesis, my grandmother, too, probably had to find subversive ways to survive in a world that provided no place for her. After all, she was, in appearance, a white woman (and remained *legally* white) who was culturally black.

In a sense, such lives—Becky's, my great-grandmother Rebecca's, my grandmother Anna's—are stories about powerlessness. When a powerless person commits an act of wrongdoing, moral and ethical issues swirl around the person like buzzards around a carcass, just as they do around the powerful. But the implications and ramifications are different.

The main point I'm trying to make here is this: Like the biblical Rebecca, a relatively powerless woman, women like Toomer's Becky, and women of my great-grandmothers' and grandmothers' generations, in order to give expression to their legitimate personal, domestic, social, or political concerns, occasionally were compelled to behave in ways that can be characterized as deceitful, mean-spirited, unscrupulous, or cruel. This is almost certainly the case with the biblical Rebecca, who was up against the power of the patriarchal family and community.

I think understanding such communities, and their histories of particulars, gives a writer the basis for understanding how powerlessness works. In the communities I grew up in, both in the North and South, I remember parents (but especially mothers) worrying about who their offspring married. I remember a neighbor woman, a friend of my mother's, going to great extremes, but in a covert manner, to try to sabotage her son's affair with a particular girl of whom she (the mother) didn't approve.

Whether or not we have power we can use openly and because we want things to go our way, we sometimes try to influence the future turn of events through taking certain actions. With her act of deception, the biblical Rebecca tries to assert her influence on the future of her family.

But does Rebecca think about the consequences of her action? As a child, I was told to think before acting. Either Rebecca doesn't think about the consequences of her deception, or she weighs the possible outcome against doing nothing and decides to go ahead with her plan because the possible problems stemming from the deception seem to her far less than the problem of Jacob *not* receiving the blessing. Or, she doesn't care.

Rebecca loves both of her sons, but Jacob is her favorite. In her own judgment, no doubt, she is acting as a good mother when she devises a scheme—

derived from her inability to act openly—to give Jacob an advantage over his brother. We all know, as painful as it sometimes is to admit, that parents have favorites.

The difficult question remains: Is it okay to commit an act of wrongdoing in the interest of a perceived good? Rebecca tricked Isaac. In a short story I wrote called, "Ten Pecan Pies," a wife (based on my other grandmother, Ada) tricks her selfish husband into turning over his prized pecans so that she can bake pecan pies as Christmas gifts for the community. Her deception, like Rebecca's, one might argue, was ultimately for a good cause.

But does that *justify* the deceitful act? That is one of the difficult questions. Yet, before we get to such a hard reckoning, we have to ask: Is Rebecca merely carrying out the wish of her husband? In other words, is she, by taking upon herself the burden of the "evil" act, letting Isaac off the hook? In this paradigm, Rebecca knows her husband so well, and is so obedient, that she saves him the difficulty of rejecting his oldest son—the rightful inheritor—in favor of his youngest, who is clearly her (and secretly his) choice for the position.

If Rebecca's deception is ultimately the act of a loyal but powerless wife carrying out the will of her husband, then she is rehabilitated, at least in literary terms, from her role as a villain. On the other hand, a deterministic reading would leave one believing that everything that happened was preordained. Such a reading would also exonerate Rebecca and Jacob of all wrongdoing. Among my grandmothers and their church friends, there was a common expression: "Well, honey, it's the will of God." In other words, they felt powerless to change the situation in question. That always puzzled me. I couldn't understand how they knew what God was thinking.

Powerless people act in ways that are not always easy to understand. When I was growing up, I couldn't count the times I saw the women of my own family take responsibilities or burdens upon themselves to protect their menfolk from having to deal with some unpleasantness. They not only accepted their place or role in both home and church but went out of their way to make life easier for the men. This may have been noble and selfless, but it was not necessarily right. Actually, I think it was, ultimately, not good for the women or the men.

But these were strong women. Rebecca, like Isaac's mother Sarah, was a strong home person. Rebecca was the manifestation of Isaac's home. Her sons were who they were culturally because of her pervasive presence in the home as its defining agent. In this sense, she reminds me of women in my own family—my mother, my grandmothers, who helped define for me my culture. I tried to pay tribute to such women in my novel *Such Was the Season*, which is about a week in the life of an elderly black woman in Atlanta.

I feel an empathy with such women, which is sometimes noted in reviews of my fiction and poetry. This identification with the female perhaps stems from my close contact with a house full of women while growing up. For example, it took courage and tenacity for women like my grandmother Anna to endure. Perhaps I instinctively understood who she was in the face of what she had to do to get through her life.

In the end, do we know who Rebecca is? Rebecca is a virgin girl by the well, who volunteers to water a caravan of ten camels; she is the same Rebecca who, many years later, urges her son Jacob to deceive his father. We know that her life has many implications. One is the notion that even from a base of powerlessness, a person can sometimes exert a degree of influence. But, as with any human life, the task is to see the whole life before passing judgment. How do those one or two moments of deception, of breaking the rules, fit into a whole life of hospitality, trust, compassion, faith, and generosity?

Ultimately, and when viewed in retrospect, breaking the rules or even breaking the law is not always bad. The serfs of Russia broke the law when they rose up against the ruling class. Rosa Parks broke the law when she refused to move to the back of the bus. Rebecca of Genesis is a good person who breaks the rules. The result is biblical history.

Wallace Thurman and the Niggeratti Manor

Perhaps best known for his successful 1929 Broadway play *Harlem* (written in collaboration with William Jourdan Rapp), Wallace Thurman is all but forgotten today. There is some documented evidence that Thurman wrote a number of other plays, none of which were ever produced. He was born in Salt Lake City in 1902, and he died in New York City in 1934, young and destitute. Author of three novels, *The Blacker the Berry: A Novel of Negro Life* (1929), *Infants of the Spring* (1932), and *The Interne* (1932), the latter written in collaboration with Abraham L. Furman, Thurman also published thirteen articles (on subjects as diverse as Christmas, Brigham Young, and Harlem). While working in Hollywood, he wrote the screenplays for two motion pictures—one about resistance to forced sterilization and poverty, and not about race in any way. He published four short stories, one in his own magazine, *Fire!!* (1926).

In the editorial comment for the first and only issue of *Fire!!*, Thurman proclaimed a philosophy of aesthetic freedom for young black writers as forceful as Ezra Pound's and Wyndham Lewis's *Blast 1* did for the expatriates. All the youthful "vortex" of what Pound called "sun, energy, somber emotion, clean-drawing, disgust, penetrating analysis" permeates the pages of *Fire!! Blast,* too, made only one appearance.

Thurman's blast against "sociological problems and propaganda" in literature, in the form of his magazine, was new on the Afro-American literary scene. The issue carried works by Gwendolyn Brooks, Zora Neale Hurston, Langston Hughes, and the artist Aaron Douglas. *Fire!!* came eleven years after *Blast* and its announcement of Vorticism ("We stand for the Reality of the Present—"), and three years before Eugene Jolas's *Transition,* with its manifesto for "The Revolution of the Word." All three efforts aimed in the same direction, stated well by the *Transition* manifesto: "The imagination in search of a fabulous world is autonomous and unconfined."

I have chosen to focus on Thurman's *Infants of the Spring* (New York: Furman, 1932) because I think it is worthy of far more attention than it has ever received. It certainly deserves a chance with present and future readers. I feel this way because the book probes—without giving any answers—important issues of race and art.

Infants of the Spring is set in Harlem, in a rooming house nicknamed Niggeratti Manor, and as such it attempts to satirize what Thurman saw as the failure of the Harlem Renaissance. The main characters are Raymond Taylor, a troubled and confused writer; his white roommate, Stephen Jorgenson, who seems to be hanging out in Harlem in order to have an exotic experience; Euphoria Blake, the landlady; Lucille, Raymond's best female friend; Aline and Janet, two young women into free love and booze and whatever else is available; Paul Arbian, a cynical and witty painter; Eustance, an opera singer filled with disdain for his own Afro-American heritage; Samuel Carter, a white man who thinks of himself as a liberal and tries his best to help the members of the artistic colony; Barbara Nitsky (the Countess), a young white woman from Greenwich Village now living in Harlem, where the living seems, for her, a lot easier; and a staggering array of minor characters, most of whom seem to be based on real, identifiable people, contemporaries of Wallace Thurman.

Raymond Taylor seems to be a persona for the author. He certainly speaks out (almost always in contradictory terms) on issues of art, race, and sex in ways one can easily associate with Wallace Thurman's own thinking on these topics. Raymond, like Thurman himself, was suspicious of the racial artistic rebirth called the Harlem Renaissance. He doubted its authenticity because he felt that it had been created by journalistic hype—"the foundation of the building [Niggeratti Manor] was composed of crumbling stone." (Whether or not this is true, it is certainly true that many movements, before and since, have been founded on questionable foundations. Two examples: The Lost Generation and the Beat Generation were journalistic inventions, yet some participants in each produced works of outstanding quality.)

As I have already suggested, in the matter of the editorial policy of *Fire!!*, Thurman took the position that Negro artists and writers of his day should be free to do what they chose (to paraphrase Langston Hughes) and not worry about how anybody might react. Well, Raymond takes that position too, denouncing any obligation for social responsibility. Yet Raymond speaks out in favor of racial pride and Afro-American cultural heritage, and keeping them ever present in art. Surely, some degree of social responsibility is expressed when the cultural heritage finds its way into a work of art no matter how free that work might be from propagandistic aims. Raymond wants it both ways, and there is nothing wrong with that. His fight is for absolute artistic freedom.

Raymond is as passionate about art as a character in a novel can possibly be. He longs to "transcend and survive the transitional age in which he was living: but he doubts that he has the genius to create a literary work of lasting quality." He no doubt echoes Thurman himself.

But it is Raymond's contradictory stand that makes him all the more human and interesting. He attacks Samuel Carter as a "phony left-wing radical." Raymond insists that Samuel is, at heart, a right-wing conservative who only pretends to have the interests of the Negro at heart. Yet he defends the Countess Barbara's right to live the sporting life, as a prized white woman, among black men. At the same time, he looks with disdain upon Janet for her attraction to Stephen ("Jesus, are you Negro women as bad as Negro men?").

When Eustance refuses to accept a job Samuel has found for him singing spirituals, Raymond is careful not to take sides. He defends Eustance's right to sing only opera and at the same time detests Eustance's refusal to embrace his own heritage by singing spirituals. Eventually Raymond tries to bring Eustace around to accepting the job.

Yet it is Raymond's relationship with Stephen that is most contradictory, complex, and subtle. He seems to have set himself as Stephen's instructor on Negro life, as a sort of tour guide of Harlem and the manor. Raymond wants Stephen to see the universal aspects of life in Harlem and at the same time to appreciate those cultural factors that are unique to the community. The two men, however, are the opposite of each other, on a surface level, and mirror images underneath. In Conrad's terms, they are soulmates. Stephen, in one sense, is slumming, and in another, he could not be more innocently serious about his interest in the people of the manor and beyond, in the neighborhood. For him they are culturally exotic, yet not in the least exotic because he *does* recognize that universal element Raymond wants him to see.

Raymond and Stephen sleep together. Although a specifically homosexual relationship is never spelled out, the emotional quality of intimacy seems to be there. Thurman has already demonstrated in his first novel an interest in male homosexuality with his character Alva. Here, in *Infants of the Spring,* Raymond seems jealous and protective of Stephen while he is carrying on with Aline. Predictably, Raymond refuses to admit his jealousy and dismisses the affair as silly.

Halfway through the book there is an important scene where Raymond is walking moodily through Central Park. Thurman would have us believe that this is the ultimate moment of Raymond's potential, and perhaps it is. Raymond dreams of breaking "the chains which held him to the racial rack. He wants to carry a blazing beacon to the top of Mount Olympus." In other words, Raymond hopes he is a genius and not simply another talented Negro with "no standards, no elasticity, no pregnant germ plasm." The narrator tells us that Raymond's mind, during this walk, is "chaotic and deranged." The tone assumed by the narrator here is a bit unexpected and not entirely convincing. Yet, at least for the moment, the condition of Raymond's mind, that is, a mind of "attractive brilliance" without maturity, saves Raymond from stupidity. And Thurman elsewhere in the book reinforces what we can expect from Raymond by quoting Maxim Gorky: "A man slightly possessed is not only more agreeable to me; he is altogether more plausible." So, we are expected to ride with Raymond's confusion, his contradictions, his "adolescent brain," and at least celebrate his potential, because again, like Gorky's ideal, this man is "not quite achieved . . . not yet very wise, a little mad, possessed."

Raymond, nevertheless, knows a few things about himself. He knows his own potential for self-destruction, his own tendency to corrupt rather than cultivate his difference. And this, I think, gets at exactly what Thurman wants us to see most about Raymond's personality: "There had been no catharsis, no intellectual metabolism." And in this moment of growthlessness, "race consciousness" is Raymond's largest trap. The fact that he sees it as a trap does not mean that he is ashamed of his heritage. On the contrary, Raymond would have the boundaries of his own cultural frame of reference enlarged and he would carry it with him to the mountaintop. He does not wish to leave himself and his history behind, but to change our perception of both. But he fails to realize that in American society his dream of freedom from "race consciousness" has no context in which it can be understood without contradiction. (This is a familiar theme in nineteenth-century American immigrant popular fiction. Bernardino Ciambelli comes to mind.) So, little wonder his walk ends in "Futile introspection, desperate flagellations . . . in darkness and despair."

Raymond's relations with the other characters also reveal his unresolved many sidedness. With his landlady, Euphoria (who has been a feminist and a Greenwich Village left-wing radical), he is strangely tolerant of human shortcomings, having no caustic responses to her many silly positions on art and life. Raymond sees in Paul Arbian a true artist and a sincere spirit. (In the end, Paul commits suicide, doomed, as the manor he named is also doomed.) Lucille is the one who meets Raymond at places beyond the manor. She clearly wants to keep her distance. Her posture seems to say that she likes Raymond but dislikes his life, such as it is. After all, he is a writer who cannot write. Raymond feels both pity and contempt for poor Pelham Gaylord, who eventually is jailed for raping a neighbor's daughter.

These main characters are probably based on real persons Thurman knew in Harlem. They are far more interesting and complex than many of his minor characters because there is evidence that the author managed to take his creations some distance from the real models and to invest them with a sort of life of their own. On the other hand, the minor characters are flat and are mainly of historical interest because they are often recognizable as figures (stick figures?) in a roman à clef. Thurman's artist friend Bruce Nugent was the inspiration for Paul Arbian. Well-known Harlem personality Mrs. Sidney was the model for Euphoria Blake. DeWitt Clint, the West Indian poet, is probably based on Eric Walrond. Sweetie Mary Carr is probably Thurman's fictional version of Zora Neale Hurston. Dr. Parks is Dr. Alain Locke? Or is Locke the model for Thurman's Dr. Manfred Trout? I suspect that Cedric Williams is based on Cedric Dover, the anthropologist and editor of *American Negro Art.*

All of these figures and more turn up for Niggeratti Manor's first and last salon. They are paraded and made to spout their points of view, often revealing narrow-mindedness, or worse, on art and race, on the New Negro, on Picasso, Matisse, Gauguin, Sargent, Renoir, Gertrude Stein, jazz, on modernism generally, you name it. (In fact, it is the soapbox forum throughout the novel that is most annoying.) Yet the dedicated trivia seeker might easily identify characters based on Aaron Douglas, novelist Rudolph Fisher, poet Countee Cullen, and others. I have little doubt that Doris Westmore, short story writer, and her cousin, poet Hazel Jamison, are based on Boston novelist Dorothy West (*The Living Is Easy* [1948]) and her cousin. In using real persons as models, Thurman attempted a difficult task. Real people and their beliefs, undigested and untransformed, never work in fiction. Dante, in his *Inferno,* succeeded because he moved beyond the original motive and turned his heretics into creations no longer linked to their models.

Infants of the Spring is not a great book but it is a serious book, a passionate and painfully conceived book. The style is often as delicate as that of F. Scott Fitzgerald's, but the point of view wobbles too much. Like Thurman's first novel (which is much better known), it has flaws, the flaws one expects to find in early work. Vincent van Gogh's "Potato Eaters," an early painting, is seriously flawed in a way that works done at Arles are not. Cézanne's early works are flawed. So are most first, and for that matter, second novels. Wallace Thurman died at the age of thirty-two. Most American writers have not published their first novels by that age. Works that show a writer or painter reaching (to paraphrase Rilke) all glory and all time, are rare. Wallace Thurman wanted to create such work but did not. There is no way to know if he would have managed to do so had he lived longer.

PART FOUR

MEMOIR

From

"Taking Chances: A Memoir of a Life in Art and Writing"

A long-standing truism holds that knowledge of one's genetic ancestral and cultural history is essential in understanding one's present condition and future prospects. Determining genetic DNA is an evolving science; percentages and geographical locations keep shifting. For now, suffice it to say that a large portion of my DNA is in Africa and Europe. Because it's based on dependable archival research, I can say with certainty that my father is descended from the Major line in South Carolina and the Lankfords and McCartys in Georgia. My mother was of the Brawner (sometimes spelled Bronner), Huff, Maxwell, and Dupree family lines, also in Georgia.

My mother and father, Inez and Clarence, married when my mother had just turned eighteen. She was a very pretty girl, and he felt lucky to get her. She was still eighteen when I was born on December 31, 1936, at 7:33 A.M. in the then "colored" wing of Grady Hospital in Atlanta. At the time of my birth, Hitler had been in power for four years. Roosevelt was president. New cars were selling for $375, but nobody had any money. Movies featured Shirley Temple, Nelson Eddy, and Jeanette MacDonald. Blacks on-screen were invariably clowns or mammies. Jesse Owens won four gold medals in Berlin. The Scottsboro Boys were brought to trial. Haile Selassie was dethroned. Howard Hughes flew a plane a fantastic 260 miles per hour across the country. Charlie Chaplin, Margaret Sanger, and Marian Anderson were household names.

My sister, Serena, was born February 19, 1938, in the same hospital. She was a big baby. One of my first memories is of pinching her when she was in her crib. Serena was smart as a whip and a more aggressive learner than I was. I followed her lead. She taught me how to tie my shoestrings, how to tell time.

We lived, at first, in a wood frame house on McGruder Street, then later on Woodrow Place, where my first memories are housed. I remember the blackouts during World War II and all of us on Woodrow Place turning out our lights and huddling together, watching the night skies and the searchlights moving across them like drugged spirits. It was more festive than fearful. When I returned to Atlanta in 1984 and walked through that area, I recognized nothing except the physical shape of the cul-de-sac.

My parents divorced in the late 1940s. My father remained in Atlanta; my mother moved to Chicago, where her sister Luvenia helped her get established. In Atlanta, my father carried on a number of business interests. At various times he owned a restaurant, a gas station, and a trucking service. We grew up mainly with our mother in Chicago. There were few trips to Atlanta to visit our father during the fifties.

In Chicago, my family lived on Oakwood Boulevard. Across the street was a popular nightclub in a famous South Side hotel. I've forgotten its name, but it sat on the corner of South Parkway and Oakwood Boulevard. In those days, you could hear some of the best jazz there. The house we lived in was owned by a woman named Mrs. Elizabeth Williams. She was something of a grande dame with old New Orleans flair. Her apartment, which was just below ours, smelled of strong perfume and powder. There was a chattering parrot in her kitchen by the bar. Elizabeth Williams talked glowingly of the old days when Count Basie and Duke Ellington rented rooms from her while performing across the street. Lionel Hampton and many other musicians stayed there too. Vibraphones—I don't know whose, Hampton's or some other musician's—were always in the living room. I grew up in this house where, in 1947, Johnny Otis's wife, Phyllis, would walk around in a bathrobe and fuss with her infant, Janice. Otis himself was rarely there. I was in love with Phyllis. She never knew it, but I was.

Forestville Elementary was a gigantic school with a vast playground. After I got over earning my right to be there by fighting off the kids who bullied me because I was the new boy, I found some time to concentrate on schoolwork. Boys were making zip guns, but in those days nobody was smoking dope. Street drugs were something we only vaguely knew about.

I started writing seriously when I was twelve. I wrote novels, stories, and poems. I was also painting and drawing a lot. In elementary school, and later at Phillips Junior High and Dunbar High School, I won many prizes in art contests. The United Nations was just beginning, and for one of my classes

I was assigned to illustrate its workings. Some teachers singled me out for special treatment, and I let it go to my head—but not for long.

. . . .

On the basis of several watercolors of figures in landscapes, I won a James Nelson Raymond Scholarship to the sketch and lecture classes in Fullerton Hall at the Chicago Art Institute and soon discovered that the city was literally full of gifted children like myself. I stayed with the arts lessons until shortly before I joined the air force. Because we were not well off, I had worked from an early age. One job I especially remember when I was about eight or nine was selling mail order salve in tins on South Parkway. I'm sure I was not yet ten. The grimness with which people walked by me was a profound lesson I never forgot. I think I went home at the end of the day with a quarter.

Years later, perhaps in the last years of elementary school, I worked in a grocery store where the hamburger was made redder with tomato juice. My job was emptying the cans beneath the meat counter. My coworkers, boys my own age, were into jazz. I first learned to respect classical jazz while listening to them.

When my mother married Halbert Ming in 1949 we moved into a larger apartment in a building near a Catholic church and school. I grew up Protestant, and the Catholics we saw in passing seemed so much saner in their faith. When Serena and I were small we were told we had to go to church. When given the choice, we went to Holy Angels, the Catholic church on Oakwood Boulevard, because there were generally fewer moral appeals and demands on us.

My mother's foster parents, Eugene and Sadie Crawford—Mom and Pop to us—lived on South Parkway. They weren't technically foster parents; they were simply people who had taken my mother in when she was a young woman and, along with Aunt Luvenia, had helped her get established in Chicago. For a while, when I couldn't get along with my stepfather, I lived with Mom and Pop. I especially loved Mom. Pop was one of the head waiters at the Palmer House, where he met many movie stars; he came home telling us about them all the time. They tipped big. Pop also brought home Palmer House Worcestershire sauce. I hated it as much as I hated Jell-O. Even today I can't stand the taste.

I continued writing stories and novels. Crude things, but there they were. My paintings were taking up so much room in my bedroom that we started storing them out in the hallway. Some of that work was good, and I now wish the good things had been saved. My mother had two works from that period, one in her bedroom and the other in her living room. Some of my teachers thought I was some sort of genius; others told me I was a misfit and that my laziness would cause me to fail in life. They thought it was a pity because I did have talent.

In high school there were a whole bunch of us, in fact, who had talent to burn—for example, the musician Herbie Hancock. One year, we were both in Mr. Green's music class at the same time. Not having the sense to be afraid to try anything, I wrote a symphony but had to ask Mr. Green to play it for me. I had this idea that if Beethoven could write music while deaf, I could try to do it purely in visual terms. Mr. Green refused but got Herbie to attempt to play it. Herbie managed to get through two or three pages of the twenty-five-page symphony before he gave up. It made no sense to him. I considered it a Dadaist symphony influenced by Bud Powell. You can imagine how disorganized it was!

I was growing up in a time when there was much to lament, but new, positive things were happening, too. *Lady Chatterley's Lover* for the first time was being sold *over* the counter in the United States. A southern black woman named Rosa Parks refused to move to the back of the public bus. Something new was in the air. The civil rights movement would soon begin.

After high school and my time at the Art Institute, where I sketched moving models or listened to lectures from Addis Osborn or Cynthia Bollinger and others, I joined the air force in 1955 to seek new adventures. The recruiters had promised me the glory of new horizons.

I worked in an office after basic training. The office was on a base in Valdosta, Georgia, which depressed me; the training had been near San Antonio, Texas, which also had depressed me. Without my friends, black guys from the North, both experiences would have been unbearable. The towns were still extremely racist with endless restrictions regarding where a black person could go and what he could do.

During my time in the air force I was reading extensively in philosophy, religion, anthropology, history, poetry, fiction, and biography. I was also writing and beginning to publish in the little magazines of the 1950s. Sometimes my friends went to dances or to the roller rink, but I couldn't dance or roller-skate (although as a child I had been a champion roller skater on the sidewalks back in Chicago, when they called me Hopscotch-Cowboy because I was equally at ease with the girls jumping rope and with the boys playing cowboy).

After I got out of the military in 1957, I started a little magazine of my own in Chicago called *Coercion Review*. In it I published the works of people I was corresponding with, like D. V. Smith and Carl Larsen. I also published an original essay by Henry Miller called "Lime Twigs and Treachery." But when it was reprinted in his collection *Stand Still Like the Hummingbird*, he did not bother to credit my magazine for its first appearance. There were also essays and poems by Lawrence Ferlinghetti and Kenneth Patchen. The activity of publishing my own magazine put me in direct contact with hundreds of other poets and fiction writers and editors all over the country and in Europe.

I found the artistic life in Chicago attractive. I used to go on weekends to a bar called College of Complexes up on the North Side with friends who were interested in art and literature. I felt weird in my own community, but up there on the North Side, among other weirdos, I felt at home. There was something different being expressed. I recognized in the North Side bohemia things I had read and dreamed about that had more to do with the expatriate literary colony and art salons of Paris of the latter part of the nineteenth century up until the beginning of World War II than with the present 1950s and 1960s values of the South Side, with its bourgeois emphasis on big cars and fine clothes.

I began a correspondence with the painter Sheri Martinelli, who had known Ezra Pound while he was at St. Elizabeths mental hospital in Washington, D.C., and who had earlier lived the bohemian life in New York, knew Tennessee Williams, and had been a close friend of Charlie Parker. She fascinated me, and I wrote book reviews for her little magazine, *Anagogic and Paideumic Review*. At one point, she sent me a book of her paintings Pound had published privately in Italy and to which he had written the introduction. I still have it and cherish it. Sheri was indeed one of my earliest mentors but also a friend, although we never met in person.

During this time, late fifties, early sixties, I also started corresponding with poet David Wang, a guest editor of an issue of the *Galley Sail Review*, where he published some of my poetry. I did not meet David until the early 1970s, when he stopped in at my Waverly Place apartment in New York only a few months before he committed suicide. I saw in his face that bewildering, almost apologetic look I later saw in the face of critic Arthur Oberg, who came into my office at the University of Washington in Seattle when I was the new guy in the department and introduced himself only a few days before he killed himself.

To get advice from a poet I admired, I sent some of my poems to William Carlos Williams on Sheri's advice, and he wrote back a long, bitter letter, leaving me with the impression that maybe writing was not worth the effort. I remember trying to understand the despair Williams was suffering, but at age twenty or twenty-one and with my optimism it was difficult. This was during the time that LeRoi Jones (not yet known as Amiri Baraka) was publishing his magazine, *Yugen*. When the first issue of *Coercion Review* appeared in 1958, Jones wrote and asked why "the campy photos." I had on the inside of the back cover photos of Henry Miller, Emilie Glen, D. V. Smith, and myself, authors represented in the issue. Jones was right: they were "campy."

Once, I kept some of Charles Bukowski's poems too long without accepting or rejecting them. He threatened to come pick them up in person and made it clear that I wouldn't like the encounter. That must have been around 1965. At that time I was publishing poems in Ron Padgett's magazine *White Dove Review*. I think Ron was still a high school kid at this point down in Tulsa, Oklahoma. I remember he wrote to me before he started *White Dove* and asked for advice on how to get started. Not long before, I had asked D. V. Smith, the publisher of my first published short story, the same question. He was still in the U.S. Army in Japan and about to bring out the issue of *Olivant* containing the story. The volume appeared in 1957 and also included works by Lawrence Lipton, Harry Hooton, Felix Anselm, George P. Elliot, Lawrence Ferlinghetti, Gil Orlovitz, James Schevill, Jon Silkin, and many others. So, my first published fiction was published in Japan.

James Boyer May, editor of *Trace*, had also encouraged me to read a wide variety of writers. He knew I was just a kid, but he had taken interest in my talent. At first, *Trace* was a writer's service magazine, but later it also became a vehicle for fiction and poetry. May published some of my things in his pages then. Little magazine writers wrote to *Trace* to bitch about various things. It was the only forum we had in those bleak Eisenhower years.

. . . .

Poet Marvin Bell lived in Chicago at this time and was a student at the University of Chicago. He and I got together socially a number of times. He was also publishing a magazine, called *Statements*. When Marvin came to my apartment on Drexel and saw how many little magazines I had, he said, "Gee, you have a better collection than the University of Chicago."

The publisher of *Big Table*, Paul Carroll, also dropped in at the Drexel place. It was a nervous meeting. He was hot at the time because the current issue of *Big Table* was under attack by the police for printing a chapter from William Burroughs's then unpublished novel *Naked Lunch*. Jack Kerouac, Paul said, had named the magazine *Big Table* for him. It was the same week I received a copy of *East & West* from India: my poems side by side in a magazine with those by William Carlos Williams. My confidence was growing.

Among the friends I was running around with was a young African American singer named Bob Ingram who had lived and studied music in Paris for a number of years. He knew Lil Hardin Armstrong, who lived near my place right there on Forty-Fourth Street, the South Side. Lil had worked in King Oliver's Creole Jazz Band in the 1920s with Baby Dodds, Johnny Dodds, Bill Johnson, Honoré Dutrey, and Louis Armstrong, whom she married in 1924. She played the best ragtime piano I had ever heard.

Bob and Lil had met years before in Paris. We used to go by Lil's house and stay up late listening to her great old recordings and sipping wine and talking art and music and life and everything possible beyond life. I now know that Lil was fragile and tolerant; we were enthusiastic and needy. But I think our youth excited her, and she warmed to it.

Once Bob gave a party at his own apartment and Lil, after much coaxing, agreed to play the piano and sing a little ditty. Her ex-husband's autobiography, *Satchmo,* had just appeared and was a best seller. She lamented that militant blacks were dismissing it as representing the vision of an Uncle Tom. Although long divorced, you could tell that some important part of her still loved Louis. She sang a tease number and then one about the infamous iceman as backdoor man ready to take care of unfinished business. She must have sung three or four. Everybody loved her humor and the scattiness. It was wonderful.

Through Lil I met her cousin the Chicago writer Frank London Brown. I heard Frank read from his work at a community center not long before his death. I remember the negative response the reactionary element in Chicago had to Brown's first novel, *Trumbull Park.* Frank died at an early age from cancer.

Another Chicago writer, Willard Motley, was not as friendly as Frank to beginning writers like myself. Young writers need to be able to meet established writers in person, just to see for themselves that those books they are reading come from human beings. This goes a long way toward suggesting the possibility of themselves as creators of books. I met Motley through his brother, the painter Archibald Motley. Archibald had paintings in Gayle's Gallery on Sixty-Third. I had met Gayle through my childhood friend Jimmie Hunter after I came out of the air force. Eventually she hung a few of my own paintings in her gallery. But the meeting with Willard was brief and tense. Although he had written to me from Mexico and asked me to visit him at his mother's, I must have arrived at a bad time. He asked me to come back the next day. It seemed to me he had a very serious hangover. I never went back.

. . . .

Omaha, Nebraska, 1962–66. I went to Omaha never intending to be there more than a few months, but I ended up staying much longer. My friend Hugh Grayson had moved there and kept after me to come out and visit, so I went. He was in a writers' group that met every Saturday afternoon. There were musicians around and a few actors associated with the Omaha Playhouse.

Long before the editor of a slick, Negro middleclass magazine for blacks in Omaha asked me to write an article on Eddie "Cleanhead" Vinson, I used to see and talk with Eddie in Paul Allen's bar, back when that place was called a dive. When Eddie worked the weekends, singing and blowing his sax on the stage at Allen's, he demonstrated for those too often inattentive people in the audience a very dramatic and important kind of improvisation. In Allen's he'd sing in his commanding voice, belting out "Cherry Red" or "Somebody's Got to Go" or "Kidney Stew Blues," then he'd pick up his alto sax and blow a rough, powerful blues-jazz solo.

It was especially painful, one time in Allen's, watching a drunk laughing at Eddie in a derisive manner and calling him a has-been. I bought Eddie a few drinks from time to time, and he told me about the great old days with Miles Davis and Bud Powell. At home, I had the Riverside recording of him with Julian "Cannonball" Adderley. When I would play that record, it was like living inside of history and culture.

The political activist Ernest Chambers was my barber in Omaha. (Ernie later became a state senator.) I remember heated discussions about politics and race relations in that barbershop. In a way, it was a good "classroom" for raising consciousness. Riots and so-called riots were spreading across America, and Omaha was on the bandwagon too. I could no longer be the precious artist refusing to take part in attempting to shape the political destiny of my country. When you are in a country that is divided over whether or not you belong, you either belong at great expense or withdraw. In my early years I alternated. I was torn between survival and principles.

Once I looked out of my second-story window and was almost shot by a nervous cop who had come to investigate a complaint downstairs. Omaha was a segregated town. It was difficult to get through even one week without being verbally abused. I held a number of unskilled jobs before teaching myself welding. I became a welder and learned to drive a crane. But there was no future for me in Omaha.

I knew that I would eventually try to live in Manhattan. In 1966, I first moved in with a friend from Omaha who had an apartment on the Lower East Side on Twelfth Street between Avenues A and B. Shortly after I arrived in New York, poet and activist Walter Lowenfels invited me to a memorial reading at St. Mark's Church for publisher Alan Swallow. Anaïs Nin was there and spoke of her late publisher. Looking at her was like seeing a transparent human being, so frail and white was she; and her voice was like that too.

When I landed a job as a teacher of creative writing at the New Lincoln School in Harlem and one as a research analyst for the Simulmatics Corporation, I was able to afford my own apartment—relations with my friend and roommate had become strained—and I moved into the building next door.

The research job was interesting. We were analyzing how people responded to the news coverage of racial violence. John Lindsay was mayor of New York

City at the time and was an outspoken supporter of the findings of those studies, which concluded that almost without exception the many hundreds of incidents of racial violence and death listed in the studies were either provoked by the police or resulted from police mishandling of the initial incident.

Early in 1967, I also traveled for Simulmatics to Milwaukee and Detroit to interview people who had lived through riots and so-called riots. I was the head of a three-man team; the other two guys were sociology students in PhD programs. Our research was directed by well-known sociologist Dr. Sol Chaneles, who interviewed us for the job on the third floor of a building on West Ninety-Fourth and Broadway.

The people I talked with in both Milwaukee and Detroit were interesting. The three of us researchers divided up the cities, and I took the ghetto each time. One of my assistants was black, the other white. The black boy had grown up in a white neighborhood. He seemed more comfortable interviewing white people, so I sent him to department stores and other kinds of downtown businesses. We hit Detroit just after the infamous July 1967 Algiers Motel incident, where three young black men were gunned down by white cops for being in rooms with white girls. The city was still steaming. People were left like cattle in trucks since the jails were filled. A barber in his shop, as he cut my hair, told me horror stories that stirred my anger and gave me a sense of despair. I went into the greasy spoons for breakfast and talked with the waitresses and the garbage men catching a cup of coffee before going to work. There was anger everywhere, some of it directed at whites, much of it directed at cops and at blacks who capitalized (in the form of theft, usually) on the chaos.

Looking back at the report I handed in to Chaneles, I find this observation: "I would discover for myself how deeply trapped in a nightmare of socially produced violence, morally rationalized racism, and economically maintained exploitation black and poor people in this country are only to see, later, Mayor John V. Lindsay mad on T.V. because Congress hadn't implemented any of the proposals." Although the Johnson administration paid for the study, the results were not what that administration wanted to hear.

. . . .

The other important detail about Simulmatics was that I met there, in 1967, a young woman I was to live with for two years. Sheila Silverstone was Jewish and had grown up in Brooklyn. While not especially religious, she called herself a "reformed" Jew. She was liberal and progressive. I remember how touched, perhaps ironically, she was when for our first Christmas my mother sent us a chocolate cake that she had baked for the two of us. Sheila had just finished earning her BA and seemed somewhat at a loss. What next? She was a moody young woman who was intellectually gifted. I liked her ability to be quiet and to read books for hours, but I disliked her smoking, especially since I had recently broken myself of the short-lived habit. I had also stopped drinking because of stomach problems. When I got my advance for the forthcoming *All-Night Visitors*—my first novel, not yet finished—we decided to go to Mexico, as my job at Simulmatics had ended and we had nothing better to do.

On arriving in Mexico City, we visited poet Margaret Randall at her home and spent the evening having dinner with her and writers Robert Cohen and Robert Sward. Margaret became a Mexican citizen. Later she wanted to reclaim her American citizenship. I wasn't to see Margaret again until 1984 in San Diego and 1986 in Boulder. This was during a time when she was waging in the American courts an important legal battle to regain her American citizenship and thereby to test and change reactionary laws established during the McCarthy years.

Within a few days Sheila and I moved on to Puerto Vallarta. It was here that she and I had our first relationship crisis. Given the culture shock, neither of us was in any shape to survive our first fight with any great degree of dignity. I thought of Richard Wright leaving his first wife in Mexico and returning alone to New York and considered doing the same thing but didn't. Instead, we wound up renting an apartment on the top floor of a house. Our place had a wraparound balcony and four massive rooms and a bathroom larger than most living rooms I had had in New York. The kitchen had a hand-laid marble-topped bar. The furniture was deep, rich mahogany, and so was the woodwork. Some rather dense Mexican paintings insulted the walls, but we were not offended enough to take them down. The building containing the apartment had just been purchased by an American woman from Los Angeles. Later, she tried to convince me to stay and work as her manager, as she didn't like Mexicans. I didn't even consider it.

I don't remember how long Sheila and I stayed in Puerto Vallarta, but I do know that we spent the last two weeks up north in San Miguel de Allende. Before we left Puerto Vallarta, Sheila became ill after we ate in a restaurant; she had a high fever and the runs and finally fell unconscious. I went racing through the night in search of a doctor. The first two turned me down. Finally, in a taxi, I was driven into the hills where I found a country doctor, an old man eating his supper, who agreed to come at once. When I got back to her with the doctor, she was beginning to regain consciousness. He gave her a shot, careful not to look at her hip, which reflected the custom of modesty there. Once I went with Sheila to a Mexican's doctor's office for a routine checkup and was surprised when he insisted that I come into the examination room too.

He covered her with a sheet and, as I watched, he examined her while looking at the ceiling.

Before going to San Miguel, we did a little traveling through Mexico and stopped in Guadalajara. We saw *Zorba the Greek* with Spanish captions. Because of my interest in D. H. Lawrence we also spent a day or two in Chapala, where the writer had spent several months in the 1920s. But in Mexico, I learned to dislike bullfights and saw for the first time the horrors of poverty worse than any I had ever seen before.

I finished writing *All-Night Visitors* in Mexico. A book described later by Greg Tate in the *Village Voice* as "'black letters' answer to *Tropic of Cancer*," it—albeit in abridged form—was published by Maurice Girodias's Olympia Press at the beginning of 1969 after being rejected everywhere. At that time, Grove Press was distributing Olympia Press's hardback line, but apparently not very well. *All-Night Visitors* remained underground and became the object of much scholarly concern during the years that followed.

The fact that I allowed *All-Night Visitors* to be published in an altered form was one of the things that came between Sheila and me. She thought I had sold out. I knew I hadn't, but there was no way to convince her. I told her that Richard Wright had been forced to cut *Black Boy* in half, leaving out the adult, communist sections. She didn't care. Our relationship ended at the beginning of the summer of 1969.

I spent the summer living in a house on a lake in the woods of Massachusetts near Lee. I felt very wounded. I kept my apartment in the city but went back there only twice during those months.

. . . .

I was beginning to gain some confidence in my ability to find publishers for the books I was writing. For years it had seemed impossible, and it still wasn't easy. In 1969 International Publishers had printed my anthology *The New Black Poetry*, and Wesleyan University Press had brought out my first commercially available collection of poems, *Swallow the Lake*, in 1970. That same year, after the Philosophical Library declined to publish my *Dictionary of Afro-American Slang*, International Publishers issued it.

The Black Nationalist writers up in Harlem had been friendly enough until I showed up once with a white date. Among that group were Ed Spriggs and other poets associated with the magazines *Soulbook*, *Black Dialogue*, and the *Journal of Black Poetry*. Spriggs, soon after the incident, led a boycott against my forthcoming anthology, *The New Black Poetry*. The conditions of his boycott were spelled out in one of the black magazines. He objected to the fact that the publisher was communist and white.

His boycott wasn't taken very seriously because many of the Black Nationalists he asked not to contribute contributed anyway, including LeRoi Jones, who was just beginning to become Baraka. After *The New Black Poetry* appeared in 1969, Kenneth Rexroth said it was the least sectarian of any of the new collections. The most nationalistic of the then Black Nationalist critics, Addison Gayle Jr., said in the *New York Times Book Review* that it contained "the best work by black American poets."

In 1971, Ted Wilentz, who had started the famous Eighth Street Bookstore, publisher of Corinth Books, issued another collection of my poems, *Symptoms & Madness*; and in London, Paul Breman, an antiquarian book dealer, brought out a slim volume of newer poems under the title *Private Line*. The following year, Broadside Press in Detroit published my *Cotton Club*, poems about various moments in black history.

. . . .

The years 1971, 1972, and 1973 were years of literary parties. When I try to think of highlights, I come up with faces, verbal tidbits, digs, compliments, and the starkness of shallow moments. I also remember a lot of celebrities.

Once at a very crowded party during one of her last trips to the United States, Josephine Baker reached through a crowd and squeezed my hand. She didn't know me, of course. But the reason that encounter is important to me has to do with the fact that when I was about twelve, in Chicago, she performed at the Regal Theatre, the place where South Side parents sent their kids on Saturday morning, often just so they could have some free time. I was overwhelmed by her elegance and extravagance in the same way I had been while seeing Cab Calloway, Peg Leg Bates, Illinois Jacquet, and many other great musicians at the Regal. (Gwendolyn Brooks wrote about those shows at the Regal Theatre!)

I met a young woman, Sharyn Skeeter, at a book party in 1971. She seemed intelligent and pleasant. I had not met many black women who were interested in literature. She was also poetry editor for *Essence* magazine. We started living together shortly after that, first in my apartment between Avenue A and First Avenue.

Novelist and poet Ishmael Reed had moved from Chelsea to St. Mark's Place, one block up from our apartment. We saw more of each other socially during this period than before or after. W. H. Auden lived in the building next door to Reed's. I used to see the great poet in the neighborhood in his house slippers. The only person I was acquainted with who had gotten to know him was poet Norman Loftis (painted by Philip Pearlstein in 1974).

At one party—for Cecil Brown's *Life and Loves of Mr. Jiveass Nigger*—I ran into the actor Robert Hooks, whom I had just seen in a movie based on a Tennessee Williams story. When I told Hooks how much I enjoyed the part he played in the film, he was not particularly pleased because, in his words, he wanted to "make black movies." Critic Christopher Lehmann-Haupt was also at this party; he had just given my novel *All-Night Visitors* a bad review.

In 1971, before Erica Jong published her first novel, *Fear of Flying*, her book of poems, *Fruits & Vegetables*, had attracted a considerable amount of attention. She and I were awarded a Creative Artists Public Service grant by the New York Cultural Foundation that year. I already knew Erica from PEN parties. The "public service" we were to perform for the $1,000 the foundation paid each of us to give a reading together in Sunset Park on June 12 in the heart of Brooklyn. We got to the park accompanied by a representative from the city and discovered there was no audience, nor were there the promised loudspeakers. No promotion had been done. So, Erica and I sat down on the grass and read our poems to each other.

One of my closest and lasting friends from this period was the poet Art Berger, whom I had met in 1966. Art, in fact, got me my first teaching job, the one in Harlem at the New Lincoln School. Later on, we team-taught one or two literature courses at Queens College, CUNY. There were times when I would go to Queens to conduct creative writing workshops in community centers he was involved in.

I met Chester Himes and his wife, Lesley, through Ishmael Reed, and we had a party in Chester's hotel room at the Park Lane in New York in 1973. The writers Reed, Steve Cannon, Quincy Troupe, and Joe Johnson were also there. It was then that I understood Chester's bitterness. He was drinking scotch. He talked a long time about his relationship with Richard Wright, since somebody, Joe or Steve, I guess, had asked him about it. Wright had dismissed as frivolous Chester's earlier relationship with an American woman Chester cared a lot about. This was during Chester's first year in Paris, at the age of forty-five. After that, Chester did not read any more of Wright's books.

I also became friends with another friend of Chester's, John A. Williams. He and I would both soon be teaching at Sarah Lawrence College. I didn't have a car at the time, so I would ride up with John. He called me his shotgun. Later, it made more sense for me to ride with Grace Paley, who also lived near me in the Village. Grace had a dependable Volkswagen Bug.

· ·

Walter Lowenfels, invited me to my first New York literary party. It was in a fancy but small hotel in Midtown and was for one of Walter's books. He had for a number of years, before I moved to New York, encouraged editors to read my work. It was Walter who, in the end, got Wesleyan University Press to take my poetry seriously, even though my manuscript was in shambles. His success on my behalf was therefore all the more remarkable.

But far more importantly, I discovered that I liked Walter's zest and his love of poetry. Lillian, his wife (whose dream was to have a grand piano on which she could keep all of her stuff), was wonderful to be around. I visited them in Peekskill two or three times, spending weekends, being overwhelmed by Walter's enthusiasm over whatever project excited him at that moment and listening to his critical responses to my own projects.

Bern Porter, publisher of Henry Miller, gathered some of my "papers" in his collection at UCLA and sent me checks from time to time in compensation for them. Porter had encouraged me as early as the late fifties. Later, he had many personal problems he only alluded to—he had been one of the physicists who worked on the atomic bomb at Los Alamos and apparently wanted to counterbalance the obvious outcome of that experience by doing constructive work for humanity. The last time I heard from him, in the 1970s, over twenty years later, he urged me not to give up my writing endeavors. That meant a lot at a time when I was in despair, feeling that both commercial and noncommercial publishing worlds were totally indifferent to my efforts.

Poet and professor William Meredith took it upon himself to drive from his home in New London, Connecticut, to Middletown to make the final selection of the poems that went into *Swallow the Lake*. Originally, Walter had sent Wesleyan a big bundle of my poems, far too many for the size of books they were bringing out. For over a year the various poets associated with Wesleyan as readers had scratched their heads over the bundle and refused to be decisive. Bill got mad and burst into the office that day and said enough was enough. He went through the bundle and came away with the poems that made the book. He handed it to the editor and, finally, after a long, long delay, the book was on its way toward production.

Norman Holmes Pearson, a professor at Yale University, had also taken an early interest in my efforts. I think I met him through Sheri Martinelli. He was collecting her papers at Yale and seemed very interested in her relationship with Ezra Pound during his St. Elizabeths years. Pearson, like Porter, got the impression I was poor. Both were right. Pearson sent me several checks in exchange for collecting my "papers." I now understand what that was about. If one had money, why not spend it this way, on something one believed in?

Between 1966 and 1970 I got to know a few of the musicians and painters on the Lower East Side. Ishmael Reed probably introduced me to more painters and musicians than anybody else did.

Around 1968 or 1969, Amiri Baraka was beaten by cops and arrested over in

Newark, so a whole bunch of us poets got together and gave a benefit reading for a defense fund at Judson Memorial Church on Washington Square Park South. I remember the audience booing Fielding Dawson for some reason. Baraka and his associates later performed at St. Mark's Church. He staged a theatrical attack on the largely white audience, using—I think—cap guns. The lights were turned off. One girl almost knocked her own brains out trying to escape from the room the moment the lights went out and the firing started.

· ·

After Sharyn and I traveled in Europe, our next move was to the Washington, D.C., area in 1975. Living in a high-rise in Maryland, I was teaching mainly at Howard University. The Howard job came about due to the kind interest the scholar Charles H. Nilon held for my work. (He was eventually tenured at the University of Colorado and was instrumental in bringing me there a few years later.) Charles was the visiting chairman of Howard's Department of English at the time and as such hired me for a two-year period. I had no idea where I would go after that. I'd been an academic gypsy since 1968. At home, Sharyn and I were suffering the pains of a crumbling relationship.

We stayed in the D.C. metro area until 1976, but in 1975, the Fiction Collective published my third novel, *Reflex and Bone Structure*. I got interested in the Fiction Collective while teaching at Brooklyn College in 1968 and 1969, where I met two of its founders, Jonathan Baumbach and Peter Spielberg. Painters had formed collectives for years, and I was attracted to the idea of writers of fiction doing the same thing. It might prove to be an alternative to the dim prospects of commercial publishing. I submitted my novel, and it earned the necessary four votes for acceptance. I had written the novel the year before, in my Waverly Place apartment in New York, in a state of mind close to that of a child playing. That is to say, I made up the rules as I went along. Writing that book at that time was a way of staying sane.

That same year, 1975, the Library of Congress held a conference on small press distribution at the Center for the Book. This was simply yet another example of business-related get-togethers. It was beginning to seem to me that the only time I saw my old friends was at such gatherings and the parties they generated. But I did meet a man I admired there: James Laughlin, founder of New Directions Publishing. He and Clare Boothe Luce were both introduced to me at the same time. I couldn't find a way to talk with him without also talking with her, so I never got the chance to say thanks for William Carlos Williams, H. D., Baudelaire, Borges, Djuna Barnes, Rimbaud, Apollinaire, Samuel Becket, Kenneth Patchen, Henry Miller, James Joyce, Ezra Pound and Tennessee Williams, writers I grew up reading and loved.

I had been an academic gypsy for years, so it was especially important to me to get my first tenure-track job at the University of Washington at Seattle. It came about, in part, due to Charles Nilon's recommendation. I went out to Seattle for the interview, met the committee members considering me, had lunch with them, and then went back to Washington, D.C. In a very short time, I received a letter offering me an appointment.

In Seattle in 1976, novelist Charles Johnson and poet Colleen McElroy became my close friends. Other people I socialized with while I was teaching there were novelist Victor Kolpacoff and some of the academics. I liked Seattle very much. The drizzle was suited to my temperament. (When I went back there later to give a lecture, I still felt close to the campus. It was one of my cherished homes.)

In Rotterdam the next year at the International Poetry Festival, an American professor, Talat S. Halman, conducted a workshop for those poets among us who wanted to try their hand at translating the work of the famous Turkish poet Fazil Hüsnü Dağlarca, who was there. These sessions were wonderful in that the participants shared an experience that brought them closer than the readings or, in some ways, the many nightly parties did.

In 1977, I left Seattle because the University of Colorado gave me tenure. Boulder, in some surprising ways, turned out to be a rather unique community in that, at least at first, it seemed friendly toward eccentrics and artists, and the university naturally generated an intellectual and generally speaking liberal community. This is not to say that racism did not make its presence felt on campus and in the community from time to time, but I was especially impressed by the lack of economic or racial ghettoes. There seemed to be a good level of tolerance for differences among people.

I remember going to one party Allen Ginsberg gave for visiting poet Amiri Baraka and meeting William S. Burroughs. We sat together on the couch. He was a very quiet and seemingly frail man with a sour face. He was complaining to me about having so little money to live on. The myth had it that Burroughs inherited a fortune from the Burroughs Adding Machine business, and I wondered if he was busy trying to counter that myth.

Baraka and I spoke together for the first time at that party, although we had read together in Harlem at the Apollo years before. He wanted to know what the Fiction Collective was, and I felt a little foolish trying to explain how it worked. I guess I was also surprised that he knew so little about a publishing co-op that had been around since the early seventies. He said he and his wife wished I "would come on it." Not sure what he meant, I did not respond.

Around this same time, Allen and I were sitting together in an audience on the University of Colorado campus listening to Robert Creeley introduce a film series. I knew Creeley from early fifties correspondence and a bit from my summer teaching at the State University of New York at Buffalo, where Creeley taught. Now, Allen wrote in my copy of *Planet News*, "For Clarence Major. Happy to be in his company, Robert Creeley talking into cinema microphone at the University, bunches of poets & students listening to the sibilant syllables—Creeley had on big cream-colored straw hat in lecture hall pit." In my copy of *Kaddish*, he wrote this: "For Clarence Major, several decades after our first poetic correspondence mid-U.S. to New York now both of us poets in the same Boulder."

My first two years in Boulder were frantic. I went to Colorado with the hope for a new life. I wanted to be reborn and to find some degree of peace and a chance of sustaining it. Although I felt lonely and alone, I trusted that I was about to break through into a whole new area of personal hope. In 1978, Sharyn and I separated, and it began to happen.

• •

Pamela Jane Ritter and I met at a dinner party in Boulder in September 1979. I fell in love with her and almost immediately we began to plan a life together. Call it love at first sight or whatever, it was the real thing.

Emergency Exit had just come off the press and the publication date was set for November, the worst time to put out a book that was not meant for the coming holiday. I went to New York for the book party, held at Carol Sturm Smith's apartment on Second Avenue. A lot of Fiction Collective writers were there, naturally, since the Fiction Collective was publishing the book, as well as Ntozake Shange and literary agent Charles Neighbors, who was first to tell me about the death of Clarence L. Cooper Jr., America's most neglected, brilliant realistic writer of the 1960s. Cooper apparently had died alone in some dingy New York room. We could make a long, long list of American writers, great and near-great, who have died alone in small, uncared-for places. Although I had never met Cooper, I corresponded with him briefly and admired his work. He was a good writer.

Pamela and I started living together on December 22, 1979. Right after our first Christmas as a couple I had to fly to San Francisco for a couple of days to appear on a Fiction Collective panel that Joe Weixlmann had organized courtesy of the Modern Language Association's annual meeting. A letter from Pamela was waiting for me at the hotel desk, which truly surprised and deeply pleased me. I called home right away to thank her and to tell her I loved her.

Pamela was working on her dissertation, a study of the fiction of Robert Coover, and our next move was in the interest of her finishing it. We settled into a kitchenette apartment in Bernardston, Massachusetts, which was a half-hour's drive to Amherst. We stayed there until December 1980. I wrote poetry and she got a lot of reading done and occasionally met with members of her committee at the university. The heavy snow came, and we spent much time in bed reading and talking and doing the other wonderful things that are so pleasant to do in bed while the whole world outside is frozen and static. We were suspended in time. We picked up our mail daily at the local post office and cashed checks when we needed money at the nearby drive-in bank. The town was dead. Teenage drunks, rednecks from the hills, and silent, suspicious farmers were the people we saw. I can imagine how puzzled they were over our presence. They never spoke, but they couldn't take their eyes off us.

While living there, I took time off from writing and drove to Albany to read poetry at the State University. Judith Johnson Sherwin (later Judith Emlyn Johnson) had invited me. I had known Judy from my New York days and liked and respected her work. She gave a reception for me in her apartment afterward.

Pamela and I also went up to Boston by car. We stayed with poet Fanny Howe in her big old house. I gave a reading one evening at MIT. After Boston we drove up the East Coast. It was winter and the drive was fabulous. All the resorts were closed, but when we needed to stop we were able to find motels. At one I encountered the usual blatant racism but refused to feel bitter about it. We were happy.

. . . .

In 1988, after years of traveling and guest teaching at other universities all over the world, Pamela and I were back in Colorado. Sick of snow, when a job proposal came from the University of California at Davis, I was immediately interested. And much of the rest of the year was spent finalizing the appointment. On July 10, 1989, the president of the University of California wrote me a letter making official my appointment to the Department of English to teach American literature and creative writing.

We moved to Davis and bought a ranch-style house on Toyon Place. Once we were settled, I was able not only to teach but to get back to writing and painting. Pamela, too, was given a teaching appointment in the composition program, which she held for many years.

Shortly after we moved into the Toyon house an earthquake hit. I was in the living room. I thought I was having a heart attack. I felt dizzy, off balance.

Then I noticed that the chandelier was swaying. It lasted only a few seconds. Later, of course, we learned that the Oakland Bay Bridge had collapsed in the quake.

One day early in the spring of 1991 I was pleased when Neil Baldwin called to ask me to serve as a fiction judge for the National Book Awards. I had had a lot of experience judging both fiction and poetry contests for various state agencies and for the National Endowment for the Arts in Washington, D.C. Tons of books arrived all summer. I spent a lot of time in the hammock in the yard reading one bad novel after another.

The other four judges—Curtis Harnack, Anne Bernays, Larry Heinemann, and Lynne Sharon Schwartz—and I kept in touch by conference calls, and finally, by the end of the summer, we had a short list consisting of five books by Norman Rush, Louis Begley, Stephen Dixon, Stanley Elkin, and Sandra Scofield. After much disagreement, in the end, Rush's novel, *Mating*, won. My friend Charles Johnson was there to present the award.

At the reception, cameras were clicking everywhere. Eudora Welty was sitting quietly in an armchair right in the middle of all the festive activities. With my little trusty camera, I snapped an excellent photograph of her. I then noticed Ralph Ellison, Michael Harper, Henry Louis Gates, and Rita Dove talking. When they saw that I had a camera they stopped and posed for me. Later, Ellison told me that I should've been in the picture too, not taking it.

Later Pamela and I moved to a new house. I once again got down to doing serious writing and painting. Remembering Langston Hughes's words in his 1926 manifesto, "The Negro Artist and the Racial Mountain," about the freedom to create, I wanted no limits imposed on me by either fashion or fear, racial loyalty or racism.

In 1992, I was approaching my fourth year at UC Davis. I had published two new books: a book of short fiction and stories, *Fun & Games*, and a collection of poems about Native American life, *Some Observations of a Stranger at Zuni in the Latter Part of the Century*. In the meantime, I was serving as director of creative writing and teaching creative writing and American literature.

That summer, I ran a fiction-writing workshop at Mills College in the Bay Area. My students were all women in their thirties and forties, all working on novels. The discussions were lively. One participant, Brenda Lane Richardson, published her novel, *Chesapeake Song*, in 1993. And, by the way, a good dozen or so of the thousands of creative writing students I worked with over a forty-year period of teaching workshops have gone on to publish collections of poems, novels, or collections of short stories. I claim no responsibility for their success; however, when they do acknowledge my help, I am grateful.

In the winter 1996 quarter at UC Davis, I was awarded a Davis Humanities Institute Fellowship, so I was able to spend more time working on my novel-in-progress, *One Flesh*. When *Dirty Bird Blues* came out, the publisher, Tom Christensen of Mercury House in San Francisco, sent me on a publicity tour to San Francisco, Los Angeles, and New York. From my own point of view, the most valuable thing that came out of the tour was that in Los Angeles, Professor Richard Yarborough came to the bar where I was holding forth promoting my new novel by signing copies and answering questions about it.

Yarborough was a professor of English at UCLA. He was also general editor of a series titled the Northeastern Library of Black Literature at Northeastern University Press in Boston. Already in the series were novels by Richard Wright, Claude McKay, and Jessie Fauset, among others. It was on this occasion that Richard told me he'd like to republish my first novel, *All-Night Visitors*, in an unexpurgated edition. I had long hoped for a chance to restore many sections I was forced to delete from the first edition. To make a long, happy story short, the fully restored edition came out with a foreword by Dr. Bernard W. Bell in 1998.

On February 20, 1997, I was once again in Washington, D.C., at the Folger Theatre giving a reading to raise money for the PEN/Faulkner Award. I had already agreed to help judge for the award. My fellow judges were novelists Annie Proulx, Madison Smartt Bell, and Rilla Askew. The ceremony would be held in May. I traveled again to Washington for that occasion. I delivered the remarks for the winning book and presented the award to Rafi Zabor for his book *The Bear Comes Home*.

In August 1998, I was finalizing the manuscript of *Configurations: New and Selected Poems, 1958–1998* just before Pamela and I flew to Paris for a six-week stay. Temporarily settled there, we rented an apartment overlooking Montparnasse Cemetery. Every morning we shopped at a nearby outdoor market for fresh vegetables and fruit. Afternoons we explored Paris, visiting museums and bookstores and sampling out-of-the-way restaurants. In the evening we ate dinner in, made from the vegetables bought at the market that day. Then we watched the news for an hour: mostly about France's former colonies and their political and economic problems.

In the first decade of the new century I made connections with several new art galleries, attended conferences, and did readings across the country. In 2001, my collection of poems *Waiting for Sweet Betty* was published. That next year, 2002, John Natsoulas selected my painting *Sweet Betty*, a large figurative work, for his annual Beat Generation exhibition. The painting was on view at his new gallery in Davis throughout the month of October. (I had curated a show at the gallery in May–June of 1992. Among the painters were Larry Clark, Robert Colescott, Oliver Jackson, Raymond Saunders, and yours truly.)

At the same time, I was looking forward to retirement from teaching, having reached the age of seventy-one. So, in the spring of 2007, I stopped full-time teaching but continued to teach for three more years in the summer school programs. I now had more time to write and to paint.

PART FIVE

POEMS

Supply and Demand

As a dishwasher
in a restaurant
I lasted only three hours.
It was a dubious role at best.
The dirty dishes kept coming
faster than I could produce clean ones.
But I could play the piano
for hours and hours,
snake across the floor
on my belly
all afternoon into the night.
As Hercules
I lifted Antaeus from the earth,
robbing him of his strength.
Always happy,
I could walk around the block
on my hands.
In a fanciful costume,
I played the joker.
With a thirty-pound sack of rice
on my head, all day,
I danced
on a stone balustrade
without falling off.
From sunup to sundown,
week after week,
I was a whole amusement park
unto myself.
I was on top of contingencies.
I defended victims of foolishness
and porous people.

I campaigned for weeks
against the greedy.
I deconstructed ancestral suffering.
I gave comfort to the feeble
and the needy.
I made marionettes dance for kids.
I played marbles with the best
and the worst.

But as a dishwasher
I lasted only three hours.

Hair

In the old days
hair was magical.
If hair was cut
you had to make sure it didn't end up
in the wrong hands.

Bad people could mix it
with, say, the spit of a frog.
Or with the urine of a rat!
And certain words
might be spoken.
Then horrible things
might happen to you.

A woman with a husband
in the Navy
could not comb her hair after dark.
His ship might go down.

But good things
could happen, too.
My grandmother
threw a lock of her hair
into the fireplace.
It burned brightly.
That is why she lived
to be a hundred and one.

My uncle had red hair.
One day it started falling out.
A few days later
his infant son died.

Some women let their hair grow long.
If it fell below the knees
that meant
they would never find a husband.

Braiding hair into cornrows
was a safety measure.
It would keep hair
from falling out.

My aunt dropped a hairpin.
It meant somebody
was talking about her.

Birds gathered human hair
to build their nests.
They wove it around sticks.
And nothing happened to the birds.

They were lucky.
But people?

Round Midnight

You know my story.
They want to make me liable
to punishment for this picture.

So my spirit is closed.
I'm a delicate engraving
outlined
with semitones, curled
at the edges,
nearly worthless,
in mysterious trouble.

I walk the beach
at Scheveningen.
Drink myself blind in The Hague.
Piss in the bushes at Etten.

I redate all my efforts.
Reconsider a cluster
of old houses nearby,
but not the church behind it.
You know why.

Midnight is round.
Asleep, we go around in it.
So what if I fail
at the total—the whole?

Judith Te Parari
couldn't care less.
She swings low
in her sweetness
around midnight as

the diggers dig
the fields stacking mud
against gold panels.

When I come to trial
you will hear
in my defense, weavers
and rug makers, potters,
old men leaning on sticks—
people I trust—tree cutters,
tree growers, folks born
in the month of March.

In Harlem or Stuttgart
you can make anything work—
jazz with hard light
against the Rhine;
even a tiny red boat
tossed this and that way
along the tired face
of night's season.

You know the story.
I am held captive by winter light
at Nuenen next to an ox,
hooked to a cart, hopeless
in its sincere effort
to go on and on.

Judith holds the end
of the winter thread,
pushes it through the needle,
then through my lip
and through midnight and
sews me and it together.

My spirit rises. I drink
nectar from her Nefertiti
moon. It's midnight, exactly
and I hear—what piano keys?—
not from Rick's. It's the sounds

of water at the Gennep
Mill, turning, and
I am a monk, waiting,
holding a gift—
a token of reprieve
placed in my hand
by my defenders
who also wait now on
benches harder than mine.

Un Poco Loco

—for Bud

To start, I have to draw blood,
find the right weakness,
show my grief,

just to get things moving:
sweep a bit,
dust my broom,
and since what I'm after
is so abstract, I bump
hard into chrome,
into the cluttered tables.

This one nearly killed me:
a lover I never wanted
to see again, a half-empty
glass of wine, lipstick
stuck in its brass tube,
a Cupid nailed to a globe,
half of an apple.

To keep going, I think
disconnected thoughts:
Chatter. Chew-tobacco.
Phoenicians. Rednecks.

To keep going I watch
my grandmother hold
the chicken by its legs—
bauk bauk bauk!
Chuck this time.
Cluck-Cluck last Sunday.

Keep going—the work
is the person said Peter
and proving it standing
there like that, silent,
before two hundred people.
That's one answer, the work
itself. No time to stop.

There's no time to stop—
for sickness or Jim Dine
or clever lines or the
upshot or the right note.

No time to remember
precisely—two glasses
left on the floor by the two
of us, gone down to
the level of plant life,
where we look so mysterious
and lovely that nobody's
going to care whether we
sprout next spring
or not. This is the problem
with a complete thing!
You can't lead it away
from the water it wants to drink.
It will kick your brains out!

Nazis drew blood a certain way.
They started something
they couldn't finish—they nailed cupids
to crosses and fed apples to snakes,
raped on the Riviera
and kicked holes through the dance
motion of abstract paintings
I expected to see later in Budapest,
where leaves on trees, birds on skies,
played Bud and whispered
Monk intimacies.
Take three. The Nazis

would have been better off
up in trees by Blue Lake.

The Pawnee is not going
to get nailed into a frame
of the Great American West.
Custer points his six-shooter
at the Indians' back:
only white space, the page's
margin between them:
the gun goes off:
a fluke of nature: I bleed.

Take four. To start again
the light has to be just right.
I'm going to shoot the scene
before me: here—
Phyllis with that calculating smile!
And perhaps your brother
at the piano with polished fingernails
making bobwhite sounds.
Start again.

Take one. There are no miracles.
Take two. Being a little crazy
isn't the result of a
volcanic eruption.
Being a little off,
places you in touch
with Jene Ballentine's
Born Free, 1968,
with Whistler's gray and pink,
with lava and its flow.

Let's do it again from the top.
It's not Art Deco,
not locomotives of
brilliant returns
from sparkling cities,
the polished nipples perched
atop Byzantine temples;

no, no—it's the return
to the unanticipated
start that continues to count:
one two three—Go!

Sure, I'm eclectic.
My colors remain pure.
My columns won't shift.
Variety keeps the boats adrift.
Blue Lake absorbs the blood
and flows on, still blue.

September Mendocino

What do you hear up here?
Same Shasta air, same Nevada air,
same Sierra Nevada air, same rainsong air
that lured Walt Whitman when he heard it.

But it is easier
to find what is left of Walt Whitman
these days, not in the sand, but
in a musty bookshop
over in Fort Bragg, where you sit,
rather than seeing him
walking a logging road,
beating the underbrush with his long stick.

Now the question is:
How good are the muffins in the morning fresh?
They taste crunchy, still warm from the oven.
Would Whitman eat one, you think?
He would, he would, but he'd smell it first.

Can you smell the misty lands of the western shore?
Yes, but not like a big net full of fresh fish.
Not like that. You smell fresh pine in the wind.
And back on the hidden road
you really smell pine and redwood
as if they were still split open like watermelons
in the grass. Which grass? And back there,
on the track of a winding logging road,
giant log-trucks shooting by the turnoff
where we bought the dulcimer
at Mick's from Deb,
these trees whisper all day and certainly at night.

Can you come here without going to Russian Gulch
or to Primitive Horse Camp, the Headlands?
Skipping these, would you go away
with less than a tourist should?

Do we any longer see what is befitting
in these mountains?
No bark a foot thick here.
No. This is 1993, tree for tree.
How many of the giant spirits
of 1874 still stand as I wash
my hands in the California coastal water?

So, is it necessary to still sing a California song?
The song has nothing to do with whether or not
this year is like Walt's year. It has to do with air,
this air, this new air, fresh still in all essential ways,
and singing through the redwoods' cold nights.

What else, then, do you hear?
We hear dulcimer strings—
that out-of-this-world sound. Nothing like it.
And other things we heard?
We heard about Jim's freshly baked muffins.
Heard about the cottage out back,
heard about the tree view,
heard about the water towers one and two.
We heard about the pine furniture.
And we heard about complete privacy.
And friendly strangers around a breakfast table.
A fire in the fireplace after dinner.
We heard people up late downstairs
talking with great excitement.
We heard old Walt's wood spirits
talking all through the night.

What do you see through the tree?
Same giant redwood stand, back farther
than we can beat our way to by land;
same cold night corner-of-Pacific
from our bed-and-breakfast window

in old Joshua Grindle's house on the hill.
Through the redwood branches
we saw Walt swimming
out in the Pacific with his boots on,
but still being clear
about "your average spiritual man,"
and clear about the "voice
of a mighty, dying tree
in the redwood forest dense."

But it's not the same there, anymore. Walt:
Not in Jackson State Forest,
not in Damme State Park,
not in Pigmy Forest.

What do you see when you stand
out on Little Lake Road
and gaze at Grindle's house?
You see the big white frame house
with wraparound ten-pillow porch;
you see your upstairs window.

What do you hear from here?
We hear other tourists at breakfast
talking about where they came from,
talking about how long it's been
since they were last here,
back when the place was owned
by somebody else, not by Jim
and his wife. But we do not hear
the crack! crack! crack!
of the chopper's ax Walt heard.
They're farther back.

How deep is the river—is it as deep as it was?
It's deeper than the gift shops are high.
That's for sure. Deeper than
Rainsong Shoes or Paper Pleasures,
Deeper than Papa Bear's Chocolate Haus
or The Melting Pot and Papa Bird's put together.
But really, how far down is that river?

Is this small cluster of shacks the remains
of the big camp shanties of the 1870s?
Pretty to think them
the ones Walt wrote about, crowded together
boastfully strung along the coast.
Do you smell them, do they stink?
Do they smell of fish?
Fishermen think fish smell pretty good.
What is their "unseen moral essence,"
compared to, say, the trendy gift shops
and their objectives?

So what is coming up the mountain road for?
For the romance of the wood spirits, still.
And for our own romance in our oceanview room
with its tiny sailboat wallpaper,
ship's table and framed pictures of paddleboats.

And when we go away from here,
what do we want to remember?
What will we necessarily remember?
What we heard in the air.
What we smelled on the air.
The smell of fresh corn muffins.
Just the things a tourist needs.

The Slave Trade: View from the Middle Passage

I

I am Mfu, not a bit romantic, a water spirit,
a voice from deep in the Atlantic:
Mfu jumped ship, made his escape, to find relief
from his grief on the way,
long ago, to Brazil or Georgia or Carolina—
he doesn't know which;
but this is real, not a sentimental
landscape
where he sleeps free in the deep waves,
free to speak his music:
Mfu looks generously in all directions
for understanding of the white men
who came to the shores
of his nation.

Mfu looks for a festive reason,
something
that might have slipped.
Mfu looks back at his Africa,
and there at Europe,
and over there at the Americas,
where many of his kin were shipped
and perished, though many survived.
But how?
In a struggle of social muck. Escape?
No such luck then or now.

And Mfu hears all around him a whirlwind
of praise, explanation, insinuation,

doubt, expression of clout—
"It was a good time to be white,
British, and Christian" (H.A.C. Cairns).
And remembering the greed of the greedy white
men of Europe, greed for—
ivory, gold, land, fur, skin, chocolate, cocoa,
tobacco, palm oil, coffee, coconuts, sugar, silk,
Africans, mulatto sex, "exotic" battles,
and "divinely ordained slavery."

And it was, indeed, with reverie,
heaven on earth for white men.

But Mfu is even more puzzled by the action
of his own village:
Mfu, a strong young man, sold in half-light,
sold in the cover of night and muzzled
(not a mistake, not a blunder);
sold without ceremony or one tap
of the drum,
sold in the wake of plunder—
for a brush not a sum of money
but a mere shaving brush,
sold without consent of air fish water
bird or antelope,
sold and tied with a rope and chain
(linked to another young man
from Mozambique's coast,
who'd run like a streak
but ended up anyway in a slave boat
without a leak or life preservers);
sold to that filthy Captain Snelgrave,
sold by his chief, Chief Aidoo.
Sold for a damned shaving brush.
(And Chief Aidoo, who'd already lived
sixty winters,
never had even one strand of facial hair.)
Sold for a shaving brush.
Why not something useful?

Even a kola nut? A dozen kola nuts?
Six dozen kola nuts?
Sold for a stupid shaving brush.
And why didn't the villagers object?
(After all, he'd not been sold from jail,
like Kofi and Ayi and Kojo and Kwesi
and that girl-man Efua.)
And now Mfu's messenger, Seabreeze, speaks:
"Chief Aidoo merely wanted your
young wife but
before he could get his hands on her,
she, in grief, took her own life—
threw herself in the sea."

Here in Mfu's watery bed
of seaweed
he still feels the dead weight of Livingstone's
cargo
on his head, as he crosses—
one in a long line of strong black
porters—
the river into East Africa;

in his seafloor bed of ocean weeds
he still hears white men gathered in camp
praising themselves in lamplight,
sure of their mission—
"Go ye therefore, and teach all
nations,
baptizing them . . ." (Matthew 28:19).

Mfu, raised from seed a good boy—to do all
he could—
never went raving mad at his father,
never shied from work, one
to never mope:
therefore, when father said hold
the shaving mirror
for the white man, he held the shaving
mirror

for the white man, teaching himself
to read
the inscription: Kaloderma Shaving Soap.

But now Mfu, like a tree, is totally without
judgment
or ambition, suspended between
going and coming
in no need of even nutrition—
gray, eternal—
and therefore able to see, hear, and know
how to shape memory into a thing of wholeness
and to give this memory
not "the Negro revenged" voice
of abolitionist Wm. Cowper—
bless him—
but to see, say, what went into the making
of what, in those days, they called
Negrophobia.

II

To understand the contour,
Mfu must tour deep into Europe first,
explore
its sense of Mother Nature: Mother Nature
in Europe is a giant pig
with a black baby at one tit
(this is good Europe: charitable, kind,
compassionate Europe)
and a white baby at the other. A sucking
sound,
plenty to go around.

And in the background,
without thought of remission, a band
of white-slave-catchers
force Africans into submission
(this is bad Europe: evil,
mercenary Europe)

in order to chain them,
hand to hand and leg to leg
and ship them into slavery
in the new land.

Both Europes baffle Mfu.
Could it be solely about greed and profit?
But he must try to understand it,
first, the good Europe.
He pictures this:
In a longhouse somewhere
on the coast
of West Africa about fifty
Africans,
in simple white cotton robes
are gathered in dim light,
each awaiting this or her turn
to be dunked head-down
into a big wooden bucket
of water.
Two rosy pink Christian white men,
in slightly more elaborate white robes,
in attendance—a link, surely, to heaven.
They do the dunking.
These are good white men
who wear Josiah Wedgewood's
medallion
of a pious African face
with inscription:
"Am I not a man and a brother?" (1787).

But what is *really* happening?
One culture is modifying another,
and in the process (perhaps unwittingly)
modifying itself, in the name of its god;
as a Liverpool slaver, with its wretched cargo,
slides easily by
headed for the West Indies
or a port at Carolina,
with bodies packed in the pit.

The good white monk on his knees in prayer,
not interested in the gold of Afric
or the Bugaboo or whether or not
a European looks more
like an orangutan
than does, say, an Ethiopian.
(And besides, the orangutan is not an African
animal.)
So, don't tell him stories
of this man-of-the-forest
kidnapping black babies,
thinking they his own kin.
Don't waste his time.
Don't tell him a good savage is one
who will climb
happily up a tree for you
and fetch you a piece of fruit like a good monkey.

Don't tell him your heathen jokes.
Don't laugh at Casper, at the birth of Christ.
Don't make fun of the Hottentots.
Don't try to convince him that Africans have
no souls. Souls are not proven. Period.
The white monk, sin or not,
has a secret vision of the Queen of Sheba,
as a healing spirit for the downtrodden
blacks,
and though this secular dream is out of rhyme
with his devotion, much of his time is
spent
on a vision of the Sable Venus,
herself a Creole Hottentot,
surrounded by chubby pink cherubs;
he prays to black Saint Martin
and to black Saint Maurice,
in armor, patron saint
of the Crusade
against the Slavs,

the monk prays to the black Madonna,
who certainly must know something he doesn't
know,
prays to all the white saints too
(and you can name them)
and to Jesus, Mary, and Joseph.

The white monk prays that these lean Children
of Ham
will be washed clean
by the spirit and say of the Lord –
made as white
as the light of day;
made to sparkle the way the little Dutch children
wanted to make
their African playmate shine from
and take to Snow-White Soap.

Anyway, at the very least,
black souls could be made pure
as snow.
No more niggling over that issue.
Pure as snow, far from the mistletoe,
that thing too terrible to touch.
And then when a French soldier
brings home
an African wife the village
grief and fear
will surely fall to the ground like a leaf.

Mfu listens to the prayer
and is puzzled by the contradiction
implicit in its quest. It conceals a tyranny
surely
not innate,
one Mfu would like to believe is not meant,
or mean-spirited.
The implication, though, is unfortunate.
But Mfu remembers many such occasions

when such good men prayed and took
action too
in the name of goodness-over-sin
that led to no good for anybody:
That out-of-breath five-year war
in Suriname (1792).

They took and hung the leader
on a hook by one of his ribs
leaving him without a tear
on the seashore to die
a slow death.
The white monk, by the way, prays
that the white Venus and the black
eunuch,
seen together like white on rice,
will remain cool, nice, and chaste.
The eunuch, after all, he knows
is not Peter Noire. And even Peter Noire
can be made to leap
out of a box
like those that French children play with:
where a black Martinican maid,
complete with apron and headrag,
springs up with a jolly smile,
ready to dust.
Or Black Peter could serve as Bamboulinette,
where we use his mouth as an ashtray.

Mfu is not sad,
but he now wonders
how necessary it is to give examples
of the deeds of *bad* white men
when there were so many jolly good sinless
deeds
of the exceptional men of pink skin.
We have so many who fought for the dignity
of all human beings. (But then,
is there not something in *all* men

that must be resisted—
especially by themselves?)
And Mfu also wonders at the noble, dignified
presence
of black intellectuals and military leaders
among the good Europeans:
There is Jean-Baptiste Belley, sad, ironic,
sardonic,
aging, elegant, in the French Army,
a captain during the French Revolution,
fighting, no doubt, for justice for all,
with strong memories
of having been born a Senegalese slave
at remote Goree (1747). Surely
this man
lived with irony as if it were a cancerous
sore
in his throat.

III

Ah ha! Mfu can now see the Americas from here.

There is a group of Maroons being ambushed
by white overseers with guns
in moonlight in the bushes,
being yanked and gathered together
on the Dromilly Estate, Trelawny.

Haitian soldiers, crushing Napoléon,
placing ropes around the necks
of French soldiers and pulling them up
by way of pulleys to hang them
dangling from stakes,
to hang in the sun till they die.
And Hansel to Gretel:
"I'm afraid to go
to Africa because cannibals may
eat me
as they do one another."

Little Red Riding Hood to her
    grandmother:
"Dig, what makes your mouth so big?"

And Ignatius Sandro, there,
    with that wonderful, whimsical
        gaze to his.
    No tears.

A crying Barbados mulatto girl on her knees
    before a planter.
His head thrown back, face drinking the sky,
    and with eyes closed, lace open,
his expression is both one of deep pleasure
    and great agony.

A Jamaican Creole noblelady sits on a porch
    while a black slave fans her.

Because of one slip,
a Sambo, white as his tormentors,
    strapped over a barrel,
    is being beaten with a bullwhip,
    and his entire backside is beet-red
        with blood.

A giant snake, sixty yards long,
    drops from a massive, ancient tree
    onto the back of a black horseman,
    right or wrong, you see,
    and wraps itself around both,
        squeezing
till the horse and the man,
    taking all they can stand,
        stop moving, then swallows first
the man then the horse.

Mfu can also see farther north—Georgia and
    Carolina:
        Black men women and children bent
            Working—out of breath—
            the cotton the corn the cane,

from can't-see to can't-see,
from birth till death,
with no stake in their labor.

Never will forget the day,
Never will forget the day,
Jesus washed my sins away.

Who is that pink-faced general, dying?
lying on the ground dying out there,
as the Battle of Bunker Hill rages on?
Another general, who will perhaps
become president, fights his way
free of a cluster of redcoats,
without feeling the slightest thrill
while, on horseback
in the background,
his slaves watch for him to botch it.

Pharaoh's army sunk in the sea,
Pharoah's army sunk in the sea,
Sho am glad it ain't me.

And a Negro soldier (strong as a Wagogo
warrior and
brave as KaMpande,
King of the Zulu)
aims his rifle at a redcoat
while a major points
the frailest pink finger
ever in danger of being shot off
in a revolutionary war.

Two white horses side by side,
Two white horses side by side,
Them the horses I'm gon ride.

A newspaper item: "And good white men
have come to believe that perhaps the sin
is not in keeping the niggers in chains but in releasing
them." ("Catch a nigger by the toe . . . ?"
"Let my people go!")

A cartoon (1789):

A black man dressed like an English gentleman
is bludgeoning a poor, suffering white man over
the head with an ignorant-stick. And in the
background: Similar configurations dot the
diminishing landscape. Message: Let them go
and they will enslave you. Rationale: Abolition
is folly.

This here is the white woman, France,
(this time without the fabled black
eunuch)
with her arms outstretched to the slaves
on knees before her,
with arms lifted toward her
thigh,
while Frossard watches with the light
of an approving smile in his eye.

Jefferson strokes his chin,
thinking about freeing his slaves.
Here they come around the bend.
But he says oh well, maybe not.
Rise Sally rise. Wipe your weeping eyes.

Washington, on his deathbed, frees his slaves.
Thanks a lot.

On my way to heaven,
Yes, Lord, on my way to heaven,
On my way to heaven, anyway.

Mfu remembers an Ashanti Juju girl
(who gave him a coin)
saying, "We must believe that the good
in human beings will prevail."
And on front of the coin:
Nemesis, antique goddess
with raised left arm.
Right hand holds olive branch.

Obverse:
Face of a young African man,
sensitive and intelligent.
And the inscription:
"Me miserum."
This relic, the best, the girl said, was given to her
by a never-mean Danish traveler from
the West Indies,
where he'd seen, without reverie,
the abolition of slavery
in 1792.

Sister Mary wore three
links of chain,
Sister Mary wore three
links of chain,
Glory, glory to His name . . .

IV

Mfu says this is to strain against the insanity
that welcomes us at the other end:
Where one does not believe there is hope,
and one strains too to keep the gentle face
of, say, Carl Bernhard Wadstrom,
white man,
bent over Peter Panah, black man,
teaching him to read.
And wish the configuration
said something more
than it does.

Mfu remembers Equiano.
Equiano (1789) said: "We are almost a
nation of dancers, musicians, and poets."
And although we're more,
much, much more,
let's have a revival—
Why not celebrate?
If nothing else,
it can't hurt to celebrate survival.

Clay Bison in a Cave

Clay-tan, eyeless,
voiceless, even in a sense weightless,
in motion yet motionless still
for centuries and centuries,
stuck in this motion
of climbing, perhaps lost, these
two Paleolithic bison,
heads lifted, strained back
to the black endless sky,
as they climb toward sunny grass.
Which black sky? Which grass?
Rock-step by rock-step,
up they go, on up and up.
The black sky at the top of the cave.
The grass that is always
more a promise in a dream
than that sweet kiss
blown by watercolored wind.

Frenzy

Here is the little earthworm-eater,
she-kiwi.

She's in her frenzy of lust.
There she goes in her flightless

night journey, in mating season,
warm in her fur-feathers

poking her long bill, beaker,
with nostrils at the tip

sniffing and drilling
scratching and uprooting

with her powerful feet
pausing, maybe, to let

herself be mounted
furiously and briefly

by a he-kiwi whose
odor is to her liking.

Then there she goes again—
through the underbrush

(followed by her
faithful seducer)

back to her *querencia*
to burrow down

and wait and sometime
later she stands up

suddenly, and hatches
a big egg

nearly half the size
of her little body.

Finished, she steps away
and the father-to-be

steps in and sits
on the egg

warming it,
sits and sits warmly,

for three months
while she-kiwi, lustful still,

goes out looking
to get laid again.

Santa Maria dei Frari

You are late for your train.
You linger anyway.
You know a Titian is there.
You looked, Madonna of the Pesaro Family.
You touched St. Peter and his great book.
You behold Madonna on her throne
formally receiving a kneeling
high military official: St. George and his soldiers.
The glitter of the swords catches your eye.
The Turkish prisoner is not happy.
Do you know the young woman
with big bright eyes? A member
of the Pesaro Family. Half-hidden
by the figure of St. Francis,
bluntly in the foreground
you watch her gaze
around the saint out directly at you,
making you self-conscious. Leaving
Frari, you wander back
across Venice. You take a boat
over to St. George's. Inside,
Tintoretto's *Last Supper.*
You—an uninvited guest—
grab its energy
as it races away in the distance
like a night train
you yourself are already on,
coming straight back
into yourself.

Plein Air

Look at Powell Street
with the trolley tracks
and the traffic jams
and the teaming crowds of tourists
and little motorbikes scooting about.

Oh, I know what the French had in mind.
Pasture with cows.
Beach house by the sea.
Hush of underbrush
where ducks suddenly shoot up
from the thicket. Last day of fall.
Sky full of dramatic clouds.
Last of the snow.
Rain over wheatfield.
Late afternoon sun
already out of sight
behind trees in the distance
and sky blazing with indirect light.
A drawbridge, a canal.
And Arles—one must not forget Arles.
Winter hills yellow and black.
Twilight on tall crop purple-green
with a touch of white light.
Midday shower in the yellow countryside.
Golden wheat harvest, no crows.
At water's edge,
empty boat slapping mossy rocks.
Summer at the beach with bathers.
And more bathers,
bathers pretending they're near a stream.

Golden autumn.
Poppy field under blue sky.
Mountain stream
with snow-capped mountains in the distance.

But what about Powell Street,
with its griminess and noise
and trolleys and crowds of tourists
and pollution with diesel fumes
billowing out of buses?
Is this not also Nature?
Who will set up an easel here,
who will defend Powell Street?

East Lansing, Michigan

September 10

There was no warning.
Rising from his rest
the dog bit the man's leg,
did it quietly,
then returned to his spot
on the front lawn to rest.
A solitary taproot
grows into a green bush
on which years later
a naked girl one day hangs
a wet bra to dry.
But the next morning
the dog's owner
came into the man's room
carrying a tray
containing croissants
and a pot of coffee,
and said, *Quick! Turn on the TV!*
Airplanes are flying
into the World Trade Center,
and the man knew then
that as fast as he would recover
from one season or reason
there would be no warning
from where the dog
or the airplane would come.
As fast as one plant dies
another grows.

The man is now a seedling
just starting
from the roots of 9/11
to grow again—but into what?

Evening Newspaper

Going home on the subway,
when you open the newspaper
you'd just picked up
at the corner
before coming down the steps,
there is always the person
next to you slyly reading
over your shoulder
and getting visibly upset
when you turn the page
before they finish the story
about some woman in Mexico or Brazil
discovering the Virgin's face in a mango
or seeing it in a puddle of water
in the road to the junkyard
or the Granada dig uncovering the bones
of people fallen in their tracks
during attacks in a medieval street battle.
Keep turning.

Father

I was there looking for the house
where my father died.
An old neighborhood,
clean and orderly,
with flower gardens flanking each front door.
Windows covered with white lace,
behind which nobody seemed to live.
Thanks to a restless cloudy sky,
a gray light hung over it all.
Despite the road sweeper's efforts
to smooth it over,
the main road was unpaved
and bore carriage tracks and car tracks.
And when I found the house,
at the deep end of the street, I knocked.
A woman came to the door
and said, Yes, he lives here
like a character in a gothic novel.
You see, when the storm came
and broke the levee, flooding the city,
leaving hundreds dead,
thousands stranded,
beach chairs and canopies blown away,
your father was a hero.
He got everyone out.
I knew it was a lie, but it was what I needed to hear.

The Young Doctor (1916)

At noon he smiles and nods
as he drives by,
thinking perhaps soon
she will be pregnant
coming to me,
but he's wrong.
He sees a long line
of pregnant women
packed like fish
in a net bursting out
the seams of their dresses.

Ah! Give me a cup of tea
and a back rub.
Blood and slime,
cupids and cherubs, no thanks.
Give me trees losing their leaves.

I'm okay. I pay the iceman,
and he brings ice
into the dark house,
inserts the block of it
into the icebox,
while church bells
go *dang! dang! dang!*
scaring the mice.

"Then again,"
as the fish man's nag
comes towing an old wagon
of trout, I turn about
to see who's driving by,

and I'm beginning to think
he is coming out of his way
maybe at least a mile
just to smile at me.
But no, that's crazy.

Against distant thunder
I watched my trout of many blues
being wrapped
in trodden newspaper
and blundered by shaky hands.
And I understand.

Morandi

London, morning: a dying rose in a dish. Camellia in a glass.
On the windowsill: chrysanthemums drooping.
Desire: an apple, red, turning yellow. Chalk Farm produce.
Wine bottle with lips like roses. Plant in a jam jar.

Last night we stayed up late eating oysters, drinking wine,
listening to the splatter on the roof. You and the scent of light.
    Aphrodite
at Turnchapel Mews. As if friends are soon to arrive.
Adjust the candles, the door handles. Think of trees; think of pears.

I think of when we met. You were sitting primly on the edge of a park
bench reading a novel. The sky behind you was a slab of slate.
How could I best start a conversation? I could say, Is that a good book?
No, I thought. And just as I was about to break the ice

I thought I might turn out to be the plot complication
you would come to hate. But, no, that's not how we met.
You were a girl squatting under the boardwalk, holding a parrot, the
parrot saying, *Teatime, teatime, mother in the greenhouse*

clipping leaves, teatime, teatime, mother in the greenhouse
clipping leaves. That's how we met. I heard the parrot.
Then I heard you say hello. Now we are here
where the road crosses the train tracks. Now is now.

This morning you have a headache. Around the round table of
    cherry pie
and tea, you stand by the stove in self-derision. You regret last
    night. But
last night was ours for hours. Happy then. Now empty jugs and mugs,
bottles and glasses. *Look at them!* Standing as if posing for Morandi.

Domestic Agenda

From outside, through the window,
you are watching the woman inside. You love her.

You left to walk the dog.
She was at the sink washing her hair.

You love her best when she is like this—washing her hair,
applying makeup, pulling on stockings.

Unconscious moments. Degas moments.
I watch you watching her.

The ocean a stretch of green,
seagulls overhead as you walk Smitty along the beach.

You pass people patiently enduring unhappiness.
You pass a pied piper, power walking,

a pack of happy kids trailing.
But who's in the houseboat making it rock?

Coming back to the smell of something baking,
cookies maybe, a warm house. She leans over the teapot,

testing it. You take a peach from the fruit bowl
on the table. You bite into its sweetness.

Water and Sand

Today. A scattering of fishing boats. A lost kite.
A scattering of geese and ducks.
Fishermen working ropes along a ropewalk.

Last night. In the night sky a falling comet,
like a stroke flashing down through the brain. No sound.
If sound, it would be that of a newborn screaming.

I need a nap. Out here on the beach a line of girls, knee to knee,
knitting a blanket spread from lap to lap. The pope resigned.
Last summer in Morocco young men gathered,

horseback riders of hope, competing in gunpowder games.
In a swelling blanket of dust they galloped across and back.
But today on this beach the comfort of the familiar.

The sky is a line of cancan girls in perfect harmony.
The ocean is clapping like a grateful audience,
regular as a train on its track.

Faith

Run free like a wild horse.
Wake the homeless weeping in their sleep on stone benches.
Rosa woke in bed at Hotel Marina.
Don't want Obi Kenobi to save my galaxy.
Pledge allegiance to the kitchen sink.
Rosa sleeping in her wedding gown.
Don't want to be inspected for perfection or rejection.
Pledge allegiance to the sky, to skylarks, to the unknown.
Don't want anybody tracking my every step.
Don't want to backtrack.
But I forgive the boy who sold me a leaky boat.
Is Rosa still in bed?
I worship the ten red apples on the window ledge.
They are my religion.

Alchemy

My senses on high alert: I see ripples in frozen water, shaded.
Evading my responsibility, I help the priest carry the cross.
I defy my boss. I see the spilling of ink and blood.
This is my untold story without glory, without the Flood.

My senses in high alert: I see veins of leaves without trees.
I hear the slapping of water as swimmers swim. Evaded,
I trim the trees. I hear the scream of a man on a flying trapeze.
I smell the splash of a cook making a washtub full of soup.

My senses in high alert: Birds and bees keep me in the loop.
I see stone blocks pitted with age and moss over rocks.
I am duped! This is my fire burning, my desire burning.
I smell cab horses, no longer restless, standing curbside,

hooked to their carriages. Without lust, I see a girl
at a window holding her cat to her bosom.
I hear the crack of rifles as men shoot ducks from the sky.
I see scraps of skin-thin paper pasted together to no good end.

No one will contact my next of kin. I am careful of what I buy.
I hear the shout of people on rooftops above shops
waving at a procession of returning soldiers.
I see in the sky a looming darkness as welded bronze.

My senses are highly alert: I hear red slabs of earth
grinding together. This is my pain, my joy on a long train ride,
my golden leaf, my relief. I am alert to all.
This is my place in the shade, my trust. My trust in all.

No One Goes to Paris in August

A Montparnasse August
with view of the Cimetière. A yard of bones.

We wake to it. Close curtains to it.
Wake to its lanes. Rows of coffin-stones in varying light.

Walking here. Late with shade low, low, long.
We're passing through, just passing through
neat aisles of gray mausoleums.

(From Paris. Send this postcard. This one.
Calm water lilies. Water lilies.
Nothing colorless.)

It's morning. Baudelaire's tomb.
Tree limbs casting shadow west.
This, a lot of time under a looming sky.
Nobody has time like this.
(Time to go to Le Mandarin for coffee
every day. We're not complaining.
They bring the milk separate.
Watch the passersby on Saint-Germain.)

Nothing to ponder. This is the plight.
Pause by Pigeon in bed with his wife—
both fully dressed.

Pink flowers, pink flowers,
just beneath de Beauvoir's name.
When she lived she lived two doors down.
Went south in August.

All of us smell of heat all the time.
We are the living. Oh dear!
There are the dead ones there.
Their thoughts more familiar, though.
Lives finished, nearly clear.
And they make it possible for us to go on living
as we do in their blue shade.

Down and Up

1 DESCENDING A STAIRCASE

Once up, nude or not,
they tend to come down—
gravity not withstanding,
with or without understanding.
They come down.
The woman carrying a lantern
comes down slowly,
inspecting the dark.
A woman fresh from her bath
comes down, damp and refreshed.
Somebody's niece or wife, in a chemise,
stands up and walks down the steps,
each one squeaking under her weight.
Two guards bring down an old woman
seated in a chair. Two boys
carry a woman, asleep in her bed, down slowly.
For the sake of art,
another woman, nursing her baby, comes down.
A man descends while reading a book
about sin and redemption.
They all come down,
down,
down
where everybody else is waiting to ascend.

2 THE UNASCENDED STAIRCASE

No one is going up—yet.
The Calvinist minister must first finish her sermon.
The old woman with one shoe must stand up.
The man refinishing antique furniture
will try his luck when he finishes.
The bejeweled wealthy woman
may be too heavy for the staircase.
She stands on the landing,
inspecting the first step for its sturdiness.
Here is a young woman,
a pimple on the tip of her nose,
skeptical eyes, tight lips,
dimples, and fat cheeks.
She's waiting for her intended.
They are intent on moving
one way or two ways.

From

Some Observations of a Stranger at Zuni in the Latter Part of the Century

I

A stranger to the desert I come here
with my jaw jammed shut
so that speech
comes out
like fish falling from a net.
Yet I speak. Having chosen Zuni
leaves no darkness roaring in my ears.
The decision is
                                        . . . a sharp fin:
We enter not by road alone. If, during the trip
inward—in an unending switch-system as
            on a train rail—the upper body
tumbles over a top-heavy house, do not
be alarmed. We are approaching the end
            of the century, yet Kothluellakwin
is where Salimopiya will continue
            to carry his yucca switches
and whistle through his blue snout.
I will be his escort between the parked
            Fords and pickups. The dogs leap
                                    —leap fast at him!
Okay, we have entered. Incest binds
the people together in the color

of Corn Mountain. Brother
and sister trusting each other's heartbeat,
swim the morningstar as it rises from
Spirit Lake. They are surrounded by
. . . powerful, powerful
medicine. Medicine men forgive them,
priests hypnotize them as they watch
themselves—reflected—lose focus in the lake.
Only where rules are unbreakable
will I break them.
With no reason to fear Unseen Hands or the ancestors
Cliff Bullneck
Dirty Water
Warmsprings
the others
"even if you become a priest" (they told her)
you will never make the prayersticks
or enter the kiva." You'd think she could
have turned to the antelope, the great Star
or Forbidden One. I could not help.
I wrote only her name with a stick in the land,
in sand. The stick
turned into a horned serpent.
One of her moccasins was stolen from her feet.
The wolves did not take it.
Spider Woman had no interest in a single moccasin.

In the house
there was a cooking bowl, a stone knife.
In the house
there was a digging stick by the door.

On the porch
there was a firestick and a portable radio.

Those who came out of the suds—
Siiwhu,
Siwa
Siiwilu
Siyeetsa

being unfamiliar with hard surfaces,
watched the white line in the middle
          of the highway with special care. Nobody
called either of the two girls a squaw.
Those times had passed.

If the head needs to be held up, use hands.
The ears will insist on a certain music.
Our Lady of Guadalupe cannot contain
          the body once it starts shaking.
The Catholic Daughters of America
          probably did not have an extra chair.

You peeped through the parsley-colored maze
     at her plumage, peeled back from her
                              shimmering body.

You wanted to seduce her for the seeds,
          in search of calmness; you had no idea
how framed and locked otherwise
                              she was. She remains.
Somewhere between Gallup
and the crow's secret you were right
                              to give up.
You had no claims on the pueblo.
Although your presence was tense
your toes might well have exchanged
                    with your heart or nose. I meant
to say all of this earlier.

I hand her a scarlet flower. The Bow Priest
will not hang me from the beam and beat me.
There are rules, laws within laws.

Yahaaaaheeeeyoohoho
Yahaaaaheeeeyoohoho

Ask me no questions—tell you no lies: Spanish
word "Zuni" is a questionable corruption
          of the Zuni "Shiwi." Pueblo's Keresan.
It sounds like Chinese and can't be linked
          comfortably with any others.

The Slavic shopowners sell junk.
The tourists buy junk.
The paddy wagons pick up drunk Indians . . .
in Gallup.
The customers of the Indian prostitutes
are rednecks Mexicans and Others.

She told me early that sheepherding
and silverwork were in their blood. I said how
long. It
didn't matter. Her own jewelry was hammered
out of her ancestor's flesh and bones.

In his red pickup, Ciwanakwa waited behind
the big rock at Yellow Rock.
He kept his bedding at Sack of Flower Place
because the lone girls came there to fill the family jugs
with clear, Spring water.
She grew up weary of errands.

She told me about being the Rat Girl singing
in the silence of her own mind, in fear
of the owl. She said
she was always among the Hawikn, shaking the gourds,
insisting on support.
They gave her oxfords—shoes—when
she graduated high school.
At Hawikuh she sang and listened to the echo
of her voice: bouncing
back from the rocks. She said the Crane
Mother protected her there.
The Great Turtle who declared a truce
with Coyote also
held her hand.
I held her hand in dusk-light.
Thin dust rose in red sunlight
as the sun sank
into sacred earth: the belly
of a starving child. First Plaza
where kachinas dance in darkness,

when they come back to touch the people.
She feared her own footprints: they might trace
                    her steps. She could hear
their hearts beating in her ears.
The dwellers woke.
          The warriors tipped out of shadows.
They ran—they ran they ran—when they saw the
                    Ghost Dancer! dancing
and they came back only when
he (her brother) took off his Ghost Dancer-mask.
They swore witchery was in the air.

Women locked windows.
Menfolk went to the kiva to pray.
Even if it was a joke, it was not funny. . . .

From

Surfaces and Masks

I

and who must remain
stuck with the idea
that the Byzantine is "unlovely"
or with the notion that
a "cultivated Negro" is necessary in a country
where one does not expect to find him,
available
and speaking many languages, causing one to
feel ignorant?
Had he been a son of North Africa
and not South Carolina—what then?
This Beloved Humorist
on the one hand
could damn the Arabs
and defend the rights of Negroes;
step into Santa Maria dei Frari
and feel outrage
in the entranceway. And why

was the gondola black?
Behind every closed window
on the Grand Canal, Othello and Desdemona.
The threat of cholera, then
hung like fog on the surface
of the page, in the end being itself
a signal
vast signs of poverty, many

beggars begging—insisting really
on their own serious anger . . .

Thomas Mann. Thomas Mann
was impatient with the closed windows,
the smelly streets,
did not imagine Desdemona
but a boy white-shod, "at once
timid and proud"
a boy, Mann's boy—and not Bordereau.
Giovane as the Fountain of Youth!

. . . something about Venetian girls, too.
Having sweet and charming
and very sad, oval faces.
And wasn't there something about
an underfed
look? Well, I never thought of them
in those terms . . .

To take a posture—"I quote the principle
parts"
"wave-washed steps" (to quote James
to quote myself) seeing this place
as a getting-away-place, away
from the hardness of plastic edges
and the sharp surface
of every secure thought I ever had,
is, in itself, a conspiracy

Left to rifle the situation
I'd hang them all in San Marco
like the French conspirators
were hanged
after the plot of 1618
was uncovered . . .
Then console myself with the music
of Schubert and Miles.
They?
Her face was framed by
a halo of thick dark hair:

she was no doubt a contessa (they
all are!)
and you could see the distant signs
of the Orient around her African eyes,
the Middle East
in the slope of her nose.
She was the summation of the human race?
Her seriousness was Greek.
There was no way to point
a reckless finger
at any part of her.

In her knit stockings,
she walks
arm-in-arm with another girl
—she parts with the friend and
calls back over her shoulder,
"Ciao, Anna!"

She is the dama Veneziana
of the 1720s,
complete with hooped
silk skirts
and a black velvet cape
which is attached
to her jewel-studded crown
and reaches nearly to the floor.
She carries in her left hand
a gold cross
suspended on a circle
of pearls.

II

They sit silently in the dark
holding hands
watching Jean Marais in *Blas*
and Lillian Harvey
and Carla Sveva
in *Castelli in Aria.*

They?
and Luchino Visconti's *Senso*
and David Lean's *Tempo d'Estate*
and a Volkoff
adventure film
starring Ivan Mosjoukine
and Max Calandri's *Sangue*
a Ca' Foscari.
They seek images
of their own memories
listen to the emperors
and to Marco Polo
zigzag mentally through Kubla Khan
and watch
William Dean Howells swim
in the Grand Canal.

III

She takes him into "The Rape
of Europa"—
he takes her by surprise
by playing the Avocadore
di Comun.
She delights him as Puttana
then again as Odalisca.
He scares her as Nobilgiovine
Veneziano
and again as Cuoco
of the Hotel Saturnia.
He scares her nearly out
of her senses
when he does his Compagno
della Buona Morte
act.
He is her cavalier-servant.
He helps her lace
her underclothes,

to take off her tight
corset.
The music they live by
is made for chambers.
He takes her duck hunting
at the mouth
of Tagliamento, in the winter.
He puts her up in the best room
at the Palazzo Gritti.
They got no interest
in Harry's, nor Martini Montgomery.
In the summer, they fight
off zanzare and spend much time
on the islands.
They go onto the mainland
Sundays or Saturdays
and drive along Monfalcone
and through Latisana.
Once with Bill and Franca,
they ate the best
spaghetti in butter
you could ever
taste
in Casale sul Sile

They toasted Carlo Goldoni's
humor
and saw in his home
the only play Picasso
ever wrote.

IV

He gave the Fascisti salute
when he stepped off
the plane . . .
there would be, I knew—
if nobody else ever knew—an endless
Sordello;

and poor "Eleanor" and all
the dream-dreamed Grecian faces
I could scare up,
the cries in the nightmares,
the Acaetes-announcements;
everything you can imagine—
least of all,
that worn-out, "Hang it all . . ."
and
and . . . worse! One could get hung
endlessly up in it all.
I said in my attempt to clear
my mind,
"Goodbye So-shu!"
and I was waiting,
on my way,
not even mindful of night
whisperings:
"Past we glide!"
There were those
willing to introduce me
to O.R., but she was too old,
and therefore
the conversation was likely to be
not worth the trip, but—
on the other hand,
there remained the quest
for kissing:

"Kiss me if you entered gay /
My heart at some noonday."

The gondolas always
repeat always—
cost too much—any year.

I was either a guilty traveller
from or to
"glorious Babylon" or else
I was less wise,

less concerned
with these surface effects.
A deep echo of Disraeli,
fearful of my plight here . . . ?
at sight of cemetery
lying there in mist, I drew
back, sharing Disraeli's fear.
Can you imagine yourself
wandering into a late-night-bar
in Venice
wearing a mask—even at Carnevale time?

We bought the papier-mâché
and covered our faces
for fun, gambling
on our luck.
(The Serenissima, in these days,
would not try us for it—)
but
poor Disraeli! "I fear I have no title"
he said,
"to admission within these walls,
except the privilege
of the season."
Only in a psychological romance!
But then you try to find a way out!
or you wait
and listen to Countess Malbrizzi,
who asks,
"Shall I tell you
your name?"
and you know
damned well
if you let her
you are going to end up
in bed with her, ah, making love,
or worse!
And once you are with her,
close to her,

in her arms, you are obliged
to not only let her tell you
your name, but to let her melt your snow.
Mount you?
Warm you?
As the countess
she will tell you
she has the power to dream
you away,
to turn you into a ghost,
make you
part of the city, fade you.
And you will be quick
to warn her that you have never had any
"sympathy with reality."
Then there's Dickens.
"So we advanced into the ghostly city"
and Dickens had had no idea
of what he was talking about!
the proof is that he went on.
" . . . a black boat . . ."
one of "mournful colours . . ."
moving
silently through the night

(I saw them
all day long, mainly—which proves
nothing—)

Yet something in you
has to go out
to that old boy, Dickens!
"So we advanced
into the ghostly city"—of
(death, death, death!)

Poor Dickens! . . .

Acknowledgments

Many people helped to make this book possible. Many thanks to Gail Fortune for suggesting this book. Thanks to Brandon Proia for recognizing the value of the project and to Lucas Church for his initial work on it. I am also grateful to Cate Hodorowicz and Andrew Winters for handling all the details involved in getting the manuscript ready for copyediting. Thanks to novelist and playwright Kia Corthron for her fine and generous foreword. Thanks also to Managing Editor Mary Carley Caviness for her fine and careful work on the manuscript. Many thanks, too, to copyeditors Jessica Ryan and Julie Bush for their careful reading and editing. Thanks to Jamison Cockerham for the beautiful design and to Rebecca Evans for the equally beautiful typesetting. In marketing, thanks to Dino Battista, marketing director, and especially to Anna Faison for her brilliant ideas for giving the book an online presence. Thanks to Leanna O'Brien for helping with the typing of the manuscript. As always, many thanks also to my wife, Pamela Major, for her expert help with the copyediting and proofreading.

Credits

The material in this book appeared in the same or similar form in the following publications.

NOVEL EXCERPTS

Dirty Bird Blues. Mercury House, 1996; Berkley Publishing Group, 1997. Copyright © by Clarence Major.

My Amputations. Éditions L'Âge D'Homme, 1986; Mercury House, 1986; Fiction Collective, 2008. Copyright © by Clarence Major.

One Flesh. Kensington Publishing Corp/ Dafina Books, 2003. Copyright © by Clarence Major.

Painted Turtle: Woman with Guitar. Sun & Moon Press, 1988; University of New Mexico Press, 1998. Copyright © by Clarence Major.

Reflex and Bone Structure. Fiction Collective, 1975; Éditions L'Âge D'Homme, 1982; Mercury House, 1996. Copyright © by Clarence Major.

Such Was the Season. Mercury House, 1987; Louisiana State University Press, 2003. Copyright © by Clarence Major.

SHORT STORIES

All of the short stories in this book appeared previously in *Chicago Heat and Other Stories*. Brattleboro, Vt.: Green Writers Press, 2016. Copyright © by Clarence Major.

ESSAYS

"Icarus Crashes and Rises from His Own Ashes." Titled "'Flying Home' by Ralph Ellison," in *Why I Like This Story*, edited by Jackson R. Bryer. Camden House/Boydell & Brewer, Inc., 2019.

"A Meditation on Kenneth Patchen's Painted Poems: Kingdoms and Utopias." Informational essay for the exhibition *An Astonished Eye: The Art of Kenneth Patchen*, September 22, 2011–January 5, 2012, University of Rochester, Rochester, New York.

"Painting and Poetry." Afterword to the exhibition catalog *Clarence Major: Myself Painting*, February 24, 2011–March 25, 2011. Center for the Performing and Fine Arts, Indiana State University, Terre Haute.

"Reaching and Leaving the Point." *High Plains Literary Review* 4, no. 2 (Fall 1989). Copyright © 1989 by Clarence Major.

"Richard Wright: The Long Hallucination." In *The Dark and Feeling: Reflections on Black American Writers and Their Works*. Copyright © 1974 by The Third Press, Joseph Okpaku Publishing Co., Inc.

"Thanks for the Lunch, Baby." In *One Last Lunch*, edited by Erica Heller. New York: Abrams, 2020.

The following essays were collected in *Necessary Distance: Essays and Criticism*. Coffee House Press, 2001. Copyright © 2001 by Clarence Major: "Necessary Distance: Afterthoughts on Becoming a Writer," "A Paris Fantasy Transformed," "Rhythm: Talking that Talk," "Don, Here Is My Peppermint Striped Shirt," "Rhythm: A Hundred Years of African American Poetry," "Struga '75," "Looking at *The Dial*," "Claude McKay: My 1975 Adventure," "Reading William Faulkner's *Light in August*," "In Search of Rebecca," and "Wallace Thurman and the Niggeratti Manor".

MEMOIR

"Taking Chances: A Memoir of a Life in Art and Writing." Originally titled "Licking Stamps, Taking Chances." In Contemporary Authors New Revision Series, vol. 337. New York: Gale Autobiography Project, 2018.

POEMS

"Bride Stripped Bare." From *Down and Up*. Copyright © 2013 by Clarence Major. Reprinted by permission of the University of Georgia Press.

"Evening Newspaper," "Morandi," "Father," "Water and Sand," "Domestic Agenda," "Faith," "Alchemy," and "Down and Up." From *Now On: New and Selected Poems 1970–2015*. Copyright © 2015 by Clarence Major. Reprinted by permission of the University of Georgia Press.

"Hair." *New Yorker*, May 7, 2018. Copyright © by Clarence Major.

"No One Goes to Paris in August" and "Waiting for Sweet Betty." From *Waiting For Sweet Betty*. Copyright © 2002 by Clarence Major. Reprinted by permission of the Permissions Company, LLC, on behalf of Copper Canyon Press, www.copper canyonpress.org.

"Plein Air," "The Young Doctor (1916)," and "East Lansing, Michigan." From *Myself Painting*. Copyright © 2008 by Clarence Major. Reprinted by permission of Louisiana State University Press.

Some Observations of a Stranger at Zuni in the Latter Part of the Century. Sun & Moon Press, 1989. Copyright © 1989 by Clarence Major.

"Supply and Demand." *New Yorker*, January 2, 2019. Copyright © by Clarence Major.

Surfaces and Masks. Copyright © 1988 by Clarence Major. Reprinted by permission of Coffee House Press.

"Un Poco Loco," "September Mendocino," "The Slave Trade: View from the Middle Passage," "Frenzy," and "Round Midnight." From *Configurations: New and Selected Poems 1958–1998*. Copyright © 1998 by Clarence Major. Reprinted by permission of the Permissions Company, LLC, on behalf of Copper Canyon Press, www .coppercanyonpress.org.